I0668827

SAGA OF A NEUROSURGEON SERIES, BOOK SIX

THE
VULTURE
AND
THE
PHOENIX

Neurosurgeon, Garven Wilsonhulme, the final great fight

Carl Douglass

Neurosurgeon Turned Author Writes with Gripping Realism

PO Box 221974 Anchorage, Alaska 99522-1974
books@publicationconsultants.com—www.publicationconsultants.com

ISBN 978-1-59433-361-3
eISBN 978-1-59433-362-0
Library of Congress Catalog Card Number: 2013930989

Manufactured in the United States of America.

Disclaimer

This is a story, a fiction, where all but a very few names have been changed to protect the people deserving of great respect and are, in all cases, cast in a deservedly positive light. They are minor characters in the book and its story. Other characters and the part they play in the *Saga* are loosely based on real people, including the author, whose names are changed; the places they work in the book are fictitious or different from where they were actually encountered by the present author. Some of the experiences described and the characters depicted are amalgamations of persons, places, and actions, and some diluted and altered autobiographical remembrances. There are healthy dollops of whimsy running throughout even the autobiographical hints.

The world of Garven Wilsonhulme is indeed fiction, but while not exactly real, it is faithful to an era of neurosurgical training and experience that is almost entirely a thing of the past. The independence and cowboy experience of being trained in a blood and guts trauma hospital in that era is not an exaggeration. There are some of those old men (and women) out there who will smile as they read and remember. If nothing else, the experiences of those semi-pioneers are the stuff of legend, humor, and pathos that invite endlessly fascinating yarns by all those consummate raconteurs.

The world of medicine and surgery is far more sophisticated and genteel now, far more of a closely controlled corporate money and legalistically driven environment. No longer can residents work 120 hours a week by federal and state law. It is all but unthinkable for a trainee to act with cavalier unsupervised independence in the closely monitored environment of the programs of the twenty-first century. A Garven Wilsonhulme would never make it into or through the training or the vicissitudes of neurosurgical practice in today's world without a very considerable amount of refinement and bowing to the ethical, moral, legal, and scientific standards of the present day. But then, neurosurgeons are eminently tough and adaptable. Maybe even Garven could make his way in the new paradigm as he did in the era of forty and fifty years ago, when this *Saga* took place. The author would like to think he could.

Dedication

The series of books is dedicated to those giants upon whose shoulders I stood, including: Harvey Birsner, MD, my partner and friend; Shelly Chou, MD, PhD, my great mentor; Kemp Clark, MD, The Chief; Stephen David Durrant, PhD, professor of biology/evolution/comparative anatomy, a curmudgeon, humorist, inspiration, and friend; Lyle A. French, MD, PhD, the grand master at Minnesota; William Wallace Newby, PhD, professor of biology/embryology, my greatest friend and help; Lito Porto, MD, The Indian; J. Charles Rich, MD, my worthy opponent in premed and the consummate neurosurgeon and contributor to the neurosurgical community; Theodore Roberts, MD, my start; Duke Samson, MD, the great builder of neurosurgery and foremost of brain vascular surgeons; Charles Sternbergh, MD, the rock of integrity; Clark C. Watts, MD, JD, my friend and support during the lean years.

Acknowledgments

The author acknowledges with appreciation the direct contributions to the books of Harvey Birsner, MD; Keith Hooker, MD; Kim Oliver, MD; Brent Pratley, MD; Charles Stewart, MD; and all of the general surgery and neurosurgery interns, residents, and professors in California, Utah, Minnesota, Texas, Virginia, and the men and women of the navy who served with me.

G arven smiled graciously as he walked up to Dr. Rosenthal. The neonatologist had worked a full head of steam. He launched into a litany of
wrongdoings by Arun and discourtesies by the neurosurgery faculty. Garven
gave him all the rope he needed. Rosenthal complained about the quality of
neurosurgical work, research, patient follow-up, and especially about their
inability to understand the problems of newborns. He paused to take a breath.

Garven maintained an exasperatingly pleasant facial expression. He smiled
slowly when Rosenthal took his breather.

"That about it, Dr. Rosenthal?"

"I guess so," the neonatologist sighed.

To say more would be repetitive.

"Then as I see it, you take exception to our diagnostic ability, to our surgical
program, to our ongoing research, to our bedside manner, to our knowledge
of pediatric neurosurgical problems, and to our grasp on interdisciplinary
courtesies. We are basically mean, stupid, lazy, and inept. Other than that, I
take it that you approve of our program?" Garven said. He was completely
civil and polite in his delivery.

"Well, Dr. Wilsonhulme...I, uh, well..." Dr. Rosenthal stammered. He had
essentially said all of that, but he did not like Wilsonhulme's summary. "I came
here, in all professional courtesy, to tell you what you should do with your resident."

As soon as he said it, Dr. Rosenthal felt that he might have gone too far with that
statement. The hard look on Dr. Wilsonhulme's face confirmed that impression.

Garven reached into his suit coat pocket and withdrew an envelope. He
handed it to Rosenthal.

Rosenthal took it and looked curiously at it. He recognized it.

"This was handed to me for action, Dr. Rosenthal. As you know, I am the
chairman of the university professional advancement committee. You have
requested consideration that you be advanced from instructor to assistant
professor. Have I got that right?"

"Yes...yes, you do."

There was a marked change in his manner. He was no longer pompous
and instructing.

"We seem to have a number of things to talk about, you and me," said
Garven. "Which of these matters do you think we should discuss first? I
rather think it best to discuss the most important things first, in case we run
out of time."

"Nothing is more sad than the
death of an illusion."
- Arthur Koestler, Hungarian novelist, journalist,
playwright, critic, and essayist.
Darkness at Noon,1940

CHAPTER
One

Medical students, interns, residents, and nurses referred to the medical school scientific laboratories as the "rat labs" or the "dog labs," and the work that went on there as "rat or dog surgery," a derogation indicative of the disdain of the clinician for the academician. The members of the university's medical faculty knew that it was their life's blood. If they were able to get something into print, however innocuous or obscure, they could keep their jobs. If they were able to do credible work, to make a real contribution, they would likely advance up the academic scale. If they were able to publish an important discovery that became widely known, they could almost name their reward. On the other hand, the best physician, the most talented surgeon, the most successful clinician or teacher would not last two years if he or she failed to list several articles in print or "in publication," i.e., to be printed.

Garven had been harboring an idea for some time, ever since he had worked with Dr. Harralsen in Phoenix. He had kept absolutely silent about it. He knew that academicians were not above frank theft of an idea; it was all part of the "publish or perish" ethic. Only the strong survived, and Garven intended, not only to persist, but to prevail in academia. His idea was insightful and simple. Spinal cord injuries that caused complete disruption of the spinal cord resulted in permanent failure of neurological function below the point of injury—quadriplegia or paraplegia, depending on the level of cord injury. Nothing anyone had done thus far had made any difference towards improving clinical neurological function. He reasoned that it might be possible to divert neurological impulses coming down the intact cord above to the level of the cord below the injury by a new technique.

Others had tried and failed by simply sewing the severed ends of the cord together, and still others had hooked up electrical connections to try and stimulate the two halves, again to no avail. Garven proposed to take the long spinal nerves coming from the cord at the chest level, cut them, and make a "bridge" around the injury to the cord by uniting a nerve above to the one below. He considered uniting several nerves for good measure, but that would have to be reserved for later. He only had time for anastomosing single nerves since his clinical schedule was so busy.

Garven had set up a very efficient lab. He trained an assistant who could do the preliminary work, even down to exposing the cord. He selected goats as his experimental animal because they had large intercostal spinal nerves that were easy to work with, and goats were inexpensive. He ordered a hundred goats, fifty to have the anastomoses after an experimental transection of the thoracic spinal cord and fifty to serve as controls. The controls were to have the cord exposed and cut, but no anastomosis. Three afternoons a week, he and his assistant, who became very proficient, did four animals. The animal lab personnel then took care of the paraplegic goats. Garven had to be patient and to wait and see if there would be either microscopic or electrophysiological evidence of transmission of electrical impulses from above to below or, more dramatically, improvement in clinical function in the lower extremities. The process took four months.

The lab work was routine and leisurely. Garven learned to relax, to drink coffee, and to read the paper and journal articles. He rapidly became a typical researcher. He improved his fund of general knowledge on current events, such as learning that the super liberal, John F. Kennedy, approved the largest budget in U.S. history, with a projected deficit of $11,900,000,000—an amount that Garven knew would lead to the bankruptcy of his country. If that was not enough to guarantee ruination, Congress began consideration of a medical-hospital insurance bill for the elderly, a gigantic federal giveaway called Medicare. Martial law was declared in Cambridge, Maryland, and National Guard troops were dispatched to that city to control race riots. That kind of problem was fomented by communist agitators, Garven decided— people like a Negro minister and self-proclaimed "black leader" named Martin Luther King. The Reverend King led a scary march of 200,000 people in Washington D.C. to protest conditions for minorities. He gave a stirring speech, something about "I have a dream…" Garven just about decided that the country would not hold together long enough to go bankrupt if agitators like the reverend were allowed to continue.

"Where was J. Edgar Hoover and the FBI while all of this was going on?" Garven muttered to himself.

He had time now to observe his competition in the neurosurgery service and to record their errors. Alfred Grossner, the neurosurgeon with the good brain and the poor set of hands, was the most vulnerable to exposure. Garven recorded a patient who had one of his major lumbar nerve roots severed in a lumbar laminotomy operation. Grossner perforated the aorta on another lumbar disc patient, and the patient bled to death in the PAR. Garven's competitor had very strange ideas for research and attempted to pursue them in humans without real thought as to the consequences. Garven scored his first coup over Grossner in the dog-eat-dog struggle for academic power by seeing to it that two of his most ill-thought-out ideas were uncovered and the patients protected.

Dr. Grossner had an interest in the serious problem of vasospasm in the cerebral blood vessels after aneurysm rupture and subarachnoid hemorrhage. The blood from the torn aneurysm spread over adjacent vessels and proved to be caustic in some way. The irritated vessel walls constricted, sometimes to the point of being mere threads so slender that they could no longer carry blood and caused the patient to have a stroke. The condition was fatal at times. No one had found an antidote. Dr. Grossner observed that bee and snake venom caused marked relaxation in the walls of the blood vessels of lower animals. He failed to take note that the venoms also caused deaths.

Grossner procured snake venom from a company in Arkansas that collected the dangerous material from a born-again religious cult that used rattlers in their religious rituals. The cult members brought in needed money by selling the snakes' venom to the drug company. He obtained bee venom from an obscure company in Vermont. When he had sufficient quantities of each, he arranged for two patients in the NICU with vasospasm after subarachnoid hemorrhages to receive the venoms by vein. Garven was informed of the plan by Pat MacNamara, who was aghast at the entire concept. Garven whispered in the ear of the head nurse on neurosurgery, and she reported the planned human experimentation to her supervisor. The supervisor and the hospital administrator, in company with Peter Lyons, head of the department of surgery, showed up in the NICU at almost the last minute before Grossner was to instill the poisons into the patients' IVs.

There was a heated argument about academic freedom and interference with another doctor's patient that made Al Grossner look more like the mad scientist than the innovative clinical investigator. Finally, Lyons had to issue an executive order for Grossner to desist permanently from his venom treatment, and in the process, the associate professor of neurosurgery was widely discredited. When the story got out and was spread around the faculty, with a little help from Garven, Alfred Grossner was made out to be a laughingstock.

Grossner had another innovative idea. Many of the neurosurgery trauma patients had multiple injuries and developed severe infections. They received large amounts of wide-spectrum antibiotics to prevent or to treat their infections. One complication of the antibiotic treatment was the destruction of the normal bacterial flora of the patients' intestines. Many of them developed an overgrowth of yeasts in the bowel that degenerated into very difficult infections related to the new, opportunistic organisms. The drug of choice to combat the systemic fungal and yeast infections was an extremely toxic chemical named Amphotericin B, and more commonly known as "Ampho-Terrible" by the house staff. In order to prevent or to cure the yeast infections without resorting to the use of Ampho-Terrible, Al Grossner hit on a novel idea.

He decided that the reintroduction of normal bowel bacteria would be the answer to the yeast infection problem. He ordered the nurses to emulsify the stool of all of the uninfected patients on the ward and to dilute it with sterile water, and, as a refinement, to add mint flavor. Every patient on the ward was then required to drink a pint of the mint-flavored diluted excreta in the morning before breakfast and another at bedtime. The nurses had to scrub with disinfectant soap and to wear gloves at all times while they handled Dr. Grossner's special medicine to prevent contamination with pathogenic bacteria from their hands. The head nurse on the ward complained to Garven that it made more sense to wash their hands after handling the medicine than before—something like doing hemorrhoid surgery.

The experiment was to be Grossner's and the nurses' little secret, but Garven knew it was too good a story not to let it get out. He put a bug in the ear of the resident covering the infectious disease service, who alerted the chairman of the department of medicine. An investigation revealed the truth of the allegations, and Grossner's experiment was summarily canceled. The treatment protocol gained notoriety and was labeled forever with Grossner's name and with a series of descriptors, the most benign of which was "detestable." It was hard for an intern or a resident to see Dr. Grossner without chuckling about his "secret minty medicine."

In mid-May, Garven's own lab experiment bore fruit. Thirty-eight of his experimental goats developed a small but dramatic return of neurological function. They were able to control their bladders. Only one of the control group regained even the slightest bladder function. None of the goats demonstrated any return in motor function of their legs, but fifteen of the anastomosed goats appeared to have some return of sensation. That finding was questionable. Garven quietly informed the neurosurgery faculty of his findings in the first faculty meeting of June. Garven's star was in an arc of ascendancy, about comparable to the arc of descendancy of Al Grossner's aspirations.

On his own, Dr. Grossner secured a position at the University of Pittsburgh, where there was a very forward-looking research professor of experimental neurosurgery. Al's genius was recognized, and he was relieved of the burden of having to perform surgery on humans. In part, that opportunity was occasioned by Garven's timely behind-the-scenes communication of his findings on Dr. Grossner's operative complications. Garven's hand in that matter went unheralded.

Garven was offered the rank of assistant professor if he would agree to continue his work at UCOMH instead of considering the three offers he received from other universities. The information about those three offers was dropped very casually and modestly in passing by Garven to Dr. Chou's secretary. No one asked for any verification of the offers; that would have been ungentlemanly. Garven had counted on that code of conduct by his superiors when he had the conversation with the secretary. He had learned a great deal about how the academic progression game was played, including the art of bluffing—perception was as important as reality—and it did not hurt to have had a couple of decades of practice playing poker with Apaches.

CHAPTER
Two

Elizabeth went into labor on June 12. Garven felt more secure about this delivery than he had for Peter Arthur's because he now had the prestige and inside track that his faculty membership afforded him. Against the advice of several of the younger obstetricians, both on the faculty and in the city, Garven had had Elizabeth see Dr. Horst Caesar, the head of the obstetrics department. His detractors accused Dr. Caesar of being both uncaring for his patients and of having only research interests. He would not give other physicians professional courtesy for their bills, Garven was told. Nonetheless, Garven went ahead and asked the professor to be his wife's obstetrician. She had not entered into the discussion, confident that he knew best. Her parents were impressed with Dr. Caesar's national reputation, and Garven's ability to secure the man to be their daughter's doctor lifted Garven a notch or two on their rating scale. Garven had been climbing that scale fairly steadily as his academic career status improved.

It was a long, hard, and fitful labor. Elizabeth had pains steadily for hours, then she quit. Finally, at nine o'clock in the evening, she was certain that this was the real thing and had Garven take her to the hospital. She was admitted to the private wing. The doctor was not in and would not be until she was approaching time for delivery, the OB nurse informed them. Her examination revealed Elizabeth's cervix to be about fifty percent effaced and three centimeters dilated at the time of admission. There was nothing to do but to wait.

The pains were moderate in intensity and came six minutes apart for the next three hours. The nurse's exam revealed eighty percent effacement and four centimeters of dilation, not a very impressive progress for all of that work. Garven asked the nurse to give his wife some morphine. The nurse was reluctant, but allowed herself to be persuaded to call Dr. Caesar. He ordered a small dose, two milligrams, and the nurse injected Elizabeth. The pain eased dramatically; unfortunately, by two o'clock, so did the contractions. The activity of Elizabeth's labor fell to near nil. Garven called the nurse.

"This girl needs some Pitocin," he said. "She'll be here forever if you don't."

"I'll ask the doctor, but he won't give her any. It's three o'clock in the morning. Do you realize who you're asking to come in here at that time? Because if she gets Pitocin, she'll go into active labor, and he'll have to come in. It's more than my job's worth to drag him out at night, if you want to know the truth."

She left for the phone only when Garven insisted.

He followed her to the nurses' station. She did not see him as he listened to her end of the conversation with the famous obstetrician.

"Hello, Dr. Caesar, this is Millicent in OB... Yes, I know what time it is. I'm sorry, but Mrs. Wilsonhulme's labor has just stopped, and her husband is insisting on her getting some Pit... I told him you wouldn't, but he was really quite pushy about it. I must say, Doctor, that it doesn't seem like such a bad idea... Yes, Sir, I know that it was his idea to give the morphine, and I do see where that got us... No, I guess that wasn't the right decision... Yes, Sir, I know who the lady's doctor is. I'll tell them. Thank you, and good-bye." She turned around and saw Garven facing her. "I guess you got the general idea of that conversation. The doctor said that he will be in to see your wife at eight o'clock. He said for you not to be a nervous husband."

"I am not a nervous husband. I am a doctor, and I know that my wife needs more care than she's getting. She is becoming exhausted with unproductive labor. Call him back. I'll talk to him."

"I can't do that, Sir. We are absolutely forbidden to let the fathers talk to the OB. Please, I don't want to get into trouble."

"I'll tell you what," Garven said, controlling his anger, "I will hold off if Elizabeth is making any progress at all. Let's go back and check her."

They did, and Elizabeth's uterus was unchanged from the last examination. Garven walked purposefully out to the nurses desk and thumbed through the Rollidex of doctors' numbers.

"You can't do that, Sir. No fathers are allowed back here. Those are private numbers. I'm afraid that you'll have to leave," whined Millicent.

Garven memorized Dr. Caesar's home number and put up his hands in surrender.

"Sure, I'll go back to my wife," he said. Instead of returning to her labor room, he went on down the hall to the pay phone. He dialed Dr. Caesar's number.

The telephone rang four times. Dr. Caesar's drowsy and irritable voice came on. "It's three forty-five in the morning, what do you want?"

"And hello to you, Sir," Garven said, scarcely masking his sarcasm. "This is Garven Wilsonhulme. My wife is Elizabeth, your patient in labor who has not seen her doctor yet."

"Do you know to whom you are speaking, Dr. Wilsonhulme? I don't care for your tone."

"Yes, Sir, I know. You are Horst Caesar, my wife's obstetrician. Now let's get down to business. I know, and you know, that Elizabeth needs Pitocin. It is past time for her labor to get under way."

"Are you an obstetrician?" Dr. Caesar's voice was acid with sarcasm.

"I am not. I am nothing but a neurosurgeon, but I know when a patient is being neglected. That is apparent. I want you either to order Pitocin or to come in and see her like you ought to. I will get my own medicine and do the job myself if you don't."

Garven's voice was cool and icy. He fought the urge to swear and yell at the arrogant ivory tower obstetrician.

"Be careful, young man. I sit on the advancement committee of this university. You may regret your outburst if you continue. I will write it off to your excessive emotional involvement in your wife's labor this time. Give me the nurse. In the future, you let me handle the obstetrics, and you go and crack people's heads. I don't think you are any judge of what your wife needs."

Garven handed the phone to Millicent.

The Pitocin was given at four o'clock on the dot. Contractions began in ten minutes and were strong and active in twenty. Millicent's serial examinations revealed steady effacement and dilatation. By ten after six, Elizabeth was fully effaced and at eight centimeters of dilation. She was also in terrible pain. Her contractions were three minutes apart, and she was unable to get any relief between them. At six-twenty, Garven confronted Millicent again.

"How about a little compassion, Millicent? This girl needs a paracervical block or an epidural, or a spinal, or gas. Something."

"I can't do that; only the doctors."

"I know that. You have to call Dr. Caesar. He needs to get in here, big professor or not. His patient needs him," Garven insisted.

He was angry enough to cause Millicent to know better than to argue. She took a big breath and called Dr. Caesar.

Garven could not hear the conversation. He did not need to. He saw Millicent's head shaking back and forth, translating the negative responses she was receiving into motor gestures. During a pause, Garven walked swiftly to where Millicent was standing with her back to him and snatched the phone out of her hand.

"This is Garven Wilsonhulme," he said peremptorily. "It's time—past time—for you to come and see your patient. She's going to deliver soon, and she needs some help. I expect to see you in no more than thirty minutes, or I will have the administrator get an obstetrician from town."

He put down the receiver without waiting for the indignant reply.

In twenty minutes, Dr. Caesar walked into Elizabeth's labor room. He was fumingly angry. Garven stood up. The delivery nurse stood so stiffly that she could have been at attention on a parade ground.

Dr. Caesar cast an abrupt and condescending look at Elizabeth and asked, his question directed to the nurse, "Is this our little girl who can't handle a little pain?"

Elizabeth was in the middle of a long, hard contraction and was crying out in severe pain and fear.

Garven transformed into a jungle animal protecting his female. He walked straight to the chief of OB-Gyn and took hold of both of the taller man's suit coat lapels. Garven propelled the astonished full professor backwards into the hallway then whipped him around so that he was flattened against the wall. There was a look of the most terrible violence in his eyes and on his face. For the first time in his memory, Horst Caesar was afraid of a man, and the fear reached into his core.

Garven's voice was barely a whisper.

"That is my wife. She is delivering a baby. She will be treated with respect and with common decency. Even a dog would be helped by a reasonable human being. Now, you will go in there, get her some pain relief, get her baby delivered; and you will treat her as if she were the queen of England. I am going to be on your heels until this is over. Two things are going to happen to you if you treat my wife with disrespect again. The first is that I am going to beat you to within an inch of your life. The second is that I am going to call for a disciplinary hearing by the state medical licensing bureau." He swept the pale obstetrician around and pointed him towards Elizabeth's door. "That way," he said with quiet malevolence.

Dr. Caesar examined Elizabeth. He looked embarrassed now, as well as angry and fearful.

"Well, young lady, you've made more progress than I thought. You're at station one. We'd better get you into the delivery room." To the delivery room nurse, he said, "Millicent, wheel her down there now. I'll change and meet you in a minute."

Without being asked, Garven helped wheel Elizabeth down the hall.

At the entrance to the delivery room, Millicent said, "Okay, Dr. Wilsonhulme, this is as far as you go. Dr. Caesar will be out as soon as we have a baby and let you know."

Garven kept pushing the gurney on into the room.

"Don't get in my way," he said.

"I don't know what Dr. Caesar will think, what he'll say," Millicent protested.

But Garven was helping to shift Elizabeth onto the delivery table.

He turned to the delivery room nurse once Elizabeth was settled and said, "You are looking at me as if I were someone who gives a damn what Dr. Caesar thinks. What Dr. Caesar thinks and says on the matter of my presence in the delivery room is irrelevant right now."

He went out, scrubbed, and donned his mask, cap, gown, and gloves.

The delivery was a fait accompli in fifteen minutes. Garven and Elizabeth were the parents of a seven-pound, four-ounce baby girl. Dr. Caesar sewed up the small midline episiotomy while Garven held Elizabeth's hand. They had agreed on Susan as a name if the baby were a girl.

"Is Susan all right?" asked Elizabeth.

She appeared wan and weary.

"Perfect," Garven said.

"Garven, I appreciate what you did. I know you took a risk by protecting me. It meant a lot. I will never forget," Elizabeth said.

She sank back on the sweaty sheets.

Horst Caesar came up to Garven in the dressing room afterwards.

"Look, I'm sorry things were unpleasant tonight. I consider this nothing more than the great anxiety of delivery, and I have no intentions of pursuing the matter further. Would you shake on that?"

Garven shook his hand. He knew it was not in his best interests to do anything more, either. He could not help but think that he had made another powerful enemy, every bit as vengeful as Henry Kowalski at the VA. He wondered when the latent animosity engendered by this night would resurface. In anticipation of that possibility, Garven made a very detailed set of notes about the case and included the pertinent information about all of the nurses who had been witnesses.

CHAPTER
Three

O f necessity, with both Al Grossner and Don White gone permanently and David Stark off politicking around the country, Garven and Steven Chou became, if not fast friends, then the best of working partners. Steven had not been able to entice anyone he was impressed with to come and join the UCOMH faculty; so, he and Garven temporarily carried the full load. The residents were busy, and the new chief resident, Pat MacNamara, was doing more big cases than he ever dreamed possible in a training program. Garven immersed himself in his work. One Monday he scheduled a PCA (Posterior communicating artery) aneurysm, a posterior fossa procedure to remove a huge acoustic neurinoma, and a large glioblastoma located dangerously close to the left hemisphere speech area.

His anesthesiologist was new, a woman. Garven arranged to do the posterior fossa case first and set the old man up in the sitting position for the procedure. The incision and bone removal went off routinely. Garven opened the dura, taking care to keep out of the large dural venous sinuses. They were very difficult to deal with when nicked.

As he was tacking the dural leaves back out of the way, the anesthesiologist said, "Dr. Wilsonhulme, Mr. Adams' BP is going down. I can't get it back up."

There was an edge of panic in her voice.

"Did you hear any air through the Doppler?" he asked.

He was worried about the passage of air from the open cranial veins passing back into the heart. The bubbles could clog the heart and the outflow vessels.

"I think I might have. The Doppler tip is right by the heart, great position. I've never done a sitting position case before, and I'm not sure what the noise is like," she said.

She manipulated the Doppler tube in its place inside the esophagus one more time just to be sure.

"You can't miss it. Sounds like a washing machine. You can't mistake that sloshing sound," Garven said.

He had already covered the open incision with a heavy gauze pad and was pouring sterile normal saline over it constantly to prevent any more air from getting into the veins.

"Uh, oh!" the anesthesiologist exclaimed. "BP is zero. Now, what do we do?" She was frankly panicked.

"Draw off the air in the right atrium!" Garven said instantly.

The anesthesiologist began to suck frothy blood from the upper cardiac chamber. Garven cranked the bed out of its upright sitting position and undid the head clamp from the table attachment. He had the orderlies help, and together they turned the patient over on his abdomen.

"BP is back!" exulted the anesthesiologist.

"Great!" sighed Garven. "How about the air?"

"Blood is clear now, no more bubbles."

"I'll close him up," Garven said. He had the nurse hand him large sutures and the team turned the patient a little onto his side to permit suturing. It was very awkward, but Garven was making progress.

"Oh, no! He's arrested. Flat line!" the anesthesiologist shouted.

Garven stopped his sewing. The entire crew set about to do the CPR. The EKG came back; it showed a normal sinus rhythm; but there was clear evidence that the man had suffered a major heart attack.

"He's had an MI!" moaned the anesthesiologist. "We're going to lose him!"

A myocardial infarction, the classical heart attack, was terrible anytime, but in the OR with an open wound it seemed to be an entire echelon worse.

"No we're not," Garven said calmly in reply to the anesthesiologist's negative outburst. "Keep working!"

They got him stabilized and into the coronary care unit. He appeared to be doing reasonably well. The anesthesiologist came to Garven crying.

"I'm so sorry, Dr. Wilsonhulme. It's all my fault. I know it. I can't tell you how sorry I am."

"Sorry isn't worth much. Learn the lesson from this case and get on with your work. It comes with the territory," Garven said, blandly.

"What are we going to do?" she asked.

She knew that her inexperience had not only injured the patient but had also wrecked the neurosurgeon's schedule. She was a basket case and could only imagine how the surgeon had to feel.

Garven looked at her for a moment then said, "Send for the next patient."

"Are you kidding?" she asked. "I don't think I have the courage to put another patient to sleep today, maybe never."

Garven said without resentment or accusation, "If you can't stand the heat, you'd better get out of the kitchen. Now, let's get back to work, it's therapeutic."

Pat MacNamara was in the hospital day and night. One weekend all year, he asked Garven to cover for him because his sister was getting married. It occurred to Garven to tell Pat what he had been told when he wanted to attend his own wedding—'that's what back stairs and student nurses are for'—but he was too soft hearted, he guessed. He agreed to cover for Pat. The chief resident looked over-tired, and Garven was afraid he would get sick and then Garven, himself, would have to revert back to being the de facto chief resident. That was a fate worse than death; so, he thought of doing the favor as the lesser of evils, a bit of insurance for himself.

The junior resident, Hartley Lithum, called Garven in to help with a GSW of the head.

"It's two fifteen, Hartley. Hasn't Pat got you doing all the head trauma at night? He's got a thought disorder if he hasn't," Garven mumbled.

"This is a big problem, Garven. The dude has a bullet lodged right in his superior sagittal sinus. It's a two man job if you know what you're doing. I never even saw one of these before," Hartley confessed.

Garven had. They were touchy. The superior sagittal sinus was a very large and critical venous channel that ran along the middle and top of the covering of the brain from front to back. If the sinus were to be cut across, there would be fatal bleeding. If it were tied off in the posterior one third, the brain would not be able to drain its blood and there would be fatal brain swelling.

"Where's the bullet, Hartley?" asked Garven.

"Where would you think? Murphy's law holds in gun shot wounds to the head just like it does in every other situation."

"Posterior third?"

"Yep."

"I'll be right in. Get the OR nurses to find a bile duct 'T' tube and some silastic hose and sterilize them. We'll need them."

"Okay, chief," Hartley said.

Garven was so often the one that the residents turned to for help and the one who taught them how to operate and to take care of patients that they were falling into the habit of referring to him as 'chief'. It was likely to prove a little embarrassing if the real chief, Dr. Chou, heard them.

Garven refused to do the operation. He made Hartley do it all, even though the resident had never even seen the procedure. Hartley did a very careful craniotomy removing the mid posterior one-third of the skull. The dural veins were plentiful there, hanging down onto the brain. It was crucial to electro-coagulate each of them and to avoid letting them start to bleed because they retracted into the brain, and it was difficult to find them and get them under control before the brain was damaged if they started to hemorrhage. Hartley did a good job.

"Okay," Garven said, "Let's cut off a piece of temporalis muscle in case everything blows up, and we have to sew in a plug just to get out of here."

Garven had Hartley put a large purse string suture around the sinus in front of the missile entry site and one behind it. The suture was left loose for future use.

"Now, let's put a big temporary aneurysm clip on both ends."

Hartley complied. There was no blood coming from the bullet hole.

"Okay, suck it up, Hartley. Time to take out the foreign body," Garven said.

The scrub nurse automatically brought up a stainless steel kidney basin to catch the bullet when Hartley performed the age-old ritual. He extracted several bone fragments, then several smaller lead fragments.

When he pulled out the last big piece of bullet, there was an eruption of bleeding from both ends of the cut venous sinus. Hartley looked slightly panicked.

"Pull the purse string sutures," Garven ordered.

Like magic the bleeding stopped. Hartley wondered if he would ever be as skilled and as cool under pressure as his chief.

Garven had placed sutures in the latex 'T' tube so that the horizontal limbs were pointing outward. He had Hartley slip the forward end of the 'T' into the sinus, then he released the purse string. Blood began to flow out of the latex diversion tube. Garven put a clamp on the latex to stop the flow.

"Suture it in place," Garven told the resident.

Hartley brought the sutures out through the walls of the sinus and tied them which secured the rubber tube in place. The sutures were in front of the original purse string sutures. Now Garven tightened that suture so that it held the tube firmly in place.

Garven had Hartley repeat the same steps on the posterior end of the tube. Garven replaced the clamp so that it was on the stem of the 'T' tube.

"Okay, open it up," he told Hartley.

Blood began to flow freely through the tube.

"Nice," said Hartley.

He had picked up a pearl that night.

"No hill for a climber," Garven said.

"So, how come we have that tube sticking out of the brain like an antenna?" Hartley asked.

"We'll have to put in a little heparin post op to ensure flow. You do that personally. That is not a job for anyone who can't run this guy back down to the OR within a couple of minutes and redo this operation. Threaten anyone who pulls this tube out with a public execution," Garven said.

He let Hartley close up. "Call me in the office," he said.

He loved saying that.

CHAPTER
Four

O ver the next two years, Garven worked to establish himself in the
academic neurosurgery world and was eminently successful thanks,
in large part, to his goats. He went from being an AIP (Almost Important
Person) when he was the chief resident to being an FIP (Fairly Important
Person) as an assistant professor. He was not yet to VIP status. With the success of his early experiments where he anastomosed one nerve root above a
cord injury to one below and the enthusiastic reception given his published
report, he had embarked on the more ambitious second half of his project.
He connected four nerves above to four below. It was like the old principle of
pharmacology: if a little is good, then, a lot must be better. The results were
more than quadruple the improvement in the paraplegic goats.

Every goat regained bowel and bladder function. Garven did 200 animals,
and of them, 174 were able to move their hind limbs, 86 could stand, and 70
were able to mount detectable movement. None of them were normal, but
the degree of improvement was undeniable, and the neurological-neurosur-
gical world was galvanized into action. None of the control animals improved
an iota. The experiments were repeated on other species with varying degrees
of success, and the nation's press ran a brief positive report. Garven had been
credited with the discovery of the method in an article written in the *New
England Journal of Medicine*. That journal had a direct pipeline to the press,
and soon Garven was being credited, in usual news media hyperbole, with
being the "Jonas Salk of the tragedy of paraplegia."

A multicenter investigation was established by the AANS to test out the procedure in humans with Garven as its chairman. UCOMH served as the collating center. The investigation proved to be an enormous windfall for under-employed neurosurgeons. Insurance companies could not deny payment for the "Wilsonhulme Cord Injury Diversion" procedure, and there was no problem in finding the 6000 patients for the worldwide study. An office with a full-time statistician was established at Osterlund Memorial, and Garven was in high demand for scientific society programs.

Knowing that he could not maintain his career on only one investigation, even though he was able to parlay the work into an even dozen articles, Garven busied himself with the publication of a number of clinical series reports—his series on transsphenoidal hypophysectomies, a collection of the results of craniotomies for metastatic brain tumors, a small series of attempts to remove skull base meningiomas that indicated a dismal future for that effort, and the UCOMH history of work on aneurysms and attempts to treat vasospasm. His success with the publication of the articles on the intercostal nerve anastomoses bred more success, at least in terms of being able to get his work published. Neurosurgery journals were flooded with articles to publish and were therefore able to pick and choose articles they wanted pretty much at their whim. They also, as a result of the glut of submitted articles, had the privilege and responsibility of careful scrutiny of what they published. Garven's name as an author all but guaranteed its publication. By June, 1965, Garven Wilsonhulme, M.D. had published or had works 'in publication' numbering thirty-one original and review journal articles, chapters in books, and inclusions in scientific program abstracts from papers he had presented.

For the past six months Garven's overriding interest, despite all the heady time he spent in the limelight, was to prepare for the neurosurgical board examination—a two day oral grilling that separated the brain surgery wheat from the chaff. Garven had been hearing horror stories about the boards since he was in medical school He was in the neurosurgical public eye, and to fail would be a publicized humiliation. Every hour he was not in the lab or operating room or engaging in his mandatory six hours of sleep a night, Garven was studying. Elizabeth told him she might as well be divorced for as much as she saw him. At least, if they were divorced, he might find some reason to talk to her. He deeply resented her inability to empathize with him. The world was her oyster, and his trevails were inconsequential in her self-absorbed prismatic view.

The test was scheduled for Friday, June 11 and Saturday, June 12 in the Parkland Memorial Hospital-University of Texas Southwestern Medical School at Dallas. Garven took a flight into Dallas a day early; so, there would be no possibility of a foul up. The orientation for the test was to begin at eight o'clock the following morning. Garven checked into the Fairmont Hotel, locked himself away in his room, and poured over his final distillation of notes—one more time over the components of the brachial plexus of nerves in the arm, one more time over the characteristic appearances of meningiomas, gliomas, and pituitary tumors on slides, one more time over the operative approach to pineal tumors. For the first time in years, he was too excited to sleep.

His alarm went off at six o'clock. He groaned. He thought that he might actually have fallen asleep for a few minutes. He had determined to be in place in the orientation waiting room an hour early. Garven hurried through his shower and morning ablutions, shaved and nicked himself and had to put toilet paper patches to staunch the bleeding. His shoelace broke. He cursed it, spliced it as best he could and jumped into his pants. It was getting late by the timetable he had set for himself months ago. His trousers zipper broke, came clear off the track.

Now, he was stuck, having to go to the most important appearance of his life with his zipper stuck open. At best he would look like a hick, at worst a pervert, he thought. He had no other pants. He had no sewing kit. He held his blue blazer in front of his gaping front and ran down to the lobby to see if the concierge had some safety pins. It took an age, but she found three of them, probably off some of the maids' brassieres. Garven thanked heaven that women always had to pin something up. He was going to be late. What had he ever done to have this calamity befall him?

As best he could, Garven put the safety pins in place. He nipped the dorsum of his penis. It hurt like crazy; but worse, the nick bled as if he had slaughtered a pig in his pants. The only thing he could do was stuff in some toilet paper to stop the bleeding and to keep the blood from soaking his dress trousers. He looked like a world class stud with the bulge in the front of his pants. He could only shake his head. He threw on a tie and his blazer and ran down stairs without even thinking about taking the elevator.

The doorman called a cab. It took forever for it to come. He would be lucky if he were even thirty minutes early. He felt panicky. In front of the hotel two little Negro girls in crisp clean and starched pinafores were laughing and singing a jive tune as they clapped each others' hands in a complicated series of maneuvers"

"Hambone, Hambone, where you been?
Hambone, Hambone, come on back again.
Do the Hambone with your hands,
Move your feet and then you stands."

The little girls' unfettered gaiety seemed woefully out of place on that awful day. Garven threw himself into the cab when it eventually got there.

"Hurry, please!" he pleaded.

"Ya'll wanna tell me where to?" the cabby drawled.

It was like seeing and hearing the world in slow motion.

"Parkland Hospital, front lobby," Garven blurted.

He shouted inwardly at himself to calm down. If he did not get hold of himself he would pee his pants during the exam.

"We is off to the 'Lands," said the cab driver.

It was a nice sunny day; the driver had had a good breakfast of grits and molasses and biscuits and gravy; and he was feeling all right with the world. He did not even mind the unusually heavy morning rush hour traffic.

In the back seat Garven was going crazy watching his time advantage tick away. He would be lucky to be there fifteen minutes early, barely time enough to get his racing mind back down into a reasonable gear. There was a hang-up getting into the entrance driveway of Parkland. Garven tried to judge the distance and the time to gauge whether or not to jump out and make a break for it on foot. The traffic moved again. Someone's old aunty had been slow in alighting from the family car. Garven gave the man seven dollars for a four dollar ride. He just grabbed the folding money stuffed in his pocket without looking at it.

"Thank ya'll, Suh!" said the cab driver.

Garven ran through the front doors. The place looked just like U.C. Osterlund Memorial, unclean and disorderly. He asked at the information desk where the conference rooms were.

"Secon' flo', turn lef', then raht. Down the hall. Turn lef' agin. Then one more raht. Cain' miss it. Ya'll have a nass day, y'heah?"

Fat chance of that.

"Thanks for the help," he said.

The elevator was out of order. He ran up the stairs two and three at a time. Same dirt, bums sitting smoking, same babies being changed on the floor of the stairwells as at UCOMH. He felt right at home. He was in the waiting room with five minutes to spare. He was pouring sweat and out of breath. He swore that he would exercise regularly if God would only let him catch his breath and stop looking like a fool this once.

Around Garven were eighteen other candidates. He knew they were there to take the test because of their gaunt faces and the haunted expressions in their hollow eyes. Some of them were in worse states of dishevelment than him.

At eight o'clock on the dot a secretary, who looked like one of *Das Gestapogehilfin*, called them to attention. Garven was relieved not to see the *Hitlergrüss*.

"I will read off your names and your room numbers. You will go there first for two hours and then proceed to the next higher room number in rotation. They have your name on their list."

Garven thought he could understand her instructions so far. It was about all he could get his mind to do. He was not sure at this point if he would be able to remember his full name let alone something about the basic sciences of neurology, whatever that was. He had to get hold of himself. He had to urinate. He would never get those safety pins undone then repinned in time. He squeezed his thighs together unconsciously.

A Parkland neurosurgeon ran into the center of the group with a wild look in his eye.

"I am not late! I am not late!" he shouted.

No one had accused him of being late. It was eight oh one. He was in scrubs, obviously exhausted after a night on call taking care of the Dallas chapter of the Knife and Gun Club. Someone had told him that he would not be admitted for the test if he came late, and he had all but killed himself to get there on time. There was blood in his eye for anyone that might have the temerity to bar him after all he had been through to prepare and then finally to get to the appointed place. Since no one seemed to challenge him, the newcomer calmed down.

The *Gestapogehilfin* had worked for the American Board of Neurosurgery for ten years. She was used to the overly wound springs that came in for the tests. She calmly went on.

"Each phase will be given by two examiners. Over the next two days, you will be examined in neurophysiology, neurochemistry, neuropathology, neuroradiology, and clinical neurology. You will each have two hours of examination on the spine and peripheral nerve section of neurosurgery and two hours on the cranial section. Lunch will be served promptly at noon each day. You will have a thirty minute lunch period."

That was generous of them. Garven strained to remember if he had even studied some of those subjects. He felt his entire mind go blank as he goose stepped behind the *Gestapogehilfin* up to the first room. It was marked with a poster: NEUROANATOMY. Two men sat behind a utilitarian table, one older, calm and friendly and one younger and intense looking. Both were dressed in tweed sport coats and hand tied bow ties. Easterners! Garven's heart sank. He knew that he could expect no mercy from the eastern establishment. They were notorious for flunking western academicians for no other reason than to advance the myth of the superiority of the eastern schools. It was very unfair. Garven felt angry and insecure. He was aware that his mind was getting away from him. He made a conscious effort to get back to reality.

"Good morning, Dr. Wilsonhulme," said the older of the two men. "I'm Ed Boldrey from San Francisco, and this is Gilmer Shapiro from Upstate New York."

Garven nodded his return greeting. It was the practice of the boards to have a younger expert in the field being examined and also an older and seasoned neurosurgeon in the room to keep things reasonable and fair. Ed Boldrey, the chief of neurosurgery at U.C. San Francisco Moffitt Hospital, was famous for his scholarship and encyclopedic knowledge of everything that had to do with the neurological sciences. Garven did not know about Dr. Shapiro.

"How is your paper on jugular vein anastomoses to the intracranial internal carotid artery post stroke coming along," Dr. Boldrey asked to calm the candidate down.

"Fine. Thanks for asking, Dr. Boldrey. I'm flattered that you are aware of it," Garven said.

He was calming down.

"Dr. Shapiro is our expert in neuroanatomy. I'm here to see that he doesn't get too technical. The fathers of neurosurgery, in their wisdom, thought that if I couldn't answer the question, it would be unfair to grade you on it. That's my *raison d'être*," Ed Boldrey said.

That was scant encouragement for Garven. Anything Ed Boldrey did not know about neuroanatomy was not worth knowing. Garven's hopes sunk a little more.

"I would like to start of with a classical little teaser," Dr. Boldrey said, "the prerogative of age. Dr. Wilsonhulme, could you please tell us the names of the nerves coming off the lumbosacral plexus starting from cephalad and working caudad and the muscles or sensory distribution served?"

Garven hesitated for a fraction, then the hours of study clicked in; and he rattled off the answer like a recorded message, "Posteriorly, from L4,5, and S1 comes the nerve to the quadratus femoris, then... "

Garven was letter perfect and used up more than three minutes. He was calm and ready to do battle now.

Dr. Shapiro took over, and the questions became harder:

"Describe the sensory nerve endings."

"Pacinian Corpuscles that serve proprioception, pressure, and touch. Meissner's Corpuscles that serve touch and pressure, the endbulbs of Krause detect cold, Ruffini Corpuscles detect heat, and free nerve endings of delta fibers, which are nearly ubiquitous, are for the various types of pain," Garven rattled.

He was on a roll. He gave a brief description of the histological appearance of each of the nerve endings.

"Tell us the contents of the floor of the fourth ventricle."

That was easy for Garven; he had looked at it surgically in his posterior fossa operations.

"Faciculus gracilis, the clave, the faciculus cuneatus... "

He listed another six or seven structures. He knew he was scoring well.

Dr. Boldrey asked Garven to describe in full and to draw the brachial plexus of the arm. Every candidate that ever took the neurosurgical boards anticipated that question, and Garven could have drawn and labeled a schema of the brachial plexus blindfolded. He planned to forget it the day after he got done with the boards. He took his time.

Dr. Boldrey nodded his approval. Dr. Shapiro kept the questions coming:

"Trace the route of the Vagus nerve from its ganglion to the heart. Describe the gross anatomy of the spinal cord as seen with a Nissl stain. Name the basal ganglia. List the parts of the midbrain."

Dr. Boldrey concluded the two hours with a simple straight forward request for Garven to name the arteries of the posterior fossa from below to above and to describe the areas of the brain they served. Garven knew he had aced this part of the exam.

He spoke rapidly, "Vertebrals, anterior and posterior spinals, basilar, PICA, AICA, superior cerebellars, PCAs."

"You may move to the next room, Dr. Wilsonhulme," said Dr. Boldrey.

Garven heaved a small sigh of relief. He was about one eighth of the way to being done. It was something.

NEUROPHYSIOLOGY read the banner over the door of the next room. This was Garven's weakest area. Theodore White was the neurosurgeon, and Thomas Perl, PhD was the researcher conducting the question and evaluation in that room. Garven introduced himself, and the questions began.

"Would you please describe the features of the Grass Polygraph, Dr. Wilsonhulme?"

Garven used the machine regularly in the lab, but would never have dreamed that he would be asked a question about it. The lab techs took care of it, and all Garven cared was that it worked.

He fumbled and faltered, "Uh, well, I confess not to be much of a hand at machinery. I know the Grass Polygraph is an instrument useful for continuous monitoring of relatively slow electrical changes as a function of time. There is a pen—I think it works by magnetic deflection—that moves across the paper at a constant rate."

Garven was aware that he had broken out into a light sweat.

"The machine amplifies bioelectric potentials and potential changes so that there can be sufficient current to make the pens move."

He floundered his way through a very rudimentary description, aware that he was making mistakes.

"All right, Dr. Wilsonhulme, that is enough on the Grass Polygraph. Now, would you tell us the characteristics of a cat with transection of the brain at the level of the pons and compare it to the behavior of another cat with a high spinal cord lesion?"

Garven knew that.

"The brain stem injury results in decerebrate behavior... "

Garven described the spastic character of the remaining movements such a cat would have. He described the high spinal injury—quadriplegia, retained flexor reflexes, and respiratory failure.

"Yes. Now tell us the effects of electrical stimulation of post central gyrus of a primate."

Garven responded correctly.

"Can you give us a word description of Fick's principle then the mathematical expression of his law?"

"*Say whaa?*" Garven said to himself.

He flipped every page in the scientific memory stored in his brain and drew a blank.

"No, Sir, I can't."

"Then please be kind enough to describe the electrophysical changes and the local electrochemical actions involved in the transmission of neural excitation."

Garven knew something about that.

"Nerve cells are specialized cells with elongation and properties unique to them of propagating excitation. The process results in a drop in voltage in a positive direction that is in the neighborhood of a hundred millivolts. At the nodes of Ranvier... ”

He felt that he had done decently on that question.

The questions continued nonstop until noon sharp. Garven felt entirely wrung out. He had forgotten the feeling of success that he had developed on the anatomy portion and was a mass of anxiety about the neurophysiology.

He did not feel like eating, but knew that he had to. His greatest fear was that he would get hypoglycemic in the afternoon and would not be able to think. He seemed to have conquered panic; and at least he still had the possession of all of his faculties, such as they were, he thought.

That was more than he could say for his old friend from Burton-Cagle prep school, Devon Upshire, who, coincidentally, had gone into neurosurgery and was taking the boards that same day. Garven had been astounded when he learned that Devon had started a neurosurgery residency at Mass General. He seemed smart enough, but not really tough enough. Garven guessed that was why he selected the Harvard system.

When Garven had asked him why neurosurgery? Devon had not hesitated a second, “Most prestige. Ever hear that old expression, ‘Well, he’s no brain surgeon.’? That means that brain surgery is the top of the mountain, the career by which all others are measured, the popular standard for intelligence. And, besides, it’s the best money in all of medicine, Garv, old Burton-Cagle buddy.”

They had both laughed at Devon’s clear exposition of the advantages of neurosurgery.

On that day of taking the boards, Devon did not look so confident or flippant. The two of them sat down to their sack lunches, and Garven thought his friend looked positively sick.

“Man, you look terrible, Devon. Got the flu?” he asked.

“Worse. I think something dreadful has happened to me.”

Devon’s face was all seriousness.

“What happened. What do you think you have?”

“I went into the first room. It was neurophysiology. It was nothing short of dreadful. I bombed. Have you had physiology yet?”

“Yeah, and I agree,” Garven said.

“Anyway, I sat in there in terror while those two grand inquisitors stretched me over the rack. I kept my shoe heels locked on the little brace thing on the bottom of the chair with my legs bent backwards during the whole session. When I got up, I expected to be stiff, but this was ridiculous. I couldn’t walk right. I still can’t. I ka-lump along with the strangest gait. I think I had a stroke.”

He looked frightened.

"I wore a new suit and a new pair of shoes; so, I wouldn't look bad; and I would be comfortable, and I wouldn't have to think about anything except the test questions. Now, I can't think about anything but having a stroke. I think I'll have to drop out. It's been a terrible day."

Garven asked, "Let's see you walk."

Devon obliged. His gait was very peculiar, but it involved both legs and did not look anything like a stroke. He ka-lump ka-lumped down the hall with an unnatural toe to heel step. Garven studied Devon generally then focused on his feet.

"C'mere and let me look at your shoes," Garven asked.

Devon looked at him strangely but came back to the table and looked at his shoes. Before he could hand them to Garven, he started to laugh. He guffawed until tears ran out of his eyes.

"Look," he said between paroxysms.

He handed Garven the shoes. The heels were missing.

"When I sat on that stupid chair in the neurophys test, I must have pulled the heels off on the brace underneath and never knew it. And I thought I had had a stroke!"

Devon broke into laughter again. This time Garven joined him. The candidates around them wondered if the two of them had gone off the deep end with the stress of the test, but were too polite and too wrapped in their own feelings of impending insanity to say anything.

The thirty minutes were up. Back to the torture chambers. Garven walked to the next room. Its banner said: NEUROSURGERY. That sounded vaguely familiar; Garven entered hoping for the best. The senior neurosurgeon was Kemp Clark, one of the officers of the board. He was a tall, patrician man dressed in a perfectly creased dark three-piece Brooks Brothers suit. Garven expected him to be harsh, but he was kind to the point of being helpful. The young Turk in the room was a neurosurgeon from the Mayo Clinic, the WFMC, named Oliver Sergeant. He had something to prove like all of those academicians who knew the books but couldn't find their way around an actual operation with the book open.

Dr. Clark, the chief at Parkland, put Garven at ease. Dr. Sergeant began his barrage of irrelevant questions:

"Tell me what you would do with an infant born with a thoracic myelomeningocoele and paraplegia?"

Garven said, "Nothing."

"What?" asked Dr. Sergeant.

Dr. Clark was looking at Garven thoughtfully.

"I think it is cruel to operate on those babies and cover up their defect; so, they can't get meningitis. Left alone they die. Treated early, they go on to live lives full of misery, operations, incontinence, and failed shunts for their hydrocephalus," Garven said.

"What would you really do, Dr. Wilsonhulme? I have heard that the English school of neurosurgeons and some benighted people west of the Mississippi practice such neglect, but I can't imagine that being a real choice. Certainly, we would not permit that at the Mayo Clinic."

"Well, Sir, nevertheless that's what I would do. I know how to put in a shunt and how to repair the spinal defect. I'll go ahead and describe that for you if you wish," Garven replied.

"Please do that."

Garven gave a description in detail.

"Would you tell me how you would go about to repair a range of injuries to the brachial plexus, Dr. Wilsonhulme?" asked Dr. Clark.

Garven gave an orderly discussion of primary suturing, lengthening nerves by dissecting them up to their bifurcations and of single and cable grafts. He added a segment on casting and post op rehab. Dr. Clark looked satisfied.

Dr. Sergeant considered himself an expert on brachial plexus injuries. He was not satisfied with Garven's answer about what he would do with a complete disruption of the entire set of upper extremity nerves by a stretching injury such as an arm being caught in moving machinery. He described a case and asked Garven for the diagnosis.

"Complete brachial plexus avulsion injury," Garven said.

He was a little confused because he thought they had just gone over this area.

"Now tell me how you would handle this problem."

Garven said, "I would leave it alone. It's hopeless."

There was a long pause. No one spoke. Garven was unsure what he should do. The questioner seemed like a typical easterner, very strange.

Finally, Garven described the alternatives of doing extensive surgery and the kinds of operations available. Still, Dr. Sergeant maintained a stiff pontifical silence. Garven looked over at Dr. Clark. The senior neurosurgeon looked as perplexed as Garven.

Finally, Dr. Clark said, "Let's go on, Dr. Sergeant. I believe Dr. Wilsonhulme has answered the question fully."

Dr. Sergeant ran Garven through a long list of questions in a rapid fire series.

"How do you treat an infected shunt in a newborn? How do you tell if an adolescent needs his shunt revised? Describe the operation for a ruptured lumbar disc."

Garven knew that procedure to perfection and stretched out his answer as long as he could.

"How would you treat this?"

Garven was shown an angiogram of a large tumor that looked like a dumb-bell occupying both the posterior fossa and the area above the tentorium. After four hours, Garven was as limp as a wet noodle. He walked very slowly out of the neurosurgery exam room. He had no more energy.

Garven and Devon went out to dinner together at the five star Pyramid Restaurant in the Fairmont Hotel. They figured that they had earned it.

"How do you think you did, Devon?"

"I sweated bullets, but I really thought I did all right except for physiology. I just couldn't get interested in that stuff. I'm really not sure there. How about you?"

"The same. I don't know if I am an 'iron man of neurosurgery' enough to go through another day of that. Maybe that's part of the test to see how much stamina you have," Garven said.

The two men renewed their fond acquaintanceship from prep school. Garven had forgotten how much he liked Devon. He was glad that his old friend had gone into neurosurgery because that meant that their paths would cross often. It was very difficult to keep up any kind of correspondence, let alone visiting schedule, with people who were not in his field, Garven had found. He had a twinge of guilt for not getting in touch with his old friends from Cipher, Arizona. He had gotten so far away from them, that he no longer admitted that he came from that little zero town. He now listed his home town as Providence, Rhode Island, where the important Wilsonhulmes lived. It was a minor concession to his entrance into the sophisticated social and professional world of academic neurosurgery.

CHAPTER
Five

The following morning, Garven went to the neurology exam room first. He was thankful to see a neurosurgeon, Bob King, in the room. Dr. King was as smart as any neurologist who ever lived, and Garven felt as if he had an ally. The neurologist looked like every other neurologist: rumpled, tweedy, gray button down collar shirt and unlatching knit tie, orthopedic shoes. He had the obligatory pipe that he chewed and poked at throughout the examination.

The neurologist presented cases as his way of eliciting Garven's medical knowledge.

"An elderly man comes in complaining of severe unilateral headache and episodic visual obscurations."

"Temporal arteritis."

"Headaches that occur frequently at intervals then are absent, only to return in a similar pattern?"

"Cluster headaches."

"Elderly woman comes to your clinic with difficulty moving especially with alternating movements of her hands, a tremor at rest, immovable facial expression, stooped posture. What does she have and what other signs might we expect?"

"Parkinson's Disease, Paralysis Agitans." Garven said. "She ought to have a festinating gate, rigidity, unblinking stare. Late in the disease she would likely have dementia."

The case histories came at Garven rapidly, and he gave the diagnosis and a short comment about each disease. He estimated that he was getting ninety percent of them. The last case was described.

"Young woman presents with unilateral blindness that clears. Then she gets weakness in her legs that clears but not entirely. Finally, when you see her, she has a tremor, a gait indicative of dysequilibrium, and a flicking abnormal movement of both eyes."

"Multiple sclerosis," Garven said as the horn sounded to shift to a new room.

The neurologist chewed on his pipe, and Dr. King looked at Garven with an unrevealing face.

NEUROPATHOLOGY, read the next sign. Garven was about to enter when he realized that the session was still in progress. In fact, he saw that there was a loud confrontation taking place. He stepped politely away. In a few minutes one of the examiners ran out of the room and caught *Das Gestapogehilfin's* arm and entered into an excited whispering conversation. She rushed to her telephone. In a few minutes security guards ran into the exam area, went into the exam room, and came out with a man Garven recognized as one of the board candidates who was now in handcuffs.

Devon sidled up to Garven and asked, "Wanna know what's going on? I confess to having eavesdropped shamelessly."

Garven laughed and told Devon that he was dying to know.

"The examinee is named Mel Farber. He's in the navy. One of the guys I talked to, a flunkee from last year, said he was here then, too. He got real excited and argued with the neuropathologist about the slides they were looking at until they threw him out. This year, apparently he was being examined by a different neuropathologist and started to argue again. This time when they threatened to kick him out if he didn't settle down, he jumped over the table and punched out the examiner. Completely cold cocked him. He went berserk when they told him that he would never be allowed to sit for the boards again."

Garven laughed uproariously at the story even though he felt terrible for the navy neurosurgeon.

"Poor bugger," he said. "I know how he feels. There, but for the grace of God, go I."

"Amen, brother. Only four more hours to go. Hang in there," Devon said.

An hour of Garven's testing time in neuropathology was used up before he got into the room while everyone was being calmed down, and the room was being restored to order. Much as Garven might have regretted not having his full opportunity, he felt that he would somehow get over his loss.

The new examiner—the previous one had given up for the day—had set up six microscopes with pathology slides under them. Garven was instructed to give the diagnosis and to describe the characteristic findings on each of the slide specimens. There were H&E brain tumor preparations, osmic acid longitudinal sections, silver stains to show cells and fine fibers, Marchi method stains for degenerated myelin, Weigert stains to demonstrate normal cord myelin, and Nissl stain to show cord details.

Garven was right on all of the tumors of the brain and of the spinal cord. He missed the multiple sclerosis plaque but recognized the Alzheimer neurofibrillary plaque. He considered himself either to be a genius or very lucky to identify subacute combined degeneration associated with alcoholism. He was accurate on herpes simplex encephalitis with its intense inflammation and pannecrosis, on a fresh infarct after a stroke, and a degenerating peripheral nerve. He was wrong on two metabolic diseases.

Garven knew full well at this point that he had not done anything like a perfect job on the boards thus far. He felt uneasy not knowing how far from perfect he could be. With that in mind, he headed into the last room, NEURORADIOLOGY.

Bassett Gilmer, one of the most renowned neuroradiologists in the country was flanked by Lyle French, the chief of the Department of Neurosurgery at the University of Minnesota. Garven had great personal respect for them both.

Dr. Gilmer led off with the controversy of the day, "Dr. Wilsonhulme, which is the preferred method of angiography?"

"I prefer direct puncture over catheter angiography."

"Why?"

"Because the studies I read and the investigation done in LA indicates that it is safer by a few percent," Garven said.

Dr. Gilmer asked, "Are you familiar with the work by Hans Newton in San Francisco or the people at the Mass General or the articles by the Russians?"

"Some of it," Garven said.

He and Dr. Gilmer had a short discussion of the two methods, enough to satisfy both examiners that Garven knew what he was talking about. They left the subject with an agreement to disagree.

"Lets get into the general field of myelography, then," Dr. French said. "Tell us about pneumomyelography, epidurography, and epidural venography, please."

Garven described and discussed the three exotic forms of myelography and concluded that he did not think much of any of them. Dr. French nodded his head in agreement, and Garven knew that he was scoring well. Dr. French was not a man to give away any free kudos.

Dr. Gilmer had Garven describe the differences between extramedullary and intramedullary lesions—whether a spinal mass lay on the outside of the cord but inside the dural covering or whether the mass was part of the cord itself. Dr. French asked him about several different kinds of trauma and about arteriovenous malformations. Garven was on altogether familiar ground and did well with all of the clinical questions.

Dr. Gilmer then showed Garven a series of myelograms and had him describe the findings and give the diagnoses. Again, Garven did well, being familiar with a wide variety of myelographic presentations from his own experience. Then Dr. Gilmer pulled out a stack of angiograms, mostly of the brain, but a few of the cord, and pneumoencephalograms. The studies had been carefully arranged to progress from easier to most difficult. By the time the two hours was up, Garven was only getting fifty percent of them. He figured that he was all right because some of them were so subtle or complicated that only a world renowned expert could have found and accurately described the abnormalities, and all three men were laughing about the absurd level of difficulty the studies presented for the test situation.

It was five o'clock on Saturday at last, and the boards were over. Garven was so exhausted and relieved to have the tests behind him that he could not worry about whether or not he had passed. He gave himself a fifty-fifty chance. As he walked towards the exit, he ran into Dr. Clark, the secretary of the board.

"Hold on a second. You're Wilsonhulme, right?" Dr. Clark said.

"Yes, Sir," Garven replied.

He was flattered that such an important member of the neurosurgical elite would even recognize him.

"I'm not supposed to tell you this; and I don't want you to spread it around that you know; but go home and sleep easy. You are one of the new members of the club," Dr. Clark told him and winked conspiratorially.

Garven wanted to shout and turn somersaults. He wanted to sing and hug homely girls and sweep up children and kiss them. He had passed the boards! He had surmounted the last great hurdle. On that day he was officially and certifiably a neurosurgeon. He was unsure if he actually walked with the soles of his feet on the ground or not when he went back to the hotel. He could not recall ever having a feeling of such elation. He was sure that the full import of what Dr. Clark had told him would make the realization even sweeter as the next few days passed. It was an incomparable elevation of his sense of self-esteem and self-confidence. Right then, Garven felt invincible.

CHAPTER
Six

Drs. Chou and Stark gave Garven a pair of one inch boards a foot long inscribed with his name and the date that he passed the 'boards' as a memento. They told Garven that now he was a board certified assistant professor. Dr. Chou and Dr. Stark now concentrated on their own research and committee work and on their few private patients at the near exclusion of the needs of the indigent service at UCOMH. That duty devolved to Garven. He was now regarded on the neurosurgery service and in the medical center as a whole as an important player. That meant that he was nearly a VIP.

He became the de facto chief for the residents and found himself pulled away from his research to teach them. He delegated greater authority and opportunity to the chief resident, but still had to be on call to help him more than Garven would have liked. Often when he planned a day in the lab, a disaster would crop up and Garven's work would have to be set aside.

Mabel Forester was a delightful woman who worked as a pink lady on the peds ward. She was an inspiration who came to do her volunteer work five days a week despite having severe pain from rheumatoid arthritis. She grew progressively ill, and one of the peds residents found that she had generalized weakness in her extremities with exaggerated reflexes, like the experimental high cervical injured cat Garven had had to describe in the boards. She was also found to be short of breath. The chief resident of neurosurgery was consulted and did the x-ray workup. He called Garven to help in the decision making process.

Mabel's spine had softened and crumpled with the chronic arthritis and her skull had settled down on the top of the high cervical spine. This narrowed the spinal canal severely and caused compression of the cord. It would only be a matter of time before Mabel would be dead. The chief resident suggested that they remove the posterior portion of the skull and do a high cervical laminectomy. Garven pointed out that those operations would only relieve the pressure from behind, not from in front where the real problem lay. He decided that they should do an experimental operative approach. He had the chief resident schedule Mabel for a removal of the top vertebral bodies from the front. They would have to go through the mouth to get to the spine.

The operation took all day, requiring the approach through the mouth and also the laminectomy as suggested by the chief resident. They had to do fusions by wiring in segments of the iliac crest from her pelvic bone. At the anesthesiologist's suggestion, they also did a tracheostomy because she was so feeble that he knew that she would require ventilation for a long time in the postoperative period. After the operation the residents worked long hours with her. She required positive pressure breathing which caused a new complication of breaking of a small lung cyst. That caused her to have a pneumothorax and to require placement of a chest tube to draw out the air between the lung and the inside of the chest wall. She developed a mucous plug that blocked off one main stem bronchus and caused collapse of that lung. She had to have bronchoscopy with placement of a tube into the air passages to remove the plug and to wash out the pus that had accumulated. Despite prophylactic antibiotics, she got pneumonia.

The chief resident, Jeff Richards, grew discouraged.

"The handwriting's on the wall for Mabel. Maybe we should just quit and let the poor lady rest. Pneumonia isn't such a bad way to go. What do you think, Dr. Wilsonhulme?"

Garven knew how Jeff felt and that he was probably right.

"We are committed to Mabel," he said. "I don't disagree with your assessment, but we have signed on for the long haul. Neurosurgery is like the devil's ball game; you can't win; you can't even break even; but you have to suit up for every game anyway. Give her a few more days."

Mabel never turned the corner and rallied to get well. She developed a new complication almost every day—antibiotic allergy or antibiotic side-effect. Her wound broke down. She couldn't eat, and she required a gastrostomy. She went into all-systems failure. Finally, mercifully, she died.

Elizabeth felt neglected but learned to savor the few evenings Garven was home and to act appreciative, at least. She bought symphony tickets and arranged a romantic date for the two of them one Friday night in December. Garven had to make a quick check on his fresh post op, one of his few private patients. It would only take a minute.

He took a shortcut through the EOR. That was a mistake. Garven should have known better.

"Hey, Dr. Wilsonhulme, we've got a train wreck in Trauma I. There's a guy in Trauma II that needs a trach ASAP. My intern, here, has never even seen one. Think you could talk him through it?"

Garven groaned. He was in his new three button silver gray suit. It was the first time it had been worn. He just knew that he would get blood speckles on it.

It was an emergency, and he knew it could be done in a few minutes.

"Sure," he said with more enthusiasm than he felt.

He set his suit coat aside and put on a gown. He and the intern did the tracheostomy in record time, for an intern. When they were almost done, Garven became aware of a peculiar warm sensation on the side of his leg. He was unsure how long it had been there because he had been hurrying so fast to get the tracheostomy done. He looked down at his leg. To his amazement he saw that his pant leg was soaked in blood, as if someone had dipped it in a vat of the viscous stuff. He could not figure how that had happened. There was no blood on the table, and the patient had hardly bled a drop when he and the intern had done the simple procedure. He pulled away from the table to inspect further for the cause.

Garven found himself hooked to the patient's IV line. It had become dislodged from his arm and the extension tube had worked its way into Garven's pants pocket and had bled away, filling his pocket and saturating the cloth of his pants as he operated. He cursed the perversity of inanimate objects. He knew that he could not go out and tell Elizabeth that they could not go to the symphony; so, he found a way to go with her. She proved to be entirely unreasonable anyway. She sulked all night in the symphony while Garven sat next to her in his suit coat and green scrub pants and one sock.

One of the worst experiences of Garven's career happened shortly after he got back from the boards. The residents had done a tracheostomy on a ten year old girl named Shigella—after the bacteria—Benson. The little girl had been the innocent bystander in a fight that broke out during the wedding of her sister. She was struck in the head with a shovel and sustained a skull fracture and severe cerebral contusion. She had required a trach because of prolonged respiratory failure, but she was improving so much that when Garven saw her on rounds he told the first year resident to remove the trach tube. Shigella was alert enough to understand and reached up to squeeze Garven's hand. He leaned down and gave her a hug.

Garven and the other residents and interns went on to the next room to finish rounds while the first year pulled out the tube. Suddenly, the nurses aide who had been changing beds in Shigella's room dashed into the room where Garven had gone.

She yelled, "We got trouble, doctahs. Y'all come in heah right smart, ya heah?"

She ran up to Garven and pulled on his arm.

All of the doctors ran into the room. A large amount of bright red blood was issuing from the tracheostomy tube.

"She started to bleed...a lot...so I put the tube back in and blew up the balloon. It didn't do no more good than a fart in a windstorm," the resident said as soon as the others gathered.

"Balls!" said the general surgery resident when he saw the bloody mess. "'Balls', cried the queen, 'If I had two, I'd be the king'," he muttered.

Jeff took his look, sighed and added to the general surgery resident's performance, "'Nay,' said the King, 'it takes twelve inches to be a ruler!'"

"Take it out," Garven ordered.

He was not in the mood for ersatz resident humor at that moment. The resident did as he was told. The blood began to pump out in a column almost half an inch in diameter. Garven had gloved his hands. He pushed a finger into the opening in the tracheostomy site and curled it in around forward and squeezed. The bleeding stopped.

"Suction her out," he asked the nurse who had come down as soon as she had learned that there was trouble.

Now Shigella was able to get a little air through. She had a panicky look.

Garven said, "It's okay, sweetheart. We have a little bleeding. We'll take care of it. You won't have any trouble. But you have to lie still."

She relaxed even though he was hurting her. Her childish black face looked at Garven with complete trust.

"What do you think is going on?" the first year asked.

Garven nodded in the direction of Jeff Richards, the chief resident.

Jeff explained. "The end of her trach tube was too low and over time eroded a hole in the subclavian artery and formed a fistula leading into the trachea.

When the balloon went down and the tube came out, the blood had easy access to the outside."

"Okay," Garven said. "I know you have to get to your meningioma half an hour ago, Jeff. When you get down there, tell the OR that I am bringing this girl down. We need a room and a thoracic or vascular guy stat."

The rest of the interns and residents scattered to their several necessary jobs; it was clinic day. Each one of them silently praised himself for not having been fool enough to get his own finger stuck in that opening.

Garven and the neurosurgery head nurse wheeled Shigella to the OR on her bed. Garven could not let go of his pressure on the artery even for an instant without causing another rush of blood. Shigella was crying soundlessly, but she kept perfectly still.

"What a tough little fighter!" the nurse said when they were on their way down in the elevator.

"She gets the prize," Garven agreed.

He hoped she would live to enjoy it. His arm and finger and his back were crying out for relief. He was in a terribly awkward position.

They were met at the entry way to the OR by the head nurse.

"I have bad news and worse news, Dr. Wilsonhulme. I'm sorry."

Garven felt a prickle on the hairs on the back of his neck. He was sure that he did not want to hear the rest of this.

"So, tell me," Garven said.

"Every room is full. They all have operations under way. I won't be able to free one up for well over an hour," she said.

"She was right," Garven thought, "it was 'bad' news."

He was not prepared for the 'worse' part of her news.

"It gets worse. Every thoracic or vascular man is either operating right now or is out of town to their annual meeting. I don't even know when they can break someone out to help. You'll have to hold your finger on the bleeder until we can find a place and a surgeon," the nurse said sadly.

"That's impossible," Garven said. "This thing will break to pieces sooner or later. We have got to operate. You'll have to make a place, even if it's a broom closet."

She shook her head, "Any serious suggestions, Dr. Wilsonhulme?"

"Set up for a thoracotomy at the end of the second hall. It's fairly wide, and it's a lot better than nothing. Let's get this kiddo asleep and out of her misery," he said.

The anesthesiology resident came to assist. He got an IV and a Foley catheter in, typed and crossmatched her, and gave Shigella some sedation. She drifted off to sleep. He held a mask flowing a nitrous oxide-oxygen mix over her nose. Garven squirmed on the bed trying to find a comfortable position. He was unsuccessful. His finger was getting numb.

Blood began to ooze around his finger. He pressed harder. More blood welled up. He shifted his finger and got a serious hemorrhage. He found his old place and got the bleeding to subside to a few spurts a minute.

"We can't keep on like this," he said. "We have to go ahead."

It was evident to everyone that what Garven had said was true. The situation was desperate. Once the bleeding erupted, the blood would fill up her bronchi; and she would not be able to move air, no matter what they did. The anesthesiology resident started a definitive anesthetic gas and poised an endotracheal tube for placement if it became necessary and possible. The nurses painted the girl's chest with iodine and alcohol and opened the pediatric thoracotomy trays and put on the drapes. Garven drew in a deep breath and took the scalpel in his one free hand, luckily his right, and made a skin incision. He had his assistant nurse suction and blot up the bleeders. He cauterized his way through the muscles of the chest wall and entered the pleural cavity. It seemed impossibly awkward. He could not both see up into the dome of the thorax and operate at the same time. He put the self-retaining rib spreader in place between the ribs.

One of the thoracic residents ran up as Garven was struggling to keep his finger on the bleeding point and to work a vascular clamp around the artery enclosed in its fascia beneath the collar bone.

"Am I ever glad to see you," Garven said.

"Well, Dr. Wilsonhulme, I am going to have to report you for stealing thoracic cases," the resident joked gently as he threw on sterile gloves and a gown.

He helped Garven ease out of the way; so, he could work. He dissected around the artery.

"Clamp," he ordered.

"Big or little?" the nurse asked.

"Big. Then we need a big cutting needle with 2-O silk to do a suture ligation of the artery."

She handed him the clamp.

Blood exploded out of the tracheostomy site around Garven's finger. He desperately tried to find the site.

"It tore loose as far as I can feel. Put the clamp on or we won't save this kid. She's special, too," he said.

The resident jammed the clamp in and closed the jaws.

Garven yelled, "Ouch! You've got my finger!"

The surgeon released the clamp. The blood was uncontrollable now. The anesthesiology resident shoved an ET tube down and Garven adjusted his finger so that it could get past.

"I can't move any air!" the anesthesiologist said quietly, but emphatically.

"I can't stop the bleeding!" Garven said, adding to the rapidly worsening situation.

The thoracic resident reapplied the clamp. The greater part of the bleeding stopped.

"Got most of it," he said.

"I still can't move any air," said the anesthesiologist.

"How long has it been since she hasn't had any real respirations?" Garven asked.

"Going on five minutes," one of the nurses said.

Shigella had a cardiac arrest. It was too late; they had nothing to work with. After forty-five minutes of futile effort, Garven called it

"We're beat. Let's stop everything. Even if we got a heart beat back, her brain's turned to mush by now."

He stepped away. The others laid down their various instruments. No one spoke. They maintained a moment of silence for the plucky little girl.

Garven's last thought, as he left to get on with his day's work, was, "*I should have gone into derm. Simple credo—if it's wet, use a dry dressing; if it's dry, use a wet dressing. No one ever gets sick; and no one ever gets well; and there's no night call, and no Shigella Bensons.*"

CHAPTER
Seven

On the strength of his work on the SupraPineal Arachnoid Body—the SPAB—Garven was advanced to the academic rank of associate professor of the University of California in 1965. Interest in the thoracic intercostal nerve anastomosis still remained high, but by 1965, it had become a standard operation for acute paraplegics and was no longer at the front of neurosurgery news and seemed to have reached a dead end clinically with only meager success for a scant few. Garven had needed a new area of success, and he went back to his interest in SPAB that had occupied his medical school summers. He kept his results to himself, not even publishing the usual preliminary results papers. He sprang his findings on the neurosurgical world in the April meeting of the AANS.

At first, the anatomical enigma had seemed to serve no purpose. That violated Garven's sense of economy and order of the nervous system; so, he dug deeper. When he found no influence by removing the arachnoid body on any normal tissue or function, he began to experiment on animals with various bodily dysfunctions and diseases—endocrine disorders, cardiac disease, neoplasms, and several genetic disorders. None of them responded. He worked with several species, most commonly with monkeys. In mid-1962, he was ready to give up and publish a paper detailing his failures and giving the conclusion that SPAB was a useless anatomical appurtenance, a sort of vestigial organ, like the appendix.

Then, he hit on a function, and when he did, he knew he had a near-revolutionary finding. Garven implanted SPAB electrodes in humans with brain tumors who had to undergo craniotomies anyway. He wanted to see what, if anything, would happen if he stimulated the SPAB. He gave small acute stimuli and monitored every function he could think of. Nothing seemed to happen. He left stimulating electrodes in place in six patients after craniotomies for highly malignant glioblastoma multiformes. The patients had no objection and did not mind doing something for the surgeon who had done all of their surgery and care for no fee. Again, Garven found no measurable change in blood chemistry, neurological or bodily function from the chronic stimulation.

But, he did make one important observation: the patients with the stimulating electrodes demonstrated a much slower growth of their tumors. They were alive and had much less neurological deterioration than those patients who were treated by any standard method—surgery, radiation, or chemotherapy or any combination of treatments.

At first, he thought that the positive results were the result of his having put every patient with a stimulating electrode on large doses of cortisone. In fact, he observed that the brain around tumors, and even in parts of the brain well away from the tumors, had less swelling. He published the results of his cortisone findings first, and received wide acclaim for that work, for that bit of serendipity. It became standard practice to pretreat brain tumor patients with cortisone and to give the hormone to people with head injuries, infectious diseases, overhydration, anything that caused brain swelling. Administering high doses of cortisone became known as the Wilsonhulme Method. Garven would have advanced academically for that finding alone. But he realized that the cortisone was not, and, in fact, could not explain the prolonged slowing of growth of the malignant tumors.

Garven's first six patients were alive and well at two years after surgery. Their tumors were present and discernible on studies, but they remained small. Most other patients with glioblastoma—the controls—were dead in less than two years. Garven got permission from the human research committee of the hospital to implant electrodes in every glioblastoma patient that he saw. He swore the committee to secrecy and cornered a number of his colleagues from the city and got their permission to implant the wires in their private patients.

By April, 1965 he had amassed data on seventy-one patients, and there appeared to be valid reason to believe that Garven had made a true breakthrough. He was honored by the American Association of Neurological Surgeons at the April meeting by giving his paper first in the program. News of his findings had gotten out, and the large hall in the Chicago Hilton was filled to overflowing. Of all the papers presented at the meeting, only Garven's made the city's newspapers. It was syndicated by the AP, and within a week, Garven was being hailed as the "man who conquered brain cancer", another inaccurate hyperbole from the press, usually reserved for reports that originated in the *New England Journal of Medicine.*

Garven had done nothing of the kind, and he not only knew it, but he explained that he had not made any such colossal discovery every time he gave a talk or an interview. It was beneficial but only palliative. His patients lived longer and better with the stimulating electrode in place, but eventually they all died from their glioblastoma. They got an additional three years, but the tumor was still fatal. And the glioblastoma multiforme was the only cancer that was effected by the treatment method. No matter how many times he said it, questions and demands from the lay public continued to pour into his office about 'the cure for cancer'. Garven Wilsonhulme was, for the moment, the best known physician on the staff of UCOMH.

There were two spin-off rewards that came to Garven as a result of his discovery and the fame surrounding it. He now received any grant money that he requested. The regents of the University of California were ecstatic with him because the money came in from sources that did not drain their corporate pocket. The other thing that happened for Garven was a rapid advancement in political neurosurgery. He was appointed to the chair of two prestigious committees—the combined grant committee of the Congress of Neurosurgery and the AANS that controlled the life and death of projects in neurosurgery that were submitted to the NIH (National Institutes of Health), and of the residency committee of the Society of University Neurosurgeons (the self-styled 'senior society'). Garven was elected vice president of the Congress of Neurological Surgeons, a post that led automatically to the presidency in two years. He volunteered to be an examiner on the Board of Neurosurgery.

His relationship with David Stark remained good, and the professor, though deposed by his subordinates, still had a very considerable influence in the national and university neurosurgical community. He was willing to help Garven, whom he considered to the his protégé, in any way he could. Garven Wilsonhulme was rapidly becoming one of the most influential and most powerful young men in American neurosurgery. Even by his own most self-effacing estimation, Garven Wilsonhulme was now a VIP.

It became apparent that the three members of the neurosurgery faculty could no longer keep up the pace of their work. The ability to juggle the several tasks of caring for private patients and helping the residents take care of the 'customers' at UCOMH, conducting a viable research program, and keeping up their important places in the national neurosurgical organizations was no longer tenable. They had to hire a new staff man. None of the current residents had the slightest interest in academic medicine.

"Too much politics for me" was the usual reason given.

Garven suggested his old friend, Devon Upshire; although he did not tell the others about their long friendship. He wanted that to be the ace up his sleeve. Devon was flown out to Los Angeles for the grand tour and the schmoozing by the neurology and neurosurgery departments. The neurologists were happy to join forces with the technicians when it seemed important. Steven Chou offered Devon an assistant professorship with the promise that he would be considered for elevation to associate professor and tenure in a couple of years. Devon would not budge on his insistence that he come in as an associate professor to begin with. After three days of partying, sightseeing, and discussing, it looked as if the academic rank was going to be the pivotal issue in Devon's acceptance and that he would leave without accepting the UCOMH offer.

On the last day of Devon's scheduled visit, the UCOMH neurosurgeons met one last time with Devon.

Dr. Chou asked, "Devon, won't you reconsider? We made a generous offer, and we think you would be a man we could work with."

Devon said, "No, we've been over this several times. The associate professorship and tenure are what I came for. Thank you gentlemen. I have appreciated your hospitality."

He rose and picked up his briefcase.

Garven had not had much to say to that point in the negotiations.

Without consulting Dr. Chou or Dr. Stark he said, "With an offer of associate professor and guaranteed tenure, how long before you could be here and ready for work?"

Dr. Chou almost jumped out of his chair when Garven said it. It was not Garven's place to make any kind of offer.

"A month," Devon said.

"Would you please step out and have a seat in the hall. We need to have a discussion about this offer, okay Devon?" Garven asked.

He had seen Steven Chou's eyebrows lift almost to his hairline.

Devon made a graceful exit and sat down with the division secretary for an animated chat about the recent sit-ins, wade-ins, library read-ins, and marches of the civil rights movement. Garven and the two professors wasted no time.

Dr. Chou said, "We have not got the money to make that kind of an offer, Garven. You should not have suggested it."

Garven said, "I think we can go about our business in a different way and have plenty of money to get the help we need. In fact, Devon can be a positive revenue source in a short time, if we are willing to make a change."

"Pray, go on," said David Stark whose attention was now engaged.

"Yes, do," said Dr. Chou.

"It's fairly simple," Garven told them. "We and all of the other academics have acted as if there were something unholy about having private practice money. We have made ourselves live within the budgets allowed by the University of California—both in the division and personally. There is no real reason why we can't change all of that."

"Go fee-for-service?!" asked Dr. Chou as if Garven had suggested that they become Mormons.

"Partly," said Garven. "We can still offer all of the indigent services and do our research. Devon can come on as a sort of junior partner with primary responsibility for the teaching and the care of the no-pay patients. We can let the word out that we are willing to take on a reasonable load of private patients. We have the best neurosurgeons, facilities, and ancillary help in the city. Why not capitalize on it?"

"Dr. Cushing and Walter Dandy would turn over in their graves," said Dr. Chou.

"That would be eminently hypocritical of them, if they did. They made plenty of money trading on their international reputations. So should we. I don't really think that the regents of U.C. would squawk that much if we brought in a few extra bucks for their hospital. I can't help but think that one day a lot of the sources of grants and even money for the charity services is going to dry up. We are going to need a hedge against that day," Garven said.

The discussion went on for nearly twenty minutes. In the end Garven prevailed because Dr. Stark sided with him. It was the first major divisional disagreement, and Steven Chou was surprised that the former chief would take up the cause for change espoused by the junior man. It was unlike him. Devon was given the job. He had no complaints about assuming the major role in dealing with the charity service since he would share in the private patient funds by a formula Garven worked out for the division. It was obvious that Garven had put in considerable preparation for that meeting.

In January of 1966, Garven was advanced to a full tenured professorship. His rapid rise was due only in part to his now prodigious personal bibliography and his eminence in national university medical circles. It was due in large part to his having arranged for a very major contribution by the Getty Foundation. The billionaire underwent removal of a chronic subdural hematoma by Garven. Ever afterwards, he sang Garven's praises for having done a new, experimental procedure on him that restored his failing mental function and saved his life. Garven reported to his colleagues that he did not know who had led J. Paul Getty to think that burr holes were 'new and experimental'. The endowment of the chair carried two stipulations. The chair was to be occupied by a full professor and its first holder was to be Garven Wilsonhulme. Garven had been on the short list for those to be advanced by the U.C. regents for some time, and the Getty endowment provided the final impetus.

Garven still took his turn in the rotation to cover the residents on the indigent service. He took call once a week, and that included going to neurosurgery outpatient clinic. He had grown away from the 'blood and guts' world of UCOMH where the victims of the 'two dudes' continued to come in on a nightly basis, where interns still wheeled gurneys along basement hallways at night and saw rats scurry along in head of them. It was not that he missed that life, but he did find a small dose of it added a little excitement to his existence.

It still amused him to come home and tell Elizabeth and the two children about taking care of a hydrocephalic girl named Peculiar Travis, a prostitute called 'Angel' whose real name was Hemoglobin Vagina Durrell. He could still evoke sympathy for a little girl with progressive blindness whose aunty refused to allow her to have a diagnostic workup—referred to in neurosurgical short-hand as the 'million dollar work-up'. The aunty preferred to have Millie treated by the soothsayer who lived in Watts. That is what she did, and yet, the aunty continued to bring Millie to the outpatient clinic regularly. The little girl slowly went blind, then became progressively demented until she became helpless; then she progressively lost wakefulness until she had to be admitted to pediatrics in a stupor. Even when she lay comatose, the aunty would not give permission to do the studies that might have led to an at least palliative treatment.

Garven could still be amused to see the occasional really strange patient admitted from the EOR. His favorite in 1966 was a twenty year old domestic who had come into the ER and was passed from the Triage Desk to the psychiatric emergency section because of her flagrantly psychotic behavior. Her sister reported that the girl had for weeks been raving about Jesus, an evident reference to a hippie who had seduced her and had made her a disciple in his traveling religious community. When she made it back home from her religious experience, she descended into madness. Finally, her sister decided that this was something more than born-again zeal and brought her to UCOMH.

While in the psych ER, the young woman had fixated on one of the psychiatry residents with a beard. When he went into the cubicle to interview her, he found her stark naked. She leaped on him and began tearing off his clothes. She was a hard working strong woman, and he was a sedentary contemplative psychiatrist. He was no match for her, and had the deputies not come to his rescue, he would have been another rape statistic.

She was placed in leather restraints on a gurney while the nurses scurried off to find a powerful injectable sedative. The other psych residents gathered around their associate who had been accosted to try and get him through the trauma that he had suffered. In the meantime the patient was able to work her hands free of the leathers and to fall off the gurney and crack her head on the floor before the nurses could get back with her sedative.

That is where the neurosurgeons entered the picture. The girl knocked herself unconscious. While she was still out, a skull x-ray was obtained to look for fractures. No fracture could be seen on the pictures, but a calcified subfrontal meningioma did show up; and the chief resident in neurosurgery was consulted. The psychotic girl was admitted for a craniotomy. Whether the meningioma was the sole cause of her being crazy or not, the operation cured her. The residents thought that was a mixed blessing. She no longer suffered from unquenchable nymphomania, and the residents recalled wistfully what it had been like for their egos to have an attractive woman battle to tear off their clothes.

The charity service also provided Garven and all of the other professors with an important resource—subjects for their research. Sometimes, as in Garven's case, private 'citizen' types were none too willing to be the heroes and heroines of the ongoing struggle to push back the frontiers of science— or, as the urologists were found of saying, the foreskins of science. Garven had a project in mind that did not lend itself to use on his private patients as yet. He was now making nearly $500,000 a year, and he did not have the slightest intention of injuring his reputation by having a problem with his private clientele. What Garven had in mind carried the potential of untoward results as did many pioneering efforts. He had to be mindful of the population in whom those 'untoward results' happened. It was possible to be sued by the private patients; a malpractice suit by an indigent was, for practical purposes, unheard of.

Garven's research idea involved an attempt to prevent stroke. It developed out of his interest in carotid thromboendarterectomies. He was impressed with the value of the operation to remove clot and atherosclerotic debris from inside the large carotid arteries in the neck. In some people, the vessel was completely blocked and surgery could not clear the fixed occlusion and restore flow. Those patients were in a category of high risk to have a devastating or fatal stroke. Garven thought it would be possible to bypass the block by sewing a graft from below the blockage in the common carotid artery in the neck to the appropriate vessel inside the head, the intracranial internal carotid artery. In great secrecy, he set about in his lab to find how that could be done.

Garven went through a number of experimental animals until he finally settled on the easiest species to learn on, then he began his work in earnest on monkeys. At first he worked on calves because of their large vessels. He was able to make an anastomosis of a Dacron graft from the neck artery to the one inside the head in a reasonable time. After a few trials, he was able to do the procedure well enough that all of the calves survived, and none of them were paralyzed.

Monkeys were much more difficult. They were smaller and had correspondingly much smaller vessels. Inside the head, the vessels were so small, that he had to use an operating microscope. There were no Dacron grafts small enough; so, Garven experimented with the use of small arteries. They tended to clot fairly rapidly and to be difficult to sew because of their thick walls. He tried to use veins, but they clotted even more quickly. He evaluated that finding and concluded that the valves inside the veins were the cause of the clotting. He reversed the direction in which the veins were inserted so it would be opposite to the way blood flowed in them in their normal position. That was worse. For a time, the problem of finding a suitable graft material stymied him.

Garven's lab assistant, who lacked much in the way of a formal education, nonetheless had a straightforward common sense approach to problems.

"Boss, how about if you pulled the veins inside out and left the valves on the outside?"

The solution offered seemed so simple-minded, even bizarre, that it was laughable. But Garven tried it, and *voila*! In eight out of ten experiments, the blood flowed during the operation, and the monkeys survived. Half of them had persistent strokes, a sobering result; but Garven chalked that problem up to the smallness of the vessels being used and his own learning curve. He was confident that he could do the procedure successfully in humans.

Garven presented his proposal to the human experimentation committee. Although several of the physicians were dubious about the operation, they were impressed with the findings Garven presented to them to bolster his argument. In his report on the results in monkeys, Garven showed them an eighty percent success rate. The charts and documentation had been prepared by his secretary, the same secretary who had been with him since the first day he opened his lab, and had enjoyed the aura that came from his many successes. She did not feel it was her place to question the laboratory data that was presented to her.

CHAPTER
Eight

E mily Robinson, a mother of five and grandmother of eleven, who worked as a part time bookkeeper for a manufacturing plant in Southcentral LA, was admitted to the neurology service after a spell of being paralyzed on the right side and being unable to speak sensibly for two days. The neurologists had the radiologists do a catheter angiogram and found a completely blocked left carotid artery. The resident contacted Garven and inquired about whether a carotid endarterectomy was indicated. He was new on the service and did not know that all such attempts had met with failure. Garven saw his chance. He accepted the patient on his service.

On evening rounds, he explained his plans for surgery to the residents. He instructed the first year to get an op permit signed. They would do her as the second case the following day.

On morning rounds, the resident told Garven that he had tried to get the permission for the operation, but that the woman had refused. She was feeling fine, and did not want to take a chance on having a problem with surgery, especially a 'spearmint'.

She said, "I don't want to have an unnecessary operation. I believe in the old rule, if it ain't broke, don't fix it."

"And, I take it that you did not use all of your great powers of persuasion on this lady?" Garven asked the resident pointedly.

"No, Sir. I frankly don't believe in the operation, myself. I think it's too dangerous. She needed to know that there was a great risk, and no one knows whether the procedure will do her a lick of good," he said to Garven.

Garven knew that the young resident expected him to admire his candor, to consider the validity of his conservatism, and to praise his attitude that the patient comes first. He did none of those things. He was angry. The young idealist had probably ruined Garven's chance to do the operation and to put another dramatic paper into the literature.

He said, "Robert, I don't have the slightest interest in your opinion about this operation. I am the professor, and I have done the preliminary work in the lab that indicates the likelihood for success. I suggest that you think twice in the future about undermining my work. Now, go find some scut work to do. I'll go in and try and undo the damage you've done. You can't be a nattering nabob of negativity and get anywhere in this neurosurgery business. You sit out of surgery for a couple of days and think about that."

Garven went in to see Mrs. Robinson. Her husband, two of her daughters, and four granddaughters were with her.

"Hi, Mrs. Robinson," he said cheerily.

"Oh, good morning, Dr. Wilsonhulme, I'd like you to meet my family."

She introduced him to her visitors.

"I need to explain your condition, Mrs. Robinson. I want you to understand why you ought to have the operation, Dr. Findley told you about," he said.

"The one where they cut out one of my blood veins and hook it up from my neck to my head?"

"You have the picture about right. Your big artery in the neck is blocked off. You had a small stroke because of that. You were lucky. One day, as sure as death and taxes, the clot in that artery is going to move on up and block the arteries inside the head, and you are going to be paralyzed and be unable to talk to your family, be unable to work, or do anything like you do now. Your family will have to take care of you, or probably you'll have to go the a nursing home for the rest of your life."

"What's the chances of that happenin'?" asked Mr. Robinson.

"Going on a hundred percent," Garven said.

He knew it was no where near that, but there was a real risk of having a frank stroke; and he was convinced that she needed the surgery. He had convinced himself that it would be beneficial. To her.

"That's purty turrible odds, Miss Emily," Mr. Robinson said. "I couldn't bear to lose you. I think you oughta think about havin' this here operation. This here's the professor doctor. He knows best."

Garven nodded sympathetically. Mrs. Robinson squeezed her temples. It was a terrible decision.

"I have a premonition, doctor. I know that don't make much sense, not even to me. I guess I oughta do what you and Cleophus say. I'll go ahead and do it. Just get it over with as soon as you can. I want to be completely out when they take me into the operating room, you hear?" she said.

"I'll see to it, Mrs. Robinson. Don't worry about a thing. Everything's going to be okay," Garven reassured her.

The operation proved to be a technical nightmare. Garven had underestimated the technical difficulty of getting a vein long enough and having a small enough end to be usable inside the head and of the difficulty of everting the vein inside out without tearing it. It was hard to find a course to run the vein from the artery attachment in the neck up into the head. That took two hours. The real difficulty came when he tried to sew the backside of the vein-to-artery attachment in the head. It was like sewing into a Dixie cup. He had his instruments held at the tips of his fingers. The sutures would not hold, and they were too big. The final anastomosis was wrinkled and looked as if the actual opening through which the blood was to flow was very small. The operation took far too long to be at all practical. Garven was not really sure whether blood was flowing through the graft when he finally closed up.

In the PAR Garven's worst fears were realized. Mrs. Robinson, who had entered the OR intact, was now completely paralyzed on the right and could not speak a word. As if that were not horrible enough, her blood pressure kept climbing and required large doses of antihypertensives. Garven did something he had never before done. He sent the chief resident out to tell the family the bad news. He rationalized that he had had to be the bearer of bad tidings plenty of times before for his professors, now it was someone else's turn. The truth was that he could not face them.

Over the course of an hour, Mrs. Robinson lost most of the movement in her left eye, then her respirations began to be irregular.

The chief resident, who had returned from his grim task, said, "Looks like she's Cheyne-Stoking, Dr. Wilsonhulme. I don't think she's going to make it out of the PAR."

"I don't think so either, Ted," said Garven. "Make her a no-code."

The two men watched Mrs. Robinson's Cheyne-Stokes respirations glumly. She breathed in a rhythm that started with very shallow respirations and proceeded in a gradual crescendo to very deep inhalations and exhalations then decrescendoed to the nadir again. After an hour, her breathing became irregularly irregular, then simply very slow and shallow.

One of the PAR nurses, a small Hispanic woman, was upset at the imminence of death, a very rare occurrence in the PAR.

"*Respire profundo!*" she begged.

Her earnest pleadings went unheeded as Mrs. Robinson's neurological and life's processes ebbed away. Finally, respirations ceased altogether. The EKG monitor recorded a heart beat for another thirty minutes before it went flat.

Garven sent Ted, the chief resident, out to give Mr. Robinson the final bad news. Garven, himself, slipped out the back door of the PAR and down the rear stairway.

Garven tried nine more times. Only one of the patients came out of the operation fully intact; six died; and the rest had strokes. Garven had a small sharp run-in with Robert Findley, the junior resident each time they had a new case. When the ninth, a seventy-three year old man, was admitted, Findley requested a meeting with Garven in his office. He had something he wanted to get off his chest.

"What is it Robert?" asked Garven.

He had a pretty good idea that this was going to be the same old litany about the danger of the operation and what they owed the patients about honesty. He was tired of hearing it.

"I didn't come to say the same old thing about the carotid-to-carotid venous bypass, Dr. Wilsonhulme. We're past that point. I am here to serve notice that if you go ahead with this operation, I am going to report you to the State of California. You have got to be stopped. These are real people you are working on. They have some rights. I guess that's all I came to say," said Dr. Findley, speaking rapidly to be able to get it all out without being interrupted.

Garven looked steadily at the earnest young man. He reminded Garven of how he might have looked a decade earlier. Had he ever been so idealistic, Garven wondered?

"Robert," he said, "what's your life's ambition?"

"I've wanted to be a neurosurgeon for as long as I can remember, Sir?"

"Is becoming a neurosurgeon more important than achieving sainthood on the question of carotid bypass surgery?"

That was a gloves off, right-to-the-heart-of-the-matter question, and Robert knew it. He thought hard about his answer, knowing that he had everything at stake here. He had never dreamed that it would come down to such a black and white choice as the one being implied now.

"I have so much invested in neurosurgery even now, I can't screw it up. Neurosurgery is everything to me, Dr. Wilsonhulme."

"Well, it seems that you have your priorities in order, Robert. I have another thought-provoking question. In a challenge match between you and me, who do you think would come out on top?"

The answer to that question required no soul searching or time.

"You, Sir," Robert said immediately.

"Um hmmh," Garven mused. "Finally, how do you suppose I would react to someone who went out of his way to make my life difficult? How do you suppose the secretary of the Board of Neurosurgery would react—that's me— to such an attack even if you chose to find another residency someplace else?"

"I get the drift, Dr. Wilsonhulme. I put my foot in my mouth. I will keep my mouth shut from now on"

He had never before been exposed to the naked extortionate power that a senior professor could wield. He did not like what he saw. He did not like the thought of his career going down the tubes just to look out for a handful of people whose names he would not even remember next year.

"You know, Robert, I really don't take to being threatened. I don't see you and I getting on too well in this residency. Don't you find this place a bit too crude and rough for your taste?"

Robert's lip quivered. He was afraid. He mentally kicked himself over and over again for opening his big mouth.

When the young resident failed to answer, Garven continued, "I know of a position that opened up in Little Rock for a first year resident. Seems one of their men developed chronic hepatitis and liver failure. The chief there, Eric Hansen, was asking if any of us in the Congress presidency knew of a good man. I think I do know a good man, Robert. Why don't you think on it overnight and write me a letter in the morning. I would be more than happy to accommodate you with a very favorable letter of recommendation. Thanks for stopping by."

Garven shifted his eyes to the pile of papers on his desk. He did not look up when Robert left.

The ninth patient died. Robert Findley was no longer in the UCOMH residency when it happened. Garven voluntarily and quietly abandoned the bypass project after that case. He did not write a paper on his efforts and results.

CHAPTER
Nine

David Stark announced his intention only to work part time. He maintained his national and international committee memberships and directorships and his positions on influential university and hospital boards. He continued to see a few private patients and to take call for the residents about once every two weeks. With Devon on the staff, the need for a new member of the faculty was not severe, but the other members came to feel that they needed someone; so, they could maintain the quality of their lives. The answer came from a conversation Garven had at his medical school graduating class reunion.

Elijah David Shapiro, his old gross anatomy dissecting partner, went to dinner with Garven during the four day reunion celebration in Phoenix. Over the salad, they talked about their families.

When it was ED's turn, he confessed that he had been married and divorced since he and Garven had seen each other last.

"Sorry to hear that," said Garven.

"It wasn't that bad, the divorce, I mean," said E.D. "Do you know why Jewish husbands die young?"

"I don't."

"They want to," E.D. said with a laugh.

Garven had forgotten his friend's sense of humor that came through even the worst of problems.

"I guess us Christians wouldn't know about that," said Garven.

"You are not so different, you know," E.D. said. "Jesus was Jewish, as you may recall."

Garven nodded, wondering where this was leading.

"Do you know how you can be sure that Jesus was Jewish?"

Garven was already laughing. Now he knew where this conversational bit was leading.

"No, E.D., I can't say that I do."

"It's obvious. He was unmarried and lived with his parents until he was thirty. He thought his mother was a virgin, and his mother thought he was God."

Garven laughed, but he looked around to see if he could smell ozone anywhere and if there was any lightening building up anywhere. He wanted to make sure that he was not sitting by E.D. if there were.

Between the entree and the cheese, E.D. told Garven about his circuitous root into the neurological sciences.

"I had to go into medicine, you know that, of course?" he said.

Garven said, "Kind of like me; I couldn't think of anything else worth doing."

"With me it was cultural," said Elijah David. "Do you know in the Jewish faith when a fetus becomes a human being?"

"Not exactly," said Garven.

"When it graduates from medical school," E.D. said without cracking a smile.

Garven laughed heartily.

"You know that everyone in my family had me slated to be a famous internist with an exclusive Manhattan practice," E.D. said. "Even in the internship at New York Hospital, I knew it was not going to be for me. When I told my parents what I really wanted to do, they all but disowned me."

"Which was?" Garven asked.

"Research. Specifically, I got a wild bee in my bonnet about studying neurological problems. I proceeded, against all protests from the establishment in my family, to get a PhD. My dissertation was on *The Association of Measles and Multiple Sclerosis.*

He gave a self-deprecating little laugh. That association had finally been disproved a year ago.

Garven chuckled as well.

"That's not so bad. I knew a guy who did his dissertation on the uterus of the gnat. He finally went into neurology, as I recall."

They both laughed.

"After I finished my orals, I thought about neurology. Besides being the world's living expert on measles in neurology patients, I came to the conclusion that I also needed to get a job where I could make some money. Neurology seemed like a good enough field. You remember the guy that went to see the neurologist about his problem of loss of memory?"

"Um mmh," said Garven waiting for the punch line, "What did the doctor do?"

"Made the guy pay in advance."

"I heard that the basis for the neurologist's fees is $60 a visit—more if you're sick," said Garven.

The two old friends laughed again.

"I take it you didn't finally do a neurology residency," said Garven.

"No. What I finally ended up doing—and you will find this hard to believe—was to do a neurosurgery residency at the Mayo Brothers."

"Really?"

"Really."

"Was there something you had against operating?" Garven asked facetiously.

"In truth, yes. Neurosurgeons have the best research projects. You are the quintessential example of that. I wanted to be free to do the exciting stuff; so, I picked out the easiest residency and finished last year. Four years ago I couldn't even spell neurosurgeon, and now I are one," Elijah David said with a grin.

Garven shook his head. "Do you have a job, E.D.?"

"Not really. I have been assisting in a private practice until I could get the right position in a university department. Heard of any good openings?"

"Matter of fact, I have," Garven said.

He told Elijah David about the situation at UCOMH. He knew it would be a real and quiet coup for himself if he could get another old friend who was a solid researcher as a junior staff man. E.D. could be another vote in Garven's favor when push came to shove in divisional meetings. Garven could foresee several scenaria where that might prove to be valuable in the future.

As a result of that chance meeting, Elijah David Shapiro joined the faculty of the division of neurosurgery at UCOMH and assumed primary responsibility for research. He proved to be a brilliant and creative researcher, and worthless in the neurosurgery OR. They all wrote that off to his education at the WFMC. He was able to handle outpatient clinic problems and was a better than average diagnostician; so, Dr. Shapiro became a valued member of the faculty to whom no one had to give up surgeries.

The service had a good crop of residents. They were smart and tough, and Garven was pleased to see how well they were learning the ropes at UCOMH as well as the didactic and clinical aspects of neurosurgery. He and Devon had come to depend on them. The new first year resident was the most resourceful, and his services were occasionally of real use to the faculty members. Nat Sykes was the world's champ at getting autopsies. At times the faculty wanted to learn something from a patient who had died. Most of the time, the families were willing to permit autopsies; but occasionally, they balked. As a corollary of Murphy's Law, when the faculty wanted an autopsy the most, the family was the most unwilling.

Garven was good at convincing people, but he had to admit defeat when his patient, Ivory Shine, died. Mr. Shine was a young man who developed a mystery disease that resulted in fairly rapid neurological deterioration that eventually resulted in loss of function of all aspects of neurological function and resisted every effort at treatment. His diagnostic tests were normal. Garven was fascinated by Mr. Shine's problem, and wanted to publish a paper on him. It was critical to have an autopsy, but the family adamantly refused.

Mr. Shine's mother-dear told Garven that they just "shoulda took him to the sorcerer and not to the big ole hospital. There was nothin' more to be done. Nothin!"

Garven sent in the big gun, Dr. Sykes, to see if he could persuade the family; and Garven went back to his lab, not holding out much hope of success. In an hour, Nat called Garven's office to let him know that he had secured permission for the autopsy. It was scheduled for that evening. Garven's secretary found him in the lab and gave him the message.

When he saw Nat on rounds the following morning, Garven asked, "I have to know your secret. I thought I was good, but you got Mr. Shine's family to agree to a post-mortem when I got nothing but complete rejection."

"Twarn't nuthen!" Nat said with a phony exaggerated shiftless Southern accent. "Ah jist chahmed those folks."

"C'mon. You have to tell me. I teach you stuff all the time. I suspect there is a real pearl to be picked up today. Tell me how you do it," Garven cajoled.

Both men were chuckling.

Nat leaned close and whispered in *soto voce*, "If you really want to know, then I am obliged to tell you, chief. But you have to promise never to divulge this secret. Promise?"

"Cross my heart."

"Okay, this is how it's done. I sit down nicely with the family, and we talk about the death of the dearly departed. Then, I explain the real purpose of that tube we put in his nose."

"Which is?" Garven asked getting ahead of the story.

"Which is to put little gold balls into the patient's stomach. Very expensive treatment. I go on to explain, nice as can be, that we either have to get the gold balls back, or the family will have to buy some new ones for the hospital. They cost boo-coo bucks, I tell them. They ask, 'how can the gold balls be gotten back?' I then explain the main purpose of the autopsy."

"Which is to get into Ivory's stomach and retrieve the accumulated gold balls and save the family a small fortune in expenses," Garven said.

"Told you twern't nuthen," said Nat.

Garven laughed on and off the rest of the day from that revelation.

The toughest feat that Nat ever accomplished in his specialty of autopsy permission getting was the case of Percy Jones. Mr. Jones had been the source of great controversy in the division. His pneumoencephalogram had revealed a fat brainstem. That element of pathology was agreed upon by everyone. Why his brainstem was enlarged was the bone of contention. The faculty and house staff were divided down the middle, half arguing that Mr. Jones had a cerebellar tumor pressing down on the brainstem making it look fat, and half arguing that it was a primary brainstem tumor. The group favoring the cerebellar tumor insisted on an operation. The group favoring the brainstem tumor insisted that surgery would only be harmful. The chief resident had been of the opinion not to operate, and he was in charge. Mr. Jones wasted away and died.

It was considered imperative that an autopsy, at least of the brain, be performed to learn Mr. Jones' secret. Since it was a critical autopsy, the principals of Murphy's Law came into force, and the family stoutly refused. They vaguely remembered that autopsies were against their religion (AME). Nat tried everything, including the gold ball approach, but could only get permission to look at the brainstem and only if it could be done without making a visible mark on the body. That was a tall order. Garven told Nat to go ahead and get that much of a permit. He would take care of the rest.

Garven arranged with the OR head nurse to bring Mr. Jones in at night and to do a transoral approach to the floor of the skull in the OR. That took some coaxing and a few markers for future demand, but the procedure was scheduled.

Garven had done transoral approaches to the front of the cervical spine and had gone through the mouth on a few occasions to relieve pressure on the brainstem from an abnormally elevated skull base or abnormally high placement of the upper cervical spine. He had the requisite skills, but there were unusual challenges attached to the problem of operating on a dead person.

The first was the social problem of wheeling the deceased through the halls of the hospital and into the operating room. Garven did not want to have to explain about taking a dead person into the OR instead of the other way around. That dilemma was solved by applying makeup. The face pinked up nicely, and the two residents who transported Mr. Jones talked to him whenever people came by. They were never questioned.

The most serious overall problem was rigor mortis. It was hard to cover limbs that were poking out at odd angles and to transport the deceased without drawing attention, especially on the elevators. The two residents and Percy entered the main elevator and the more junior of the two held the rigor mortis stiffened arm and spoke soothingly to his patient who was covered with a sheet.

The more senior resident asked a pretty young girl accompanying them onto the elevator, "Ya'll mash four, please?"

The girl pressed the elevator button for the OR, and the handsome resident engaged her in conversation. The elevator trip was thereby accomplished without undue scrutiny. In the OR there were two advantages: dead men do not bleed, a factor that made dissection much simpler and faster; and dead men do not need anesthesia, a factor that helped keep the number of spectators to a minimum. The few people who did know about the operation taking place on the dead man did not find it all that unusual. People who died in surgery or just after coming up from the EOR or in the PAR often underwent procedures by interns and residents as a teaching opportunity.

The only serious disadvantage for having a surgical procedure when recently becoming deceased, so far as the neurosurgeons were concerned, was the presence of rigor mortis. Usually, the living patient undergoing a transoral procedure was done in the sitting position. Since Mr. Jones did not bend at the waist, he had to be supported on the operating chair like an oblique board. It was monumentally difficult to get Mr. Jones' mouth open sufficiently to permit access to the back of his throat and his palate. Garven and the resident had to straddle his chest and take turns working away at the skull base. It was very tiring.

They got a biopsy; it turned out to be a brainstem glioma proving the chief resident to be right. They were able to close the incision with small sutures, and to leave an almost undetectable closure. Garven let the residents cope with the problems of getting Mr. Jones back to the morgue, another one of those perks of being the boss.

CHAPTER
Ten

Although Devon had the major responsibility for running the everyday service at UCOMH, the custom developed for Garven to be the final arbiter and judge in cases of accusations against residents, and there were many of them. Garven was inclined to be very lenient, knowing the difficulties involved in doing the resident's daily thankless job. His main problem was to smooth the anger of the accusers. He faced a rich variety of allegations in the course of his judgeship:

The first year resident was caught in a compromising position with a student nurse. Student nurses seemed to have a peculiarly enhanced libido at UCOMH, the rest of the faculty observed. Perhaps it was something in the water. They had been in that position in a laundry room when an older night nurse came upon them. They were unaware that they had been observed. The nurse quietly locked them in the room and fetched the supervisor. Word got out, and a crowd comparable to the Court of King Karackticus gathered outside the laundry room. Garven tried to prevent the girl from being fired—he remembered a few trysts in similar laundry closets—but was told that her fate was none of his business. He gave the resident a public verbal reprimand. The ward secretary, the only public present, found the tongue lashing hysterically funny. In that way, no written notation was made.

Another resident ran afoul of Garven's old friend, the head nurse of the OR. The resident was operating on a young girl that had been struck in the head with an ax. It was a hopeless case. The resident had the mangled brain exposed and knew that there was nothing useful he could do. He called out for the nurses to allow the girl's priest to come in and perform extreme unction. It was a common occurrence in the hospital.

The priest was extremely nervous. He was a sweet old man who had never seen anything to compare to the horror of that operation, and he was terrified that he would do something to interfere. The resident told him to go ahead and perform the last rites while the OR crew went ahead with the operation. The priest insinuated his hand beneath the drapes and applied his oils and intoned his prayers. The resident looked away from the craniotomy for a moment. When he looked back, he saw that the priest's hand had crept up over the edge of the operative site and his fingers were applying the sacred oil to the very surface of the exposed brain.

The nurses shrieked out loud at that gross breach of sterile technique. The poor old priest was destroyed. He thought that what he had done had killed the little girl from his parish whom he loved. He started to cry. The resident shushed the nurses, put his arm around the kindly old priest's shoulders and drew him back up to the operating table. He told him it was all right to put his hand on the brain. The old man gave the final measure of the last rites and left the room greatly relieved because the specialty doctor had reassured him that he had done her good.

The nurses reported the resident's misbehavior to their head nurse, and in turn, she came to Garven. Garven very soberly told her that he would chastise his resident severely. That mollified the nurse. He called the resident in. Their conversation went as follows:

"I understand that you encouraged a gross break in sterile technique in your patient last night," Garven said.

"She was all but dead," the resident explained. "I just let the priest do last rites. He got carried away and put his hand in the wound."

"That must have been a thrill, seeing a couple of ungloved fingers coming up and lying on the brain."

"It was different, all right."

"My spies tell me you soothed the poor old priest when the battle-ax nurses were beating up on him."

"Yeah. He was about destroyed. It would have ruined his life to have been left with the thought that he had hurt that little girl."

"So, what do you think I ought to do with you?"

"How about giving me a couple of tickets to the Dodger and Phillies game? I don't think I deserve the key to the city."

He said it with a completely straight face.

Garven liked his moxey so much that he told the nurse that he had cut off one of the young man's hands. She scoffed at him, but presumed that some sort of justice had been done. In actual fact, Garven got the young man and the nursing student of his acquaintance a couple of free tickets to the Dodgers and Phillies game.

Another resident was accused of purposefully causing a faculty member public humiliation. Dr. Emmett Bushel, the anesthesiologist who was most preferred by the neurosurgical service, was a sensitive fellow, who went into anesthesiology because he did not want to deal with any given awake patient for more than a few minutes at a time. He studiously avoided the limelight even to the point of refusing to serve on hospital committees. That kept him from advancing in academic rank above assistant professor level, but that was all right with him.

Dr. Bushel was surprised to hear his name paged to come to the main lobby one morning. When he arrived, the secretary who had paged him, pointed out a patient, saying that that was the man who paged you.

"He kept saying over and over, 'Dr. Bushel is my doctor. Dr. Bushel is my doctor'."

When the anesthesiologist investigated, he learned that the man had been operated on the neurosurgery service for a severe head injury. It was Friday, and the patient had a chit to come to the neurosurgery clinic, but because of his severe post brain injury dementia, he had no idea where or even what the neurosurgery clinic was. The only thing he knew for certain, was that "Dr. Bushel is my doctor."

Dr. Bushel would have written that occurrence off as just another of the strange things that happened all the time at UC Osterlund Memorial, had it not been repeated several dozen times over the next several weeks. Poor flustered Dr. Bushel would be paged to one place or another in the hospital to find some unfortunate demented person saying to any and all that would listen, "Dr. Bushel is my doctor."

The nurses and secretaries did the natural thing and paged the hapless patient's preferred doctor.

It became embarrassing and troubling to the good doctor. He had no idea what to do with these people, and it was frustrating to him. He became upset at being called out of his operating room so frequently for such nonsense. Some one put a bug in his ear that the neurosurgery residents were playing a joke on him. The informant told Dr. Bushel that the neuro residents spent long hours with the brain injured patients.

It was their usual method of testing to lean down to the patient and say, "Hey, Lenny, how'ya doin'? Can you recite the Pythagorean Theorum for us?...How about your first name?"

Every time they went past one of the brain deficient patients, the residents would have the patient repeat the phrase of the day: "Dr. Bushel is my doctor."

Dr. Bushel heard through the grapevine that it was Dr. Marshall, the first year resident who had been caught in the laundry room who was behind it all, and reported the serious breach of professional etiquette to Dr. Wilsonhulme.

Dr. Wilsonhulme had some prior knowledge of the practice of having demented patients recite "Dr. Bushel is my doctor."; so, his conversation with the accused resident, Dr. Marshall, went like this:

"What do you have to say for yourself, young man?" Garven asked within the hearing of Dr. Bushel.

The anesthesiologist, confident that the professor of neurosurgery had the situation well in hand turned and left. He hoped that Garven would not be too hard on the young man.

When they saw the door close behind Dr. Bushel, both Garven and the resident broke out laughing.

"This is serious," Garven said and almost choked.

"What I can't figure out, is why it was me that he got all bent out of shape about?" Dr. Marshall said, still laughing.

"I can't imagine how that particular rumor got started myself," said Garven.

He could not keep talking because of his recurring fits of laughter.

"Dr. Wilsonhulme! Did you let that little idea get out by any chance?" Young Dr. Marshall said.

The light had just come on in his head.

"Me?!" asked the senior professor.

The two men had to sit down.

Back in control, Garven said, as he usually did in cases of serious misconduct such as this one, "What do you think I should do with you?"

Dr. Marshall just shook his head. He could not speak. It had been a long hard day, and the cathartic effect of the laughing jag was not yet complete.

"Consider yourself reprimanded, young man. I don't want to hear of anything like this happening again!"

He gave Dr. Marshall two tickets to a Dorothy Chandler Pavilion production, some strange Greek production that he would not have dreamed of going to himself.

Dr. Marshall said, "Thanks for the tickets. I think I deserve the key to the city you keep talking about just for never telling poor little Dr. Bushel that it was you that started instructing the dements to say that, 'Dr. Bushel is my doctor'."

Among the complaints that came to Dr. Wilsonhulme, there were some that were a serious threat to the career of the young surgeon being accused. The university acquired a new neonatologist, Dr. Howard Rosenthal, a specialist in the problems of the first few weeks of life. He became the chief of the pediatric intensive care unit, and guarded his fiefdom with all of the proprietary zeal of a mother bear defending her lair. He was very taken with himself and made a law that every consult for a specialist require that the specialist see Dr. Rosenthal both before and after they examined the little patient. He also required that every order on his unit be counter signed by him, something of an implicit insult to the licensed physicians.

The edicts were too new to have been fully disseminated among the many specialties in the hospital. The chief resident of neurosurgery, Arun Morashivadun, the first Indian resident to go through the UCOMH service, was called to the peds ICU on an afternoon when Dr. Rosenthal was at one of his crucially important committee meetings. The baby had a mass on its forehead that protruded very prominently. It appeared to be a frontal encephalocoele, a portion of the front part of the brain that pushed itself out of the cranial vault and appeared on the surface, covered only by dural membranes and skin.

Dr. Morasivadun gave his opinion, discussed the problem with the peds residents whom he complimented for their astuteness, and left to schedule the baby for surgery the following morning. Dr. Rosenthal somehow missed the transaction and arrangements with the neurosurgeon and was not yet on the unit the following morning when Dr. Morasivadun took the infant to surgery.

The lesion proved not to be a congenital anomaly, the frontal encephalocoele, that the chief neurosurgery resident had diagnosed. Instead, it was found to be a highly malignant, rare developmental tumor. Dr. Morasivadun did a masterful job and got all of the tumor out, a gross total removal. The baby was returned to the neonatal ICU where the pediatric residents took over. The baby had difficulty with respirations, difficulty with managing fluids and electrolytes, and periods of irregular heart beat for the first two days after the major operation. By the end of the first week, the child was well. The residents and nurses all had reason to hope that the infant was cured and could be normal.

On Friday morning, Garven's secretary brought him the daily mail. There was a letter from a Dr. Howard Rosenthal in the pediatrics department, a man whom Garven did not know. The letter was vitriolic. Rosenthal named Dr. Morasivadun as menace; a child stealer, a kidnapper who had wrested an infant from his intensive care unit bed and had taken him to the operating room without permission. There, the letter stated, the neurosurgery resident had done the wrong operation for the wrong diagnosis and had brought the baby back to the ICU in shock and near cardiorespiratory arrest. Only the expert ministrations of Dr. Rosenthal—the modest Dr. Rosenthal—had brought the tiny infant through the neurosurgeon created crisis, Dr. Rosenthal humbly added near the end of the letter. The last sentence was a demand that Dr. Morasivadun be fired.

Garven called Arun Morasivadun to his office.

He showed the chief resident the letter. Dr. Morasivadun was a brilliant and extremely conscientious man. He looked at the text of the letter as if it were smeared with sewage. He dropped it to avoid further contamination.

Garven said, "Arun, tell me about this, please."

Arun told Garven the whole story. He was astounded at the accusations. After all, the child was doing perfectly well. No one had made the slightest complaint in his hearing.

"Arun, you handle the consultations on peds the way you think best. Go about your work the way you always do. We'll talk again about this."

Arun had a question on his face.

"I'll take care of Dr. Rosenthal in my own way and in my own time."

Relations were frosty between Dr. Rosenthal and the neurosurgery service. The faculty of neurosurgery refused to comply to the neonatologist's demand that only an attending be permitted to see his patients. As was the service custom, Dr. Morasivadun continued to respond to all consult requests. There were some changes. Before Dr. Morasivadun would see any of the peds ICU patients, he required that Dr. Rosenthal himself hand write the consult and present it personally to Dr. Morasivadun. Until he did so, the patient could not be seen. That infuriated Dr. Rosenthal who had to disrupt his work every time a neuro consult was necessary, which was frequent. And it put him in the position of having to play the game in a way that Dr. Morasivadun could win a small skirmish. That was not what Howard Rosenthal had intended, and he had not had satisfaction from the neurosurgery faculty.

Dr. Morasivadun added a small, minor but irritating note to the ongoing cold war. Whenever he wrote a consult or an order on the peds chart or an entry in the progress notes, he misspelled Dr. Rosenthal's name. They were simple mistakes that anyone could make, but they happened too frequently to have occurred by chance. 'Rosenthal' became 'Rosenthale' and 'Rosenberg' and 'Russenthal' and 'Rubenthal' and on and on. Dr. Rosenthal, for whom the sound of his name was the most beautiful word in the language, found himself responding by making a very prominent correction whenever he found his name misspelled. Everyone likes the sound of his own name; but for Dr. Rosenthal, neonatologist, it was music, a spiritual thing. Mispronunciations and misspellings were like a burr under his saddle.

The little war festered along for three months. Finally, Dr. Rosenthal called Arun to tell him of the birth of a baby with a thoracic myelomeningocoele. He insisted that Dr. Morasivadun call the attending neurosurgeon at home that very night. When he learned that Garven was the only member of the faculty present in LA that particular weekend, Rosenthal demanded that Dr. Wilsonhulme come in to see this baby himself. It was eleven o'clock pm.

"If you insist, Dr. Rosenkranz..." Arun said.

"It's Rosenthal."

"Yes, Sir," said Arun courteously. "I will call Dr. Wilsonhulme, but I can tell you now that he is not likely to come in. He is very busy."

"I am far busier than that man, Dr. Whateveryournameis, I expect to hear from him within the hour."

"I will call him as soon as we get off the phone with each other, Dr. Rubenstein. If that is all for now, I will be about that task."

"*Rosenthal!*" the neonatologist shouted and hung up.

Arun called Dr. Wilsonhulme and told him about the call.

Garven said, "I'll take care of it, Arun. I haven't forgotten our first meeting on the subject. There is a time and a season for everything. Tomorrow will be that time. You can tell the man to call me in the morning."

Garven did not see the infant that night, and he did not speak to the neonatologist. The following morning at five after seven while the residents, interns, and Garven were making rounds, Dr. Rosenthal marched into the middle of the group and interrupted Garven mid-sentence while he was explaining why it was necessary to do a ventriculogram rather than a PEG on a patient with a suspected tumor.

"We really must talk, Dr. Wilsonhulme. I have a very critical patient, and you must see her. This is a problem for someone above the resident level," said Howard Rosenthal pompously.

His chin was jutting forward like Il Duce in a nonverbal challenge.

Garven was the very picture of cool politeness. He did not raise his voice nor complain that he had been interrupted.

He said, "Dr. Rosenthal, I have to finish rounds here. It should be no more than ten minutes. Why don't you have a seat by the nurses station, grab a coffee and a doughnut, and I will be with you shortly?"

Dr. Rosenthal shrugged. What else could he do? It was apparent that this technician did not know how important his work was. No one kept him cooling his heels. Still, it would be worth it to put the surgeon in his place. Rosenthal walked slowly to the nurses station and sat down.

It was fifteen minutes before Garven dismissed the troops and turned to go and talk to Dr. Rosenthal.

Arun asked, "Do you want me to go with you, chief?"

"No, thanks, Arun. That won't be necessary. I told you from the beginning that I would take care of this matter. You won't have anymore difficulty after my little talk. Get those sluggards to work. See you in the OR. I'll be there about nine when you have the crani open."

Garven smiled graciously as he walked up to Dr. Rosenthal. The neonatologist had worked a full head of steam. He launched into a litany of wrongdoings by Arun and discourtesies by the neurosurgery faculty. Garven gave him all the rope he needed. Rosenthal complained about the quality of neurosurgical work, research, patient follow-up, and especially about their inability to understand the problems of newborns. He paused to take a breath.

Garven maintained an exasperatingly pleasant facial expression.

He smiled slowly when Rosenthal took his breather.

"That about it, Dr. Rosenthal?"

"I guess so," the neonatologist sighed.

To say more would be repetitive.

"Then as I see it, you take exception to our diagnostic ability, to our surgical program, to our ongoing research, to our bedside manner, to our knowledge of pediatric neurosurgical problems, and to our grasp on interdisciplinary courtesies. We are basically mean, stupid, lazy, and inept. Other than that, I take it that you approve of our program?" Garven said.

He was completely civil and polite in his delivery.

"Well, Dr. Wilsonhulme...I, uh, well..." Dr. Rosenthal stammered.

He had essentially said all of that, but he did not like Wilsonhulme's summary.

"I came here in all professional courtesy to tell you what you should do with your resident."

As soon as he said it, Dr. Rosenthal felt that he might have gone too far with that statement. The hard look on Dr. Wilsonhulme's face confirmed that impression. Garven reached into his suitcoat pocket and withdrew an envelope. He handed it to Rosenthal. Rosenthal took it and looked curiously at it. He recognized it.

"This was handed to me for action, Dr. Rosenthal. As you know, I am the chairman of the university professional advancement committee. You have requested consideration that you be advanced from instructor to assistant professor. Have I got that right?"

"Yes...yes, you do."

There was a marked change in his manner. He was no longer pompous and instructing.

"We seem to have a number of things to talk about, you and me," said Garven. "Which of these matters do you think we should discuss first? I rather think it best to discuss the most important things first in case we run out of time."

The subliminal message was loud and clear. Dr. Rosenthal understood how the game was played well enough to know that he had just met a master.

"In view of your tight schedule, professor, perhaps it would be best to take up the matter of my request."

"Good," Garven said. "I like that as a priority—personal development. Sometimes I look at that as being even more important than some of the things that seem so earth-shaking but are so temporary and forgettable, don't you?"

He smiled. It was genuine and free of any hint of being fulsome.

Dr. Rosenthal smiled in return and nodded his agreement. The two men walked into the hallway lost in conversation.

"Now, about your request for advancement, Dr. Rosenthal. Although you have not been with us on the faculty for long, and the subspecialty of neonatology is suspect in many institutions, my personal view is very favorable. Why don't you tell me more about yourself?" Garven was saying.

There were no further problems between Arun Morasivadun and Dr. Rosenthal or with anyone on the neurosurgery service. Garven forgot about the incident entirely. Dr. Howard Rosenthal, however, was like Shylock. He did not forgive or forget, and he vowed that, one day, he would exact his pound of flesh.

CHAPTER
Eleven

1967 was an eventful year in the life of Garven Wilsonhulme. He was able to open the brain tumor research building on the UCOMH campus, a project that was his brain child, and the product of a great deal of his effort and sweat. Arthur Fletcher, his father-in-law, died in February. Garven learned from the Maricopa County Coroner on the quiet that he had been actively engaged in an "aerobic exercise activity" at the "No-Tell Motel." Garven saw to it that that bit of information was kept from Elizabeth and the rest of Fletcher's family but filed away a notation in his now rather large private notebook. Half of his estate went to his daughter, Elizabeth, his only child. Mrs. Garven C. Wilsonhulme, already wealthy in her own right, became the richest woman in California.

In April, Peter Wilsonhulme died in the Emmett Community Hospital in Emmett, Arizona. He had been in the Sarah Daft Rest home for more than five years. The locals referred to it as the Sarah Daft Home for the Daft. At first, it was his heart. He became unable to do anything more than sit up in bed. Then his mind deteriorated until, at the last, he could not recognize his doctor. He went into congestive heart failure and was transferred to Emmett's only hospital. He died two days later. Garven had been meaning to go see the old man, but something always interfered. Then, when Peter, Sr. became so demented that he could not recognize anyone, it did not seem worth the effort. His adopted son had not seen Peter Wilsonhulme for six years before he died.

Garven's mother completed her last year of teaching in Cipher in June and went into retirement. Garven had been in London presenting a paper on *The Tumor Angiogenesis Factor* at the International Neurosurgical Association meetings. Those meetings only convened every fourth year, and it was Garven's only chance to get world-wide recognition for his current project. Otherwise, he would have been at the program in his mother's honor. She moved back to Phoenix. Garven had not yet received notification of her new address. His meager conscience was assuaged by the fact that he sent her enough money every month to allow her to retire in real comfort.

One of his old professors from the University of Arizona Faculty of Medicine School contacted Garven about an Indian who had come into the hospital with advanced liver cirrhosis, an alcoholic named Edward Sespootch. The reason his old professor contacted Garven was that Edward had persisted throughout his hospitalization to tell any and all about his friendship with the "famous brain surgeon, Garven Carmichael." The professor was curious to know if, in the Indian's ramblings, there was anything to his knowing Garven, the mistaken last name notwithstanding.

When Garven looked into it, he found out that Edward had reached the bottom. He was at the point that further drinking would kill what remained of his liver, and that would not be very long. Garven flew out to Phoenix and talked to Edward before he was released from the hospital. He got the Apache to agree to come out to California and to work in Garven's lab. He also got Edward, who by now had awakened somewhat to the grim reality of the condition of his health, to agree to go into a drying out clinic at Garven's expense. Lyle Durche brought Edward to Los Angeles. He looked so bad himself, that finally both men entered the alcohol and drug rehabilitation center together.

In that way, Garven came to have two permanent personal employees and semi-permanent house guests. The two desert rats were given a small house on the grounds of the Wilsonhulme estate in Beverly Hills. Garven never treated them as hired hands, and they cleaned themselves up and tried to make a contribution for all the living they received. They dropped in at Garven and Elizabeth's exclusive home whenever they wanted without knocking and at all hours. Elizabeth did not like their lack of courtesy, nor them, for that matter. For some reason, she was a little afraid of the two hard looking, sun wrinkled men. Garven seemed to be completely at home with them; so, she only complained occasionally but wondered if Garven did not have a small touch of insanity.

1967 was a year in which Garven's career soared due to two unrelated circumstances—his latest research and to the decline of Steven Chou, chief of the division of neurosurgery. Garven's publications on his tumor angiogenesis factor research were heralded as one of the most dramatic contributions to the understanding of and the treatment of brain tumors in the past fifty years and led directly to his being able to obtain public and private funding for his dream of building the brain tumor research facility. Garven came upon the idea of tumor angiogenesis by a simple route and with very little actual effort.

Garven had practiced the tumor protocols for brain tumor chemotherapy exactly as outlined by the NIH. The National Institutes of Health in Washington was able to get all of the nation's researchers to agree on protocols so that there would be an orderly accumulation of information leading to the increased use of good drugs and the abandonment of bad ones. The process was tedious and generally unrewarding. Only about every three or four years did a new drug make the grade and enter the field as an agent to be used in practice. Garven's success in the development of new agents had been the same as everyone else's for the past three years—nil.

In early 1964, a young investigator by the name of Gordon Styvescent, M.S., was referred to Garven by the NIH. Garven held the position of final arbiter for grants by the NIH for neurosurgically related projects. The entire field of brain tumors was so designated and fell under Garven's purview. Styvescent was working on his PhD at the University of North Dakota, where there was no neurosurgery department. He and his work were obscure, and he had no other hope of getting grant money if Garven's committee did not give him a positive recommendation.

The abstract submitted by the investigator with the master's degree described a chemical factor, as yet undefined, that was produced by malignant glioblastomas, and caused the growth of abundant blood vessels, tumor vessels, that served to nourish the tumor at the expense of the surrounding normal brain. There appeared to be some quality possessed by the "vessel growth factor" as Mr. Styvescent described it, that not only robbed the normal brain of its vessels, but also resulted in a change in the brain so that it progressively changed into the malignancy it bordered. The "vessel growth factor" was, in effect, a tumor growth factor. Although the work was preliminary, enough had been done to make it apparent that there was, indeed, a chemical process that lay at the core of tumor growth.

On the committee, the members were assigned to review the submitted abstracts and to present the promising ones to the group as a whole. The rejected projects, of which there where hundreds, were thereafter ignored and simply withered on the vine for lack of monetary nourishment. Garven was the only member of the committee who had seen Mr. Styvescent's paper—the original manuscript. He made a copy of the paper and called Mr. Styvescent.

"Hello, is this Gordon Styvescent?"

"Yes."

"I am the chairman of the NIH grant committee. We have been looking over your submission and find it interesting. There are several on the committee who question the validity of your evidence for the existence of the "tumor vessel growth factor." They have indicated that they cannot authorize a grant without a thorough review of your raw data. Will you submit your work to us?" Garven asked.

"Of course, Sir. Anything. Where do I send it?"

Garven gave him the address of the committee in the NIH center in Washington, DC.

"Flag it, 'Tumor Vessel Reviewer', if you please."

"I'll put it into the mail this morning," Styvescent said.

He was so excited by the prospects of getting a grant that he did not realize until he hung up that he had not even gotten the name of the reviewer who had been kind enough to take time to call him.

In a week, Styvescent's envelope was in Garven's hands. It had been routed from the NIH to his office at UCOMH as matter of routine. As soon as Garven saw the raw material, the culmination of two years work by a very careful and talented young researcher, he knew that he was looking at the nucleus of a major discovery. He also realized that he was looking at Styvescent's original paperwork, not even duplicator copies. Some of it was hand written. It was altogether possible that he had in his hands the only copies of the work.

Garven let the work sit on his desk for a month. In the meantime, he thought about the consequences of what he was contemplating. Garven had come to grips a long time ago with one facet of his own personality; he was a sociopath. He had either been born without a conscience, or he had lost it along the way. When he had such thoughts about himself, he remembered being deserted by his biological father and his vow to succeed at all cost. He was not bothered by pricklings of an outraged superego or any fear of a god or a devil when he made decisions and assessed results. He was a nearly unadulterated pragmatist. He had first known that about himself for sure on the night when his psychology professor, Dr. Simpkins, had fallen to his death during a confrontation with Garven. The question for Garven was one of finding a solution to his task, that of using Styvescent's material without him being the wiser.

Finally, Garven simply sent an NIH form letter of rejection to Mr. Styvescent's department head at the University of North Dakota. The young researcher tried in vain to retrieve his lab notes or even to find out from the NIH who might have them. Since there was to be no money for his project, he eventually went on to another project, this one not in the neurosurgical field. He had heard that certain South American frogs exuded a stimulant on their skin, and that the natives licked the amphibians' skin to get a chemical high. He was determined to find out what was involved and received a grant to do a field study along the Orinoco River.

Garven set in motion every resource in the UCOMH labs. Fresh glioblastoma cells were plated, ground up, filtered, and the chemicals were fractionated. Garven's techs isolated a crude chemical that was an angiogenesis factor. When concentrated, it was very a potent stimulus to the production of abnormal tumor vessels in mice. Having established the reality and reproducibility of the chemical, he requested the biochemistry department's help in isolating, identifying, and finally synthesizing the material. Garven would not let anyone publish the slightest hint of the discovery.

The UCLA zoology department had a large primate collection, and had done preliminary work in inducing various tumors in various parts of monkey bodies. Macacca mulatta monkeys, cousins of the famous rhesus monkeys used as lab animals in the study of polio, had been found to be good subjects for the induction of malignant gliomas of the brain. Garven procured a dozen animals which already had tumors growing and injected the angiogenesis factor into them intravenously and also directly into the tumors. The tumors grew almost explosively with the direct injections and increased in size geometrically even with the venous route because of the tumor activated break down of the blood brain barrier. The link of the chemical, now identified and synthesized, with glioblastomas was now firmly established. It was no feat of imagination to presume that the link would be the same in humans. Still Garven insisted on secrecy.

Next, he pressed the entire neurosurgery lab, the department of pharmacy, the department of pharmacology and the department of biochemistry into a meticulous search for a practical antidote to the tumor angiogenesis and growth production factor. To keep them from demanding credit, Garven compartmentalized the work and paid them for their efforts on a fee-for-service basis. Antibiotics, antimalarials, antifungals, tumor chemotherapeutic agents, solutions of heavy metals, specific antibodies, and every anticonvulsive agent were all tried. Some of them denatured the tumor promoting factor, but in doses that also killed the monkeys.

A young hematologist mentioned to Garven about the many products that were being found in blood elements that had effects on any number of bodily functions. Garven halted the drug investigations temporarily because of their lack of progress. He paid the hematology division to process blood and bone marrow cells to see what possibilities there were. The hematologist with whom Garven had talked about the idea of using blood found a material in blood platelets which when extracted and concentrated, was dramatically effective against the tumor angiogenesis and tumor growth factor in tissue cultures.

The excitement of discovery kept Garven so exhilarated that he had trouble sleeping. He concentrated all of his efforts on the refinement of the platelet factor. After a crash program lasting four months, he had a purified protein that did not produce allergic responses that were uncontrollable, and was effective when administered by vein. Given directly into the tumor vessels of the malignancy itself in addition to the IV dosage, tumors literally melted away.

He took his work to the human experimentation committee and gained permission to use his new treatment on the next ten glioblastoma patients who came to the neurosurgery service. The results were very promising. Combining surgery, radiation therapy, and "Anti GBM Concentrate", as Garven styled his platelet derivative, the malignant tumors were reduced to virtual invisibility. Still Garven held off from publishing his results.

He wanted to try one more thing. With the human experimentation committee's permission, he added another facet of treatment to the next ten Glioblastomas who came in. He implanted SPAB electrodes and caused the stimulating currents to run at a higher than previously employed level. By late 1969, when Garven was ready to publish, none of the patients in the treatment group had demonstrated recurrence of a visible tumor. The longest survival in the group was only two and a half years to date, but with no evidence of recurrence present in any of the patients, there was no question of the revolutionary nature of Garven's discovery.

In 1970 Garven did a unique thing with his preliminary findings. He hired Jones, Leipzig, Shimataki, and Lender, an intellectual properties patent law firm in Irvine, California and obtained a patent on his materials and his treatment protocol. He did that very quietly. Then he sold the patent to a major drug firm on the promise of anonymity as part of the contract. Then, at long last, he published.

Garven had written a paper at each stage of the progress of his investigation. Now, he began to publish them one by one. There were six in all, and he spaced them out at monthly intervals. Garven Wilsonhulme became the most sought after speaker in all of neurosurgery. Even with careful screening, he averaged ten major addresses a month. His work spawned hundreds of other papers, review articles, newspaper editorials, and write-ups in magazines. He was famous. Even Hollywood personalities strove to include him on the guest lists of their parties for the glitterati. Garven Wilsonhulme, M.D.'s name had become synonymous with neurosurgery. By all accounts, the young coyote from Cipher, Arizona had become a world-class VIP.

CHAPTER
Twelve

The only downside to the success of Garven's efforts was that he was home very little during the period. Unfortunately, with the death of her father, Elizabeth needed him more at that time than ever before. Both children were away at boarding school, and Elizabeth felt that she had no one to turn to. Once again she became snippy and complaining. Despite her own needs, her spiteful feelings and sense of being neglected caused her to all but lock Garven out of her bed. They made love only rarely now.

Occasionally, Garven felt deprived enough to challenge his wife on her moody ill-temper and it's effect on their love life.

"You don't understand, Garven. It's a hormonal thing. I can't always help it. I wish you could be the woman for just one month."

"The old PMS excuse again," Garven challenged.

He definitely did not believe in all the hormonally based excuses. They were as flimsy as the old "I've got a headache" routine so far as he was concerned.

"I heard that there's going to be a new all-women package delivery service," he said.

"Don't bother telling me," she snapped.

She did not like the kind of jokes he brought home from that hospital.

"It's going to be called UPMS," he went on unswerved by her objection. "They deliver whenever they bloody well feel like it."

"Thanks for understanding, Garven."

She wore her usual hurt expression. Garven knew that his wife had an ego that was as fragile as a Fabergé egg, but he could not be sympathetic. It turned Garven off completely.

"I should have admitted to myself from the beginning that we weren't going to be compatible in that department," he countered with a note of cruelty in his voice.

"What do you mean? We had a good marriage until you started into training!"

"Yeah, it was about then that we got the water bed, and your half froze."

"Very funny."

Garven was so busy with his practice, his research, his public engagements, and with his small contribution to the residency program that he did not pay attention to what his colleagues in the department were doing. David Stark had become the President of the AANS and, at the same time, of the American Board of Neurosurgery. Devon was promoted to full professor and Elijah David's sterling work with the basic underlying factors of the dementia following head injury, had elevated him to associate professor. Garven began to pay attention when Steven Chou, the division chairman had a problem during an operation

The operation was a routine craniotomy for removal of a chronic subdural hematoma. Unlike most of his colleagues, Dr. Chou preferred to do the major craniotomy instead of just doing burr holes to remove the crank case oil-like old blood clot. His reasoning was that there were frequent recurrences after burrholes owing to a membrane that formed around the clot and could not be removed successfully with the more limited procedure. His patient was a wealthy retired executive of Occidental Oil. Dr. Chou was trying out a new power driven instrument for removing the skull bone called a craniotome that day for the first time.

Garven and the rest of the division members preferred the old tried and true method of using an old fashioned brace and bit to drill four holes then using the simple and safe Gigli saw to cut the bone between the holes. Steven liked new gadgets. He drilled a burrhole with the craniotome, then put on the saw blade head of the drill. He wanted to show the chief resident just how slick this new gadget was. He put the saw tip in the burr hole then very quickly zipped the bone off, a clean, neat saw cut; it took a tenth of the regular time, and in that sense was impressive.

The most impressive thing about the maneuver, however, was that Steven cut too close to the great midline vein of the dural covering of the brain, the superior sagittal sinus. He split the sinus right down the middle. Blood poured out from beneath the bone saw line in a torrential flow.

Dr. Chou reacted as if he had been struck a blow in the chest. He squeezed his eyes closed as if to blot out the evidence of his horrendous mistake. The outpouring of his patient's life's blood was still there when Steven opened his eyes. He and the chief resident removed the skull as fast as they could and packed the huge tear in the superior sagittal sinus. The blood continued to pour out. They clamped the sinus in front of and behind the area of the split, but nothing worked. The human body has between five and a half and six liters of blood. Below a certain retained blood volume, shock sets in and the machinery of the body begins to shut down. Steven's patient was old and could not adjust to the blood loss and had a cardiac arrest. He died in the OR.

Dr. Chou was sued, not an unexpected result. He became morose and depressed, more than even the terrible outcome and the suit should have caused in a seasoned senior neurosurgeon. It was the first suit in the history of the division, and his colleagues attributed Steven's prolonged and unapproachable dejection and his associated psychomotor retardation to that fact.

Dr. Chou became nonfunctional, and was the talk of the hospital. He developed into a recluse, staying days on end in his office without talking to anyone. Garven took it as his responsibility to find out what was going on and what could be done about it.

He made an appointment with Steven to be sure that there would be no mistake that resulted in them missing each other. When he entered Steven's office, he turned on his pocket tape recorder.

"Hello, chief, how are you feeling today?" Garven asked for lack of anything more appropriate.

"Not that great, Garven. Not that great."

It was unlike Dr. Chou to admit to feeling poorly. He was one of the 'iron men of neurosurgery' who advocated coming to work sick or well and of ignoring minor social problems like marital discord, death in the family, or malpractice suits.

"I gather as much, Steven. Look, I know this suit is a terrible blow to you; but you have to get on with your work. It's not the end of the world. You have a defense. You have a good lawyer. And this is California; the process will take years in this idiot malpractice justice system that we have to put up with. You can't mope around for all of that time," Garven said.

"Garven, sometimes the obvious is not the whole explanation. Things are not as simple as they seem," said Steven.

His voice was quiet and subdued. Garven thought that the man looked ill.

"I like to think of us as friends, Steven. Why don't you share whatever is wrong with me. You can trust that I will keep your confidence; I think you know that. I might even be able to help."

"I wish I could believe that, Garven. I mean, not about trusting you, but that you could help. I'm afraid it isn't possible."

"You are really down in the dumps. You don't look altogether well. Steven, is there something else? Please."

"I have been keeping something from the university and from my colleagues. Yes, I am disturbed, disturbed to the core over this malpractice suit and more than that by what I did. I guess it's rather a *res ipsa loquitor*—'the thing speaks for itself'—case. But, there is something else. And you are right. I am sick. I have a systemic lymphoma. Apparently, it is some sort of resistant form; and nothing seems to effect it. My bone marrow is shot. They give me a couple of years. I just want to be able to keep my position. Neurosurgery and being the head of this division are my life. You know that my wife died some years ago. I have no other family. I have no outside interests"

"I can't tell you how sorry I am to hear that, Steven. I wish that there was something I could do," Garven said sadly.

"There is, Garven."

"Name it."

"Keep my secret and help me hang onto my position as long as I can. I am going to City of Angels Hematology Center and get a transfusion. That will give me a lot more pep for a while. I have always wanted to spend a little time in Hawaii. Six weeks from now, I have a chance to stay in a friend's house on Kauai. I want to make it into a little sabbatical. I am frankly afraid to leave. You know what happens around here when someone goes away for too long."

He gave a wan smile. The reference to Steven's having been given the divisional chair while David Stark was away was not lost on Garven. It was a dog-eat-dog world in academic neurosurgery. No one needed to tell Garven anything about that.

"How can I help?" inquired Garven, who was genuinely curious.

"Just keep the wolves at bay while I'm in Kauai. That's all I ask. I know I can get to feeling better with a little rest. Then, I can come back and take on the world again. Will you do that for me?"

"I'll do my best, Steven. I will do the best thing I know how," said Garven.

"That's good enough for me, Garven. You are about the only one I can count as a friend, and I appreciate you coming by. Now, go on back and get to work, or the wolves will think we have a lame duck department all the way around."

Steven left in September for his Hawaiian sabbatical and named Garven as the acting chairman in his absence. The anti-glioblastoma multiforme angiogenesis and SPAB stimulation procedure with all of its offshoots of activities and dramatic earnings was essentially on automatic pilot. Garven hired a public relations and accounting firm to manage the spin-off for him. They, quite naturally, found the descriptive name rather daunting, and simplified it to the 'Wilsonhulme Procedure'. Although the efforts were all conservative and free of overt advertising or any other unethical or despicable practice, Garven came in for a measure of criticism both in the press and in the neurosurgical world for the "mercenary character" of the patent and the drug company business contract.

Steven Chou left behind unfinished work in all spheres of his activities in neurosurgery. Garven took up the slack by working longer hours—a necessity that further antagonized his wife—and began to bring order and completion to Dr. Chou's unfinished business. Since he had to put with the downside of Dr. Chou's affairs, the extra patient load, the grant requests and administrative backlog, Garven felt entirely justified to complete Steven's paper on thalamic stimulation for pain. Steven was one of the pioneers in placing stimulating electrodes in various parts of the brain with emotionally charged collections of neurons and in the thalamus, a segment of brain with discrete segments that sits at the top of the brainstem. He was on the verge of a breakthrough in treatment of inoperable back pain.

Garven did a few more cases, found the exact locus in the thalamus that corresponded to the portion of the back involved with the pain, and wrote the conclusions of the paper. He put his name as first author and Steven's as second. Dr. Chou had put in three years of painstaking work to see his name in second billing.

CHAPTER
Thirteen

G arven's work became a model of almost martial efficiency. The residents worked up his private cases, set them up in the operating room, and opened for him. Garven was able to keep three operating rooms going all day, three days a week by spending no more than thirty to forty-five minutes in actual operation time with each patient. The residents did the closures. Garven spent only a few minutes on daily rounds. The division's billing department kept a separate file on Garven's income, which was becoming prodigious. He forgot to call or to write to his mother, but he did keep her in mind enough to buy her a mortgage-free house in Scotsdale near the famous Camel Back Hotel.

The chief resident set up a teenager named Ronnie Heiden who had bilateral huge acoustic neurinomas in his posterior fossa. The resident was in the operating room for twenty-six hours, and Garven was there for six. The resident had the pleasure of taking care of the young man postoperatively, and Garven had the task of collecting the fee from the insurance company. Garven was in the operating room for five minutes on carpal tunnels, the junior resident for fifteen; and the fee was five hundred dollars for each operation. Garven let it be known that UCOMH was a center for doing carpal tunnel operations, and the referrals from the California Workman's Compensation Board were so numerous that it was as if Garven had signed a low-bid contract.

The surgeon collected forty percent of every surgical fee billed, and the hospital collected sixty percent from which they paid expenses. David Stark and Steven Chou had been neglectful of the accounting aspects of the service and had lost large quantities of money. Garven was so successful in collections that the university administrators monitored his methods, and his fellow faculty members realized a thirty percent increase in their incomes the first months of Garven's acting chiefship. Garven gained an appreciative following among the younger faculty members, not just those on the neurosurgery service, for his efforts.

Devon Upshire was a good surgeon, but lacked full confidence in major cases. He regularly asked Garven to be there when he put a complicated operation on the schedule. Once, on a woman named, Birdie Mason, he had a huge frontal arteriovenous malformation—AVM—open and ready for removal. Garven scrubbed in and held a sucker in one hand and the electrocoagulating Bovie in the other.

"So, go ahead, Devon. We ought to be able to do this in eight or ten hours if you move right along," Garven said.

"If we're lucky and our bladders can hold out," Devon responded.

He always felt more at ease having the chief scrubbed in with him.

Devon started to work on the lesion.

"Garven, did you buy your son an encyclopedia?" he asked.

"No," Garven said. He's only fourteen years old."

"I think that's great. Rich as you are, and you're going to let him walk to school like the rest of the kids," Devon said chuckling.

Garven said, "Surely, you can do better than that, Devon."

"I know. It's hard to find for love nor money a joke that's clean and also funny. I'll try harder. You hear about the six year old kid who goes to Beverly Hills grade school where the teacher was starting the new sex education program?"

"No. I'm not sure I want to either."

"Sure you do. The teacher assigned the boy to go home and find out what a penis is. So he goes to his dad and asks, 'Hey, pop, what's a penis?'

"His dad pulls down his pants and says, 'That son, is a perfect penis.'

"The kid goes back to school and meets one of his friends. The other boy says, 'Jeez, Tommie, I forgot to find out what a penis is. Can you help me out?'

"The first kid takes Tommie into the boy's room and opens his pants. He points down and says, 'Tommie, if this was two inches shorter, it would be a perfect penis.'"

Garven laughed and said, "That's closer to your usual standard, Devon."

He and Devon worked efficiently together dissecting, electrocoagulating, and cutting the host of small arterioles leading from the brain into the mass of abnormal vessels. The procedure was tedium itself.

Arteriovenous malformations are abnormal collections of blood vessels on and in the brain wherein arteries connect directly with veins instead of having intermediary capillaries. The veins are huge and bulging under abnormally high pressure since they receive the head of arterial pressure undiminished. One of the maxims of operating on AVMs is that the arteries must be meticulously electrocoagulated or tied off first. If the veins are tied off while the arterial flow is still coming in, there is no runoff for the blood and the mounting pressure will cause massive enlargement and eventual rupture of the huge veins with consequent massive hemorrhage. In the course of the operation on Birdie Mason, while rapidly and efficiently buzzing and cutting arteries, Devon clamped off two veins in a row.

In seconds, both veins blew up like automobile inner tubes with a weak spot on the wall. One after the other, the veins burst; and blood swept over the operative site. Other veins burst, some internal to the superficial mass of abnormal vessels; and suddenly, Birdie Mason's frontal lobe started to swell up out of the cranium. In a matter of seconds the pressure would destroy her brain.

Garven sucked up blood as fast as he could. Devon tried to clamp off the vessels. The vessel clips and mosquito and Mayo clamps fell off. Electrocoagulated vessel ends broke open. Where originally two vessels had started to bleed, there were now dozens, and soon hundreds of bleeders. It was impossible to get at them all, or even to see a few of them because so much blood was coming in from so many different loci. Devon was desperate and began to panic.

"We're going to lose her, Garven!" he shouted.

He dropped a moist lap cloth over the bleeding as much to hide it from view as to control bleeding.

"No we're not," Garven said with an icy calm voice. "Now get back in there."

"And do what?! I've tried everything. Nothing, but nothing works. She's bleeding out!"

"Two choices," said Garven. "We can tie off both carotids, or we can take off the frontal lobe. Choose!"

"I can't make that choice. Both of them are fatal. We are going to be sued big time!" Devon whimpered.

He was so frightened that he was ineffectual now.

Garven looked hard into the eyes of his friend and saw a man who was defeated. Devon's hands sagged. Blood was pouring out onto the drapes and was dripping onto the floor, right over the drain were Garven had insisted that all heads be placed during operations. He shrugged and stepped into the place Devon was occupying.

"Chet," he said to the anesthesiologist, "T&C eight more units of blood stat."

He reached out a hand to Lisa Conners, the scrub nurse, without looking at her.

"General surgery pool sucker, please."

To the circulating nurse he ordered, "Candy, turn up the Bovie to eight."

The blood was flooding out of the craniotomy opening now.

Garven wielded the outsized sucker and began to remove a wide line of brain behind the rapidly hemorrhaging AVM. He bovied every large and small bleeder he saw, most of them before they had chance to bleed. In a few minutes he had neatly cut off the frontal lobe. It now lay suspended by a mass of huge tangled arteries and veins connected to the major intracranial vessels coming in from below. The bleeding was gaining in ferocity.

"Big bowel cross clamp!" he ordered.

He worked the clamp across the entire huge cable of vessels and clamped it shut. The bleeding diminished dramatically.

"Another one!" he ordered.

His voice was quiet and commanding. Aside from his words, the only other sound was the respirator and the suction apparatus. The OR staff and Devon were all holding their collective breaths.

The tethering bunch of vessels was huge, nearly an inch and a half across. Every vessel was many times its normal size.

"Mayo scissors," Garven requested.

The scissors were large and crude by neurosurgery standards. This was something less than a delicate procedure by any standards. Garven made sure he was well away from the main intracranial internal carotid artery and the optic nerve then cut through the vascular bundle. The frontal lobe with its meshwork of abnormal vessels now fell free. Garven lifted it out carefully. Devon suctioned all of the remaining blood from the cavity created by removal of the brain and lavaged it with sterile normal saline until all wash water came back crystal clear.

"So, how do we tie off those vessels?" Devon asked looking at the grotesquely large clamp sticking out of the brain. "I don't think that aneurysm clips will hold, do you?"

Garven said, "Not a prayer. I'm going to ligate them."

"They'll pop a ligature off like nothing," Devon said. This loomed as a major problem in his mind now.

"Watch," Garven said. "Two-O silk ligature, Lisa."

She placed the suture across Garven's fingers that were waiting palm side up. He double wrapped the suture around the vessel stumps behind the clamp and slowly and cautiously cinched down a surgeons knot. The large vessels grudgingly yielded, narrowed and did not tear open. Garven had Devon release the clamp and slide it forward away from the ligature but still on the vessel stump. There was a gap of two millimeters.

"Two-O suture-ligature, now, Lisa."

The scrub nurse handed Garven a needle holder with the requested suture. Garven rejected it.

"Can't be a cutting needle. Give me a round needle. Hurry, my hands are getting tired," he said.

She gave him the proper needle and suture.

Garven ever so carefully eased the needle into and then through the mass of vessels in the two millimeter opening between the first ligature and the cross clamp. He pulled the suture through, then put figure of eight double tie around the vessel stump. Devon cut the suture ends.

"That ought to do it," sighed Garven.

He gingerly removed the clamp. There was no more bleeding. With the removal of the AVM, the vessels were already beginning to shrink in size.

"You saved my bacon, Garven. Thanks. You have always been a guy with four balls; today proved that for anyone who might have doubted it. I just hope she hasn't been gorked. The most we can hope for is that she didn't loose anything more than violin lessons and grade school," Devon commented.

"She'll be fine. Wait and see," Garven assured his friend. "This was no hill for a climber. See you at lunch."

Devon had to smile at his old friend and new chief's chutzpah.

Postoperatively, Birdie had no problems and resumed her original IQ.

Devon paid Garven surgery's highest compliment, "I have to hand it to you; it's better to be lucky than good. I never expected Birdie to be able to put on lace-up shoes again. What a great result!"

Garven just shrugged and said, "You don't think with AVM. I didn't take out anything she couldn't easily afford to lose. As one of my favorite residents used to say, 'Twern't nuthen'."

CHAPTER
Fourteen

A committee of neurologists and surgeons asked to see Garven on a formal basis when Dr. Chou had been away for a month. The meeting was scheduled in Warren Hickman, the chief of neurology's office. To Garven's great surprise, the call came from David Stark; and he referred to himself as the chairman of the deputation asking to talk to Garven. Devon Upshire accompanied the deputation by invitation. For all of its formality and austerity, Hickman's office showed that its occupant was a man with a sense of humor. A sign on the secretary's desk read: "DYSLEXICS OF THE WORLD, UNTIE!"

"Dr. Wilsonhulme," said Warren Hickman, spokesman for the group. "I'm sure that it will come as news, as a surprise to you that a search committee has been established to find a new chairman for the Division of Neurosurgery. For some time there has been a concern among the faculty that Dr. Chou is unable to discharge his duties in an acceptable manner. We have done a quiet investigation of his laboratory research, his operative activity and results, and of his administrative performance. Without boring you with the details, let me drop right to the conclusion of the investigators: Dr. Chou was found wanting in all aspects. We were dismayed when we learned that with his own performance so questionable and in need of improvement, the man has taken leave of his senses and is even now vacationing in Hawaii.

"We reached a unanimous conclusion that if the division of neurosurgery is to maintain its standard of excellence, there will have to be a new chairman."

Garven said, "Don't you think that this should wait until Dr. Chou can get back from Hawaii?"

Dr. Hickman said, "Pointedly, no. We are all men of the world here. We know that Chou can mount a troublesome counteraction if he's here. In the end, the result will be the same; but we are determined to avoid the public spectacle of a succession fight. Dr. Chou has tenure and will continue to be able to function as a full professor in the U.C. medical school system. I really think that Steven would welcome the chance for a rest once he is handed a *fait accompli.* I must say that he has not looked well to me for some time."

"What role do you see for me in this search effort?" Garven asked.

His heart rate was beginning to climb.

David Stark came into Hickman's office. "Sorry I'm late. Don't let me interrupt."

"I was just about to pop the question, David. Dr. Wilsonhulme, the search committee has come up with a name, and we all seem to be in enthusiastic agreement that you should be the next chairman of the division of neurosurgery," announced Dr. Hickman.

"I know you to be a fair man and a friend of Steven Chou's, Garven," said David Stark before Garven could give a reply. "We think the change should be made now unless you know of anything that Steven could do that would turn himself around. We don't want to rush to judgment, but the handwriting does seem to be on the wall for us on this matter."

Garven detected what he interpreted as a hint of wavering on the part of the other members of the search party. He had waited a lifetime for this moment. Steven Chou was an acquaintance, a colleague, but not a friend. In the world of fang and claw where they lived, Garven did not feel that he owed Steven anything. This chance at the brass ring might never come around again.

He said, "Gentlemen. I regret that I do have something to add. I learned this in confidence, and I hope it will not go beyond this room. There is an entirely justifiable excuse for Dr. Chou's shortcomings for the past year or so. He has a widespread lymphoma, and he tells me that his doctors have given up on treatment. They give him something like two years to live. Perhaps it would be best to let him hang on."

To David Stark, it was pure justice. Steven Chou would go out as painfully as he, himself, had done.

"No, Garven. I think I can speak for the rest of the committee, and I know that I can speak for the rest of the division. We can no longer afford lame duck leadership. We all want you to be the chief."

Garven paused before answering. There was something he wanted.

"I am willing and flattered to accept, but there is one condition, I am afraid I would have to insist upon. That is that neurosurgery be elevated to full department status. We can no longer function as division under surgery. We are quite able to stand on our own. I must insist on fulfillment of that condition."

Dr. Hickman was taken aback. That was an entirely new situation. If neurosurgery were to become a department, it would occupy a full class level higher than neurology with its division status. He did not know if he could countenance such an imbalance.

As if reading Dr. Hickman's mind, Garven continued, "And I frankly cannot, for the life of me, understand how neurology can continue to be regarded as a division. The eminence of the service and its faculty and their scholastic standing is so high that it seems to me to be no longer tenable that it remain under medicine's heavy thumb."

There was nothing that Garven could have said that would have endeared him more to Warren Hickman.

Hickman said, "At long last there is something that a neurologist and a neurosurgeon can agree on. Tell you what, Garven, my friend. You and I will mount a campaign together. We will see our services be departments inside a year. You can count on that!"

"That is good enough for me, Warren. I accept the position without reservation. Thank you for the confidence you have all shown in me," Garven said.

He was quiet and humble with a strain of resoluteness that further impressed the search committee members. They expected great things.

Garven left the office early and went home to celebrate. For that one night, he and Elizabeth set aside all of their growing differences and celebrated with their wealthy neighbors and with Edward and Lyle. Elizabeth could only shake her head at that social aberration, but it was Garven's night. It was truly Garven's night.

CHAPTER
Fifteen

By 1970 after he was elevated to the chairmanship and the division became the newly established department of neurosurgery, Garven was riding along the crest of the peak of his career. He had come out of abject poverty and deprivation, from a town that was so much a nothing that it bore the name of Cipher. He had clawed his way to the very top, and it was sweet, indeed. He was not a brilliant man, but his work was solid enough and backed by an organization of brilliant assistants who turned out a continual series of neurosurgical research articles with Garven listed as first author. The members of the neurosurgery faculty were his hand-picked friends, men he could count on, and who would protect him should he dare to leave town. They were his insurance as well as his friends—to him what the papal *Uomini di fiducia*, the "Men of Trust" were for the pope. As a matter of fact, there were more than a few of his underlings and other medical school faculty members who had taken to calling him "The Pope." All of his now fifteen residents did. Nobody called him that to his face. He knew about it, of course, and was secretly amused.

Garven's standing in the university and scientific community was established; he could now list one hundred eighty-three publications in his bibliography. By virtue of his considerable reputation in the neurosurgical world and his position as the chief of one of LA's three major neurosurgery training programs, Garven attracted more well-to-do patients and exciting and important cases than he could handle alone. He helped his faculty colleagues to enjoy his success and income by easing some of the cases to them.

As a senior faculty member of the University of California and a major attending staff member of UCOMH, Garven was able to work his way into several very important and influential positions on hospital committees. He maintained his place as chairman of the faculty advancement committee, was now the vice-chair of the disciplinary committee, served on the professional standards committee, and as the representative of the neurological sciences on the governing medical executive committee. Garven no longer took anything for granted. He kept careful and collated records of the favors he was owed by various other faculty members, and also of the indiscretions communicated to him in unguarded moments. He felt keenly the need for self-protection in the rarefied atmosphere he now breathed. His expensive, small, spy tape recorder was regularly in play.

He was the surgical representative of the three member advisory board of the mayor of LA and served on the twelve member board of medical consultants to the California State Assembly. He was one of three senior physicians serving on the California Board of Medical Licensure and was the chairman of the disciplinary subcommittee of the license board. In that capacity, he learned a very great deal about the individual practices and personal lives of physicians from around the state. There were many men and women whose careers had hung in frightening jeopardy and who, in the end, believed that they owed their salvations—their probation status or suspended sentences rather than loss of license or even criminal prosecution—to the critical intercession of Garven Wilsonhulme. He was offered bribes; some of the sums were staggering. He always smiled and jokingly told the doctor offering the bribe that he himself might be in need of a favor one day. He was only too glad to be of help to his fellow physician who was beset by the unfair outside attackers.

Nationally, Garven had graduated from his role in the Congress of Neurological Surgeons some time before. He was elected vice president of the much more prestigious American Association of Neurosurgeons in 1968, an automatic step on the ladder to being the president. In the April, 1969 meeting he was slated to be put in as the president-elect, and the following year, he would just as automatically become the president of the nation's most important neurosurgery body. He was on the board of directors of the 'Senior Society', The Society of University Neurosurgeons, the WOMs—Wise Old Men—of brain surgery. Garven Wilsonhulme was enjoying the fruits of the golden years of his entire career.

He spent little time with the residents other that when they assisted him or did one of his cases. Like the rest of the professors at UCOMH, Garven did not discuss with his patients the fact that the chief resident would be doing their surgery many times. If pressed, he mentioned only that the resident would be present. After all, he explained, UCOMH was a teaching institution.

Garven had his share of difficulties and nerve-wracking experiences allowing the residents to act as surgeons. He never quite became patient enough to let them fumble along inexpertly without causing himself gastritis. He was uniformly polite and understanding externally. Aneurysm surgery, being the most delicate of brain operations, brought the most anxiety to Garven.

In the late-sixties, it became popular to coat aneurysms and aneurysm clips with a variety of materials to prevent post operative clip slippage and aneurysm rupture. Aneurysms were wrapped with muslin, silk, and the patient's own plasma. The process of wrapping was difficult and tedious. Someone somewhere discovered an extremely rapidly drying epoxy glue made in Japan and that it coated aneurysms, even wet ones with an extremely adherent and very tough membrane. The glue was intended for plastics and was not approved by the FDA. It should not have been used without that permission, but in a matter of months, neurosurgeons all over the country found their own sources in Japan, and introduced the coating material into their aneurysm surgery practice. The Japanese 'superglue' came in two separate vials that had to be mixed at the last minute then applied.

By the grapevine, Garven learned the three rules of using the glue. 1. Once the glue was applied, never put anything into or onto the glue. 2. Never let a drop of the glue get into your own eye because it burned terribly. and, 3. Don't write in the operative note that the glue had been used. He conveyed the rules to Damon Carter, the chief resident on the first day they were to use the glue on an aneurysm at UCOMH.

Damon was a nervous operator. He insisted that all of the OR doors be kept closed; no radio could be played during his operations; and the nurses were forbidden to use the intercom system. He sweated all the while he operated and never told jokes or participated in chitchat. He had good hands and in two hours had the aneurysm exposed and dissected under the operating microscope. Garven assisted, willing to remain quiet during the procedure. Orders were whispered, and that was a remarkably effective means of communication. Everyone listened, and no one said "What?" or "Huh."

Aneurysms are delicate and easily ruptured. The moment of truth, the moment of greatest tension in the aneurysm operating room comes when it is time to clip the lesion. Under the operating scope Damon gently slid the tiny vise-grip clip's jaws open and insinuated them around the small neck of the bulging turgid structure. He bumped the edge of the aneurysm with the blade of the clip. Everyone held their breath. The aneurysm did not rupture. Damon wiggled the clip in its holder until the blades passed neatly across the neck. The tips of the blades showed beyond the neck; so, Damon and Garven could be sure that no unwanted structure was in the blades. Damon very slowly and gradually closed the blades. They tightened down onto the neck and finally occluded it entirely. Then Damon released his grip on the clip holder to leave the clip in place.

The clip remained stuck in the clip holder. Damon began to sweat. He growled curses, but his hands remained perfectly steady. He moved the clip holder back and forth. The clip released only part way.

Garven suggested, "Why don't you use a 'thing-with-a-hole-in-it' and push the clip off the holder?"

"Okay. Good idea, boss. Mary-Ellen, put a 'thing-with-a-hole-in-it' in my left hand. Gently, gently, now," Damon whispered as if there were some secret about using the Olivacrona periosteal elevator.

He inserted the tip of the smooth shaft of surgical steel into focus under the operating microscope.

"That's it," said Garven. "You've almost got it."

The elevator was gradually easing the clip off the holder. The aneurysm was hardly moving.

"Gently. Not too fast; so, it doesn't spring back," Garven whispered.

"Boss, that's like telling Werner Von Braun how to light the match in an A bomb test," Damon whispered back.

He did have some sense of humor. Garven realized that it was unnecessary to tell his very skillful resident that he needed to be careful.

The clip was off. Damon removed the instruments. The clip was in perfect condition. The aneurysm was trapped and now harmless.

"Nice job, Damon," Garven said. "Another notch on your gun."

"Thanks, boss," Damon said and heaved an audible sigh of relief.

His nervousness would not abate until he had the patient safely in the PAR.

"Now for the famous belt and suspenders part of the operation," Damon said. "Mary-Ellen, get the two vials of 'super-glue' up and ready. I need a little insulin syringe and a small spinal needle, say a 20 gauge."

The nurse mixed the contents of the two vials into a dry watch glass. Wetness caused the glue-hardening reaction to be accelerated. She drew up the glue in the slender syringe as instructed and handed the syringe to Damon. Damon aligned the tip of the spinal needle over the tip of the clipped aneurysm and gently dropped three drops of the crystal clear glue over the aneurysm and the clip. The glue instantly spread all around the aneurysm.

Damon was very nervous, now.

"Quick. It all ran off. I have to save some of it," he said.

Before Garven could react, Damon took up a cotton swab and probed the base of the aneurysm to push the glue up into place.

"Don't," yelled Garven, but he was too late.

The cotton on the swab stick was instantaneously caught in the glue. The stick end poked ludicrously out of the opening of the brain dissection. That foreign body could not stay there.

Damon was beside himself with anxiety now.

"Hand me that tongue depressor. I have to get the swab off."

Mary-Ellen put the thin wooden stick in the doctor's hand. Damon quickly nudged at the cotton trying to dislodge it. Garven's worst fears were realized. The tongue depressor became fixed in the glue alongside the cotton tipped applicator. Now, there were two absurd looking sticks poking out of the cra-niotomy opening into the depths of the patient's brain.

Damon was frightened. He pushed the forefinger of his left hand into the opening and attempted to push the tips of the sticks off the sticky aneurysm.

"Don't do that!" shouted Garven. "You'll break off the aneurysm neck!"

"I'll be careful. I'll just flick it a little," Damon reassured him.

He was careful and did not break the delicate tissue enclosed within the aneurysm clip blades. He did get the latex covered tip of his finger caught in the glue. He could not move for fear of disrupting the aneurysm. He had an agonized look on his face. Were it not for that, the absurdity of the situation might have been laughable. No one laughed. There was a grim tension in the room. Garven shook his head.

"Fine dissecting scissors, please, Mary-Ellen," Garven requested.

She placed the scissors in his hands with a gentle and firm plop. Garven worked the scissors tips into the wound and brought them into focus under the scope. They looked huge, magnified ten times by the microscope. They were in proportion to the assemblage of sticks and fingers stuck in the glue on the aneurysm. It was difficult to manipulate. Garven held his breath and steadied his hand on the edge of the patient's skull. He very slowly began to snip. First he was able to cut off the end of Damon's glove, thankfully, without taking any of the young man's finger. The process of getting off the pieces of wood was more difficult. Garven gnawed away at the ends until he had freed them from the bulk of the swab stick and the tongue depressor. The pieces of latex and sticks looked grossly out of place there under the microscope. There was no question of trying to remove them. They were now an integral part of the patient's anatomy.

"I'm sorry, Dr. Wilsonhulme, I acted like a real buffoon," said Damon.

Garven could almost see him mentally flagellating himself.

"She'll get infected. I know it," moaned Damon.

"Give her some prophylactic antibiotics. She'll do fine," Garven said. "Don't sweat the small stuff."

"Dr. Wilsonhulme, I appreciate your help, but I have to tell you that it's easy to hate someone with ice-water in their vascules," Damon said, starting to calm down now.

Garven laughed. "If you can't stand the heat, you'd better get out of the kitchen," he said.

The patient did well, just as Garven had predicted. He did not tell Damon how much he sweated over leaving the foreign bodies in place. No one told the patient or the family about the absurd situation in the OR, and Garven called the entire house staff and attending faculty together to instruct them on the use of the fast-drying glue. He was not about to have another such prematurely aging experience. Damon thankfully attributed it to the intercession of the pope—the real one who lived in Los Angeles.

At the end of the week, Garven left for Atlanta and the AANS meetings. It was an important meeting for him. He was scheduled to report the findings on the manpower study; he was now its chairman. The neurosurgery manpower committee had been assigned the volatile and charged task of evaluating whether or not there were too many neurosurgeons in the United States, and if so, what to do about it. He was also up for election to president-elect. The election was ordinarily a rubber stamp affair with the current leaders giving their recommendation for the new president, and the body of the membership giving their approval. There was no campaigning, no behind the scenes maneuvering, and no additional candidate once the leaders had named their choice. The nation's neurosurgeons considered themselves to be above the pettiness of politics. That denied the intense infighting among the committee before the new president-elect candidate was chosen. It was better that the membership was spared knowledge of a process that had more vicious infighting than the selection of a new pope.

Garven was in possession of rather startling information derived from the two year long study of the numbers of neurosurgeons and their practice characteristics. David Stark's committee had done a preliminary study years ago with the same findings. Garven was certain that his message would be well received, because it was likely to result in greater security and business for the average neurosurgeon then in practice, and Garven considered himself lucky to be the bearer of good news.

He walked over the lush hotel carpet towards the large meeting room for the business meeting of the association. Along the way he exchanged greetings on a first name basis with the leaders of neurosurgery from around the country and from two dozen different foreign countries.

"Garven, we need to get together for the president's committee lunch!"

"Call my secretary, Jim. I don't have a clue what my schedule is."

"Hold up there, Garven. You're a hard man to catch. The membership committee for the Harvey Cushings is having a little get together tonight. You need to be there."

"What time? I have my residents' reunion dinner at six thirty."

"Everybody's having their dinners tonight. That's why we made the committee meeting at nine."

"What a bunch of gluttons for punishment," Garven smiled. "I'll be there. Save a little Jack Daniels for me."

"Dr. Wilsonhulme, you haven't forgotten about meeting with me and the young fellow I told you about. He would be perfect for your program. I can vouch for him myself. Our program is filled up."

"We'll have to squeeze in a time between the SPAB seminar and my paper on carotid endarterectomies. Can you get your guy and meet me in the slide preparation room at eleven ten?" Garven called as he entered the room and headed for the podium.

The meetings were run with a Prussian efficiency. Neurosurgeons love to hear their own voices and would rather talk about their pet projects than eat. Given the chance, they would run overtime until the speakers at the end of the day and the end of the week would never be heard. Devon Upshire was the monitor of the business meeting. He banged down his gavel just as Garven took his seat on the stand. It was four o'clock on the dot.

CHAPTER
Sixteen

"Members, we have three matters of business on the agenda. Please take note of the packets on the chairs. All the information you need to have about the manpower study by Dr. Wilsonhulme and about the election is in the package. Let's start with the budget for the upcoming year. The Harvey Cushings will be in Los Angeles next April, and we expect an increase in costs of ten percent. That is reflected in the budget. Is there any discussion?" Devon asked as a matter of form.

Two Indian neurosurgeons from San Francisco rose to protest the increase in membership fees and the added cost for the upcoming meetings. As a solution, they suggested charging the residents twenty-five more dollars and the residents' wives another thirty. The comments from the rest of the speakers from the crowd were couched in polite terms but made it abundantly clear that it was considered stingy and mean-spirited to pick on the residents. The budget passed with a unanimous vote.

"Thank you. We are right on schedule," said Devon when he stood at the podium again. "Now, the highlight of this meeting—the manpower study. We purposely reserved this topic for the closed business session because we did not want the press or the public to have access to this information. Garven Wilsonhulme, chief at UC Osterlund Memorial in Los Angeles, and his committee have spent the better part of two years in collecting and collating this material. This is the most definitive set of data ever collected. I think you will be surprised at some of the findings. Dr. Wilsonhulme."

"Thanks, Devon. Fellow members of the AANS. Please turn your attention to the two slides on the screens in the front."

It was the first time two screens had been employed. The members nodded their approval of the innovation. It was going to be a test of their concentration and ability to absorb numbers with two sets of data coming at them at once.

Garven described the numbers of neurosurgeons in the country including those who were AANS members and those not, those board certified and those not. He gave a quick rundown of the demographics of practice—how many in practice, how many private, how many in academics, how many retired and disabled. Then he read a summary of the most important types of problems and types of operations done by neurosurgeons and gave averages of how many each neurosurgeon did. The members were mildly shocked at the realization in black and white of what they knew from their own experience was true.

Garven summed up the grim findings, "The average neurosurgeon serves a population of less than a 100,000 where a decade before he served half a million. The Canadians serve a million. In some major urban areas there are so many neurosurgeons that they serve populations approaching only 20,000 each. The average neurosurgeon's practice is seventy to eighty percent spine work. Twenty years ago, eighty percent of the work was cranial. Twenty percent of our number have stopped doing brain surgery altogether because they see so few head cases that they cannot keep up their skills. The average neurosurgeon does one aneurysm a year and less than ten craniotomies."

The neurosurgeons in the room listened in dispirited silence.

Garven completed his rendition of the statistics.

"Gentlemen and ladies—there were three female neurosurgeons—the conclusion is inescapable. There are two many neurosurgeons. If we did not produce another neurosurgeon for ten years we would only then break even. The committee was so alarmed by our findings that we decided to overstep our mandate and to make a proposal. We put it to you. The residency programs should cut down their intake of new residents by half. The programs that take two a year should take one, and those that take one a year should cut down to one every other year. We feel that this is a matter of such overriding importance that it should be debated by and voted upon by the membership. I open the floor to your comments.

The response was a shock to Garven, to the officers on the dais, and to the manpower committee. Men rushed to the microphones scattered at appropriate intervals throughout the spacious room. They jockeyed for position.

They interrupted each other in an ungentlemanly fashion. There was a passion in the deliveries that had never been seen before in a business meeting or for any neurosurgical subject before.

Daniel King, the chief at Cornell, with his stentorian oratorical voice won out over the others and was given the nod first. He spoke for the university professors.

"I can only say that Dr. Wilsonhulme has sandbagged us. By 'us' I mean the program directors. I take great umbrage at learning about this material for the first time today. I for one do not believe it. I do not think for a minute that the average neurosurgeon does nine and a half craniotomies. Cutting down on our number of residents will bankrupt our hospital. There is no way we can take care of our responsibilities to indigent patients if we have to pay the salary demanded by the average neurosurgeon. I suggest, Mr. Chairman, that this entire matter be tabled and restudied. Maybe we can look at it again in about ten years," he added sarcastically.

The next speaker was Dick Lathrop from Riverside, California.

"I'm in private practice in California. I saw those numbers that say California is specialist overcrowded, and that we have about as many neurosurgeons as we do lawyers. I know you big professors think we are dumb out there; Professor Wilsonhulme in his ivory tower there in LA is out of touch with the mood of the real head cutters. Those of us out in the trenches are not about to let you academic types run everything. Now you want to control the number of neurosurgeons coming out into practice. Soon you will determine where they go and guys like me will have to kiss Wilsonhulme's ring to get a new partner. I am plenty busy enough to need one, thank you, Dr. Wilsonhulme. If we let you get away with this, the next thing you will want to do is to revive your old commie plan to create regional centers where all of the cranis have to go—a center for aneurysms, one for carotids, one for backs. Old Joe over there in Moscow would love that plan. No, Sir. I don't think us guys in practice will be voting in favor of cutting our own throats, thank you!'

The phraseology was usually more polite, but the sentiments expressed by the crowd were pretty much in tune with those of Dr. Lathrop as the meeting wore on. Devon gave up any hope of keeping to his schedule. Garven was shocked. He had expected the university professors to be universally behind him in an enlightened effort to save the profession, and he had expected the town men to line up with him to put the university professors in their place and to make them stop the glut that was diluting their personal practices and presumably their incomes. He was aware that he had never been so intuitively wrong in his entire career. Devon looked at Garven and shrugged a small gesture of hopelessness.

Garven leaned over to him and said, "This is absurd. They ought to realize that if we don't control ourselves, the government will. We will see socialized medicine telling us how many head cutters there can be if we don't police ourselves."

Devon whispered, "Or worse, big business will figure out that they're paying too much, and they'll take over and cut us off at the knees."

He shook his head.

Garven stood up and called for an end to the debate.

"I think we have gone over this enough for one night. Maybe what we should do is to send out a questionnaire and find out what the consensus of the membership is before we do anything hasty."

"You do that," someone yelled from the crowd. "Recrunch your figures or better, let some one else do it," came another impolite voice.

Garven could not recall a heckler shouting from the crowd in all the years he had been attending the business meetings. The negative political tenor was electric in the air that evening.

There was no vote on Garven's proposals. He said nothing more about the proposals or the manpower study per se. Devon again assumed his position at the podium.

"Now for the election. As is customary, the leadership has chosen a slate of nominees for the various positions. We have Jack Langtry for secretary, Avvard Jenkins for veep, and Garven Wilsonhulme for president-elect. We ask for your sustaining vote for these men who have given so much to the organization. We think they will be great leaders for the next several years."

"Let's have a real vote. Closed ballot just like this was America," one of the neurosurgeons shouted.

The voice was heavily accented. Garven could not place the voice nor the origin of the accent. It was another first; there had not been a closed vote on the leadership's proposed candidates in all the time he had been a member. It was a crushing blow to his ego. Devon looked at Garven helplessly. Garven shrugged to indicate that there was nothing else to do but to have a vote.

Devon said, "Okay. You have the slate of candidates before you. It's in your packet. You can mark a check for the men on the list, or you can fill in names for anyone else you might want in the space at the bottom of the page. You do not need to put your name on the paper. When you're done, pass the papers to the aisles, and the sergeants-at-arms will collect them. As always, we will count the ballots and announce the results while we wait. This may take a minute; so, why don't you catch a few winks while you have the chance."

"Don't patronize us, Upshire!" a voice from the darkened room called.

"The natives are restless, Devon. Better not let anyone walk up behind you, and maybe you'd better hire a food taster," joked Garven although he was not in a jovial mood.

There was considerable heated conversation in the hall as the votes were cast and collected. A delegation from the crowd was appointed to count them. It was a measure of the animosity rife in the room that night that an independent group to do the counting should be considered necessary.

There were 1859 voting members in the room. No one was sure what percent was required to declare a winner. Before the results were tabulated, the ad hoc committee took upon itself the right to declare that a simple plurality would be enough. Instead of the four candidates on the original list, votes were cast for fifteen neurosurgeons. Most of the names were unknown to the members of the ad hoc committee or to the leaders. Garven won by a plurality 431 votes. He never mentioned the manpower study again, never suggested to any colleague that there might be too many neurosurgeons; and he was content, as were the other members of the manpower committee, simply to let the matter drop into oblivion. He was becoming a true politician, practicing the art of the possible.

CHAPTER
Seventeen

Garven was content to go back to Los Angeles with a meager victory and a title and to let it go at that and not to dwell on the limits of his success. However, he recognized that it was a small, but telling chink in his armor. He was not accepted as the pope by everyone. He plunged himself back into his work. Now he had the lab geared up to electronics to pursue nervous system stimulations for pain. He reasoned that if stimulating the thalamus in the brain could give some people a substantial measure of pain relief, there could be other areas for different kinds of pain. Devon signed on to investigate several pains that were limited in the number of people suffering from them, and Garven concentrated on back pain.

Devon and his PhD neurophysiologist associate implanted electrodes in the limbic system, the cingulate gyrus, and in the midbrain. They had only a handful of patients in each category of pain, but achieved a modest amount of success. They, like Garven, were hampered by the problems of addiction, personality disorders, and workman's compensation psychosomatic overlay, and out-and-out craziness. They were able to crank out a paper a month on the average. Garven and Devon agreed on a mutually beneficial arrangement whereby each of them would be named as the other's coauthor thereby raising the number of their publications significantly.

Garven elected to implant electrodes on the spinal cord itself, some inhibitory and some excitatory, by a trial and error program. He began to find a fair percentage of people with relief from stimulation of the section of the spinal cord at the very back—the dorsal columns. It was unclear why the stimulation worked since none of the fibers in the dorsal column directly subserved pain impulses. Then, his patients began to develop complications.

Wires broke; wires disconnected from the implanted battery boxes; scars formed on the spinal cord; some people could not tolerate the buzzing sensation that the stimulation caused; others had unpleasant sensations in different regions of their bodies. Garven suspected that many of the men with work-related back pain had no intention of getting better; and some of them, even with real pain relief, refused to admit that they had been made well for fear of losing their compensation. It was nerve-wracking to see the complaining, drug seeking, work avoiding people day after day. Garven thought that he would give in to his logical urges and punch one of the chronic complainers and give him a lecture on the Protestant work ethic; and at times, he feared that he would go crazy himself. The last straw for Garven came when he implanted fifteen stimulators in women.

Five of these women, for reasons that were completely unexplainable, developed a peculiar complication, and all of them demanded the removal of the stimulators immediately. The women had in common a very strong moral sense even though they were of widely different cultural backgrounds—a Mormon, a Catholic, an Hasidic Jewess, a Muslim woman, and a Presbyterian who was an unflinching believer in hell-fire, damnation, and John Calvin. The complication was that the stimulators caused sexual arousal at low intensities, at a level that would not take away the pain for which the stimulator had been implanted. At stimulation intensities that did do away with pain, the five women suffered multiple orgasms. Each of the women of punctilious rectitude came to the immediate conclusion that the spinal cord stimulator was the work of the devil, and demanded that the stimulator be surgically removed. Pain was preferable to the unspeakable complication that they were forced to endure.

Garven wrote off the project in disgust after a six month trial. He concluded that the thalamic stimulations were the only practical mode of central nervous stimulation that had any future promise. He left the field, even the lone authorships, to Devon.

In much the same way that he found the inspiration for his tumor angiogenesis research and antitumor therapy, Garven was able to come up with an additional two projects. He was in an unassailable position, and when he published a paper that used the kernel of another young neurosurgeon's work, it was impossible to trace the maneuver back to him with any certainty. No one was about to accuse the president-elect of the AANS and UCOMH professor with the power of project life and death over NIH grants of flagrant plagiarism without rock solid proof, and that was hard come by. Garven had not even been accused.

One of the ideas Garven expropriated was from a Mexican researcher in epilepsy. The research project submitted by the worker involved surgically splitting the corpus callosum—the large cross connection of white matter from one side of the brain to the other. The researcher, Jose Ortega-Otero had done enough preliminary work in his Guadalajara hospital to warrant serious interest in his method of dealing with otherwise unsuccessfully treatable seizure disorders. The worker was so obscure that Garven summarily turned down his request for NIH funding, and took over the project idea as his own. He published a paper on 100 patients from all over the United States, and the paper was well received. Garven did not see Jose Ortega-Otero's name on any other paper, even in the Spanish language literature.

The other idea concerned the use of papaverine for vasoconstriction after rupture of aneurysms and accumulation of subarachnoid hemorrhage. Don Ketchum, from Atlantic City, had proposed intravenous and intraarterial injection of the drug that caused vessels to dilate. Garven knew that it was unlikely for the drug to reach the cerebral vessels in any concentration that would be beneficial. Garven adopted the idea of using papaverine, but he instilled the drug in suspension directly into the cerebral spinal fluid in the head by doing a small operation. He received full and unacknowledged credit for the idea, and the accolades of his fellow neurosurgeons for his contribution. He added the "Wilsonhulme Vasoconstriction Procedure" to the neurosurgeons' armamentarium of "Wilsonhulme Procedures."

Garven and Elizabeth attended the Screen Designers Awards at the Beverly Hills Hotel after Thanksgiving. It was a black tie affair, and they were invited because the producers of the awards program wanted to diversify their audience to include community leaders. Elizabeth was thrilled to go; she loved dress-up affairs. Garven sought every excuse that he could find to get out of it. The prospects of spending an entire evening with Hollyweird types was daunting. But he knew that he had neglected his wife in the past year. The only other black tie party they had attended had been the AANS banquet in April. He gave in and even tried to put on a pleasant face about it.

The people were genuine, unlike the other movie and TV affected sycophants he always seemed to encounter at the entertainment world's soirees. They spoke of technical concerns of their craft and art and seemed to evince an authentic interest in his work. Unlike physicians, the most boring conversationalists in the world, these people were capable of discussing a wide range of topics, and Garven found it refreshing. He did not notice when Elizabeth left his side to mix, mingle, and integrate.

He fell into conversation with a stunning young blond woman who had never been to an award presentation before and was glad to encounter another novice.

She said, "It's nice to meet at least one someone who is not connected with the business."

"What's your connection?" Garven asked her.

"Peripheral," she answered, "I'm in modeling."

"Is your escort in films?"

"My escort is my roommate. She is a high fashion designer who gets the odd bit of business from the film people. She came for business reasons."

"How about you?"

"Mainly because I'm bored, but I presume there are people here that it wouldn't hurt for me to meet. They need to hang the rags on somebody; it might as well be me."

The statuesque girl looked at Garven for a moment and smiled.

"What?" Garven asked.

"Oh, I was just thinking how different this is. I think you are the first man I have met at a Hollywood party that asked about me, talked about me, and didn't automatically hit on me. It's rather novel...and nice. Usually, the men I meet are producers who have a wonderful bit part for me...you know what I mean. I always feel like I have to do up my buttons again when they get done talking," she said.

She had relaxed with Garven. He could sense that she had let down her guard and was not trying to impress him nor to conduct one of those plastic showbiz conversations.

"Well, at the risk of being too forward," Garven said, "My name is Garven Wilsonhulme."

"Everyone knows who you are, Dr. Wilsonhulme. Ever since you took care of Senator McMurtry when that crazy shot him, you have had a persona. I'm glad to get to meet the person behind the persona. Oh, yeah, I forgot; I'm Jenny Lakewood."

"I am pleased to meet you, Jenny. I mean that. I've never thought of myself as being in the public eye, and I'm not sure that I like it," Garven said. "I think of myself as being a private person."

"I think I'd like to get to know the private person a little better. Think that's possible?" asked Jenny.

"It is. I'm married. I hope that won't preclude us getting to know each other," Garven said.

He was careful to keep his expression neutral.

"Thank you for telling me. I feel like I can trust you since you have been open with me. I'm unattached—'between engagements'—as we say in the 'biz'. I wouldn't want to make any trouble."

"I wouldn't foresee any problem, Jenny. My wife and I live very separate lives of late. Just one of those things. I don't see why you and I couldn't become friends. You are a very pleasant woman. I presume we could be friends without romantic entanglement. Are you free for lunch this Wednesday?"

"Not free, but I'm willing to negotiate a good price," she laughed, a full deep laugh of a woman comfortable with a man. "And don't be too hasty about the 'romantic entanglement' decision. It might be fun. We can make all the stops along the way, as Frank Sinatra would say."

"He ought to know," Garven said.

He took down her name and number, and they agreed to meet at The Brown Derby for lunch on Wednesday.

Garven mingled with the crowd and looked for Elizabeth. He had time to think despite the noise of the partying crowd. This was where he had been very early on when he had gotten to know Martha Storm but before he had allowed a romance to develop. He shuddered at the memory. He could ease away from this girl now, and no one would be hurt or embarrassed. He certainly did not want to get into the same kind of snarl that he had experienced with the VA secretary. In the end, he admitted to himself, Martha had entangled him in a Gordian Knot. Like Arthur, he had been unable to untie himself and had had to resort to ex caliber.

He shook his head then looked around embarrassedly to see if anyone thought he was hallucinating, talking to people who were not there. No one paid any attention to him. He could not shake the image of Martha. It had been a sobering experience, and he was determined to remember the lesson he had learned.

He guessed it was best put by his old friend Lyle Durche, the only person in whom he had confided: "Don't let the little head tell the big head what to do."

He could see Martha wearing more provocative clothing, even at work, as he tried to back away from the relationship.

He could hear her whining voice, almost pleading, "What have I done? Why don't you like me? Why are you so mean?"

He shook his head again.

"Don't get your tail where you get your mail," he remembered grimly.

Martha got hold of his unlisted home number and called at times when she knew he would be home alone. She drove by his house. She found pretexts to page him and get him to her office. Garven had been weak and wholly responsible for the mess himself, he knew that. As often as not, when Martha did get him alone, he succumbed. After a while, he began to feel a sense of self-loathing. Not conscience or remorse, exactly; it was more like fear or being caught up in an addiction. He felt himself being swept by an undertow, and he could not find a way to extricate himself. She was aggressive, and the little head was swayed by the flattery that pursuit engendered.

Finally, she became too bold, almost obsessive. She began to make private scenes; at least, she was discrete enough not to let her emotions get the best of her around others. She hinted little threats, couched in joking terms, about showing up on his doorstep in a nightie or of mailing anonymous letters to his wife. She began to ask what she meant to him, really. Why couldn't he ditch the shrewish wife who would not even try to understand him and his career? Did they have a future together? She made him anxious and desperate at the end. He could envision Martha destroying everything he had built up. He lost any affection he felt for her after a few months. His lust for her gave way to a calculated determination to disentangle himself from her pursuit.

He confronted her with his desire to break off their affair. She had cried and even begged. He was afraid of what she would do; so, he let it go on. He confronted her again; and on the last occasion, she decided that he was, at last, completely serious. She threatened him. She softened then and assured him that she could never do anything to hurt him; she could be a better wife than that Elizabeth had ever thought of being. Garven knew that he had to find an oblique but irreversible solution. The woman now posed a threat to his career and to his well-being. Garven Wilsonhulme had never permitted such threats, even from the time he was a boy in Cipher.

As he walked through the strangely dressed crowd at the fashion designer's party, he conjured up the picture of his solution, a thought he had worked to put away from his consciousness. Garven began making the calls to his old friends around the country's VA hospitals, the professors who were the movers and shakers in the system, and some of whom owed him favors. He made deals and concessions, and without divulging his dilemma in so many words, he got Martha a transfer to Washington D.C. at the Veteran's Administration Headquarters. The move was a major promotion, and cost Garven more markers than he cared to think about. He did it all without telling Martha, herself. He learned from the administrator's office at the Rosewood VA in Los Angeles, that Martha was reluctant to leave. They could not imagine why anyone would balk at such a step up. The administrators made the offer an all or nothing on: accept the promotion, or face demotion.

The next part of Garven's slashing of his Gordian Knot had required him to overcome her reticence to move. He did that by mounting a careful campaign of undermining her work. He was able to convince the administrator that Martha Storm was disloyal and was keeping records on him in order to get his job. She was cunning and patient, Garven had secretly let the administrator know. It was only a matter of time. The administrator began to make life unpleasant for Martha, nothing overt or in writing, but effective nonetheless. Finally, Martha brought up the entire subject of her job offer to Garven, confident that it would be news to him.

He had acted convincingly surprised and genuinely saddened, but had allowed that it was probably for the best. He and Martha were star-crossed lovers, meant to love from afar. She was not unintelligent. She could see that her affair was going nowhere. She shared his sadness, and tearfully parted from him.

Garven had taken his family out to Knott's Berry Farm for an entire weekend to celebrate. Elizabeth was unsure why Garven had seemed so lighthearted; but she liked the change in him, and made no complaint. Now, here he was on the threshold of another relationship, he thought. He really should nip it in the bud and just call the girl and break it off before it got started.

But, she was easily the most beautiful and alluring woman he could every remember being that close to.

"*Is that little head talking?*" he pondered with a small inward laugh.

Elizabeth interrupted his thoughts. She was ebullient. He had not seen her that way for a long time. There was something about that public display of zestful enthusiasm and disinhibition that was out of character and faintly disconcerting. It took her giving him a big public kiss to realize that she had a strong odor of expensive alcohol on her breath. Elizabeth was drunk. Garven had a sudden feeling that he had been missing something in his recent arm's length observation of his wife's life.

CHAPTER
Eighteen

It was hard for Garven to concentrate the following Monday. He had to go to the indigent neurosurgery clinic, a distracting experience at best. He had no patience with the questions.

"Is you ma doctah?"

"Does Ah takes ma ekalectic conversion pills three times in a day or do ah takes 'em all at onct?"

"How come mah liters still hurts, Huh? I done had the operation awreddy. Ah'm beginnin' to thenk it warn't nuthen but a 'spearmint."

"How come ah'm still ahavin' trouble wi' ma nature? 'Splain that if ya'll can."

"If ah has dat head operation lak you say, will Ah be on the pitiful list? Ah had an aunty that died in there. Ah don' wan' nuthen to do wi' that."

Garven was only half there.

The half that was present listened absent-mindedly to the complaints and bits of personal history:

"Ma haid smahts. That dude done come upside mah haid wi' a pool cue right smaht. Ya'll goin' to gimme that pain pill that starts with a 'D'? Somethin' lak Dem...Demerol. Somethin' lak that? Ah am hallergic to everythin' else, ya heah wha' Ah'm sayin'?"

"How much Ah been drenkin'? Aw, mebbe two beers on a weekend, thass all, doctu. Use to drenk a whole lot, but Ah quit."

"Where was Ah shot, you ax? At Main and Pico."

Garven raised his voice a little and repeated, "Where were you shot?"

"Oh, whyn't ya'll ax me inna first place. In the right sidda ma head. Thass how come Ah walks so funny."

Garven was getting a headache. He had been there the whole morning, and they had scared up only one surgery. Even that one was doubtful. The patient still had to consult her witch doctor. He found himself asking the standard questions.

"Do you have insurance?"

"You been drinking?"

"Are you a veteran?"

"Do you want to sign out?"

"What do you mean, there were eight of you in one little car and nobody speaks English?"

He found himself slipping back into his EOR 'Pit Boss' routine.

"Do you hurt all over more than any place else?"

"Yes, Sah."

"Have you had a hair cut? the bad blood?"

"Not as Ah knows of."

He was surprised when the time approached noon, and he would soon be able to get out of the clinic and back to civilization. His mind was so preoccupied that he found only faint amusement in the patients' names or the oddities of their examinations—a girl named Female, pronounced Fa mahl ee, a boy named Wurthles, and a pair of twins named Si-Philis and Gonora. The residents showed him tattoos, something that always gave him a chuckle, other than today. Under the areolae of one woman was "Hot-cold" and another, "Sweet-sour", and on one foreskin a handsomely depicted fly, and on another the words, "Little Henry."

"Hey boss," said the middle year resident after they had evaluated the works of penile art, "you hear about the guy that had a tattoo on his pecker?"

"Besides these two fine citizens?" Garven asked, willing to be the straight man.

"Yeah. His wife thought the word on her husband's pecker was S-W-A-N, and his girl friend thought it was S-A-S-K-A-T-C-H-E-W-A-N."

That set off an intrusive and inconvenient train of thought. Garven felt that he was acting like a schoolboy, but he could not get the anticipation of Wednesday's lunch date to quiet down in his mind.

Monday afternoon he helped the chief resident with an aneurysm in the back part of a woman's brain, the posterior fossa. He was very competent, and needed no direction, just competent assistance. Garven was able to do his part without really putting his mind to it.

He finished up the day going through his mail and the LA Times- ANGELA DAVIS SEIZED; Black militant UCLA communist was arrested in New York City after a courtroom shoot-out in San Raphael, California. ORGANIZED CRIME CONTROL ACT PASSED; President Nixon pledged "total war against organized crime."

Wednesday morning dragged. Garven spent the morning in the lab injecting viruses into the layers of rat's dura to see if that would cause the formation of meningiomas. It was dull stuff, and his mind took him to the lunch room with Jenny Lakewood and his fantasies carried him to still other, more comfortable, rooms. He left early and was seated at a table in the Brown Derby fifteen minutes before the time of his date.

Jenny arrived fifteen minutes fashionably late.

"Sorry, got held up in traffic," she said breezily. "Heard that one before?"

They both laughed at the quintessential Los Angeles excuse.

"I am glad you made it. I was a little afraid you would forget," Garven said.

"No way, Garven. I have even been doing my homework about you. What an impressive career! I didn't even finish college. You are a brain surgeon. That must be the hardest thing in the world to learn. Wow!"

She smiled fully, telling him that of her admiration with her eyes and her smile as well as her words. Garven blushed.

"I'm starved. What should we eat?" Jenny asked enthusiastically.

"I thought about ordering before you came, but I didn't know what you like. I wasn't sure if you were one of those bony models that eats nothing but unbuttered popcorn and fresh lettuce."

"My motor runs so fast all the time that I can eat just about anything I like...as long as I lay off the double Dutch chocolate cake."

Garven liked to hear that the attractive woman had a lusty appetite. He had a theory about lusty appetites and their association with lustful appetites. Thoughts of her flitted through his mind even as he sat looking at her. It was an intense involvement for so short an acquaintance, at least on his part.

They looked at the menu for a few minutes, then she said, "I can't decide; I like it all. You order for me. I know it'll be great!"

They started with young white asparagus tips dressed with Hollandaise sauce. The entree was fillets of sole sautéed amandine and garnished with fresh lemon and parsley, rice pilaf, and glazed carrots. The effect was right, Garven thought, just French enough; and it did not make him seem like he was trying too hard. They drank water and refused dessert. The portions were generous, and Jenny ate heartily and without affected manners. She was comfortable with him. He liked that.

As they ate, he watched her. She caught him from time to time and rewarded him with a little appreciative laugh. She was beautiful with classical high cheek bones. She wore a simple blue dress with large brass buttons. The V of her neckline hinted at a classical form beneath, offering only the slightest indication of pink. Her blond hair was swept back from her ears, and she wore no jewelry. She ate as if it was fun. She looked at him and enjoyed his appraisal of her. She talked sparingly and drew personal disclosures out of Garven that he would ordinarily have kept reserved. By the end of the meal, Garven felt himself ensnared in a tender trap.

"I have a job at two. I know it's terrible to eat and run, Garven, but I really have to be there. Please, let's do it again. Could you get away for a little tête-à-tête at my place sometime? I have a gig in 'Frisco on Wednesday and Thursday, but I'll be back for the weekend—Friday night," she said.

Garven nodded his approval.

Jenny said, "Friday, then? I cook up a mean filet mignon and little new potatoes. Maybe you could bring some Chianti or something."

Garven felt like he was being swept along by a forceful girl, and it felt good.

"Friday. Seven okay?"

"Great!" she said with enthusiasm. "Until then," she put her finger to her brightly lipsticked full lips and pressed it to the back of his hand and was gone.

Garven savored the moment. When he drove back to the hospital, he underwent a minor mental-psychological tug-of-war. At once, he thought about calling it all off before the real trouble could get started and also thought about her in her apartment, warm and inviting. He scolded himself for his illicit eagerness; she was young enough to be his...well, his niece. He prided himself, a forty year old, on having captured the interest of such a lovely creature. He had a fleeting thought about being caught, exposed, and thrown into divorce court, facing the austere university faculty board with all of the attendant repercussions. He had a long thought about Jenny's living quarters and the activities that could be imagined there. On the elevator, he decided to call her and put a halt to the foolishness. In his office, he called his wife and told her that he would have to stay late in the lab for the rest of the week, but that he would make it up to her on the weekend. It was true that he needed to bring his current project to completion before Christmas and had planned to be in the lab Tuesday, Wednesday, and Thursday. The inclusion of Friday had been an afterthought.

Garven took Elizabeth to lunch on Thursday at the Escoffier.

"To what do I owe this unique privilege?" she asked.

There was an edge to her voice, or maybe he just imagined it. He tried not to look blameworthy—like the silly men who came to the G-U clinic at UCOMH and were found only to have the g-c—not the gonococcus, the guilty conscience.

"I feel guilty about not being home for the next few days. I wanted to get us out together, that's all," he said lightly.

She looked at him with an expression that approximated a sneer. It was uncharacteristic of her, and he wondered at her behavior.

The gourmet meal was wonderful, and her air of reproach and unfriendliness cleared as the courses came and went. It was an operating day for Garven; so, he did not touch any alcohol. He watched Elizabeth quaff down an aperitif, white wine with her fish, and red wine with her chocolate mousse. She sipped a cognac as they talked about the children, her activities in the Japanese-American Friendship League and at the Museum of Modern Art. He made a point of not talking about himself or his work, and of not noticing her alcohol consumption.

When they separated, he watched her being curt to the doorman. She forgot to tip the valet who brought her car. She laughed raucously when she dropped her keys and wobbled slightly as she picked them up.

Garven mused to himself, "I wonder how long this has been going on?"

He had scheduled a three o'clock starting time for a private patient to have a craniotomy to clip a very difficult aneurysm. He hurried back to the hospital. Mrs. Fendell was the wife of a roofer with good insurance through her husband's union. She was the mother of six. Two weeks previously, she had walked into her kitchen to prepare breakfast for her family. To the horror of her children, she had suddenly clapped her hands to her temples and cried out in agony. She collapsed to the floor and was brought to UCOMH to the EOR stuporous and vomiting. She was found to have a neck that was stiff as a board. The 'Pit Boss' had done a lumbar puncture, found gross blood, and referred her to the neurosurgery service. It was Garven's turn to take the private patients coming in from the clinic, the EOR, and from consults.

In previous years, Mrs. Fendell might have been operated upon immediately to prevent her from rebleeding and having disastrous consequences, even death. Those operations had always been bloody and difficult due to brain swelling, and the mortality and morbidity statistics were too high for anyone to be comfortable with them. In recent years, as a result of a number of articles in the literature, the patients were operated only after fourteen days in the hospital. They were placed on a drug, Amicar—epsilon amino caproic acid—that hardened the clots and prevented rebleeding. The operation after the subarachnoid blood had had a chance to clear was much simpler and safer. It bothered Garven that some of the patients rebled and died during the waiting period; but overall, the results seemed better. At least, it was easier on him to do a clean and easy operation.

Nothing about Mrs. Fendell's case looked to be simple. She had a carotid-ophthalmic aneurysm that was very large and appeared fragile even on the angiograms. The worst thing about it was that the lesion was located immediately above the process of the pituitary, almost flush with the skull floor. The question was whether there would be anything of a neck to put a clip on or would Garven have to be content just to apply some Japanese superglue.

The operation was hampered by firm clot in the area of the vessels that contained the aneurysm. Garven suspected that the Amicar might have created the hard and undissolved clot, but he had no scientific evidence that the drug caused that effect. He slowly and painstakingly cleared out the blood until he was looking through the objective of his operating microscope at a throbbing giant aneurysm. The wall of the blister on the vessel wall was so thin that it was possible to visualize blood swirling around inside. The dome of the aneurysm could not even be touched. Garven worked for two hours in a space about the size of a thimble to free up the vessels, the optic nerve, and the aneurysm in order to isolate a clippable neck. He was sweating. The room was quiet, none of the usual joking and banter.

"I think I have enough neck, here," Garven finally said. "Give me a big upcurved Mayfield clip first," he asked his scrub nurse.

The junior resident was assisting.

"Isn't that just a temporary clip? Dr. Upshire always says they are. He thinks they will fall off," he said.

"That's a legitimate concern. I want to be able to put a temporary clip on the carotid, above and below the 'rism to trap it if I have to. I'm just trying to check the fit," Garven told him.

"Looks huge under the scope, doesn't it?" commented the resident as the clip was moved at various angles to see if it could prove useful in an emergency.

"Sure does," said Garven. "I can hardly see the aneurysm when the clip is in the scope's field. It would almost be easier to put the clip on with the unaided eye than under the scope, like we used to do in the old days."

Having satisfied himself that the clip would do in an emergency, Garven asked the scrub nurse, "Big McFadden clip. The biggest."

She handed him the tight spring clip.

"Okay, everybody quiet and hold your breath," Garven announced to the OR team. "I'm going to try and clip it."

He looked at the permanent clip under the operating microscope.

"Take her BP down to sixty systolic, Jed," he said to the anesthesiologist.

For this procedure, Garven had used the old technique of hypothermia and had insisted that the room temperature be reduced to fifty-five degrees.

The circulating nurse had complained that "it is cold enough in here to hang meat."

Hopefully, now Garven's extra precautions would pay off.

There was great tension in the room. Garven's breath came in slow breath-holding, concentrated, efforts. He eased the clip into approximately the correct position. It seemed too high on the fundus of the aneurysm. He brought the blades of the McFadden clip out again and aimed them at a more oblique angle for the next try.

Before he could move the small steel clip towards the aneurysm neck again, there was a sudden explosion of the large thin-walled structure. Blood splashed into the small operative field and visualization was completely obscured. Garven could not do anything with the clip because he could not see.

"Suction," he requested calmly.

Both he and the resident put large bore suckers into the gathering pool of blood and drew up the viscous stuff until they could see intermittently. There was nothing left of the aneurysm. Where it had been, there was now a pencil sized geyser of blood.

"What's her systolic?" Garven asked the anesthesiologist.

"Eighty, I'm taking it down," was the reply.

"Give me the Mayfield clip," Garven ordered.

He put it down towards the source of the bleeding. "Too big. Get me a smaller one, same curve."

She handed him the clip holder. He struggled to get the tips of the clip below the bleeding point. He cursed.

"Too low. We are in real trouble. Give me some fine rongeurs. Daniel, you suck for me."

Garven nibbled off more of the anterior wall of the pituitary fossa—the sella turcica or Turkish saddle. He tried the clip again. It was still far from perfect. He pressed down hard and situated the blades of the clip as far into the carotid canal as he could and closed the tips. It did nothing. Blood continued to erupt.

He removed the clip and placed it on the intracranial portion of the small internal carotid artery. That did nothing to staunch the flow.

"Start a unit," he asked the anesthesiologist. "Occlude the carotid in the neck. I can't get control from below."

Nothing happened.

"Are you on the carotid?" Garven asked the anesthesiologist.

"With both hands," he answered.

"Mash on both of them. She's getting cross fill, and there is no decrease in the flow."

"I have them both closed off, Dr. Wilsonhulme," the anesthesiologist said. "Slowing down?"

"Not a whit," said Garven.

His voice was more strained now. Blood continued to pour into the suction apparatus. Under the microscope it looked like the Red Sea overflowing its banks, but Garven knew that it was still a manageable amount.

"Give her another unit, and you'd better T&C four more. Make two of them stat uncrossed."

He paused to think and to take stock. He placed clips on the opposite internal carotid artery inside the head. That did nothing.

"Call Dr. Upshire. Tell him to get down here stat. And Caroline, open up the carotid tray. We are going to have to tie off one and maybe even both of her carotids in the neck."

The circulating nurse shook her head sadly and complied. She knew what an act of desperation that would be; the woman would stand a great chance of having a stroke, even a stroke on both sides, and would likely die.

Things went from terrible to worse. The temporal lobe of the brain behind where they had been working began to swell markedly for no apparent reason.

"What now?" Garven moaned.

It was the first time he had allowed himself to give vent to his feelings. The swelling brain forced itself into the space. Now the two surgeons were unable to work.

"I think somebody sprinkled goober dust all around this lady's bed," Garven said recalling one of the superstitions heard in the neuro clinic. "And tomorrow she's gonna wake up dead."

His voice was bitter.

"What are you going to do, chief?" asked Daniel Lemming

He was clearly shaken by this turn of events.

"I was thinking about giving you my sucker and the clip holder and going to the office. Call me when you get the bleeding under control," Garven said in a bit of gallows humor.

"Great plan, chief."

The very thought of having primary responsibility for this progressing train wreck scared the wits out of the young resident.

Devon Upshire entered the room, scrubbed and ready to go.

"Caroline filled me in, Garven. Still need the carotids tied off?"

"I hate to say it, but yeah; go ahead. I am up to my knees in alligators here. Now the temporal lobe has decided to blow up. You're on your own," Garven said.

He was already suctioning out large segments of the temporal lobe. Daniel tried to keep up with the problem of suctioning out the blood coming from the aneurysm site and from the new bleeders Garven was creating by the second. Finally, there was room again and some ability to see.

"Got the first side, Garven," said Devon.

He packed the neck incision with antibiotic soaked sponges and began to open the right side.

The bleeding continued unabated.

"How many units so far, Abe?" Garven asked the anesthesiologist.

"Six. I sent for another four. You know she's only got six liters; we've about given her a complete exchange. We'll have to start some platelet packs."

"Do it," Garven said.

He watched the bleeding continue with a feeling of helplessness.

"Devon?"

"Yeah, Garven?"

"Do you have a clamp on the carotid?"

"It's occluded: I have still got to tie it off."

"Thanks. Good work."

As incredible as it seemed, the bleeding did not abate in the slightest.

"Give me two straight 'rism clips," Garven said and extended his hand towards the scrub nurse without looking up.

"What are you going to do, chief?"

Daniel asked apprehensively. He could not see any better way to put a clip on the aneurysm bleeding point now than he had thirty minutes ago.

"Clip the posterior communicators. She's got huge vertebrals supplying blood from behind and in addition to the carotids. I'll do the right one first in case it makes any difference to her speech areas."

He cross clipped the small artery. The bleeding seemed to decrease a little.

"Not good enough. Here goes."

Garven's voice was grim. He applied the last clip, stopping off the last major supplier to the bleeding artery and to almost the entire brain. Now the blood flow cut down to a steady annoying trickle.

"It hardly seems possible," said Daniel. "She's not supposed to have any other supply."

"A few collaterals, Daniel. Enough to get on our nerves but not enough to save her brain, I fear. Put a cottonoid on the bleeding site and suction on it. It'll stop. At least, let's make sure the operative bed is dusty dry before leave," Garven said dejectedly.

Mrs. Fendell did not have a chance; he knew that.

"Devon, let Daniel close up. I'd like you to go out and talk to the husband with me."

Miriam Fendell survived a day and a half in a grotesque decerebrate state. Garven canceled all of his other commitments and spent the time with the family. He had to tell the grim story and answer the questions for every member of the large family one at a time. They seemed unable to accept anything second hand.

"Thanks Doctor," said Jake Fendell, pale faced and wan, when Garven gave him the final bad news. "I know you did the best you could, and I know that you care. That means a lot to me. She's in a better place, now. She was a good lady, a good mom; but she had a hard life. I hope she has some rest now."

CHAPTER
Nineteen

Garven was in a low state when he arrived at Jennifer Lakewood's apartment just before seven on Friday night. He was not hungry, and he was not in any kind of mood for romance. He would have canceled the rendezvous had he not received such a frosty reception from his wife, Elizabeth, when he called home to get the family news. It had made him angry on top of the rest of the rotten week.

"Come in, Garven," Jenny said and took both of his hands and pulled him into the entrance hall.

She was going to pull him to her for a kiss, but saw that he was troubled.

"What's wrong?" She asked. "You look lower than a snake's belly with fallen arches."

"I'm afraid I won't be very good company tonight, Jenny," Garven said noncommittally.

"Bad week?"

"The worst."

She led him to her couch, put both hands on his chest and gently pushed him down. She took her place next to him.

"Tell Mama Jenny all about it," she said in a soothing warm liquid voice. "Let it out."

Garven Wilsonhulme never confided his troubles to anyone. He did not really trust anyone; and right now, he did not trust himself, fearing what might come out if he ever released the flood gates of his emotions, even a little. She rubbed his tense neck. He began to open up and told her about

Mrs. Fendall. She kneaded the stiff muscles of his upper back. He told her about the tensions of being the chief and always in the medical spotlight. She had him lie across her knees and massaged his sore lower back. He relaxed and got drowsy. He told her about the problems he was having with his wife and about his suspicions that she may becoming an alcoholic.

Before dinner, Jenny had soothed away all of Garven's tensions.

The weekend with Peter Arthur and Susan was pleasant; Garven took them to the beach because Elizabeth was ill. She would not talk to her husband about her 'illness', but there was no doubt about its authenticity. She was tired, nauseated, and pale. Her face appeared edematous and her eyes swollen. She shooed the rest of the family out insisting that all she needed was rest. Although the two of them argued about her condition, and Garven tactfully questioned her as to the merest possibility that she might be having problems related to her alcohol intake, Elizabeth refused categorically to see a doctor. When Garven left for rounds early Monday morning, she was no better, and the issue was unresolved.

Garven had developed a peculiar practice with regards his work and sleep habits. He arose at four o'clock in the morning and was on the hospital ward or in the NICU before five. That way, he was most efficient in getting his work done because he did not have to stop and chat with other physicians he might encounter at a more leisurely hour. He needed time to himself as well, and the only period of the day when he could work undisturbed was in the early morning hours. He tried to get in a nap in the mid-afternoon, but most days, it was just too hectic. Unless he had something important to occupy him, he had developed the practice of going to bed at nine.

Devon was aware of this, which to him was a monastic existence and quoted to Garven the old adage, "Early to bed, early to rise, makes Jack," with ill concealed scorn.

On this particular Monday, Garven needed to see his rather famous new patient, Jack Clyde Powers, the pastor and owner of the Amazing Grace Full Gospel Cathedral. He had the largest Protestant congregation in the state of California, and he had the largest craniopharyngioma Garven had ever seen. The tumor sat in the midline of the base of Pastor Power's skull above the sella turcica. He was slowly going blind, had become impotent, and was beginning to experience generalized pituitary failure. Garven wanted to check for himself if the pastor had been given his critical extra dose of cortisone in addition to the daily maintenance dose prescribed by the endocrinologists when the patient had been admitted. He was scheduled for surgery at nine that morning. Garven and Kent Ashcroft were on the schedule to do the case.

At seven, Garven went to the OR to see how Jim Bettman, the chief resident was doing on his case. Jim was a free-wheeling cowboy who never looked tired or out of sorts. Dr. Stark and Dr. Chou looked at Jim's antics as if he were a loose cannon on deck, but he had never had any real trouble, and Garven was glad to have someone around who was almost constantly cheerful.

When Garven entered the room, he knew he was in the right place.

He heard Jim singing as he worked, "Catch a falling star and put it in your pocket. It will burn your balls away!"

He had an awful voice and made up for his lack of quality with an increase in decibels.

"Hi, chief, how's it hangin'?" he asked as soon as he saw Garven.

"I'm okay. How's your case coming?"

"Couldn't be better. This is a secret 'spearmint'. One of those very exotic cases that the head cracker should get fifty thou for, you know."

"It's an acute subdural, Jim," Garven said sticking a pin in Jim's oratorical balloon.

"But the patient doesn't know that, and neither does his insurance company," said Jim with undampened spirits.

Garven looked at the plastic bag of the patient's clothing. They were filthy and ragged, the obvious apparel of a street person. He laughed at Jim's hyperbolic economic expectations.

"And what insurance does he have?" Garven asked.

"The famous No-charge No Pay Company, chief. The favorite company for our elite clientele. Are you going to do Jack What's His Name, the preacher today?"

"At nine."

Jim hummed a little more of "Catch a falling star" as he secured the red rubber catheter drain to the scalp with a silk suture. Then, as if he remembered Garven's clinic and just made an important association, he recited, "Jack be nimble, Jack be quick, Jack jumped over the candle stick! Great balls of fire!" and he began to hum Jerry Lee Lewis' great song. Garven felt his spirits lifted by his zany resident.

He did not want to be outdone.

"Did you hear about the horse that went into the bar, Jim?"

"Nope...Unless he was the one that the bartender asked why he had such a long face, yuk, yuk," he said.

Garven grimaced. "Heard it, eh?"

"Sorry, chief."

"I'll have to come into your OR and pick up some newer material, I guess," said Garven.

"Hear about the two Irish queers?"

"No."

"Old John Fitzpatrick and Patrick Fitzjohn?"

"That's pretty weak."

"I'll try harder. Do you know how tell which is the Mexican at the cockfight?"

"Um mmh."

"He's the one with the duck. Do you know how to tell which one is the Italian at the cockfight?"

"Um mmh."

"He's the guy putting his bet on the duck. Do you know how to spot the Mafia wiseguy at the cockfight?"

"Um mmh." Garven was chuckling.

"The duck wins," Jim said and laughed loudly at his own joke.

The nurses rolled their eyes.

Garven could not resist a parting shot.

"Do you remember Cary Limpole, the surgery resident we saw in clinic?"

"Oh, yeah," Jim said.

His voice was serious now. And respectful.

"That was the greatest call I ever saw. He came in with a little patch of numb skin on the back of his hand, and you got a biopsy and proved that it was leprosy. That was incredible. You really made your bona fides that day."

"Well, I have an update for you. Did you know that he can never finish a game of cards now?"

Jim was suspicious.

"Really, how come?"

"He always has to throw his hand in early."

Garven had a straight poker face.

"And you say I'm terrible."

He thought his chief was a great guy. Garven had treated the surgery resident's Hansen's disease with sulfones and had probably gotten a cure or at least a complete remission, and nobody outside the department and the patient knew anything about it; so, the poor guy could go on practicing.

"Well, wish me luck on the pastor, Jim. See you at evening rounds. Any trouble and you can call me in the office; I'll be there most of the day.

Garven made rounds with the other residents and interns then came back down to the OR. He wanted to be there when Pastor Powers went to sleep;

so, the well-known clergyman would know that Garven was present and would presume that the neurosurgery professor was going to do the case himself. In reality, Garven planned to let Kent Ashcroft do the case. It was not a particularly difficult one.

Garven sat in the doctor's lounge and swapped stories with the orthopods while Kent got the pastor shaved and in position. The pods were wasting away their lives waiting for an x-ray to come back, as usual. Kent called Garven when he was ready to make the first burrhole.

Garven scrubbed and was gowned and gloved by the nurses. Before he could take his place at the table, an oxygen tank came loose from its connection to the feeder lines and flew dangerously around the room punching dents in the wall and knocking over one of the Mayo stands before finally rolling to rest on the floor. Everyone in the room had taken cover and had to rescrub, gown, and glove.

"I hope that's not some sort of harbinger for the rest of the case," Garven sighed when it was over, and they were ready to go again.

Fortunately, no one was hurt, and only about fifteen minutes had been wasted.

"Ready?" Kent asked.

Garven said, "Go for it. Let's don't make a career case out of it."

Kent placed the skull perforator bit on the thin skull of the temporal bone and began to work the brace around, slowly grinding off the bone. Garven began to hum, "Forever and Ever." Kent moved along more bravely.

"Seems dull," Kent observed as the perforator ground at the skull rather than making clean swirls of bone as it penetrated.

"Only the poor carpenter blames his tool," said Garven.

Kent leaned into his work and began to made more progress.

Garven looked at Kent and was about to caution him not to put his weight onto the brace and bit when suddenly the perforator plunged through the last portion of the skull and into the underlying dura. The perforator sank to its hilt. Both surgeons could envision in their minds' eye the devastation wrought in that tenth of a second. Kent whipped the perforator out of the hole so quickly that anyone not paying attention would have missed the catastrophe. He had a stricken look on his face.

"Oh, no," he moaned, "I hurt him. I really hurt him."

He looked at Garven for some sort of reassurance.

There was none to give. What was done was done.

"You've pithed him," Garven said quietly. "Now we have to see what we can salvage."

In his own mind, he could see himself explaining what had happened to the family and the eminent members of the clergy who were in the waiting room communing with the family. He shook that thought and all other extraneous considerations from his mind, and soberly went on.

"Do you want to take over, Dr. Wilsonhulme?" Kent asked, crestfallen.

Garven shook his head.

"It's your case."

Together, they did a formal craniotomy, opened the dura widely and followed the ragged hole through the brain down, down into its core. The point had plunged to the midline immediately above the craniopharyngioma destroying vital structures all along its path but leaving the tumor completely unscathed in a perverse rendering of Murphy's Law. The first order of approach was to stop the bleeders; some of them were large and undoubtedly important arteries. They had to go. Garven electrocoagulated each of them in its turn, wincing a little every time. They debrided the destroyed edges of the artificially created tunnel until there was healthy brain everywhere.

Kent asked, "Want to close up, now, Chief?"

"No," Garven said, "might as well do what we came to do. If nothing else, you'll get the experience. Can't hurt, might help, and besides, you haven't done one."

Kent shrugged at the logic of the old surgical training dictum and set to work. He had calmed down and now worked as if the tragedy had not occurred. He carefully and completely removed the large craniopharyngioma with Garven's expert help, succeeding even in getting all of the capsule off, a very delicate operation. The two men waited anxiously in the PAR to see if they would get a miracle and the pastor would wake up. Garven idly examined the perforator from the craniotomy set. Kent had been right, it was dull and the cutting surfaces were nicked. That had been the cause of the plunge, at least partly. Murphy was right; Nothing is as easy as it looks, and Mother Nature always sides with the hidden flaw.

Pastor Powers never awakened. He could not have been expected to; Garven knew that. His midbrain and hypothalamus had been gouged to pulp. Forlornly, Garven made his way out to the waiting room.

A congregation arose from their seats in expectation and in respect as the eminent neurosurgeon entered the room. Garven had practiced keeping his face bland.

"Mrs. Powers," he asked, not seeing the pastor's wife at first.

"Here, Doctor," came her thin voice.

She had been sitting between two portly matrons, and their bulk had obscured her from view. Garven walked over to where the worried little woman sat. For some reason, she had chosen to wear plain black.

"How grimly appropriate," Garven thought to himself.

He said, "Mrs. Powers, the operation is done and the tumor is completely out..."

Before he could complete his thought, she exclaimed, "May the saints be praised. The Lord has worked through your hands, Dr. Wilsonhulme."

Her eyes looked skyward.

It flashed through that portion of Garven's mind that harbored protective irrationality to leave it at that and to let the bad news filter in gradually. He had a strong inclination to say nothing about the plunge of the perforator, to let her think that it had been in the nature of unexpected complications of surgery that he had failed to wake up despite an excellent operation—God's will.

But he knew better, and his rational mind gained supremacy. Nurses had been there, and there was no plausible way to deny what they had seen even if he and Kent stuck to a lie—a conspiracy of silence. Such conspiracies were more often attributed to doctors and nurses by disgruntled patients and self-interested lawyers than they occurred in fact. One of Garven's colleagues, bitter at the failure of his doctor friends to protect him when he was sued for malpractice, had had a pithy remark about instances of the vaunted closing of ranks for their own by physicians.

He said that it was one of those concepts "like hobby-horse turds; everyone's heard about them; but no one has ever actually seen one."

Garven launched directly and unreservedly into a description of the operation including the fatal operative accident. He mentioned briefly the condition of the perforator tip but made no real effort to shunt blame away from himself. He did not describe Kent Ashcroft's direct roll in the mishap but shouldered the entire responsibility himself. At the moment, Garven did not look on that omission as a lie, exactly. Rather, he was thinking of the 'captain of the ship' principle that left the blame squarely on himself. From his dim dark memory he dredged up Peter Wilsonhulme's rendition of Kipling's lines: "When the buckled girder lets down the grinding span, the blame for loss or murder lies upon the man. Not on the stuff, the man." And Garven had to regard himself as 'the man'.

At first there was a stunned, unbelieving silence, then a look from many of the people standing there that read: "This can't be real. We're talking about Pastor Powers. Tell us this is a joke."

When Garven's face conveyed as much as his words, Mrs. Powers began to sob. Dozens of excited people clamored for Garven's attention, everyone wanting a personal communication about the tragedy. Garven wanted to flee, but stayed and answered every question, some put to him half a dozen times—some by the same persons. It was as if they wanted to be sure that some sort of warp had not occurred in the ether of space that distorted the meaning of words. Finally, Garven led Mrs. Powers to her husband's bedside along with her three grown children. The four immediate family members wore expressions of benumbed shock.

Garven was sensitive to every nuance. He looked into the eyes of several of Dr. Power's pastoral colleagues. There he saw most unchristian glares. It seemed cold in the room.

Jack Clyde Powers died that night. Garven and the family were in attendance. *The Los Angeles Times* carried a front page article about the pastor and his untimely death. U.C. Osterlund Memorial Hospital and its 'neurosurgery staff' were not spared in the slightest, as if the reporters had smelled blood. The article speculated on the possibility of the "malpractice suit of the century."

CHAPTER
Twenty

Notification of the suit was four months in coming. Garven was having a mildly bad day that Friday. He had installed an intercom system from his office to the neurosurgery operating room without its presence being known to the residents. The system had only worked intermittently and had required a costly set of revisions. The money had had to come from the research funds, and Garven felt angry about that. He was angry about a lot of things since the Pastor Powers operation. For him, there was an air of tension and anxiety in all of life. He felt like he was waiting for the second shoe to drop.

He was listening to the intercom. Jim Bettman was helping Kent Ashcroft do a back. Jim made several disparaging remarks about the staff men, obviously intended in nonmalicious jest.

Of Garven, he joked that, "The chief went to the beach today. Thought it would be a nice day for a plunge."

"Oooh, bad," Kent's voice came over the intercom.

Garven could not resist revealing the secret of his new toy. The comment about the 'plunge' had stung, mainly because Garven was still smarting from the incident and from the unfavorable news stories about the accident. One of them had managed to dredge up his name.

He spoke into the microphone, "Bettman, if you could operate as well as you talk, you'd be a long ways ahead. I'd like to buy you for what you're worth and sell you for what you think you're worth."

He could hear titters of nurses' laughter in the background.

"Do better work, or I'll get you that job in the laundry room I keep promising."

He put down the mike. It was adolescent, he knew, but the rancor he felt had to come out somewhere.

Jim and Kent jumped when they heard their chief's voice coming out the tiles of the operating room wall. They grimaced at each other and decided that it would be unwise to make a comment. In a world where professors had all power, and never said a 'thanks' for hours and days and weeks of hard work, they considered their positions precarious enough to need to keep quiet, if not actually to grovel.

It was Garven's turn to jump almost as soon as he put down the microphone. His faithful secretary rushed in with a slit open envelope. She opened all of his mail, a fact that prompted Garven to instruct Jennifer Lakewood never to write anything to him in the course of their now torrid affair.

"You need to see this right away, Dr. Wilsonhulme."

She held the envelope so that he could see the return address of the law firm printed in bold letters in its upper left hand corner.

Garven glanced at the unfamiliar attorneys' names then quickly pulled out the heavy bond paper letter. The message was simple and to the point. He and the hospital were going to be sued by the wife and family of Jack Clyde Powers, and this was his ninety day notice.

Although he had been half expecting such a letter for the past four months, it still came as a rude shock. Suits were what happened to someone else, to lousy doctors, to doctors who made mistakes. He looked at his own name under the box marked "Defendant." Kent Ashcroft's name was immediately below his in that box. Now, he shifted his hurt and shock to the names of the plaintiffs' lawyers. Suits were caused by avaricious unprincipled lawyers. He felt victimized.

"Thank you Mrs. Danziger," he said to his secretary without looking up from the letter.

He was fixed to its terse message by a sort of morbid fascination.

He forced himself to say, "Get hold of the administration office, and let the malpractice insurance company know. It's Traveler's, I think."

He then sat quietly, musing.

"What are you going to do, Doctor?" Mrs. Danziger asked. "This is terrible, ridiculous. There ought to be some kind of a law. Los Angeles is going suit crazy. I wonder where it will all end if the most important professor of neurosurgery in the whole country can be sued by just anybody!"

"I am going home and slit my wrists. Tell the rest of the faculty that I won't be in tomorrow. Dr. Upshire can have my office and the booze in my fridge."

"Dr. Wilsonhulme! Don't joke about such things! I'll get right on this. I am sure there is some mistake!"

She was flustered and now absorbed her confusion and upset in a flurry of activity. In ten minutes Garven had a phone call from Anthony (Toby) Pingrath, the senior partner of Pingrath, Olsen, and Catterman, Traveler's Insurance company's favorite malpractice defense attorneys.

After the usual brief greetings, Pingrath got right to the heart of the matter.

"Don't talk to another soul about this, not your secretary, not the administrator, not the family, not your colleagues, all right?"

"I won't," Garven said.

He felt like a criminal.

"And whatever you do, keep your hands off the hospital chart. Don't you dare change that record in the slightest way, no matter how compelling you think it is or how easily you can get away with it. You may not have committed malpractice, but if the plaintiff can find any kind of record change, you will lose the case irrespective of its merits. Do you understand that, as well?"

Garven nodded at the phone.

Then, realizing that his gesture could not be heard over the telephone line, he said simply, "I won't make a move without you."

"Good. Then maybe you will turn out to be a decent client. I would like to see you this very afternoon to talk about how we defend this case. That convenient for you?"

"No, but I'll make it convenient," Garven responded.

He knew that this would be only one of many of his days that would be trashed before this sordid affair was over.

Toby Pingrath came at two. Garven cleared his schedule for the afternoon, a painful decision. He would be all that much further behind on the mountain of paper work in his in-box. Mr. Pingrath as a tall graying man in a perfectly fitting, very expensive dark blue suit. He wasted no time.

"Dr. Wilsonhulme, we are both very busy men, both experts. Let's get a couple of things straight from the first. You are an expert in neurosurgery, and I will rely on you for that expertise throughout. I am an expert on the law. Specifically, I am an expert on conducting the defense of physicians who have been sued for malpractice. I ask that you defer to me in that regard so that we do not waste unnecessary time and energy in arguments over how the case is to be handled. Are you with me so far, doctor?"

"I'm glad to have you on my side, Mr. Pingrath. I'll do my best to be a good client."

"Remember that promise, Dr. Wilsonhulme. Doctors are lousy clients generally. You know too much. You have egos that are too big and too fragile. I don't know if you think you are tough, but this is going to be your chance to prove it. I presume that you feel wounded and affronted by being sued; all doctors do. Remember this is not about your feelings, and it's not even about how you see the medical aspects of the case necessarily. It is about winning. I intend to win. I have a vested interest in this as well as you do. I have never lost a case, and I don't intend to start any kind of losing streak with you. This is a war. The plaintiff has attacked. Forget about any niceties like fairness or justice. We will work together to win. You let me handle the strategy, okay?"

"Okay. What are our chances?"

"Obviously, they're not perfect. But doctors almost always win, partly because juries don't like them to lose; they don't like to see doctors knocked off their pedestals. You can bet the farm that we'll win in the end. Not the house, just the farm."

"Thanks. I'm ready."

"Good, with that out of the way, we can get down to business. I have a photocopy of the hospital record, and I see that you have your office records. Tell me everything you know about the case, and especially about the operation."

Garven talked for over two hours. He was interrupted only occasionally by Toby Pingrath for clarification. Mr. Pingrath did not try to slant the facts or Garven's concept of them in any way but would not let Garven get away with any face saving reconstructions. When Garven indicated that he was finished, Pingrath thumbed through his notes and asked a question.

"Is Dr....let's see, Dr. Ashcroft, a licensed physician in the state of California?"

"Yes."

Pingrath opened the hospital chart and checked something.

"On the OR schedule sheet he is listed as the surgeon with you as the assistant. Is that accurate? Will the OR nurses testify that that was the case?"

"I presume so. But I don't see what that has to do with anything. I was the surgeon of record, the patient's doctor, and I was the captain of the ship in there," Garven said.

"This is one of those legal points, Dr. Wilsonhulme. You are making legal observations, not medical ones, although you commonly view your responsibility in those terms. The state may not necessarily take that view. Now, once again, was it Dr. Ashcroft who had the drill in his hand when it plunged into Pastor Power's brain.?"

"Yes, technically."

"Not 'technically'. He did it, or you did it. Which was it?"

"He did."

"You see, Dr. Wilsonhulme, you regard that young man as if he were a student, a trainee. I believe that a case can be made that he is a duly licensed physician in this state with all of the independent responsibilities that entails. You don't countersign his orders or notes or anything like that, do you?"

"No."

Garven was not sure that he liked the implications of Mr. Pingrath's line of reasoning.

"Would you know if he has malpractice insurance coverage through the hospital the same as you?"

"I believe there is some sort of blanket coverage that does not specify the individual intern or resident and has rather small limits. Usually it is the professor who bears the brunt of the attack, and the hospital covers him. I think the residents are either dropped early on so the plaintiff's attorney can efficiently go after the 'deep pockets' defendant, or are assessed only a small amount of damages when a judgment is rendered against them," Garven said, remembering his own misgivings as a resident.

"My investigations into this subject have indicated that you are partly right. Most charity hospitals and universities save money by accepting responsibility for the incident rather than trying to cover all of the individual trainees. Your Dr. Ashcroft, like most residents, could be dropped early on. But, I am afraid that he is not actually covered by the hospital's insurance," Pingrath said.

His face showed no doubt.

"Boy, that puts him between a rock and a hard place," said Garven.

"Indeed. Dr. Wilsonhulme, this is a big case; and our position on the merits appears bad, very bad indeed. I have to tell you that. At the beginning of our talk, I think you indicated that you wanted to win and were willing to trust to my judgment as to the winning strategy. I will be meeting with the hospital's and the plaintiff's attorneys in the next week. I believe I know how to get you out of this. But you will have to focus on winning, not one any kind of romantic notion of justice or of what you may think of as some sort of moral principle. Forget about both justice and morality; this is a lawsuit. I will be back in touch with you in a week or ten days. Don't talk to another person about this. Not even your wife. Certainly not Dr. Ashcroft. And remember, I am your lawyer, yours alone. I work for you. Only for you."

CHAPTER
Twenty-One

It was past nine when Garven returned home. The routine work of the day had been pushed back by the attorney's visit, but could not be ignored. He had cleared the last piece of paper out of his in-box, seen every patient of his own, talked with the resident on call, and smoothed the ruffled feelings of one of the neurologists who accused Jim Bettman of stealing another case from his ward. He was tired and felt weighed down. It was all well and good for the attorney to tell him not to worry and to let him handle the malpractice case; it was quite another to put it out of his mind. Garven seldom took his medical cases home with him however bad they may be going, but he could not shake himself free of this legal case.

"Hi, Daddy!" came the musical voice of his daughter, Susan.

She jumped into his arms for a hug and babbled on for five minutes about the harrowing events and great angsts of her young day.

That was enough, and off she went again.

"Dad?"

Garven turned to see Peter Arthur. How big the kid had grown. Garven had a flash of guilt that the boy always seemed to grow so much because it was so infrequent that the two of them had anything more to do with one another than to wave and say "hi" and "bye."

"Yeah, PA?" Garven responded.

"Wanna wrestle?"

Garven groaned inwardly. He hoped his weariness and desire to slump into his overstuffed chair did not show too plainly on his face.

Chapter Twenty-One

"Sure," he said.

Peter Arthur took his brief case and held his hands out to take Garven's suit coat.

He assumed the stance, flexing his muscles and glaring defiantly at Garven like a cartoon character or TV wrestler.

Garven laughed. His weariness was pushed back a little; and he, too, adopted a murderous stance. PT hurtled through the air and tackled Garven around his trousered legs. Garven had underestimated his son's increase in size and had to catch himself as he fell. They were near the entry hall mahogany occasional table. PA's leg neatly caught the Chinese vase (pronounced "vaz" as opposed to a "vace" which costs less than twenty dollars) and tipped off onto the floor. There was a resounding crash. Elizabeth rushed into the room and eyed the culprits lying on the floor, weak with laughter.

"Isht's not funny," she said angrily.

PA turned silent in an instant. Garven caught the hint of slurring in her voice. He wondered whether that was the cue to which his son reacted or if it was fear of a punishment more severe than Garven had ever known to be administered in his house.

"I know, I'm sorry, dear. We were just spending a little "quality time" as the liberals call it. I'll get a new one," said Garven apologetically.

He knew that Elizabeth truly cherished her things and this one probably had a history like the rest of the junk she collected, and he could not get interested in.

"Don' bother, Garman, it's irreplash, irreplaceable. I wish I could rely on you for reasonable care. I feel like I have three shildren."

Her face was flushed, all out of proportion to the situation and even to the degree of anger she was evincing. Garven kept hearing the little slurs in her voice. Someone who did not know her well would probably have missed them.

Susan started to cry, a soft disappointed cry rather than an upset or frightened sound. Garven got up and put his arms around her; and, to his surprise, she clung to him tightly, burying her face in his shirt front. Peter Arthur scurried to pick up the pieces of broken vase. He did not look at his mother as she towered over him menacingly. Garven became aware that something was amiss in his household that went well beyond the breaking of a vase, however valuable.

Elizabeth said nothing more. She turned and walked towards her bedroom. There was a slight sway to her gait. Garven dried Susan's tears and helped his son finish cleaning up.

"I like the table better bare; how about you?" he asked PA.

His son smiled at his dad, and he began to relax.

Garven herded the two children into the kitchen. It was neat, even sterile. There was not a thing out of place, no food on the counter tops, no old magazines or newspapers. There were fresh flowers in a crystal vase on the round kitchen table. The maid was fastidious. The children took seats at the table and sat with folded hands. It was unnatural. They did not talk or laugh or banter the way kids were supposed to do. They did not even touch the table, perhaps for fear that they might disturb something.

"C'mon and help me make some supper," Garven asked.

They were reluctant.

"We already ate, Dad," said PA.

He sat as if the seat of his pants had been glued to the chair.

"That's okay. I need the help. I'm tired, and I'm hungry. This place needs a mess. Come over here and help me dirty some dishes and get some crumbs on the floor. I don't think it's healthy to have a floor so clean that you could eat off it; how about you guys?"

Susan giggled. PA's face lightened up.

"We're not supposed to, Dad. It bothers Mom when she's sick."

"And is Mom sick pretty often?" Garven asked.

The two children looked at each other before PA answered.

"Pretty often," he said.

Garven got the kids up to help, and soon they were laughing and joking and making a royal mess.

"Mom will have a hyssy fit," PA said when he dropped a dollop of mayonnaise on the floor.

Susan dropped a piece of ham.

"Hey, look you guys, we might try and use the counter. We don't have to make the lunch on the floor," Garven said.

They looked at him to be sure that he was not angry then laughed uproariously.

Garven had his sandwich and milk supper and tucked the children in for the night. PA seemed a little embarrassed.

"I'm too old for that, Dad," he said when Garven leaned down to kiss him.

"No you're not. Nobody ever is, son. Don't you forget that."

He saw a small tear form in the corner of PA's eye. The boy threw his arms around Garven and squeezed him until Garven gasped for breath. The two of them laughed again.

"Good night, son."

"Good night, Dad."

Garven went to his room and changed into sweat pants, a tee shirt, and slippers. He padded over to the door to Elizabeth's room and knocked softly. There was no response; so, he knocked again more loudly.

"Go 'way," came Elizabeth's voice.

Garven opened the unlocked door. His wife was sitting up on her bed watching Johnny Carson. A tumbler sat on the bedside table a quarter full of an amber liquid and ice cubes.

"You feeling better now, Elizabeth? I put the kids to bed."

"Big deal," she said, "once every three or four months you come by and play big daddy."

"I didn't come in to have a fight, Elizabeth. I needed to talk to you," Garven said. "I have a problem, and I need you."

"The great professor of neurosurgery—the pope—needs little Elizabeth!" she snapped sarcastically. "I have a hard time believing that. Or is that just an excuse to get into my bed?"

Elizabeth had an expression of theatrical lust, a very unattractive expression to Garven.

"Do I need an excuse?" Garven asked, aware that he had been sidetracked.

She turned her face back to Johnny Carson. They had been through the "you aren't interested anymore" conversation too many times. She did not feel like getting into it again. They always ended up trading complaints about each other's failings, and frequently the conversation deteriorated into insults. She took another sip of her drink.

"Look, Elizabeth. I guess we can let my problem go. But I am concerned, I mean, really concerned about your drinking," Garven said, knowing that it was a touchy subject, especially when she was under the influence even as they talked.

"You should talk. You're the one who had the problem," she snapped.

She immediately returned to her television program.

"Elizabeth, you need help. I am worried about the children. You can ignore me, I suppose; but if you don't get some professional help, I am going to take steps to protect Susan and Peter Arthur."

"I'm going to take steps to protect precious Sushan and Peper Arthur," she slurred in a slightly failed attempt at mockery.

Garven sadly turned and left the room. That night he talked with Jenny Lakewood by phone until one in the morning.

News of the malpractice suit buzzed around the surgery suites, but there was confusion as to exactly what was involved. Garven told questioners that he could not answer any questions—lawyer's orders. When he went to the surgeons' lounge, or when he operated, or even when he ran into a friend or colleague in the hall, the topic of conversation always drifted to his suit. When he failed to be forthcoming, his well wishers fell back on the recourse to share the latest lawyer joke.

An OB man said, "Garven, I heard about your suit. You know I lost one last year. Preposterous thing—some baby was born with cerebral palsy. They said it was my fault. I have to pay for the kid's needs for the rest of his life. I don't care what my son wants to do, except if he even thinks about going into the law, I'll disinherit him so fast, he won't know what happened to him!"

"I know how you feel, Chet," Garven had agreed.

"Say, are you being sued by the same bunch of reptiles that had my case— you know, Dewey, Cheatem, and Howe?"

Both men shared a laugh.

In the surgeon's lounge, Peter Lyons stopped his conversation with one of the ENTers when Garven walked in to change.

The chief of surgery said, "I hear you're being sued by Dwight Lethbridge. Is that right, Garven?"

"That's right, Dr. Lyons," he said. "I hear I am in good company with that distinction."

"So I hear, " said Lyons. "I heard a funny thing about his kid the other day." He smiled at his dressing room audience. "Seems the kid's teacher asked them what their dads did for a living. One kid said his dad was a banker, another, a farmer, and Lethbridge's little boy piped up and said,

"'My dad plays the piano in a whorehouse.'

"The teacher looked a little shocked but didn't want to say anything to the little Lethbridge boy. Instead, she waited until parent-teacher day to talk to Dwight.

"She said, 'I don't want to upset you, but your son, Tom, told the class that you played the piano in a whorehouse for a living.'

"'Oh,' says Lethbridge, 'I did tell him that. I'm actually a lawyer, but you can't go around telling a seven year old a thing like that.'"

The men in the lounge laughed and started another round of jokes about lawyers and other reptiles, as Peter Lyons put it.

In the OR the circulating nurse asked Garven if he knew how to tell the difference between a dead snake lying in the middle of the road and a dead lawyer. Garven smiled and shrugged as she put on his gown and gloves.

"There are skid marks in front of the snake," she said and like everyone else that day, laughed joyfully at her own joke.

Not to be outdone, the scrub nurse asked, "What do you need when you have a couple of lawyers up to their necks in cement?"

"I give up," said the circulator.

"More cement," said Garven with a mean smile.

"Killjoy," said the scrub nurse.

Beneath the camaraderie and the jokes, there was an uneasiness about the lawsuit throughout the hospital. Garven ordinarily liked anti-attorney jokes and the shared antipathy towards lawyers, but the emphasis on that kind of joke and comment whenever he came around began to wear thin on his nerves. He noticed that a percent of the consults shifted to his fellow faculty members.

The OR nurses pointedly checked instruments and made little disclaimer remarks, like, "I don't know who's responsible for the sharpening around here, but if it were me, I'd take every one of these drills back."

The unnaturalness of it got on Garven's nerves.

It was a month before his lawyer, Toby Pingrath got back to him.

He called Garven and said, "Why don't you come by my office tomorrow? We need to have a conference, and I need to have a couple of my people come in with us then."

"I can get there around noon."

"It would better at one for me," said Pingrath.

"I'll be there," Garven said.

He frowned because the later time meant that he would have to cancel his little midday tryst with Jenny. He found himself looking forward to the time he spent with her more than he liked to admit. She gave him the solace that Elizabeth did not.

Pingrath's office was large and opulent, full of deep rugs and heavy chairs. The lawyer was punctual to the minute.

"I'm glad you could make it, Dr. Wilsonhulme," he said.

Garven was seated in the large conference room in an armchair pulled up to the gleaming cherrywood table.

"This is my paralegal, Mindy Scofield, and one of my associates, Jeffery Webster."

Garven acknowledged the introductions.

"We have been busy gathering information, Dr. Wilsonhulme. Briefly, we have learned that the surgeon responsible for the operation, that is, the surgeon who actually wields the knife and gives the directions can be considered the one with the major responsibility, and perhaps all of it. At least, it is an argument that we can use in your behalf. I have done just that in the meeting with the plaintiff's attorneys and the lawyers for the hospital.

"We have come to a sort of agreement. If you concur, then we can have an actual settlement with very little fuss and no publicity. I take it that you would like that sort of turn of events?"

"Probably. I would like to hear more about that 'settlement' you are talking about before I get too excited. I had hoped to fight this thing all the way, and maybe get acquitted altogether. 'Settlement' sounds like I admit guilt and pay a fine," Garven said.

"Take it easy, a minute, Dr. Wilsonhulme. Hear us out. First off all, this is a civil case. It's not about 'guilt'; its about win and lose. You don't get acquitted; you win. That's what we have for you, a way to win."

"I jumped the gun," Garven said. "Go ahead and finish."

"Yes. Now let's see...We put it to the plaintiff's attorney, Mr. Lethbridge, that it would be tough; and we would fight like wildcats to prevent him from making you the goat in this case. On the other hand, we told him we might concede that the Reverend Dr. Powers, the deceased, had suffered at the hands of a surgeon. If he could see his way clear to drop you, you might consider giving testimony against Dr. Ashcroft."

Garven gave a little gasp and started to protest.

"Hear me out all the way. Remember, this is lawyer stuff. Everything is not always what it seems to be. There's a lot of smoke and mirrors."

Garven nodded and made a sewing motion along his lips.

"The hospital and the university have the same insurance company as you, and agreed that they had nothing to gain by your involvement as long as Dr. Ashcroft remains in the picture. Their main concern was that the hospital not be seen to bear the full blame. They would accept that the drill tip was dull. They would also be willing to give testimony against the local company that does their sharpening and against the company that made the perforator drill—V. Mueller, I think it is.

"To tell you the truth, with you out of the picture and willing to give the necessary evidence if required, the plaintiffs benefit by a speedy solution and payment. Now, what they don't know, is that Ashcroft is not covered directly by the insurance company, and the hospital can wiggle out of this one day down the line since he is considerably more to blame than they are, dull perforator notwithstanding. We can drag it out for so long that only Ashcroft will be left. A couple of years from now, he can be told to get another lawyer because of our representation of you and because of our dealings with the hospital, there is a conflict of interest. As I see it, Ashcroft is a poor resident and will be totally unable to meet the financial obligations of any judgment that is gained against him. He will have a quickie California bankruptcy and won't be out more than a few thousand dollars in lawyer fees and minor court costs. It's the best deal we could broker, and Lethbridge went for it. Of course, he thinks he's going to get his from the hospital and V. Mueller. He may have a nasty little surprise."

"And all you have to do is to sign a waiver promising not to sue Lethbridge or the Powers for filing of a malicious suit."

"And screw Dr. Ashcroft," Garven said with bitterness.

"I wouldn't put it quite that way, Dr. Wilsonhulme; but however you look at it, you know that someone has to go down. It is all but a *res ipsa loquitar* case. This is a real world situation. Frankly put, Doctor, are you willing to flush your career for some noncontractual verbal agreement with Ashcroft?"

Garven felt morose. He hated the idea of watching one of his residents get hurt, especially so early in his career. He rationalized that Kent would be able to go somewhere and set up practice where no one would have ever heard of this case. He would not really lose much in the way of money. It would be far worse for Garven than for Kent, Garven reasoned.

"I will agree. I don't see any other way. Let's keep this thing quiet, all right. We all need to get on with our business, and this does no one any good," Garven said to Toby.

Garven was quietly dropped from the case after giving his deposition and laying the blame squarely on Kent Ashcroft. He prayed that Kent would never see that deposition; but, as he had said in the meeting with Toby, there was really no other choice. There was nothing to be gained by both of them going under in this mess.

CHAPTER
Twenty-Two

I nterest in the malpractice suit diminished in inverse proportion to the amount of news let out to fuel the excitement. People forgot about Garven, the defendant, and once again looked on him as the peerless researcher, professor, and clinician. At the end of academic year 1971, Kent Ashcroft, now a second year resident, came to see Garven in his office.

"Dr. Wilsonhulme, I just learned that the hospital can't defend me. They say there's a conflict of interest or something. Anyway I have to get a new lawyer. It looks to me like they are going to get the OR nurses to testify against me. I wish I could have gotten out of it like you did, but I guess they look at me as the surgeon responsible. They say we're going to trial in three or four months if we don't settle. What do you think I ought to do?"

Garven took a sober interest.

"Kent, I think you're caught between a rock and a hard place. Candidly, I doubt if you can win this case; and you will spend a fortune defending yourself. I have given this thing a lot of thought. Here's what I would do. I would settle now before you incur any more costs. It doesn't really matter what the amount of the settlement is, you don't have that kind of money. I know this is tough to swallow, but I would simply file for bankruptcy once the settlement is reached. You don't make anything as a resident, and you have three more years to go. You might even add a sabbatical. I can arrange that, and that will add another year."

Kent sighed.

"Just what I wanted to hear, another year of beating my brains out, and be completely broke to boot."

"It's crappy, but it's not forever. You get to keep your means of transportation, your residence, and one gun under California's Homestead provisions. That's something. I have another suggestion in addition to the idea of the sabbatical. You would probably be better off to finish your residency outside California. That would put you more out of sight and out of mind."

Kent hung his head. He knew he had to capitulate.

"Anywhere in mind for the sabbatical and for the change of residencies?" he asked, and Garven knew, with that question, that his own problems with the Powers malpractice suit would vanish.

He had a small pang of guilt about it, but he did not let it get in the way of what he had to do.

"I think you could profitably spend the year in France with Professor Guiot. If you want, I will contact him. The University of Miami program is getting underway. I can get you in there as a third year when you get back from France. What do you think of that?"

"Better than a poke in the eye with a sharp stick, I suppose," said Kent.

With the options open to him, he could see no better possibility. At least he would be able to finish his residency and get into practice. He really appreciated Dr. Wilsonhulme for sticking by him. A lot of profs would simply have thrown him to the wolves. And Dr. Wilsonhulme quietly provided the funds; so, he could live for the next year through a secret account.

Garven knew he had dodged a career bullet or had been granted a miracle. He had a momentary thought about taking up religion. This fleeting aberration was partly in response to an item he saw on the back pages of the *Times* in the church section. The ad was for "The Church of Monday-Night Football", a California chartered institution (only in California, of course). Maybe that was where he should join up.

Kent Ashcroft went to Paris in July. He was promised the position in Miami; but, a year later, when it was time to go there, the Miami chief was sorry to tell him that the position had been filled. They had had to place a black man in the position because of a new government program called 'affirmative action'. He regretted the inconvenience, and wished Kent well. The judgment in the Power's case was for two million dollars with V. Mueller being assessed ten thousand, the hospital fifty thousand, and Kent the rest. The terms of the bankruptcy proceedings required Kent to pay anything he made over three thousand a month to the settlement fund. He finally decided that it was not worth it to go through the rest of a neurosurgery residency and then to be in hock for the rest of his life, working in semi-servitude. He joined a general practitioner Greenville, Mississippi and never worked a dollar harder than $3000 a month.

The children told Garven that their mother was sick most of the time now. He hired a live-in nanny, and she reported abusive behavior by Mrs. Wilsonhulme and quit. Garven gave her a generous severance in return for a signed affidavit regarding Elizabeth's behavior and drinking. The nanny threw in a paragraph about Elizabeth's having slapped Peter Arthur. Relations between Garven and Elizabeth deteriorated to the point that the only time they spoke was to conduct a little essential family business.

When she went to see her internist, Garven followed up and told her doctor about Elizabeth and her drinking. The doctor tried everything she could to get Elizabeth into treatment, into AA, anything. Elizabeth began to lose weight, and was finally forced into UCOMH by the development of jaundice. She had early alcoholic cirrhosis, and was warned that she would kill herself in two years if she did not stop drinking.

At Garven's strong request, she was seen by one of the psychiatrists in the university, a man who was in Garven's hunting club. Garven had introduced him to Grantland Kurze in Texas, and the psychiatrist friend had nothing but good to say about Grantland and about Garven ever afterwards. Kendall Draper, the psychiatrist, offered the opinion that Elizabeth was out of control and would require in-patient psychiatric therapy to get over her problem with alcohol. Elizabeth would have none of it, and Dr. Draper stopped short of declaring her suicidal or incompetent as Garven wanted.

The arrangement at home in Beverly Hills became so intolerable that in December, 1971, Garven finally moved out and got a condominium of his own. His lawyer told him to make sure that Jenny Lakewood never came there since that would give Elizabeth a lever against him in the inevitable divorce action that was looming. When Garven protested that Jenny was the only thing that made his life bearable, his attorney had chastened him with the threat of never getting out of his marriage and never getting what he wanted out of the marriage.

"Don't let the little head do the thinking for the big head," his attorney had warned.

It seemed to Garven that he had heard that someplace before.

The news of his marital difficulties moved sluggishly through the hospital. Garven never talked about it, and since there was nothing official, no one pressed the issue. Divorce was very poorly thought of in the ultra-conservative U.C. system, and Garven wanted to keep his private affairs as private as possible for as long as possible. He confided in Devon and Elijah David, the two men he esteemed as his only real friends—his "Men of Trust."

When Garven moved to the condominium, Devon sent him a card that read: "Do you know which word doesn't fit in this grouping? AIDs, Herpes, Gonorrhea, and condominium?"

On the flip side of the card was found: "Gonorrhea. You can get rid of it."

CHAPTER
Twenty-Three

Devon and E.D. threw a bachelor party for him that cheered Garven up. He missed Jenny terribly and called her every day. After a month, she began to hint that she could not wait forever. He agitated over that threat until he left the protective confines of his condo and took her out to the premier of a movie and to several parties in Orange County that were filled with fun-loving glitterati. That eased the tensions between them by satisfying some of Jenny's feeling of being neglected.

Another result of the exposure of the loving couple to the outside world was that some one who knew Elizabeth and apparently disliked Garven gave Elizabeth a call. When Garven came to the house to pick up the children to spend the weekend with him, he met a very sober and furious Elizabeth.

"Are you going to subject my two children to your chippie?" she carped.

No "hello", or "how are you?", and not "here's the to-do list for the kids."

Garven was shocked, taken aback. It was as if he had suddenly discovered that he was not invisible; or like the emperor, he was discovered in his nakedness, deluding himself that his expensive new clothes were real. He had presumed that he had covered his tracks and had hidden his activities so well that no one but he and Jenny were aware of his affair. He blushed. It was not from guilt, but from embarrassment that he had been so naive and careless, a practical sort of abashment related to a negative reflection on his social skills.

"It seems that we need to talk," was the best he could muster.

At least, he had had the presence of mind not to blurt out a confession.

"I think we do, Garven," said Elizabeth.

Her voice was hard and brittle, but free of passion or over recrimination. She might as have been announcing the closure of a house sale to a real estate colleague.

"Come in, please."

Very polite. Correct.

It seemed quite odd to Garven to be admitted into his own house as if he were a guest, or worse, a stranger. He resented it. He followed her into her personal business office. There was to be nothing of nostalgia or home in this place or at this meeting.

"Won't you take a seat," she offered.

He wanted to shout at her, "Do you even know who you're talking to?! Do you have any idea why I strayed?!" to break the stranger to stranger quality of the confrontation, but he simply and quietly took the seat offered him.

"Are you going to try and deny it?" she demanded.

There was a little more emphasis, a little less indifference. Her cheeks colored; maybe that was a good sign.

"I don't suppose it would do much good. You have your mind made up and wouldn't be interested in anything to the contrary of your mind set," Garven said.

He had worked out an elaborate and to him, plausible, denial as they had walked down the bare wood hallway to the office; but he thought to himself, "What's the use?"

"That's one thing you've gotten right. It is probably beside the point, anyway. We do not have a marriage. We have a financial and social arrangement that is sterile and unrewarding for me and has been from the beginning, I am sad to say. The worst thing about it is that I have to admit that my father was right. He did know better, I guess."

She was more sad than angry.

"Maybe it has been for you as well, I don't know."

Now she was more pensive than sad.

"Things have been a lot less than ideal for some time, I'll agree to that much without argument," Garven said.

He looked at her for a minute or two as if searching for a reason to argue against the inevitable that he could see and hear.

"What do you have in mind?" he asked, finally.

"The obvious...A divorce..."

There was only a trace of hesitation in her delivery of the answer.

As he had done, she looked at his face for a reaction; and, finding none, made a nervous dry cough and went on, "I propose that we make it simple, both go our own separate ways. You go to your movie starlet, whatever her name is, and the children and I go on with our lives without you. That wouldn't change the status quo by a great deal."

He could tell that she was fighting back tears and stubbornly refusing to let him see her emotion or faltering control. Now that the gloves were off; and it was going to be an openly declared fight; he took pleasure in her discomfiture.

"You don't really expect me to agree, do you? I don't want a divorce. In fact, a divorce will do me untold professional damage; but, of course, you already know that. You think you have a trump card to use against me. This is no game for me, Elizabeth. I do want the kids; and then, there is always the subject of our assets."

He had regained his composure entirely. This was a cold Duel—a knife fight—and he had no intention of letting his emotions interfere. He was now the ice-blooded neurosurgeon, calmly working to contain a growing disaster.

"Since when have you ever cared a whit for Petey and Susan?" she snorted. "And you have the assets of your practice; what else could there be to discuss about finances. I paid for the house, the cars, the furnishings, the clothes—everything. They are mine, pure and simple, just like the trust from my grandpa. You can make it uncomplicated and quick by remembering that fact of life."

"I see your logic, Elizabeth. 'Simple', 'quick', and totally one-sided and self-serving. Was that little speech prepared by the family attorney?" he demanded with a cold sneer.

He was fighting angry now, but he worked to keep his voice in check. He knew that his ire was showing in his naturally expressive face. He regretted that he was constitutionally unable to be inscrutable.

"You haven't got a leg to stand on, mister."

She knew that he hated to be called 'mister' now that he was a doctor as much as he had hated being referred to as a 'boy' when he became a man.

"You are the family deserter, the adulterer. I am the one with the money. No judge in the state would grant custody of the children to you and a whore. And you have a bat in your belfry if you think you are going to lay your greedy little hands on even a penny of my money."

She was floridly angry now. Her face revealed every opprobrious feeling she had about him.

Garven infuriated her with one of his long, thoughtful silences. He looked at her eyes all the while she was speaking as if to goad her. He silently dared her to interrupt his unresponsiveness. She had an obloquy in mind, but it would keep until he had made his next unacceptable speech, his counter-offer. She knew it would be unacceptable before he even said it.

"Elizabeth, you want this divorce, and I don't. That gives me the upper hand. I might accommodate you on a couple of conditions."

She looked at him ruefully.

He went on, "you take my conditions back to your attorney and consider them very carefully before you think to turn them down. I will only make the offer once. The first condition is that we have joint custody of the two kids. I get to see them without difficulty on my part on a regular and frequent basis."

She wrinkled her brow as if to interrupt, but he put up his hand to stop her; so, he could finish.

"Next, we divide up all of the assets of this marriage and each take a full fair half. I will not, under any circumstances, discuss any difference between your inheritance and the proceeds of my work. Better get that straight at the outset. You will recall that we did not sign any kind of a prenuptial agreement. This is California, and California is a community property state. We have had a long term marriage under the definition of the law which requires an equitable split. You are stuck with that fact."

She flashed him a heated look.

"In fact, to protect my interests, I am moving back into our house."

He emphasized 'our'.

"Garven!" she interjected.

"I haven't quite finished—one more sentence," he overruled her. "We can work this out like ladies and gentlemen; or we can fight it out fang and claw, your choice. Don't forget my abilities in a brawl."

His face was implacable; his eyes shone with the cold hard glint that she hated and feared.

"Never!" she raged.

She was angry with herself for losing her control. She needed a drink. She wanted him to go; so, she could pour herself a stiff one.

"You won't get a penny of my money! Shame on you. It's unmanly!... un-American!"

Now she wished that she had accepted her attorney's offer to be there with her. She had insisted that she could handle the impending confrontation with her estranged husband perfectly well alone. Now, she knew she was making a mess of it.

"We'll fight it out, then," Garven said with provocative evenness.

"Get out!" she hissed. "Get your loathsome, adulterous…man's body out of my house!" she yelled.

He did not make a move and did not seem upset.

"Now!" she screamed, her face turning something near the color of an egg plant. She really needed a drink.

Garven knew there was no use talking. She had thrown down the gauntlet; and he could not fail to take it up, or he would lose everything. He was about to tell her to calm down and to discuss this situation rationally; he had a counter plan that he had worked out weeks before in anticipation of this very confrontation. Now he thought better of saying anything. He might as well speak Kurdish to the family dog. He got up and inclined his head in her direction in polite excuse. She thought he had capitulated.

He walked to his car, and she was glad to be quit of him for at least another day. As she saw him walk out of her life, she was surprised at her own reaction; she had imagined that such a parting would be very difficult after all of the years of marriage. But, it was easy for her, a relief.

To her utter dismay, he opened his car door, picked up a small suitcase and turned back toward the house. She flew down the front stairs and clicked the lock on the front door. Garven did not even head for the main door. He went down the sandstone pathway beside the house in the direction of the rear entry. She raced to beat him and locked that door as well. He hardly paused. He used his key and opened the door as naturally as if nothing had ever changed. Elizabeth kicked herself for having forgotten to change the locks.

Before she could get her wits together, he was already in the house. He was in her kitchen.

"No-o-oo! she shrieked.

She had lost any semblance of her former hauteur or control. She rushed at him with her bright red painted nails flared like talons. She swept up a butcher knife from the cabinet top as she went; her vision was a red blur of rage; and she had no rational plan, just animal rage.

Garven kept his eyes focused on the erratically swishing blade. It swept disconcertingly close to his face as he backed away. It was Wednesday night and the Mexican maid, Maria-Theresa, was in her room watching *Room 222* and *The Smothers Brothers*. When she heard the commotion, she rushed into the kitchen to see her mistress make three or four ardent slashes at the man of the house who was bobbing and weaving and ducking to keep out of harm's way. Elizabeth was distracted for a moment by the maid's entrance, and she looked over at the tiny Mexican-American woman long enough for Garven to catch her wrist in his strong left hand. He gave the wrist a brutal twist and would have broken her arm had Elizabeth not fallen to the floor. The knife clattered harmlessly across the limestone tiles towards the maid.

Maria-Theresa picked up the knife and put it will out of the way of both Wilsonhulmes. Elizabeth sat in a fetal heap on the beige tile floor and sobbed convulsively. The maid was an illegal alien like the maids in virtually every other house in their posh Beverly Hills neighborhood, and her English was halting. But she was able to get Elizabeth to stand up and to go to her room.

"Chall I call *La Polizia*?" she asked Garven when Elizabeth had been put to bed.

"No, Maria-Theresa," we don't want anything said about this to outsiders. This is family, you *comprende*?"

"*Si, señor Doctor*," she said.

She stood in the center of the kitchen, docilely awaiting instructions.

"Maria-Theresa, I want you to give the lady a couple of pills," her face was quizzical; he was going to rapidly for her. "*Aspirinas*," he said; and she understood.

Garven found two blue Valiums from her cache in the bathroom. Maria-Theresa drew a glass of water.

"Take the day off, and don't worry. No *preocupe sobré esta problema*, okay? Here's a little bonus; so, you can have a good time."

He handed her a crumpled hundred dollar bill. She looked at him with pleased astonishment.

"And, Maria Theresa,"

"Jess, *señor*?"

"I want you should remember what happened here today, *entiendes*?"

"Oh, si *señor*!" she answered enthusiastically.

She understood full well. She liked the *professor-medico*. He was great man and so nice She knew what everyone meant when they said that the lady was 'sick'. She would have no trouble remembering how the lady had gone crazy and had tried to cut the *caballero*.

While Elizabeth reposed in her deep twenty milligram Valium sleep, Garven made a concise, fact-filled note in his omnipresent self-protective note book. Then he made a quick trip to his bachelor apartment and picked up a large bagful of his belongings and brought them back to the Beverly Hills house. He took them to his room and dumped them on the bed. Then, he remembered about the two children. He went to Susan's room. Their little TV set was playing *The Courtship of Eddie's Father*, one of the childrens' favorites, but they were unaware that the set was even on. The two of them were there huddled on her bed. Susan had been crying. PA was white faced. Both children appeared confused and frightened, like war waifs. Garven guessed that that was what they were, in a way. He sat on the bed with one of them under each arm and consoled them.

"Is Mommy sick again?" asked Peter Arthur.

"I'm afraid so," Garven said.

"Are you coming back to our house, Daddy," asked Susan.

"Yes. I am going to take care of you. Everything's okay."

"Sometimes Mommy is mean when she gets sick," PA said with an angry and determined look. "I don't want to be with her."

There was no going to the beach as planned. Garven called Jenny, and she was miffed. It seemed like every time she planned anything nice for the two of them, he had to go to the hospital. Now it was his kids. She looked at the attractive picnic lunch she had taken such pains to make and angrily dumped the entire basket in the trash.

The children took naps. Elizabeth had drained a tumbler full of straight whiskey the size of a mixing bowl on top of the Valium that Maria-Theresa had given her. She would be out for the rest of the day. Garven had time to think. Her drinking problem was out of all control. She was acting like a twelfth century fishwife over his affair instead of a 1970's California woman. She had not given the slightest consideration about how he felt or of what had provoked him to stray. He concluded that she never would. She had announced herself to be his avowed enemy and had essentially declared war on him. He figured that her lawyer would egg her on to a prolonged battle that would make the lawyer a rich man, and make Garven into a wreck and a laughing-stock among his colleagues. He had to do something to protect himself.

He picked up the telephone and dialed.

"Hello, Travis? This is Garven. I know it's Saturday, and I wouldn't bother you if it were not important. I have a problem with my wife, and I need your help."

Travis Longman was a newly created associate professor on the psychiatry service. Garven had helped to grease the skids to get the young psychiatrist the coveted position of tenure over another, more politically savvy, competitor. That other applicant had made the mistake of trying to bar Garven from going onto the psych back wards and finding the patients with meningiomas, which caused what looked like an irreversible psychosis, and had been missed by the psychiatrists. Travis had been considered to be too young, but Garven had championed his cause and had won the young man's undying gratitude.

"I'm only too willing to help," Dr. Longman said.

He asked very few questions as Garven poured out the sordid details of Elizabeth's drinking, her erratic behavior, her neglect of herself and of her family, and finally, of the precipitous knife attack witnessed by the family maid that very day. When the two men were done with their telephone conversation, it was determined that Elizabeth was a threat to herself and to others and that she would have to be admitted, against her will, if necessary, to the psychiatry service's locked ward and heavily tranquilized. The psychiatric hold could be for two weeks without court action, and Travis Longman hoped that he would be able to persuade Elizabeth to stay on for another six weeks of detox and alcoholic rehabilitation.

The ambulance arrived thirty minutes later.

"Boy, she's blotto, doc. I'm sorry to have to ask this, but what did she take? Is this all booze or did she OD?" asked the lead EMT.

He knew Garven from his time in the Pit.

"I don't know," said Garven, appearing distraught. "She is a very heavy drinker, but sometimes she takes sedatives, usually Valium, as well, even forgets that she takes them. I try to keep them away for her, but you know how it is."

The EMT indeed knew. He felt sorry for Dr. Wilsonhulme. The guy was a big shot at UCOMH and had to be saddled with this kind of a wife. He thought Dr. Wilsonhulme qualified for a minor sainthood for staying with the wretched woman.

"Yeah, doc, we understand," he said sympathetically. "You can't watch them all the time. We'll take good care of her. Now, don't you worry none. She'll be good as new after the shrin... I mean, the people at the hospital work with her. Thanks for writing out all of her information; that'll save all of us time and aggravation when she's admitted. Get some rest yourself, Sir. You look beat, if you don't mind me saying so."

Garven did not mind. He nodded his gratitude for the EMT's solicitude toward him.

"Mind taking a couple of Polaroids of her...condition? Might help in her treatment," Garven asked.

"No problem. The instant photographs revealed a comatose, completely disheveled woman obviously heedless of her appearance on a long term basis.

The ambulance pulled away. The EMT recorded his impression: "Acute and chronic alcohol abuse, probable superimposed drug overdose, and possible psychosis. Violent and a danger to her husband and children."

CHAPTER
Twenty-Four

Elizabeth awakened nineteen hours later, dazed and confused. The surroundings were unfamiliar and frightening as she fought to become alert. When she finally realized where she was, Elizabeth became hysterical, cursing Garven roundly and swearing at the nurses. They tried to calm her, and she reward their efforts by clawing and scratching at them. The nurses called in the burly psych orderlies and the group of attendants wrestled Elizabeth into a strait jacket and gave her a hefty dose of Thorazine in her buttock. As required by hospital regulations, they duly recorded every action of Elizabeth's including a video of her violent behavior.

She was trussed up securely and stuporous when Garven came in to see her. He requested that she have no other visitors. Aside, he asked Dr. Longman to be sure that her lawyer did not sneak past the buffering nurses. He was likely to upset her. Dr. Longman understood and agreed.

Several days later, the young psychiatrist conveyed to Garven the baleful news that Elizabeth refused to have Garven visit her in the hospital. Dr. Longman explained that it was just one more symptom of her psychosis, and that he should not take it personally. Mental illness was like any other illness with characteristic symptoms and signs.

Garven shook his head sadly, "You know what's best, Trav. Keep me informed."

"There is something of a problem, Garven. You know how people love to talk. You're something of a celebrity, and this is likely to get out eventually despite everything we try to do to preserve privacy and anonymity. I put her in under an assumed name, but somehow it'll get out. Brace yourself."

Chapter Twenty-Four

Garven shrugged and wrinkled one corner of his mouth.

"Thanks, Trav. Not to change the subject, but what's your working diagnosis?"

"No question about it by the staff. She's officially listed as acute and chronic alcoholism, Valium overdose, and acute paranoid schizophrenia. I can seal the records and can probably soft pedal the 'psychosis' part, if it'll help," Travis offered.

"Not necessary," said Garven. "I certainly wouldn't want to alter her records in anyway. Just do your objective best. That's all anyone can ask. We'll have to stand up to the facts as painful as they are. The records may become important in a variety of legal proceedings down the line. Let's don't make that too difficult."

His face was pained.

Travis Longman gave Garven's shoulder a brotherly pat and shook his head. It was tough. Everyone in the place felt for him. Garven signed the commitment papers and took his leave.

"Thanks, again, Trav," he said in parting.

Garven did not look all that pained as he left the hospital that evening and headed up Sunset to Jenny Lakewood's apartment before going home to see his children. She was an invaluable source of solace.

Elizabeth was released from the hospital with arrangements for outpatient follow-up and group therapy three months later without having spoken to Garven or to her children during the entire hospitalization. She was dried out, ten pounds heavier, and had a light tan and even some evidence of muscle definition from the PT she had thrown herself into during her stay. She was an official enrollee in Alcoholics Anonymous and had just completed her fifth step—the painful complete confession to another (not Garven).

She entered the house and acted as if Garven were not there. She created an invisible and impermeable barrier between her quarters and his portion of the large Tudor house. On her first day home, she called the two children and Maria-Theresa together in her drawing room and gave them an elaborate apology for her past behavior. Garven listened from the hallway and presumed that Elizabeth must be going through one of the twelve AA steps. Evidently, it did not include him. As he did in his professional relationships, Garven recorded the entire detailed and incriminating confession.

The first time the Wilsonhulmes spoke to each other was three weeks later at her lawyer's office on Wilshire. Garven chose to attend the meeting without representation of his own despite the very strong advice of Elizabeth's attorney that he bring counsel with him.

Elizabeth was composed and appeared to be fully self-assured and comfortable on her side of the table flanked by her three attorneys. They were large men and conveyed the impression that they were giving her needed physical protection as well as legal representation. Garven sat across from one of the larger attorneys, a man who sat and stood a full foot taller than the short neurosurgeon. It was not lost on Garven that he had been given a large uncomfortable straight backed hardwood chair that accentuated his smallness. He resented the effect, and it furthered the fighting mood he had had when he walked into the tasteless art deco room.

"Good afternoon, Doctor," said the lead attorney.

He had long hair from the right side of his head combed across the bald pate of the middle of his head. The hair had been greased down. Garven thought it gave him a comical look. He held on to that thought as the man spoke.

"I trust that you are well."

He sounded syrupy and silvery.

"I'm fine, thank you," Garven said frostily.

He had avoided shaking hands with any of the attorneys at the outset, a fact that was not lost on them. It set the tenor of the meeting.

"I'm sure you're busy. Let's get on with it."

"I agree. There's no reason to prolong things. We have a divorce settlement proposal for you—a simple document that will allow a rapid solution to the problem, we believe," the lawyer continued and smiled his cloyingly sweet smile.

He handed the document to Garven.

Garven scanned it rapidly and set it down with a look of mild disdain. It was obvious that he could not have digested the contents in any degree of thoroughness during the brief time he had looked at it.

"No," he said.

"No?" said Elizabeth's lawyer, a little less syrupy now.

He was professional enough to keep the smile, however, the smile that seemed painted on his mouth and did not include his eyes.

"Just like that? Being stubborn will only make things worse, Doctor, more prolonged and painful. We're only asking you to be reasonable. Mrs. Wilsonhulme has gone the extra mile and has graciously granted you visitation rights with the children that are more generous than the usual arrangement when she might well have been quite severe about it."

His smile was more pinched now. He looked at Garven for a cue and, finding none, went on.

"For that matter, the rest of the items of the agreement are pretty standard, as well. There is a small alimony, almost negligible, really, small child care provision commensurate with the rights of visitation; and she gets the house as is the general rule."

The last half of his sentence was so decrescendo that Garven found himself leaning forward to be able to hear.

"I'd say you are getting off easy because she wants to get this over and done with in the least amount of time and with the least degree of distress. If you had brought your lawyer with you today, I'm sure that he would tell you the same thing."

The attorney's tone was ever so slightly chastening. Garven was attuned to nuances. The attorney looked at Garven expectantly.

Garven purposefully allowed an awkward silence to develop.

Then he broke the spell and asked sharply, "Have you finished?"

"Yes, unless you want to go over the fine points."

Garven shook his head.

"Now, here's what *I* want," Garven said curtly.

He did not like lawyers, especially this oily trio. They could have been the models for a movie shyster firm. He handed Elizabeth's lead attorney a neatly printed short list.

The attorney read the list quickly. At first he was inclined to treat the document as a joke; but when he looked into Garven's unfeeling eyes, he thought better of that inclination. He looked at Garven in disbelief.

"Really, Dr. Wilsonhulme, you can't be serious. This is unheard of! One half of the estate?! To you?! She pays alimony to you?! You keep the children?! You don't strike me as being an ingenuous person. Let me remind you that it was she who brought the Fletcher fortune into the marriage and generously provided for you, Sir!"

He could not keep the contempt out of his voice or off his face.

"That money is hers by every legal and moral right. No judge would dream of forcing her to part with her legacy. And no judge in the state would dream of violating the most sacred tenet of family law and take the children away from their mother. Get serious, man! We need to approach this like men. We need to get down to business!"

He looked at Garven as if he were dealing with one of those dead heads who followed the Grateful Dead rock and roll band around the country, the fans whose heads glowed in the dark.

"Oh, I assure you that I am perfectly serious, and this is no whim. I will go one step further. Elizabeth, herself, will agree to these requests," Garven said flatly.

Elizabeth winced involuntarily when Garven spoke her name.

"I would like to speak to her alone for five minutes. I believe we can resolve every difference during those few minutes. That is what you want, isn't it? You can still gouge your fat fee from her. You won't be able to suck any more of my blood in that event; but you can't have everything."

Garven had to work to keep an overt display of derision off his face.

"Now see here, Dr. Wilsonhulme, there's no need for any of us to be uncivil!" ejaculated the attorney. "And, as you had to expect, the answer is an emphatic, 'NO'! for any such meeting between you two litigants. It is not done!"

"Elizabeth?"

Garven asked fixing his gaze on her. He looked at her with an expression of calm reason, unthreatening and benign. She was sedated with Miltowns and Thorazine to fortify her against the stress of the confrontation. She found it difficult to experience fear, animosity, or anything approaching pleasure or joy. The hills and valleys of her emotions were significantly leveled.

"What can five minutes hurt?" she asked her lawyer.

He put a cautionary hand on her forearm. She gently lifted it away.

"I'll be all right," she said. "He's not a monster," she added doubtfully, and as an afterthought, "altogether."

"I don't approve, and I advise you against any such meeting, Mrs. Wilsonhulme," he said to her. "But, if you insist, we will step outside. Five minutes, no more. We will be right outside the door if you need us," he announced avuncularly.

When they were alone with the lawyers only looking on from outside the glassed-in enclosure of the meeting room, Garven waited for Elizabeth to speak first.

"Well, what is it, Garven, grandstanding? some hare-brained proposal? are you going to beat me up? You're just making this whole business difficult. Why fight it? We're finished," she said caustically.

The presence of her lawyers in the background lent her courage.

Garven did not speak. He handed Elizabeth an envelope from the inside pocket of his blue blazer. He made a point of keeping his mouth tightly shut and of not making the slightest move towards her, always looking directly at the kibitzing attorneys. She spread the photocopied typed sheets of paper and 8 X 10 glossy photographs before her on the table and took out her reading glasses.

He finally said, "These are copies. I have the originals, in case you are interested. These constitute the evidence that I will use to establish that you are an unfit mother."

He was as matter-of-fact as if he had been discussing the evening's TV schedule. She looked at him with undisguised loathing.

"Go ahead and read them. We have plenty of time."

He was completely relaxed and confident. She knew that Garven was no poker player. He could never bluff. For the first time, she felt a deep surge of anxiety course through her.

"I can tell you that every individual who has written one of these papers is ready to testify before a family court judge."

Now she read the papers and the photographs intently. As she did so, Elizabeth's face set into a mask of antipathy. There was an affidavit from her very own maid, the ingrate of a wet-back that Elizabeth had been so good to, and to whom she had even gone so far as to make a formal apology. There were reports by the EMT, the ambulance drivers, the admissions clerk, two psychiatric nurses, and her own doctor, Travis Longman, all attesting to her mental illness, to the instability and fragility of her personality, and to her penchant for both neglect and violence including against her own children and her chronic severe alcoholism and drug abuse. The photos were of excellent clarity and showed a disheveled drunk, a violent out-of-control harridan, and a maniac in a straight jacket.

Dr. Longman's affidavit, duly notarized, swore that Elizabeth's mental condition was such that her children should be removed from her temporarily until she could adjust to life on the outside of the psychiatric center. Even after the children were returned to her, Dr. Longman averred, Mrs. Wilsonhulme should not be allowed to be with them without another responsible adult appointed by the court being present. He went on to indicate her ongoing need for medication and for attendance at Alcoholics Anonymous meetings for the rest of her life. Elizabeth felt betrayed by her doctor.

"You set me up. That is despicable!" she snarled, barely able to keep her voice down.

"No. You set yourself up. I didn't want to do this. Read on," Garven said and handed Elizabeth a second envelope.

Both of her children had hand written short statements to the effect that they feared their mother and that they wanted to stay with their daddy. There names were signed in large block letters in their unmistakable childish writing.

"You rotten..."

"Now, Elizabeth. Wouldn't you rather spend our remaining moments in coming to a compromise?" Garven said. "I am tired of being vilified. If you make one more nasty comment, I am going to walk out of here with my evidence. Suit yourself."

"What do you mean, 'compromise', Garven?"

It was the first faint glimmer of rationality and hope she had heard from him or vice versa.

"What do you really want? I can't have this filthy stuff made public. It would kill the children...to say nothing of my mother."

"I have one more paper for you to look at, Elizabeth. Think of it as the cost of doing business."

He handed her another envelope, this one unsealed. The attorneys were all but pressing their noses against the plate-glass windows. He gathered up the other papers, replaced them in their envelopes, and returned them to his jacket pockets. Elizabeth opened the new envelope and drew out the single sheet of paper. The essence of an agreement between them was spelled out: He gets one-half of the entire monetary estate, including the trust fund and inheritance from her family, and two cars including his favorite $3,398, 1970 Opel GT. She gets the house and the other half of the entire estate and the other, better, two cars including the big Mercedes which made her the slight winner, financially, on paper. She gets sole custody of the children. He gets generous visitations rights. There is no alimony or child-care support from either party to the agreement. He promises not to discuss with any other person, Mrs. Wilsonhulme's incapacities. She promises not to publish abroad any comment about Dr. Wilsonhulme's social life and activities nor to disclose to anyone the details of their agreement or of the discussion leading to that agreement.

"This is blackmail. That's what this has been all along, hasn't it? An elaborate and cruel way to get hold of my money. You never cared for me from the first minute we met at the Fitzpatrick's party. You don't give two hoots about the children. It was just money. How could a man stoop so low?" she asked, staring daggers at him.

"Elizabeth," came his hard and uncompromising voice. "That is it on the insults. I told you that before. I have had all of them I am going to put up with for a lifetime. I have not abused you for being a commode hugging, falling down, public drunk or for neglecting the kids shamefully. I have not put it up to you for being a frigid, spoiled little rich girl who thinks she can buy anything she wants. I won't have your snotty, self-praising clap-trap. I'm done. See you in court—courts."

He stood up abruptly and started for the door. The attorneys started to move back to let him through.

Elizabeth was still in the very early healing process from the self-loathing she felt for her excesses under the influence. He could not have hurt her more if he had backhanded her across the face. She gritted her teeth and squeezed her eyes shut to hold back the sting of tears that were welling up. She drummed her gold Cross pen on the table top several times. Then, without speaking, she signed the agreement papers—two copies of each, one for her, and one for Garven. This was a precaution Garven had added to avoid interference from her attorneys. He had walked slowly enough to give her time to do the sensible thing. As soon as she did, he stepped swiftly back, swept up the papers, and went to the door.

"Come in, gentlemen," he said pleasantly, and returned to his seat in the conference room.

The attorneys looked at Elizabeth's ashen face.

"He didn't..." one of them started to ask.

"No, nothing like that," Elizabeth said very quietly. "I have signed an agreement. We are settled. Now, I'd like to get out of here; so, I don't have to look at him."

The three attorneys looked at the simple agreement in bemusement. They were rife with speculation about what Garven could have said that would make such a radical turn in the day's negotiations.

Garven stood up and said, "Good day, gentlemen. Send me the formal papers for signature when you have them prepared. Send her the bill."

He stepped away from his chair and left the room.

The final divorce papers were delivered to Garven's office at UCOMH by courier one morning two weeks later. He signed them without a passing thought. Garven Wilsonhulme was not one to look backwards at events or at his sins. To himself, he said, remembering lines from the Rubyyiat of Omar Khayam: "*The moving finger writes, and having writ, moves on. Nor all your piety nor wit can alter half a line, nor all your tears wash out a word of it.*"

Besides, he had a new attack to defend against.

CHAPTER
Twenty-Five

When word of Garven's impending divorce leaked into the hospital rumor pipeline, Dr. Hickman, head of neurology, came to Garven's office to chat with him and brought the conversation around to Garven's social life.

"I had to make a deal with my wife," he said after a wide ranging conversation about the neurological professions, the sad state of baseball, and hiking in Southern Utah. "We had the devil's own time getting along what with both of us being working professionals. Finally, I said, 'Look, you don't tell me about your day; and I won't tell you about mine.' That's worked pretty well for a grumpy old pair."

Garven chuckled politely.

"In truth, we had an old fashioned marriage," Dr. Hickman said, warming to his audience of one. "On our wedding day, we decided that I would make all of the important decisions."

He smiled. And paused.

"And she would decide which decisions were important."

Garven laughed genuinely then.

"In all seriousness, Garven, I have heard that you and your lady are having something of a spotty time of it. I don't mean to intrude, and I certainly do not want to spread rumors. That's why I came directly to you. You may stop me anytime, Garven."

He gave Garven a chance.

"Is it so?"

It was a question that would never have been asked in polite company and was only brought to the surface by Dr. Hickman because of the serious implications of divorce for a senior faculty member for his or her career with the university.

"I have tried to keep this thing very private, Warren. You can imagine that it has been painful. Yes, I'm afraid it is so. My wife, who is a fine woman otherwise, has had a drinking problem for some years. Recently, her behavior has gotten to be so erratic that I have had to hospitalize her on the psych service. She has been diagnosed as having a mild case of schizophrenia; hopefully one that can be controlled most of the time with medications. She developed an obsession in her mind that she had to get a divorce in order to fulfill her own personal destiny. She cannot be reasoned with. I think she bought into the claptrap from the shrinks and the twaddle from one of those man-hating woman's groups. She has filed all the formal papers through her lawyers who seem to egg her on. It seems inevitable now."

"Sad," said Warren Hickman, and he meant it. "I am also afraid that there are likely to be repercussions a bit more far-reaching than your own family boundaries.

"What sort of repercussions?" Garven asked ingenuously, but with some well-founded apprehensions.

"Well, you know the general stand in the faculty councils against taking on divorced people?"

Garven nodded at his friend.

"There are those who are looking askance at your situation. It will be the first divorce on the senior faculty since the school opened. We had young Butler from pediatrics who divorced about ten years ago—ugly thing, that situation."

Hickman gave a small shudder.

"Well, anyway, he eventually had to resign. I have to tell you, Garven, that you have some enemies; men and women who would like to see you out of your position. They are just looking for an excuse."

"Men like whom?" Garven asked.

"It would be uncomfortable to say," Hickman answered.

"Not nearly as uncomfortable as my not knowing," Garven countered.

"Your point is well taken and fair. I don't see the harm in it. They certainly don't make any bones about letting everyone know of their animus towards you. There's Kowalski from anesthesiology at the VA. I don't know the man. Howard Rosenthal, from Pediatrics. He's now on the Medical Ethics Committee and is something of a Torquemada at heart. Never cared for the man, myself. But the one to be concerned about is Horst Caesar. For some reason, he seems to have sworn out a vendetta against you. I can't, for the life of me, fathom why. He has real power, and he wields it like a club. From his position on the faculty review board and the medical director's committee, he can be a good friend or a bad enemy. In your case, I'm afraid it's the latter. They all serve on the faculty review board, for that matter," Hickman told Garven.

The names came as no surprise to Garven, but that the three men involved could hold such long term grudges for such petty grievances seemed disproportionate. Garven did not believe in coincidences, and having all three men on the same influential committee that could attack him where he was vulnerable was well beyond coincidence.

"They know that a divorce is, by itself, a weak basis to force a chief of a department to step down. They have been moving around rather vigorously. I am on that same faculty review board and the medical director's committee, myself; and I have been hearing some negative things about you. I thought I would look for first-hand evidence. Garven, the three of them are telling anyone who will listen that you are having an adulterous affair with a young lady, a movie starlet, I've been told. Would you care to comment?"

"For the record, counselor?" Garven said to Dr. Hickman, with faint sarcasm.

Hickman shrugged good-naturedly. The men shared an antipathy towards attorneys that characterized the feelings of ninety-nine percent of their fellow doctors.

Garven's first, second, and third inclinations were to tell Warren Hickman in varying forms and intensities to butt out of his private business.

But, he responded to his fourth inclination instead, and said, "Warren, it is true that, since my marriage went sour, I have been seeing a fine woman. She is somewhat younger than I and is employed in the design and fashion industry. She has nothing to do with the movies. Our relationship is discrete."

Warren looked at Garven a moment. He forbore to ask directly whether The chief of neurosurgery was carrying on a flagrant adulterous relationship. He decided that he had his answer.

"Well, Garven, I respect and appreciate your candor. I fear that you will not have heard the end of this after today's conversation, by a long shot."

"It's hard to believe that I am hearing this. It is 1971, after all. And this could hardly be considered a Catholic country, or city, or university, for that matter," Garven said. "Where I come from, a man's private business was considered to be just that—private."

"And where was that?"

"Where did I come from?" asked Garven.

"Yes."

Chapter Twenty-Five

"Providence."

"Ah, yes. The banker Wilsonhulmes, I presume? I knew several of them from horsy circles," Hickman said, glad to be able to shift to less charged subjects for awhile.

"Yes, that's the family," Garven answered.

"Well, brace yourself. This is a fishbowl. California is not Rhode Island. Discretion among gentlemen went out with high button shoes, I'm afraid. Don't be too shocked to see some of this business in the newspapers. I wouldn't put it past my colleagues to advertise and would expect to see those reptiles, the lawyers, hawking their wares any time. Nothing is sacred anymore.

"I am going to have to run, Garven. I'm sorry to appear brusque, but there is one more thing. Your malpractice suit has added fuel to the fire. I wanted to be the first to tell you, to warn you. Caesar has put your divorce and your malpractice suit on the agenda of the next medical director's meeting. They are going to offer you an invitation to attend."

"A subpoena," Garven said morosely.

"More or less. I think you should take it seriously, start rounding the wagons into a laager, as it were. Better call in your markers on this one. I think you may need them."

Garven Wilsonhulme was the first item on the agenda of the monthly medical director's meeting after coffee and petit fours. Garven could not help but notice that there was a stack of charts sitting in front of Horst Caesar, the chairman. He had not heard that he was going to be the subject of any kind of chart review, and he was unprepared.

"So much for due process," he thought.

When the subjects of Garven's private social life were introduced, David Stark, whose standing was every bit as lofty as that of Horst Caesar, came to Garven's defense. He politely but firmly informed the assembled men of the august body that this was the twentieth century, and that their organization were not dictated by the Presbyterian Church or the Star Chamber. It was time for them to recognize that significant changes had occurred and were even now taking place, with California, as usual, moving ahead of the other states. They could not hold their heads underneath the sand on the subject of divorce forever, he told them.

"And if every man on the faculty who has played the extracurricular slap and tickle game were to be kicked off the staff, we would be reduced to a couple of

Mormons, a Catholic priest, and old Mudgers, who fell astride the wagon shaft as a boy," he said by way of argument about the 'charge' of adultery.

"Sir, perhaps you did not know that adultery is a crime," piped up Dr. Kowalski.

"A blue-law crime that was put on the books two hundred years ago and hasn't been enforced for a hundred," Stark said sarcastically. "I would like to ask a serious question of this body. How many of you really want to pillory Dr. Wilsonhulme on the charge of adultery? Before you answer, consider the Pandora's box that will be opened by so doing. Any of you ready to cast the figurative first stone?"

There were a number of quick life reviews and consideration of the consequences to themselves of introducing adultery as a cause for dismissal from the faculty. Although there was a mood of general disapproval of Garven's actions, the consensus was that they were not hearing just cause for a professor to be removed from office. And none of them stooped to pick up a stone.

"I would like to move on to the subject of a chart review of Dr. Wilsonhulme's patients," said Horst Caesar, feeling that he was losing support for his dump-Wilsonhulme campaign. "I believe we should start with that of the recent malpractice suit of which you have all heard so much."

The group of senior professors discussed the patient, the Reverend Dr. Jack Clyde Powers, and the role played by Garven Wilsonhulme and Kent Ashcroft, the resident. The discussion took place in front of Garven in full frankness and without asking him to clarify, elucidate, or to explain any of the events leading up to the suit. Dr. Stark was, once again, Garven's chief defender.

His posit was basically that, "This is surgery; things like this happen, unfortunately."

"I've heard that old, "*Inshallah*" argument too many times. It glosses over any and everything," said Dr. Rosenthal sharply.

He was tired of the hackneyed old surgeons' excuses.

However, the other surgeons on the panel were distinctly uncomfortable with criticisms of surgeons over complications, reasoning, "There, but for the Grace of God, go I."

When it was finally deemed to be time for Garven to offer a word or two in his own defense, he described the case, and particularly his role as an assistant rather than having full responsibility. He concluded with something the others did not know.

"Although I would never make a light thing out of a man's death," he said, "in all fairness, the suit has proved to be a tempest in a teapot. I was dropped from the case, and Ashcroft settled. He was a stand-up fellow. Shouldered the blame and saw to it that I was exonerated. That is how the case stands as of this moment. There is no suit against me. The point is moot."

Heads turned and nodded to their neighbors. Surgeons breathed a literal sigh of relief.

David Stark asked Caesar, "Is that the worst case up for review, Horst?"

"Well, I think it probably is," Caesar replied reluctantly.

"Then, I wonder if we couldn't table the reading of those remaining charts to another day. Better, perhaps they should be heard at a lower level—in surgery committee—where they belong; and then they can send a report on up the line to us. What does everyone think?"

"Hear, hear," chorused the tired and overworked physicians.

None but the three who bore their animus towards Garven on their sleeves were in favor of continuing the mini-inquisition. There did not seem to be an adequate reason to pursue the matter further, and the three were outvoted.

"But, it is important to consider the cumulative character of Wilsonhulme's customs and practices," protested Caesar knowing that he was flogging a dead horse.

He had already lost his audience and his crusade, at least for that night. He sounded whiny. The heads of the other fifteen men and women in the room shook in negative unison.

"Until another day, then," Dr. Caesar conceded.

Only he and Garven knew that he was not referring to the chart review, but to another battle in the undeclared war being waged by Garven's three nemeses who were sure that Garven would provide them more fuel for their fire eventually.

CHAPTER
Twenty-Six

When the divorce was final, Garven wrote a letter to the chiefs of neurosurgery and neurology services around the country and the world. He knew that divorce was like the fifth horseman of the apocalypse to most of the ultraconservative men to whom he was writing. He could only fail to communicate with these influential people at his professional peril. It seemed prosaic and none of their business to Garven's way of thinking; but nevertheless, it had to be done.

> Dear ——,
>
> I feel the need to let you know of a major transition in my life. My wife, Elizabeth, and I have long been under a strain; and finally, we have chosen to divorce. Some relationships were not meant to be, and ours has not been a happy one for some time. Elizabeth is a fine person and has my utmost respect. We remain on congenial terms.
>
> I hope this transition in my life will in no way hinder our association. I value your friendship and seek your understanding in this difficult time in my life. Let me assure you that the program at the University of California Osterlund Memorial Hospital is unaffected by my personal problems. We continue to strive to offer the best possible care for our patients, the most advanced research; and we will continue to participate

to the fullest in the affairs of the world's outstanding neurosurgery academies, congresses, and associations.

Thank you for your kind consideration and support, I remain,

Sincerely yours,
Garven C. Wilsonhulme, MD, FACS
Professor and Chairman.

Garven told his friends, Devon and Elijah David, about his troubles at
dinner a week after he held the decree of divorcement in his hand. It was
the first time that he had been able to summon the courage to have them
meet Jenny Lakewood, and the only time he had discussed his divorce and
malpractice suit outside the official chambers of attorneys and the medical
establishment. The ostensible reason for the dinner was to announce his
engagement to the attractive young model. Both Rachel Upshire and Miriam
Shapiro heartily disapproved of Garven's affair, his choice of women—young
and beautiful—and the announcement of his engagement; but wild horses
could not have kept them away from that dinner.

"So, that's about it, my tale of woes. I suppose that I can take solace in the
'all's well that ends well' argument," Garven concluded after telling the two
men and their wives of the snarl his life had gotten into of late.

Jenny sat and listened without interrupting.

Devon said, "You have two sources of trouble, Garven—informers and
enemies in the institution, and lawyers, it seems to me."

Garven nodded agreement.

"All I can say about the institution is that you'd better watch your back all of
the time. I don't think your enemies there are going to give up. The slightest
pretext, and they'll be on you like hyenas again. Remember the old wisdom at
the VA - 'never let anyone walk up behind you'," Elijah David said.

"And as for lawyers," Devon said, "they produce more of them every year.
They have less and less work all the time. We can expect a lot more malpractice attacks, mark my words. I predict a real crisis one day. Our only hope
is that they will multiply until they starve themselves out or cannibalize one
another. I suppose we shouldn't stand around on one leg waiting for that day."

E.D. asked, "Do you know what you have when you've got only on lawyer
in a town?"

They all shook their heads.

"Too little work. And what do you have when there are two lawyers in a town?"

They shrugged.

"Too much work," he said with a grin.

They all smiled in agreement.

"Oh, oh, lawyer jokes are like potato chips," said Devon, "once you start with one, it's tough to quit. So, one time the big gates between heaven and hell were stuck closed and needed repairs. Saint Peter hollered over to Lucifer. 'Hey, Lucifer, it's your turn to repair the gate.'

"'Sorry, my workers are too busy bringing in a new load of coal for the furnaces. We aren't going to bother about a simple gate problem,' the devil hollered back.

"'But we have an agreement,' yelled Saint Peter.

"'Tough,' yelled Lucifer.

"'I'll sue for breach of contract,' threatened Saint Peter.

"'Go ahead,' said Lucifer, 'but where're you going to find an attorney?'"

Garven was in a good mood. He started to tell his favorite joke, but Jenny interrupted him. She looked apologetic.

"I'll forget if I don't tell it now," she giggled.

He gestured for her to go on.

"Did you hear about the lawyer that was so successful that he was able to buy his own ambulance?"

The doctors tsk-tsked and laughed heartily.

It was Garven's turn.

"My attorney in the Powers case told me that the California bar has become concerned about the image of lawyers. They have been suffering a lot of criticism of late. So, they have gotten into the arts to give people a gentler view of attorneys. They're doing a modernized version of "Faust." In this version, the main character is an attorney.

"The devil comes to Faust, the lawyer, and offers him fame and respect within his profession, a fortune in fees, youth, and the adoration of the public.

"The lawyer asks, 'What must I do?'

"The devil states simply, 'You must abuse your wife and give her to Arabs for prostitution, sell your children into slavery, and betray your friends and business partners. For that, I will give you fame, fortune, and youth.'

"The lawyer looks at the devil questioningly, strokes his beard thoughtfully; then with a bewildered look, asks, 'Yeah, and what's the catch?'"

Jenny poured them each a small snifter of cognac.

Garven raised his glass for a toasts, "Confusion for our enemies," he said.

They were all happy to drink to that.

After dessert, Pedro Domecq sherry, and more light-hearted shop talk and lawyer bashing, Devon asked Garven to come by and see a patient with him in the morning. Garven and Jenny walked the two guest couples to their cars. Devon and Elijah David's cars were parked next to Garven and Jenny's cars. Miriam Shapiro saw the problem first.

"Look," she shrieked and pointed to the tires on hers and ED's car.

All four tires had been slashed and lay flat on the asphalt.

The others quickly bent to look at the tires on their own vehicles. Every tire on every car was flat.

"Elizabeth!" said Jenny in a whisper to Garven.

He nodded his head in agreement.

Devon snarled his judgment, "Vandals. No place is safe, not even Camelot here! There're j.ds everywhere."

They all trudged back into the house and called for emergency service. The wrecker driver had been told the sizes of the tires on all of the cars.

When he was done replacing all of the tires, he thought to himself, "*Maybe I outta hire a few hoods—I should say, 'underprivileged youth'—to come around here all the time. I haven't made this much dough in an hour since the last riot.*"

Garven was frustrated. He would never be able to prove that Elizabeth had been behind this. He knew she was; this was only the latest in a string of incidents since the divorce—spray paint on the front walk, unsigned poison pen letters to him and to Jenny, and distorted, nasty letters to faculty members and to the priest and deacon at their Beverly Hills Episcopal Church. Short of moving out of town, he guessed that he would have to try and ignore her.

Garven thought to himself, "*Cheer up; things could be worse. So, I cheered up; and sure enough, things got worse.*"

He also wondered when the black cloud over his head would finally go away.

CHAPTER
Twenty-Seven

Devon's patient was a twenty year old girl who had been drunk on her motorcycle and had wrecked while riding around in the Anaverde Hills near Palmdale. She had fractured the body of her twelfth vertebra, and had an unstable spine as a result. She was in pain, but was neurologically intact. Garven considered this an intern's case; treat the woman with bed rest for four months at home and avoid an operation and the potential for surgical complications. He waited to hear why Devon wanted his help at all.

"I need you to be there when I meet with the family," Devon said as if Garven had sent a telegraphic message. "Her uncle is a lawyer, apropos of our conversation at your dinner last night. He is an obstreperous and litigious ambulance chaser. He has been hostile and threatening all along. I just want to have a significant witness with me; help me say everything right," Devon told him after they had seen the young woman, a pleasant and much subdued former drinker.

Devon had the girl's x-rays with him. The floor nurse brought the family into the patient's room. The two neurosurgeons met them, including the uncle, who spent most of the twenty minute interview scowling. Devon put up the films, and to be on the safe side, read from the radiologist's official report. The diagnostic impressions were routine and listed the differential diagnosis of the obviously badly disrupted vertebral body—the usual things: fracture, cancer, infection, TB.

The girl's uncle had apparently been elected family spokesman or had usurped the position, more likely.

He said, "That's all well and good, gentlemen; but we wish to take Emily to a major hospital where she can have the best. We want her transferred to UCLA, their Westwood hospital."

Emily had a surprised look indicating that this was as new to her as it was to the two doctors.

"Fine with us," said Devon, quickly.

"*Maybe a little too quickly,*" thought Garven.

"We will make arrangements as soon as possible. You have our opinion about the diagnosis and about treatment. We advise a conservative approach," Devon said, gritting his teeth slightly.

"Frankly, the opinion of peripheral doctors such as yourselves is immaterial, Doctor. We are not overly impressed with what might come from an indigents' hospital in the heart of darkness. We are going to hear from physicians at the major center. I will be in my office. You can call me there when arrangements have been made. You can go now."

Garven thought of a number of speedy and nasty retorts, about giving his opinion about the World Famous UCLA (WFUCLA), or simply knocking the snob's teeth out. He was proud of himself when he was able to do nothing. The lawyer was not worth it.

Emily was transferred to the WFUCLA where, not unexpectedly, she underwent a laminectomy, fusion, and placement of Harrington Rods—as much surgery as could be done on one back. Garven groused that UCLA would surgerize anyone whom they could get to hold still long enough and who could pass the wallet test. She did well and was on her feet, healed and well, at the end of four months. The orthopedic surgeons at UCLA kept Darven and Devon well informed of the girl's progress as a professional courtesy.

The day after Emily's last clinic visit at UCLA, Garven and Devon were served notice of intent to sue by the young woman's lawyer uncle. Garven looked at the service papers perplexed. He had no recollection of who the woman was whose name appeared in the plaintiff's segment of the formal papers. He had to look up the hospital chart to refresh his memory. When he learned who she was, he was even more perplexed. He could not think of a single reason why anyone would sue him on that case. He called his old friend, Roderick Naffziger at UCLA and asked how Emily had done and was now doing.

"Great!" came back the reply to both questions.

Garven was really perplexed.

It took Garven and Devon's attorney two weeks to get a telephone call through to and back from Emily's attorney uncle. The uncle was very forthcoming in his answer.

"Simple open and shut case. It is a new theory of law; frankly, I hope to see this as a precedent setting case that will open the way for more protection for poor abused patients in the future. What happened to my niece, what caused her such trauma and infliction of mental and psychological injury, was that she was exposed to inordinate fear. The doctors at the peripheral hospital presented to her a whole list of terrifying diagnoses and left her with lifelong scars resulting from her fear that, besides being hurt, she had cancer, tuberculosis, or other infections!"

"That's it?!" queried the defense attorney incredulously.

'That' was, indeed, 'it'. The entire cumbersome rigmarole of the litigation began to grind its way into and through the legal system with Garven's insurance company steadily paying the defense attorneys' fees that would never be refunded by the plaintiff, even in the instance where the plaintiff lost. The case went on Garven's record. Whether he won it or not, having another malpractice case on his record was going to hurt him.

The worst thing for Garven was that the new case provided additional fodder to feed the ill will of his avowed enemies on the faculty committees, a side issue to the litigation whose importance did not escape him. A month after the suit was filed formally and made public, Garven received another notice to appear before a board of inquiry, this time, the critical Faculty Review and Promotions Board. Ominously, he was invited to bring his lawyer with him.

He asked Devon and Elijah David, "Do you think I really need to take a lawyer? Has California come to this? Has the practice of medicine come to this?"

"Yes, yes, and yes," said E.D. "Every indication is that we need protection all the time. I'd like to have one of those reptiles with me on rounds if I could afford it and if I could stand being with them."

"And in this place, at this time, *you* need all the help you can get," added Devon.

Garven shrugged. It was a nuisance. He was too busy to have to put up with this. He found an attorney through the same firm on Wilshire Boulevard that was handling his defense against Emily and her avaricious uncle. Together, he and the new attorney, MacArthur Copeland, reviewed the known accusations, and Garven got the list of the patients' charts that had been stacked against him in the last hearing.

On the night of the meeting, Garven knew he was in trouble as soon as he saw the agenda. The only item listed was "Dr. Garven C. Wilsonhulme."

He soberly handed the agenda sheet for his attorney's perusal.

Dr. Horst Caesar had recently been elevated to the chairmanship of the Faculty Review Committee which made him the most powerful man on the UCOMH faculty and hospital medical staff and number two man in importance for the hospital itself. He was standing at the head of the long conference table when Garven and Mr. Copeland took their seats at the other end. Shortly, other men and women strode purposefully in and took their seats. It troubled Garven a little that they all avoided sitting right next to him as if he had missed his shower or had something contagious. He recognized most of the people, but not everyone. There were more in attendance at this meeting that had been at the last one.

Dr. Caesar looked at his watch.

"It is seven on the dot, ladies and gentlemen. We can start on time for a change. First, we should have some introductions; so, we can know the players. Would each of you stand and tell us your name and your faculty position or your purpose here?"

The physicians sat together along one side of the table. Especially, Dr.s Caesar, Rosenthal, and Kowalski sat together.

"*Thick as thieves*", Garven thought.

Garven also thought it was something of a coup to have gotten all three of them on this prestigious committee. There were seven heads of departments and four other physicians present. The hospital was represented by the top three administrators. Two hospital attorneys stood up and gave their names and the name of their firm. Garven's lawyer was next, then Garven. No one smiled or acknowledged anyone else as the introductions moved around the room.

"Thank you, colleagues, ladies and gentlemen," said Dr. Caesar. "Now to business. We are here on an extraordinary matter. May I caution you at the outset that the proceedings of this meeting are not to be discussed outside this room. The hospital and each of you individually and collectively are liable for any communications beyond these doors. You cannot be sued for your actions and statements here. State hospital law protects you. Also, Mrs. Worthington, my worthy secretary," and he could not suppress a little grin at his witticism, "will be taking down what is said, verbatim. She will keep the only transcript. To make it possible for her to do her job, you will have to refrain from talking when someone else is talking. Everyone here will get his or her chance to speak."

Dr. Caesar asked Dr. Rosenthal to review the minutes of the meeting of the Medical Director's Committee when Garven had first had his feet held to the fire. He seemed to take genuine pleasure in presenting the condemnatory material.

Garven spoke up when Dr. Rosenthal finished, "I thought that was satisfactorily dealt with in the previous meeting, Mr. Chairman," he said.

"Dr. Wilsonhulme, you will be given your chance to communicate after a while. For now, please try not to interrupt. That material was included only for the sake of background," Dr. Caesar answered in a chiding tone.

Garven felt as if he were being treated like a naughty school boy. He did not like it at all.

His attorney whispered to him, "It may be background, but it is certainly prejudicial."

Garven flattened his lips feeling provoked.

"Dr. Ivins will present the new case of malpractice committed by Dr. Wilsonhulme," the chairman announced.

"Alleged malpractice. I trust that some of the rules of American jurisprudence apply here," said Mr. Copeland.

"Your point is well taken," said the hospital attorney, "alleged malpractice."

"Mrs. Worthington, would you note that in the record, please," said Dr. Caesar, the very soul of protocol. "Now, Dr. Ivins."

Bartholomew Ivins, the head of the division of hematology, quickly read a prepared synopsis of the history of Emily's course in the hospital and afterwards and read the particulars of the legal complaints against Garven. The accused was heartened to see the looks of confusion and doubt on the faces of the men and women in the room, even Dr. Caesar, when the summary was presented.

"Is that all?" Garven's attorney asked after a few minutes of awkward silence.

"No, not quite," answered Dr. Caesar dragging out the suspense as long as he could. "I have here a set of documents that will be entered in toto into the record. I want to save all discussion until the end, if you don't mind. We can look at the whole picture and render our judgment at that time. I have requested that Dr. Steven Chou from the department of neurosurgery come and present these papers and the background pertinent to them."

Garven gave his attorney a quizzical look of raised eyebrows and shrugged his shoulders. Mrs. Worthington stood up and walked to the side door of the meeting room.

"Dr. Chou, would you step in now?"

"I'm sure you all know Steven Chou. He was Dr. Wilsonhulme's predecessor in the department chairmanship," Dr. Caesar said, "and a man of integrity."

The last phrase, given parenthetically, was taken by Garven as an implicit observation that he suffered in the comparison. He gritted his teeth at the rather bald insult.

All heads in the room inclined in small bows of recognition. Dr. Chou was well thought of throughout the university and around the hospital. He was also an object of sympathy. He looked as if he were knocking at Death's door.

Dr. Chou started his communication as soon as he was standing at the head of the conference table, "The first of these documents, a letter, came to me almost by mistake. It was addressed to me as head of the department, a mistake, as you know. I thought nothing of that small oversight and opened it. I will read the letter in its entirety and without editorial comment. It comes from a researcher named, Gordon Styvescent, presently working at U. Mass in Amherst. At first, I thought it was a crank letter. I checked Dr. Styvescent out and spoke with him. He is the genuine article.

"Excuse me for that bit of digression. This is the letter..."

Garven strained his memory to get a handle on who Gordon Styvescent might be as Dr. Chou proceeded. It was all too clear before the third sentence was completed. Garven knew he had not met the writer of the letter, but his name blazed before Garven's eyes as the accusation came out. Dr. Styvescent accused Garven of having used his position as the NIH Neurosurgery Grant Committee chairman to take advantage of the idea submitted, the most craven act of plagiarism.

Garven felt like he had been hit in the face with a pole. He felt faint.

There was more.

Dr. Chou then said, "I could not be certain that this had any truth to it. I certainly hoped not."

Garven did not like the use of the past tense. He waited for the other shoe to drop.

"So, I communicated with the security people at the National Institutes of Health in D.C., and that set off a four month investigation of Dr. Wilsonhulme's practices while he served on the grant committee. He still serves on that committee, for your information."

"Why wasn't my client informed of any of this before tonight? It is hearsay, and the accuser can't be questioned. Due process and common decency cannot be said to be in force without the elemental opportunity to review accusations and to prepare some kind of defense," Garven's attorney said.

He had risen to a standing position.

"Sit down, Mr. Copeland. You will get your chance. I believe I made that clear at the beginning of this meeting," said Horst Caesar, brusquely

Mr. Copeland reluctantly re-took his seat, shaking his head.

Dr. Chou continued, "The NIH people looked into papers submitted to Dr. Wilsonhulme and compared them to Dr. Wilsonhulme's own publications. They came up with two additional instances of what they felt were irregularities. I have their full report here, but perhaps the official letters that were requested by the NIH from the other researchers will suffice for now."

He read a letter from Donald Ketchum from Atlantic City and one from Dr. Jose Ortega-Otero of Guadalajara, Mexico. Despite himself, Garven reddened as he envisioned the proposal from Dr. Ketchum about using papavarine to combat vasoconstriction after subarachnoid hemorrhage that had launched the now widely accepted, "Wilsonhulme Vasoconstriction Therapy Method."

He had not thought ever to hear or to see the Mexican neurosurgeon's name, Ortega-Otero, again. Now he was hearing, in perfect English, a denunciation of himself for having plagiarized the concept of splitting the corpus callosum of the brain to treat intractable seizures. He tried not to look as guilty as he felt. He told himself to put an expression on his face like a biscuit and to keep it there.

"I would like to see the evidence behind those scurrilous accusations," demanded Mr. Copeland.

"In due time, Mr. Copeland. Keep your pants on," said Horst Caesar, who was obviously enjoying this.

"From what I have studied about hospital law over the years, these proceedings fail to meet even the most minimal standards of due process. There is no way that you are going to be able to remove a tenured full professor from his position on the basis of what I have heard to date. If you make any of this public, you will invite a lawsuit for libel that will make Dr. Wilsonhulme the new owner of this institution. There needs to be more than this. In the first place, these accusations have nothing to do with his performance at this hospital or, are at most, trifling matters of reputation that could impact on his standing," MacArthur Copeland persisted despite Caesar's admonition.

One of the two hospital attorneys spoke up.

"Please wait before you make your own assessment of Dr. Wilsonhulme's culpability and jeopardy, Mr. Copeland. We have not finished. Do not in any way think that these matters are being taken as 'trifling', to use your word, by any one in this room. They are considered to be most serious and to fall within the old law school dictum, *'De minimus non curat lex.'*"

For the first time in his adult life that he could remember, Garven had a serious use for all that time he had spent in Burton-Cagle School learning Latin. "The law is not concerned with trifles," he translated to himself.

The opposing attorney translated for the other members of the committee, and added, "And neither are we."

"As if what you have heard was not damaging enough, I hasten to tell you that the worst is yet to come," said Dr. Caesar with something that approached glee in his eyes.

Garven groaned inwardly and silently.

"What more could there possibly be?" he asked himself.

CHAPTER
Twenty-Eight

I t was his own worst nightmare, and he was awake.

"Mrs. Wilsonhulme," Mrs. Worthington called into the adjoining room. "Come in now, if you would."

Elizabeth Wilsonhulme walked into the room accompanied by a severe looking woman in a plain suit and gray hair done up in a plain bun. Garven had not seen Elizabeth looking so strong and healthy, so vital in several years. He was impressed at how well she had gotten herself back among the living. She did not even deign to glance in his direction. Mr. Copeland looked questioningly at Garven. Garven shrugged his shoulders in ignorance of what this was about.

"Thank you for coming, Mrs. Wilsonhulme. I know this is an imposition," said Dr. Caesar as she and her companion took their seats.

"I consider it to be no less than my duty, Dr. Caesar," she said.

Garven shivered.

'Duty', in Elizabeth's dictionary was shrouded in many dark Old Testament overtones.

"Ladies and gentlemen, this is Elizabeth Wilsonhulme, the former wife of Dr. Wilsonhulme. Madam, we won't waste your valuable time. Why don't you tell us what you have learned?"

"My former husband and I have two children, a boy and a girl. Our daughter, my daughter, is named Susan; she's eight years old..."

Elizabeth looked as if she were going to cry. She got control of herself and took a long deep breath.

"She has reported to me that my former husband, Dr. Garven Wilsonhulme, has...has...how can I say it? He, uh, has done things."

The assembled committee audience looked bemused at the oblique references made by Mrs. Wilsonhulme.

"What sort of 'things', Mrs. Wilsonhulme?" asked the head of obstetrics and gynecology, Dr. Caesar. "You can speak frankly here. We are all doctors and attorneys. I don't think anyone will be shocked."

Garven was sure that he would be at least one exception to that statement. He waited with baited breath to learn exactly what it was he was supposed to have done.

"Well, you know. Not the right sort of things. I mean, you know."

She was twisting her handkerchief and avoided looking anyone in the eye. The woman who accompanied Elizabeth kept her ax-like expression and sat grim-lipped and like a dark shadow in the room.

"Come, now, Mrs. Wilsonhulme," said the woman across from her who was the Chief of Pediatrics. "It's a little late for daintiness now that you have started this line of implication. I think it is time for us to hear exactly what your daughter told you."

The shadow beside Elizabeth spoke for the first time.

"Perhaps I can be of assistance. Allow me to introduce myself. I am Dr. Mildred Pearson-Wight. I am a child psychologist. I have interviewed the little girl in question. Would you like me to elaborate?"

"By all means," said Dr. Caesar pleased with the bit of theater that was unfolding.

"I must object," said Mr. Copeland. "This is the worst of hearsay evidence. We are twice removed from the actual witness."

"Save your objections, counselor. This is not a court of law. I want to hear about this, and I think that I speak for everyone. Stop with the lawyer jargon and the interruptions. We are a fact-finding group. What is to be done about the facts we elucidate will be a matter for a subsequent meeting, or perhaps for the board of directors of the hospital. Now, go on, Dr. Pearson-Wight."

"The subject, Susan Wilsonhulme, age eight, was brought to me for psychological evaluation by her mother. In the course of my examination the little girl told me that she had been sexually molested by her father, Dr. Wilsonhulme."

For a few seconds the room became as quiet as if a stun grenade had just exploded, and everyone there was holding his or her breath collectively waiting for what new misadventure would be visited upon them.

Someone gasped, "No!"

Garven roared, "WHAT??!"

His attorney restrained him from leaping across the table and throttling the imperious woman. He shook his head vehemently at Garven to prevent him from saying anything more.

"Yes, sadly, ladies and gentlemen, the act that cannot be spoken. Incest. There it is, out in the open. Incest. This defenseless little girl was raped by the father she trusted!" said Dr. Pearson-Wight.

She no longer looked like a severe shadow. Her eyes blazed with messianic fervor. Her face and hands were as animated as a demagogue addressing a rally.

Garven was on his feet.

"That is a cold calculated lie and a blasphemy concocted by my angry and self-styled 'scorned' wife and her henchwoman!" he shouted. "I don't believe that my daughter ever said any such a thing whatever persuasion was used. It is a rotten absurdity!"

His face was fiery angry.

"Sit down, Dr. Wilsonhulme!" called Dr. Caesar.

He did not like to see the meeting he had so carefully orchestrated getting out of hand before the complete impact of his anti-Garven symphony was fully played out.

Garven ignored him.

"I can believe that Elizabeth would say such things. Her mind's unhinged. She has been doing all sorts of vandalistic things against me ever since our divorce. This is the lowest thing yet—the lowest thing possible!"

MacArthur Copeland prevailed on Garven to sit down and to be quiet. Dr. Caesar excused Elizabeth and the psychologist. The men and women who remained behind were drained. They slumped in their seats totally unsure how to react, what to believe. Incest did not happen in good families or among educated people. They were sure of that. They felt bombarded. Now, they were not sure of anything.

Mr. Copeland was steely calm.

He said, "It is finally my turn, ladies and gentlemen. As you can see, my client is as shocked by this as everybody else. I suggest that we take some time to assemble witnesses and real evidence, not just inflammatory statements by an aggrieved wife and a person whose credentials have not been examined, taken alone. The little girl can be independently examined. For one thing, a competent pediatrician or gynecologist can ascertain if the alleged crime ever took place, in fact. The wife can be subjected to proper cross-examination. The accusations and evidence about plagiarism can be perused and verified or denied. In the meantime, in the name of common sense and common decency, let us keep this under our hats. This institution will crumble if these accusations are made public. I plead with you to adopt the same cool objectivity toward this matter as you do with your other professional responsibilities."

The hospital lawyers both spoke up in agreement. Dr. Caesar adjourned the meeting greatly pleased with his own skillful performance.

He could not quite restrain himself from throwing out a parting jab, "Not quite the pope anymore, eh, Garven?"

He drew Garven's name out into three long syllables.

Garven frosted him with a look but held his tongue.

"What on earth should I do?" Garven asked once he and Mr. Copeland were alone.

"Nothing right now. Go about your work as if none of this had ever happened. I think you need to look hard at the effect these accusations will have on your professional standing, even if...when, in the end, they all prove to be unsubstantiated. Such dark accusations take on a life of their own once they have been loosed, like the evils in Pandora's box. It is very difficult to undo what has been said here tonight," Mr. Copeland told Garven.

"But I must attack them head on. Every one of these charges must be gotten rid of if I am going to be able to do my work. Reputation is everything in medicine, and it is a fragile entity. Elizabeth knew that. This is her 'most unkindest cut'. And all of that about plagiarism—that's nothing more nor less than envy for my successes. So what if ideas abound out there, and I become the one to take advantage of them. Louis Pasteur put it well when he said, *'Dans le champs de l'observation le basard ne favorise que les espirits préparés'.* [In the area of scientific investigation, chance favors only the mind that is prepared.]

"I agree with you about Elizabeth's motives. I must say that I have never heard of such a scandalous accusation to be used as a weapon against a divorced spouse. Her hatred must know no bounds. However, on the practical level, it may well be that she has done you irreparable harm, even if the charges on a formal basis are withdrawn. You may have to face negative options such as filing suit against Elizabeth and the hospital for defamation of character and risk laundering your dirty underwear in public.

"The charges of plagiarism are another matter, one that may be addressed by evaluating tangible evidence. I am convinced of the venomous intent of those people. I sat and watched them in that room. You have real and determined enemies. I know you know that. The Zulus had a ceremony they performed just before starting a bloody raid that was called 'washing of the spears'. I think at least three of the men in that room already have their spears nice and clean."

"It sounds like my options are public spectacle or sniveling unconditional surrender," Garven said ruefully.

"Unless those in a position to do so drop their accusations, the extremes you describe will be major options in reality. I would be doing you a dis-service if I told you less, at least by my present reading of the situation. But, you hired me and my firm for a reason. I have not yet begun to fight. There is another approach, maybe two."

"I'd like to hear them, Garven said, grasping at any straw offered, and without any great hope.

"You have been around here for a long time and know all about political infighting. Make no mistake; this is political. You may have to make promises, give favors, make compromises, and call in every marker you have out there. Maybe that way you can defeat them politically. But even in victory, you will be effectively emasculated. The other tack is to consider what in lawyer argot is called, "plea bargaining'. You accept a penalty of sorts that lets you out of answering to or defending against the major charges. Make no mistake, Dr. Wilsonhulme, serious charges, even felonies, have been described. I want you to think about this 'plea-bargaining' concept," Mr. Copeland said.

They had hashed the subject as much as they could usefully do without a view of the evidence. The two men agreed to do their own background work and to get back together in a week.

David Stark called Garven that night. Garven's voice was tired and hoarse.

"Have a hard day, Garven?" asked Dr. Stark.

"No thanks, I just had one," Garven joked wanly.

"I just wanted you to know that you still had friends."

"I can't tell you how much it helps to hear it, thanks boss," Garven said.

The two men arranged to meet three days later.

Garven huddled with his three remaining friends on the neurosurgery staff. David Stark was tired, and his alcoholism had drained his will to fight any more. He was unlikely to be much of an ally; but at least, he cared enough to stand on Garven's side of the line drawn in the sand. He had no good ideas for the moment, however.

Devon told Garven of the swirling gossip that surrounded him—talk of his having a mistress, of his divorce, and of his doing battle with the powers that be in the hospital and in the university. At least, none of Elizabeth's damning accusations had surfaced.

It was the conventional wisdom around the little town that was the hospital, Devon said, that Garven's days were numbered. He had very few supporters left, the popular gossip went, Devon said.

"And I thank you for being the nucleus of that support. You are my real friends; your presence here tonight confirms that. Thanks," Garven said with feeling.

Garven very frankly told his friends about all of the accusations. They shook their heads in disbelief.

"I see myself as the lone knight tilting against an array of the forces of evil," Garven exaggerated, allowing an unwanted note of self-pity to creep in for the first time.

"Garven," said Elijah David. "It's time to look at this objectively so you can make sensible decisions. You need to try and see this from your enemies' point of view instead of your own for a change. Remember in Burton-Cagle when we made fun of Robert Burn's *To a Louse*? Garven had to smile at the irreverence he and his friends had shown to everything artsy when they were in prep school. He nodded his recollection.

"There was some wisdom in that for you, Garv. Remember:

"O wad some Power the giftie gie us
To see oursels as ithers see us!
It wad frae monie a blunder frae us,
An' foolish notion:
What airs in dress an' gait wad lea'e us.
An' ev'n devotion!"

The point was not lost on Garven. He took his friend's advice and thought long and hard about his present status, his political assets, his considerable public relations deficits. He had to see more clearly now than ever before. What he saw in considering his situation objectively, in seeing himself as others might see him, was a weakened state. It was like quicksand, the more he struggled, the deeper he was likely to sink.

Nor was the news from his attorney uplifting.

"The long and the short of it, Dr. Wilsonhulme, is that the evidence about plagiarism is backed by careful work. Your detractors are serious people. The NIH investigators have no ax to grind. What they have to say will be very telling. The hysterical accusations by Mrs. Wilsonhulme about your daughter will probably never gain enough strength to land you in court, but the publicity will kill you. That's what she's counting on.

"We have hired a private detective at your expense. He has dug up some dirt on the psychologist with the phony hyphenated name. First of all, she has been involved in six or eight of these cases, all coincidentally brought on by accusations from angry divorced wives. 'Hell hath no fury like a woman scorned', I guess. I think Dr. Pearson-Wight is impeachable. For one thing, she only has a masters. She is not 'doctor' anything. And I find it amusing that her two last names are those of her two husbands. She kept both of them, and she's divorced them both. She's what people used to call that kind a 'ball-breaker; nowadays, they call them 'fema-nazis'."

Garven laughed.

"More telling is the fact that she keeps no tapes or records. No one knows how much she is pumping into the kids' heads. Her work is suspect, at best. My colleagues in the family law field tell me that much. I don't worry over much about what will come from the long run of that accusation. It's the short haul that disturbs me. It serves as a great lever against you, make no mistake, the vultures are hovering."

Grimly, Garven had to agree.

"Isn't that obvious? It's almost impossible to defend against such a charge. It's the old 'have you stopped beating your wife' question."

"There was a very specific accusation—that of rape. We can have your daughter examined," Copeland suggested.

Garven looked sad and shook his head.

"There has to be another way. I don't want my daughter subjected to that if we can help it. Let's hold off as long as we can."

"Until you do, Elizabeth has you by the short hairs."

"What do you think I should do? From your perspective, anyway?"

"I'd like to see if we can't get them to agree to a cooling off period—three or four months like I suggested in the meeting. We all agree to maintain the status quo for that period, and we all agree to keep a lid on it. I think Dr. Caesar can get your wife, your former wife, to contain herself for that long. During that time, the hospital attorneys and I will work out a compromise of some sort. I will very gingerly look into the criminal allegations that have been made. Fortunately, none of this is in the hands of the authorities, yet."

"So, I go on with business as usual, eh?"

"Not quite. If I were you, I'd lay low. This is a good time to be inconspicuous. Aren't there some meetings to attend somewhere? Some writing to be done? Some put off vacationing to catch up with?" Copeland asked by way of suggestion.

"All of the above, I guess," Garven said. "My first inclination is to stand toe to toe and duke it out with them. Hiding is a miserable option in my book."

"This is not going to come out all in your favor. I'm afraid you're going to have to face up to that, and the sooner the better. You have to look at it from a damage control perspective, and that requires compromise. You will have to do some soul searching to decide just what is most important to you, short run and long run. And you do need to let me do my work. I am a negotiator. That's what I do best. I believe I can get you the most possible out of this, but I can't make a silk purse out of a sow's ear, as the old saying goes. To do that you have to start with a silk sow's ear," Copeland said.

CHAPTER
Twenty-Nine

Two days later, Copeland called Garven to suggest that it would be timely for him to start his absentee period now. Garven had his travel agency arrange for him and Jenny to go to the pre-AANS, AANS, and post-AANS meetings and added a week of vacation tacked on the front and the back of the three weeks of meetings. He scheduled himself in the lab for the month of May, and he accepted a long standing invitation to be guest surgeon-lecturer in London at the Queen's Square Neurological Hospital for the summer. That would be at the restful English pace, and he would not be allowed to do any actual surgery, since he would not have the necessary English license to practice. He could just walk around the hallowed halls looking scholarly.

Garven secretly relished all the side-long glances he got as he waltzed Jenny around the hallways of the neurosurgery meetings and at the obligatory cocktail parties and social events held in conjunction with the meetings. He had to admit to himself that he had never felt more virile. There was the usual sucking up to him by the residents since he was an influential senior academician with potential careers to offer. There were interminable meetings of committees, but the very boredom generated by the gatherings and the prattle of the often self-important moderators was soothing after the confrontational atmosphere he had left. From old pals there were a few envious snide comments about how nice it was for him to bring his niece along to the meetings, but it was all very polite. Even the threatened older wives were women of class, and they avoided open displays of hostility. It was not the first time these women had seen a beautiful young usurper coming on the arm of one of the older brain surgeons who had gone crazy and dumped his wife of many years during a mid-life crisis.

Jenny's best quality, and one that partly made up for her grave flaw of having youthful beauty, was that she knew when to be quiet. She was friendly but not forward, and soon enough the novelty of her newness on the scene and her striking attractiveness began to wear off. The wives did not really accept her, but they tried not to be mean about it. The men obeyed the one absolute cardinal rule of neurosurgery society—other men in the club's wives were sacrosanct. Every man Garven and Jenny met was the picture of propriety with her.

London was nothing more than he had anticipated. He was bored with the proper English pace after a few weeks. He found himself longing for the fast-pace action of Southern California. Garven liked the power he had in his own institution and felt frustrated and bored at Queen's Square for all of its prestige in the neurological world. There was not much news coming from Los Angeles. Copeland kept him up to date on the negotiations which seemed interminable from Garven's vantage point thousands of miles away. His attorney continually warned him that he would have to be ready for compromise. Devon stopped writing in mid-July. He begged off, citing the press of work with the service being a man short. He was now the de facto acting chief and had a pile of administrative duties as well.

The lectures to bright and curious students were the highlight of Garven's stay. He was respected, and his advice was sought with regularity. He made a full lecture series with slides and diagrams and bibliographic citations. He was pleased to see an increasing attendance at his lectures. He needed a small success. Most of the students could be seen taking careful notes. It was not the life for Garven, however. He had to get back to where the action was. He decided to return to Los Angeles two weeks early.

His attorney, MacArthur Copeland, sent Garven one more admonition about compromising along with the welcome news that it looked like things had been worked out. Garven's mood lightened considerably as he set out for home on the thirteenth of August.

CHAPTER
Thirty

After clearing customs at LAX, Garven collected his luggage and caught a cab back to his apartment. On the way, he read the *Times* and realized that one of the things he liked about his own country was how vibrant and exciting it was. The newspaper bristled with news and with action in contrast to the insipid British newspapers. In England he had seen small scandals blown out of proportion, especially if they involved the royals; then the scandal stayed in the front of the paper for days on end. Garven found that as boring as stories about movie celebrities in the LA papers.

The *LA Times* carried editorials that day favoring the admission of the People's Republic of China to the United Nations, an opinion that made Garven angry, although he could not really say that it surprised him, since the UN was nothing more than a communist front, in his opinion. Garven liked it better when Red China did not exist, at least so far as the U.S. government was concerned. "Red China does not exist", the wags used to say at Stanford. The front pages were full of flag burnings, bra burnings, a picture of U.C. San Francisco students with their "Death to Corporations" placards, and of Americans in Helsinki participating in the SALT talks. The paper made Garven perplexed, confused, sad, angry, and made him laugh. He knew that he was back in America.

Jenny was in Vermont on a modeling assignment, a "photo shoot", as she so ungrammatically put it. She had flown out of Heathrow a week before him. The apartment was empty and seemed sterile, unlike his former Beverly Hills home that had been so filled with the two children and their half-drunk mother. He missed the children and determined to see them that day if at all possible. First, though, he called MacArthur Copeland.

"Whitney, Jones, Copeland, and Closs," the secretary said with practiced efficiency. "How may I direct your call?"

"To MacArthur Copeland," Garven said.

"I'm sorry, sir. He is out of town. May I leave a message? Is there anyone else who can help you?"

"Just tell him that Garven Wilsonhulme is back in the country and have him call me at his first convenience."

"Happy to, Mr. Wilsonhulme," she said.

It always grated on Garven a little to be called "mister."

He made a half-hearted attempt to deal with the stacks of mail that the building manager had been keeping for him. Aside from the usual annoying bills and junk mail, there were two hate letters from Elizabeth that he threw into the junk mail pile as soon as he recognized that he was looking at the usual diatribes. He made himself some lunch, a can of Spaghetti-Os and a piece of cheese from which he had to remove spots of mold. He told himself that he could not forget to do some grocery shopping.

Garven put on his best dark blue suit, white shirt, and red "power" tie, and drove into Central LA to the hospital. As he passed through the half deserted streets on the approach to the sprawling medical center, he observed to himself how little had changed since the first time he had driven those lonesome streets. The same lonely old men in their grey-white tank top underwear shirts leaned out of second story windows staring blankly at the world as it passed them by.

A little alarm bell went off in his head when he found his private parking place occupied. He recognized the car but could not immediately associate an owner with it. He purposely walked by the space and saw that the painted name designator on the tire stop had been blackened over, presumably by the grounds crew who were repainting and upgrading the parking lot. He felt a little foolish and paranoid.

Two seconds after he was back in the welter of human activity and misery that was UCOMH, Garven felt oddly at home, as if he had never left. Despite all rationality, Garven rather liked the place for all its noise, dirt, and manifest ignorance and suffering. He felt that he was a part of it and that he belonged, a feeling that he did not quite have anywhere else.

A little boy ran away from his mother and collided with Garven's legs as he crossed to the bank of elevators.

The boy's harried mother said, "Scuse my little boy, mistah. He ain't got no behavior."

"It's okay," Garven said, "I have kids, too."

She was relieved not to have someone else on her case that day.

He went to the ward first. Nothing had changed. There were people walking around in large head bandages, hemiplegics—the whole gamut of the blind, crippled, and crazy; a man had a fit as Garven walked down the aisle between the rows of beds. Garven recalled his aversion to the hospital's food when he saw an older woman, posey-belted into the ward's adult high chair, holding a bowl of gray-green soup.

He smiled indulgently at the woman's empty expressionless face, and asked, indicating her bowl, "What are we having for lunch today?"

She looked dully at him and answered like an automaton, "It's puke," she said.

Garven could not help himself. He inspected the bowl more closely. It *was* puke. He was glad he had asked. He moved more briskly up the aisle and curbed any further curiosity and questions.

The nurses were sharing a joke when Garven came up to the charting desk.

"Hi, Dr. Wilsonhulme," the charge nurse called to him as he drew close.

"Hi, Angela, glad to see you."

"Welcome home."

"Thanks. Anything up?"

She laughed.

"Not really. You need to see one thing, though. Should liven up your day."

Garven had been educated to be suspicious of things that would 'liven up his day'.

He said, "I'm rested up; show me your worst."

Angela smiled broadly.

"Come with me," she said.

Garven followed her back down the aisle. The other nurses tagged along.

In the private room segment of the ward, they ran into a doctor in a crisp lab coat carrying a stethoscope and a harried expression. There was something odd about the man, something about his movements and a rather vacant look on his face. Garven wrote that off to the probability that he was just a neurology resident.

Angela stopped. Garven and the other nurses stopped. Garven looked at the charge nurse quizzically. She was laughing, and the rest of the nurses seemed to be in on the joke.

"What?" asked Garven, more leery of whatever was afoot than before.

"Just watch for a few minutes," Angela directed.

Garven watched the only thing there was to watch, the neurology resident.

The young doctor went hurriedly from room to room. In each room, Garven could hear laughter. He raised a questioning eyebrow at Angela.

She said, "Listen what is said in the next room."

Garven was intrigued.

He and Angela pressed close to the door and heard the doctor asking the patient, a retired army general, "What's your name? Tell me the Pythagorean Theorem."

After a short pause, punctuated by chuckles from the patient, the doctor could be heard tapping his stethoscope on the metal bed frame impatiently.

"Now Tommy, what's your name? Tell me the Pythagorean Theorem. Repeat after me: 'My doctor's name is Dr. Wilsonhulme.'"

Garven understood immediately and perfectly what was going on. He had not been a house staff officer at UCOMH for six years for nothing. He broke into a completely cathartic laugh. He really was back home. When the white coated doctor came out of the room, Angela had one of the other nurses take him back to his bed on the ward.

"He's a dement from a murder-cycle accident," she said. "Dr. Radcliffe, the first year, got him the coat, and even had his name embroidered on it. We got him the stethoscope. He makes rounds with us then spends the rest of the day making rounds on his own. He's harmless, and the people who can think, like the general, are nice to him. They get a kick out of him."

Garven laughed some more.

"You know, Dr. Wilsonhulme, Dr. Radcliffe reminds me of someone I once knew on this ward a few years ago."

Garven could not imagine whom she was talking about.

"You know the guy, the one that secretly told the patients to 'repeat after me; my doctor's name is...whatever that poor retardo anesthesiologist's name was."

Garven still had a look of complete innocence and ignorance.

"The same guy that used to put the patient's trays at the end of the hall and go around and tell the patients that this was the 'Darwinian Test' - 'Anyone who could make it to the lunch trays would be a keeper. The rest would have to be discharged to the rehab'."

Garven could not keep a straight face. He and Angela laughed until they were tired.

"Can't have any secrets around here. Like that obnoxious comedian says, 'I don't get no respect'. I am thinking that you might really like your new job in the laundry, Angela. Just keep it up."

"The truth hurts," she said.

"*Mea culpa*," he said, "*mea culpa, mea maxima culpa.*"

It was good to back home with his real friends.

Dr. Radcliffe buzzed through the ward to do a little scut work chore as Garven was about to leave.

"How are things going, Dan?" he asked the resident.

"Fine, Sir. Couldn't be better. In fact, I'm off to do the best thing there is," Dr. Radcliffe answered.

He had a boyish smile.

"Operate?" asked Garven knowingly.

"Yep. The only thing that's better than sex or watermelon. I have to rush. Did you need me for something?"

"No, go ahead, make a great save. I'll see you at ward rounds tonight," Garven said.

He almost envied the young resident for his freshness and enthusiasm as he rushed off to do his purposeful work.

Garven boarded the elevator. There was a very well endowed young woman, an obvious hippie, and a couple of older Negro women on with him. The young woman vaguely reminded him of Jenny, but a more robust and less sophisticated rendering of her well tabernacled form. He responded to the girl by absentmindedly staring at her. She seemed not to notice at first. Then she suddenly turned and looked at him frankly. He looked away, embarrassed. "This what you're looking at, Doc?" she taunted.

Then she whipped up the front of the beaded vest that covered her straining front and exposed her breasts briefly as they bounced free of their restraints. Garven took a large step back away from her and blushed scarlet. The two older women gasped audibly and reproachfully. Garven was glad to get off the elevator at the next floor. He laughed at himself and UCOMH all the way to his office door.

When he stepped up to turn the knob to the office door, Garven experienced a momentarily unbalancing feeling of *jamais vu*, the opposite of *déjà vu*. He felt disturbingly unfamiliar in a place that was as customary to him as his own home. He took a step back and looked up and down the hall to count doors. He presumed that he had been preoccupied and had turned in at the wrong door. The bright gold lettering on the glass of the door read: DEVON UPSHIRE, CHIEF OF NEUROSURGERY.

Garven required almost a full minute to absorb the obvious as it was presented to him on the door of his office. His former office. A rush of anger coursed through him heating up his arteries. He felt betrayed, murderous. His fists clenched and unclenched, and he fought for self-control. He weighed his options at computer speed. He knew that he would be better off to walk away right then and to find out the details of what was going on. He should call MacArthur Copeland. He could not walk away; his legs would not obey his brain's pleading command. He opened the door and strode over to where his secretary was sitting. She looked at him in befuddlement and transparent discomfort.

"Uh, Dr. Wilsonhulme, how nice to see you," she stammered.

It sounded as feeble to her as it did to him.

"So, I take it that you have a new boss, Kerstin," Garven asked with an unmistakable note of demand in his voice.

"Well, yes, Sir...I presumed...uh, at least, I thought...when Dr. Upshire was made chairman...I, uh, naturally presumed..."

She was having difficulty working this out.

"That I would be the first to know?"

"Well, yes, something like that. I'm sorry. This is so awkward," the secretary said.

"Kerstin, you've been around here long enough to know how things are done. You were David Stark's secretary first, then Dr. Chou's, if I recall correctly," Garven said, his words and face angry, as if this were somehow her fault, as if she were an accessory after the fact.

He regretted his manner as soon as he said it.

"Sorry. I shouldn't take it out on you. It's just that it is something of a shock."

She relaxed a little and looked sympathetic.

"No, actually, I started with Dr. Sundquist, the one before Dr. Stark. You know, he was away to a meeting when Dr. Stark replaced him," the elderly secretary said working her brow as she sought the memory.

"I detect something of a pattern," Garven said. "Again, I'm sorry, Miss Dutchen. Is Dr. Upshire in?"

"No offense taken. I understand; and no, he isn't here, I'm afraid. He won't be back until day after tomorrow."

"Hey, we have time to put Dr. Shapiro into his office and to get the lettering changed on the door, if we get right to it. You probably know just who to call," Garven said with petulant humor.

Like a child who has just had its bottom patted, Kerstin Dutchen looked into Garven's face to see if he was being angry or if he was making a little joke. She was relieved to see that it was more the latter than the former, and she managed a small laugh.

Garven left. He steeled himself not to show his inner turmoil as he walked down the back stairs hoping not to meet anyone he knew. His world had caved in, and he was afraid that he might look as if he were staggering. He was no longer the pope. The vultures had won. It was only in his mind, but the whirling of his thoughts was vertiginous. He thought about calling Elijah David but decided against it. He needed to talk to Copeland at first.

CHAPTER
Thirty-One

H e drove to Beverly Hills like a homing pigeon, walked up to the front door of his house, his former home, and knocked. It nettled to have to knock.

Maria-Theresa answered the door, "*Muy buenas dias, Señor Doctor!*" she said with authentic enthusiasm and affection.

"Glad to see you, Maria-Theresa. Are the kids home?"

"Oh, jess, Señor. They weel be so *alegre* to see you! I weel get them!"

Garven knew that the maid must have had instructions not to let him into the house; so, he waited on the porch to keep her from having a problem with Elizabeth. He looked around to make sure that his former wife did not run out from underneath the porch and bite his leg. He could hear the raucous joyful voices of his two children rushing pell-mell down the curved staircase rattling the balustrade. Maria-Theresa shouted belated cautionary admonishments behind them. Susan and Peter Arthur rushed into his arms.

"Daddy, are you coming back? Are you going to stay?" bubbled Susan.

PA said, "Don't be silly, Suse, Daddy can't stay, here. They're divorced."

It hurt to see his son so adjusted to the abnormal world of having divorced parents. Half of PA's friends were in the same condition; so, Garven knew it was not as traumatic for the boy as Garven might have imagined.

"I will be taking the kids to the beach, Maria-Theresa. You can tell Missus Elizabeth that. Don't know when we'll be back," Garven said above the din of the excited children.

"Oh, Hi don' know, *Señor* Doctor..." her voice trailed off, worried. "The keeds... I yam suppos' to keep them *aqui*."

"It's okay, Maria-Theresa. I have visitation rights, too, you know."

She guessed so and made no further protest. She feared for her job when Mrs. Elizabeth got back. She wished that those two were Catholics; so, they couldn't be having this divorce thing.

Garven kept the children for the entire weekend. They all played at the beach and slept on couches and on the floor at his apartment as if it were a slumber party. The only negative note for the entire three days came when Garven called Elizabeth to tell her where the kids were and when he planned to bring them back to her.

The frolic with his children was rejuvenating after the shock of seeing that his name had been removed from his old office door. First thing Monday morning, he called MacArthur Copeland's office again. This time, the secretary told him to plan to come to Mr. Copeland's office at ten.

He was there on the dot.

"Have a seat. I take it you just got back," Copeland said as soon as he ushered Garven into his private office and closed the door behind them.

"I have been here for three days," Garven said.

"I hope you had a good stay in Britain. You'll have to tell me all about it," Mr. Copeland said looking as if he had all of the time in the world to chat.

"Later, MacArthur. I have been to the hospital. I have seen my office—what used to by my office. My stuff has been moved to the broom closet. Why don't you just fill me in on the missing details. I'll try not to interrupt."

Mr. Copeland coughed a couple of times.

"Yes," he said, "Well, that would be best. A lot has transpired in the last couple of weeks. I had nowhere to get hold of you, as you recall."

Garven nodded his acknowledgment.

Copeland went on.

"We finalized the understanding with the hospital. There is no written contract, nothing to sign; there is only a gentlemen's agreement. I thought that best since it removes any taint of the record of the accusations."

"Which ones are the 'gentlemen'?" Garven asked caustically.

Mr. Copeland shrugged it off.

"Let me lay out the terms of the agreement. First, between you, the hospital, and the university. You step down as chairman of the department, but stay on as a full-salaried and tenured professor; and there is no record kept of any accusations from anyone. You agree not to interfere with the department's activities, to give up all of your committee positions, and, in general, to take a low profile. If you wish, you will be permitted to retire early at age sixty, with seventy-two percent of the pension that you would get if you elected to stay on to age sixty-five."

He paused to let Garven digest the unpalatable terms.

Garven said nothing.

Copeland continued, "They have been given a decree by the National Institutes of Health, and that organization is also desirous of hushing this whole affair up. You are not to do any more research, even clinical. You quietly drop out of your NIH position without raising a stink. If you publish or make it difficult for them to get you off their committee, the NIH will turn over the three accusatory letters and all evidence to the major neurosurgical societies, to the police, and to the news media. They are determined to play hardball all the way and won't budge a nanometer on any of their demands."

"A nice bit of blackmail," Garven said morosely.

He indicated his readiness to hear more of the unwelcome news. Might as well get it over with.

"That covers the university and the NIH. Now for the hospital: you can take call and see patients from the indigent service, the 'War Zone', I think everyone around there terms it. You may see a limited number of private patients, but you may not do seizure surgery or have anything to do with subarachnoid hemorrhage patients. I have to tell you, the professors with the apparent clout seemed to be very confident that there would not be many private consults coming your way."

"So, I'm to be the UCOMH leper, eh? Do I get an office, or do I work out of my present broom closet?" Garven asked, his sarcasm revealing his deep anger.

"Something like that. It was a hard fight to get these terms, believe me. At first, Caesar, Kowalski, and Rosenthal would consider nothing less than a public *auto de fe*. Anyhow, you are now in the office that Dr. Shapiro occupied when he first arrived and will share a secretary with him."

"Whatever did Elijah David do to deserve being banished to outer darkness with 'Garven, the Leper'?"

Copeland shrugged.

Garven did not have to have anyone draw him a diagram. The other side was wreaking such devastation on Garven's career that had not been seen since the Romans vanquished the Carthaginians in the third Punic war in 146 A.D. They were making the arrangement humiliating enough that he would have no face-saving choice but to resign. It made him coldly furious.

"Go on," he said, resignedly.

"I know you're angry and upset, Dr. Wilsonhulme. Let me assure you that all of the other options offered during your absence were worse. They seem to be confident that they have built up a very serious case against you. While you might possibly win in the courts, it would be a close thing; and it would take years. If you were to lose, you would probably lose your license to practice at all. If you were to launch a civil suit, they would be within their rights to prevent you from practicing in the hospital for the duration of the suit. This is California. They can drag a case like this out for so long that you will be withered and gray before it was ever heard. That's the rub in a nutshell."

Garven shook his head in loathing.

"Now that I'm emasculated by taking their deal, what about my sweet wife? Is there an agreement with her? Let me guess, she was not entirely independent of the rest of those jackals."

"There is. And it is not altogether in your favor, either, I'm afraid."

Garven could not even feign surprise at that revelation.

"Stick it to me," he said.

"No joint custody. She gets full and final custody, and the children do not get to express their preferences. You do get visiting rights,"

Garven moved his hand in a sarcastic rendition of waving a "Yea!" flag.

"Your ex and her battle-ax friend fought me to make those visits supervised ones in view of the allegations of sexual abuse. I finally got Mrs. Wilsonhulme away from Dr. Dyke long enough to get a more reasonable deal. She agreed to keep any and all charges of child molestation secret in perpetuity, as long as you 'shut up', her words, about her 'alleged' drug and alcohol use and about her psychiatric hospitalization."

"That's one up for her, but okay, I guess," Garven said.

"You get to visit on Wednesdays. Elizabeth will be out of the house. The kids have to stay at home. That's part of the deal, and because of their home work. You do not get to enter the house. You can only be with Susan and Peter Arthur on the grounds. You do get to keep them every other weekend and every other summer for a month. You may not take them out of the state."

"What about Elizabeth? Does she get to take them wherever she wants?"

"She has to inform you; but otherwise, she has unrestricted custody, access, and travel rights, and parental privilege."

"Now, that sounds fair," Garven groused.

"Nothing's fair in love and war, and this involves both," Copeland said. "There is something I should add. She could move and take the children with her. If you then wanted to be with them, you would have to go to the state where she chose to reside. You would not be able to take them out of that state. It is possible, in the worst case scenario, that the new state, say Arizona, would impose even further impediments."

Garven had to take a minute or two to absorb all of that.

"That's about it," Copeland concluded.

"I should hope so," Garven said dejectedly. "How long do I have to think about this?"

"The university and hospital committees meet during the third week in September. They have agreed to keep this matter open until then and no longer. They want this to be decided before the new students come in. And, I forgot to mention an important proviso. You have to meet them in person in the Executive Committee on the seventh. They want to make sure there is no possibility of misunderstanding the terms of the deal."

"And to rub my nose in it. They can hardly wait to watch me twist in the wind on the end of the rope they made for me," Garven said.

"I'm afraid there's a lot of truth in that. Your three special pals want to see you sweat. They would give just about anything if you would give them a cry. It would be a genuine disappointment for them and a diminished victory for them if you are civil, calm, and brief."

Garven got the message.

"MacArthur, you can count on me. I will as docile as a lamb being led to the slaughter. I will take a few days to sort all of this out and to make my decision. I presume that you will be in attendance on the seventeenth?"

"Absolutely."

"Well, until then," Garven said and eased himself out of Copeland's comfortable chair.

CHAPTER
Thirty-Two

At two o'clock the same day, Garven walked into the office of the chairman of the department of neurosurgery, past Kerstin Duchen who only had time to gasp, "Dr. Wilsonhulme, please..." and through the door of the private office.

Devon Upshire was at his desk facing a man in a three piece suit even though it was a scorchingly hot day. Garven recognized the man as one of the legions of assistant administrators of the hospital. Garven pushed a pile of papers off a chair and plopped himself down.

"Ah, yes, Dr. Wilsonhulme, come right in, take a seat. I'm not busy," Devon said, with irony.

"Thank you, Dr. Upshire, don't mind if I do," Garven said with exaggerated affability as if he had been invited by the duchess.

"Now, see here, Dr. Wilsonhulme," said the assistant administrator, "this is a scheduled and official hospital meeting. You have no right..."

Garven's masseter muscles clenched. His eyelids narrowed, and he looked at the young man with an implicit physical threat so strong that the man recoiled and could not tolerate the gaze. The assistant administrator had heard about this rude interloper, that he was capable of just about anything.

"Get lost, pipsqueak," Garven said in a quiet opprobrious voice.

The hospital functionary looked to Devon for help. Devon shook his head.

"Let's discuss this matter another day, Mr. Abraham. My secretary will get with yours. I apologize for Dr. Wilsonhulme's egregious behavior. He doesn't know any better; he's a neurosurgeon. But I had better take care of this business now."

The assistant administrator left in a huff.

"Nice touch, Garven," Devon said when the door closed.

"Well, old friend, old confidant, old buddy," Garven said and looked daggers at Devon.

What went unsaid was, "This had better be good."

"You have been right here in my exact position, Garven. Don't get holier than thou with me. You know how the game is played. If you can't run with the big dogs you better not come down off the porch. The faculty set up a search committee; they selected me. If I had refused, they would have found someone else. You were dead the day you left your office for Europe. It just took you the rest of the summer to start to stink. It was none of my doing," Devon said unemotionally.

It was an obviously rehearsed speech.

"And you fought them tooth and toenail, right? You defended me right up to the bitter end. They had to drag you into this office kicking and screaming, didn't they old confidant, old buddy, old friend?" snarled Garven as insultingly as possible.

"It was out of my hands. I don't know what they had on you, but it must have been powerful jou-jou. They knew that you would not be able to fight them."

"Happened on the other shift, eh, my friend?" Garven said, giving Devon none of the benefit of the doubt.

"Have it anyway you want, Garven. However it happened, I am now the chief, in fact, and officially. You are the professor of neurosurgery, and that ain't chopped liver. And we have to find a way to accommodate."

Garven's demeanor suddenly changed. He became quiet, waiting for all traces of anger and resentment to clear from his face, willing his fight tense body to relax. He even managed a smile.

"You betrayed me, Devon."

He was friendly; it was almost as if he were conceding a tennis match.

"I should have watched my back, only friends can stab you in the back. You win. You get all the marbles. It's the game we play in the great ivory towers of academe. I wish you luck. Uneasy sits the crown on the new king's head."

"Are you going to fight me or try to undermine me?" Devon asked seriously.

"Not in the least way, Devon. Your status here will suffer no threat from me. You don't have to watch your back around here at all so far as I am involved. That is something you can take to the bank."

"So, we can let bygones be bygones, old buddy?" asked Devon hopefully. Garven nodded.

"No grudges, no ill will?"

"I don't know that I would go that far, Devon. But you can be completely at rest about one thing, I will not try to take your job back, and I won't help anyone else to do it, either."

Garven smiled, got up, and left. It was only after Garven closed the door that Devon realized that they had not shaken hands. He did not like the implication of that minor omission. Garven, he knew, had a long memory.

There was considerable apprehension in the air at the September seventeenth faculty meeting. Despite MacArthur Copeland's assurances that Garven would behave himself, the members were jittery. They were all seated when Garven entered. He nodded an affable greeting to each one of the men and women in the room and took his seat. Copeland was glad to see that his client looked calm and at ease. He was not completely sure about how Garven was going to act himself, and he was totally uninformed about the neurosurgeon's decision. This round of diplomatic courtesies was a good beginning, at least; hopefully a harbinger for the rest of the evening.

Horst Caesar did not have the fire in his eyes that he had had on the previous occasion. He felt himself to be the winner; and more, he had accomplished a manifest bit of good. He could afford to be courteous, even to appear magnanimous. He did not need to gloat; he was too much of a gentleman for that, he liked to say.

Caesar called the meeting to order, "Colleagues, ladies and gentlemen, we have placed Dr. Wilsonhulme as first item on the agenda for his convenience. I believe the details of an agreement have been worked out amicably by the good offices of the hospital attorneys and Dr. Wilsonhulme's counsel."

Each of the lawyers nodded in the affirmative.

"Well, then, all that is left to do is to read the details of the agreement and to have each side acknowledge its acceptance. I have to say, that, on his part, Dr. Wilsonhulme as been most cooperative. I understand that many of the terms of our agreement have already been put into effect. Thank you Dr. Wilsonhulme," Caesar said.

Garven seethed inwardly at the patent condescension but kept his face rigidly agreeable.

"Well, then, Dr. Kowalski, would you read the entire agreement, please?"

The Veteran's Administration Hospital anesthesiologist read the document carefully, enunciating clearly. There was no mistaking anything he read.

"Is that your understanding of the arrangement, Mr. Copeland?"

"Yes."

"And yours, Dr. Wilsonhulme?"

"Yes."

"And members, any questions? Any complaints?"

The members all had copies of the agreement before them. No one demurred.

"I will speak for the university—I have the verbal clearance to do so from the board of regents—and for the faculty," said Dr. Caesar with an air of pontifical authority and finality. "We accept the terms and will live by them. This is, of necessity, a verbal contract; but we are ladies and gentlemen here. We consider it to be a covenant, a binding contract."

There was a unanimity of head nods.

"Mr. Copeland?"

"We will abide by the agreement."

"Dr. Wilsonhulme?"

Garven said, "Yes."

"It is done," said Caesar and settled back in his chair to relax fully for the first time that night.

Garven reached into his suit jacket pocket and extracted an envelope. He stood and walked over to Dr. Caesar and handed it to him without speaking. The committee chairman looked at Garven and then at the envelope as being out of synchrony with the well-timed and well conducted meeting with its conclusion in a smooth agreement. He opened the envelope and removed the single page inside. It was a photocopy, brief and to the point:

Regents
University of California

Gentlemen:
Effective today, September 17, 1971, I resign my chairmanship of the department of neurosurgery at the University of
California Osterlund Memorial Hospital in Los Angeles. I
resign my position as professor of neurosurgery including
all rights, privileges, and tenure. I resign from the physician
staff of UCOMH and surrender my privileges of admission,
surgery, and performance of diagnostic procedures.

This is a voluntary decision of my own and is not related to any disciplinary action or censorship.

Respectfully,
Garven C. Wilsonhulme, MD, FACS

Dr. Caesar stared at the terse document before him for a full thirty seconds. He passed to his co-victors, Drs. Kowalski and Rosenthal. They looked it over with undisguised elation. It was more than a victory; it was an annihilation. They could not keep smirking grins from their faces as they passed the paper on down the line. For several weeks they had been privately referring to themselves as "The Three Vultures" and reveled in how sweet it was to be able to pick at the erstwhile pope's last vestiges of flesh. It was all the sweeter, that the grand old man was leaving not with a bang, but a whimper. Still, it seemed so out of character.

"I trust that the regents will accept this resignation as a matter of course. On behalf of the faculty, the staff, and the administration, we accept it as well. It is probably for the best, Dr. Wilsonhulme, for everyone concerned," said Dr. Caesar, still a little overcome with the new development. "Have you anything to add, Dr. Wilsonhulme? Anyone?"

His questions were asked so perfunctorily that Dr. Caesar did not really look to see if anyone did have anything to say.

"Then consider it done," he said. "Congratulations. This was kept in-house. We policed our own, contrary to what our dissenters, the Trial Lawyers Association, would have you believe," Dr. Caesar concluded.

Garven and his attorney stood up to leave. He saw Drs. Caesar, Kowalski, and Rosenthal exchanging grins and winks. In those expressions he saw his career being flushed away. His eyes fixed on the architects of his ruin. Mr. Copeland started to draw him away.

"Good-bye, Garven," called Howard Rosenthal as Garven started to exit.

The tone was gloating and mocking, that of an ungracious unconditional victor.

Garven turned back and looked into the eyes of Horst Caesar, then Henry Kowalski, then Howard Rosenthal, each individually in his turn.

He caught their attention with, "Gentlemen."

All eyes or the men and women remaining in the room turned towards him. He looked only at the three men still seated together at the head of the table.

He spoke softly, "I will ruin you, gentlemen."

He turned again and left the room.

CHAPTER
Thirty-Three

G arven C. Wilsonhulme, MD, FACS, PC, sat in his office catching up on the mounds of paper in the in-box generated by his busy and successful private practice of neurosurgery. He picked up yesterday's newspaper and speed-read through the *Times* article headlined, "COMMISSION QUESTIONS CIA ON DOMESTIC ACTIVITIES." He was tired. In the four years since he had left his professorship and entered practice with four other neurosurgeons in Los Angeles he had expected to feel less harassed and to be in a simpler, less hostile environment than the one he had left at the medical school. That had not proved to be the case.

He rubbed his sore eyes. He had been up all night taking care of an indigent. Even that had not changed. Rivalries and jealously guarded lines of patient referral, litigious patients, avaricious lawyers, and uncooperative hospital administrators made the social and political arena of private practice no better than the fang and claw jungle of academia. The money was better; the prestige on a local level was better in his private practice. On a national level his standing had evaporated. He had to admit that, at times, he missed the heady atmosphere of national and international committee involvement, and the accolades of his contemporaries for his research. At other times, though, he wondered why he had ever thought it mattered. After all, he was making nearly three times the money he had during his tenure in academia. He had no money worries as a result of his partial pension from the University of California, his own lucrative investment portfolio, and, yes, the three-quarters of a billion dollars he had netted from his divorce settlement with the richest woman in California.

Garven was not inclined to look backwards. He was not nostalgic, just making a pragmatic comparison between his two careers. The *Times* article told about President Ford's appointment of an investigative body to evaluate whether or not the CIA had overstepped its charter by engaging in domestic intelligence operations. There was evidence that the CIA had unlawfully maintained surveillance on 300,000 people and organizations. The evidence was very suggestive that former President Nixon had used the organization against his political enemies. Garven understood what had prompted Nixon; he empathized with the man for having been forced to resign.

He could not concentrate on the paper and dropped it into the waste bin beside his desk. He had an hour to kill before going over to St. Patricia's Hospital to start his day's work of cracking backs. It was unexciting, but it was a living.

After his night up taking care of the woman with the acute ruptured disc and progressive leg weakness, Garven had made rounds at five o'clock in the morning. The nurses and his patients all thought he had taken leave of his senses, but he was already up; so, he made use of the time. Now he tried to nap during the hour he had left, but he could not get to sleep. He stood up and walked over to the mirror in the mini-bathroom in his office. He took a good long look at himself. The hour to wait gave him time for a self-assessment.

Garven did not particularly like what he saw: forty-four years old and looking every day of it—paunchy, temples beginning to gray, something of a prison pallor from too much time in the OR and clinic and not enough time at the beach, on the golf course, or in the mountains. There was a quality to his look that was like many of his colleagues, not easily defined, somewhere between anxious and bored; everyone knew the correct phrase—"burned-out." His brow was permanently lined from the stress about confrontations every time he sucked in a breath and went to meet a patient or a family member. He found it hard to remember a pleasant interchange; it seemed as if everyone he encountered professionally had a chip on his or her shoulder, an antagonistic question, a criticism, implicit or explicit, a disbelieving expression, or was threatening to sue; even children had learned the attitudes and the quasi-legal jargon. The bags under his eyes looked as if they had been packed for a long trip.

Garven looked candidly at what he had become and where he was headed. He had done all of the operations known to neurosurgery, most, many times.

Chapter Thirty-Three

They all seemed routine now, like work. He had seen the successes and cures, the complications and failures, the seemingly endless stream of oddballs, both on the side of the patients and among his colleagues. He was no longer certain that he could always tell the inmates from the keepers. In the final analysis he had no great interest in his work. It was no longer fun like it had been in the days of his impoverished residency. That was it in a nutshell. The fun of medical practice had gone.

Garven made a handsome living from neurosurgery, and he knew that he could not complain. He took in $700,000 before taxes last year added to the incredible amount of income from his investments and from the interest bearing accounts. The money meant very little to him since he had almost no time to spend it. He was his own boss and found himself to be a hard task-master. The vast amount of money he had gotten from Elizabeth alone had made him independent; he could have lived very well if he had not worked another day after his divorce from his first wife.

His social balance sheet left room for improvement as well as did his physical inventory, he had to admit. On the plus side, he had been able to hire a private detective to document his former wife, Elizabeth's, slide back into alcoholism and Valium addiction. He arranged for the director of the private school attended by his children, Peter Arthur and Susan, to receive incriminating photographs and information without himself being known to be involved. The director had done her duty and had filed a report to the juvenile authorities. The authorities had contacted Garven to assume tempo-rary guardianship of the two children while they carried out an investigation of Elizabeth. When Elizabeth entered the Betty Ford Rehab Center, Garven sought and was awarded full legal custody of the children. The shoe was on the other foot. Now Elizabeth had to come, hat in hand, to her visitations with the children, and they had to be supervised by a dour old caseworker. She had aged twenty years in the last five.

For Garven, it turned out to be something of a Pyrrhic victory. He had bested the woman he hated in a very telling way and had rendered her *hors de combat* for future efforts at getting back the children. He had snatched old Fletcher's fortune. Once he was in control of the children, he had taken his daughter, Susan, to the chief of pediatrics at UCOMH for a complete examination and had exacted from him a statement that Susan had never had sex, let alone rape, and her hymen was perfectly intact. The lie that he had sexually molested his daughter would never resurface in the face of such over-whelming evidence that the whole story was a fabrication. But now, he was saddled with them. He almost felt like it was a trick, a trap into which he had fallen, all the more bothersome because it was one he had set himself. There were rides to school functions, soccer games that took up every free Saturday, church youth activities that wasted every free Sunday. He had all but given up his personal social life.

Even after five years, Elizabeth still got in her foolish little digs, a punctured tire or scratched paint job, a poison pen letter to Garven himself or to the state medical society, and limitless servings of vitriol for the children when they visited her. She was consumed with hatred and malignancy towards Garven, and the children did not like to hear it at first and found their visits with their mother unpleasant, and eventually they refused to go with her at all.

CHAPTER
Thirty-Four

Garven's marriage to Jennifer Lakewood (She had insisted on keeping her own last name) had been a victim of the trap, and that was the greatest debit in his social ledger, at least the most recent serious casualty. She had soon tired of her initial pride of being, "the wife of the brain surgeon" and of the novelty of having children around. It was no life, so far as she was concerned. The two of them seldom went out, and as often as not, when they did, he had to drag along his two irksome teenage children. The two spoiled brats had never taken to her for some reason despite all her efforts to be friendly, nor she to them as a consequence. Jenny did not like the fact that Garven had torn loyalties, and was unwilling to see things from her perspective. She had had enough of seeing things from his viewpoint. It was a boring outlook; she had come to realize.

Jenny liked the fast life of New York and Paris that her modeling career provided. She had landed two bit parts in movies and walk-ons on TV. She had hopes and aspirations. Garven could not or would not make the effort to go out and meet the glitterati who could further her fledgling career. She became bored with Garven and his stodgy life and attitudes. He was a political Neanderthal and a social slug. The reality of marriage to the famous brain surgeon had not been nearly as much fun as the clandestine meetings and hurried entanglements of their sneaky backstreet courtship when he was the pope. Finally, she opted out.

When Jenny's lawyer served intent-to-divorce papers on Garven, Jenny learned about a side of her husband that she had only glimpsed previously.

He was an implacable unrelenting foe; devious, secretive, and even mean. He locked her out of the house, instead of the other way around as it was supposed to be. He charged her with desertion, citing her many modeling assignments abroad from their home. Finally, he had the audacity to charge her with adultery—Garven Wilsonhulme, who had more scalps on his belt than a tribe of Comanches. The trouble for Jenny was that Garven had photographic proof, obtained by one of his private eyes.

In the end she went away with no more than what she had come in with. There was a prenuptial agreement that made divorcement simple and painless for Garven, and simple and unprofitable for Jenny. His lawyer successfully argued that she was wholly independent, emotionally and financially, and should have no alimony or other support. The houses and cars were all in Garven's name because he had paid for them. In a moment of weakness Garven allowed her to have the 1973 BMW, while he kept the 1970 Opel GT that cost him $3,398. Other than that she left the marriage with nothing to show for the nearly five years she put into it. She considered herself lucky not to have to contribute to the support of his children after his lawyer got done with her.

The only other major item in his personal social column could arguably be placed in either the credit or the debit side of the ledger depending on the point of view one chose to take. Garven had established a liaison of sorts—it would be an exaggeration to call it a real affair—with a woman he had met in the course of his practice. Her mother had had a stroke on a night when Garven was on call for the group. The Los Angeles Neurosciences Medical Group included both neurologists and neurosurgeons and also a psychologist. Helene Eamon had been distraught over her mother's illness. It was clear from the onset that the matriarch of the large family was going to die. It was only a matter of time, and not much of that. Her six brothers and sisters accepted the inevitable, but Helene had been unable to do so.

Both she and Garven had been at a vulnerable point in their lives. She was freshly divorced and very leery of men. He was going through the last antagonistic days of his dissociation from Jenny. She had tearfully told Garven that her platter had been over full with grief from the divorce, and her mother's stroke had left her feeling completely and unreasonably bereft. For some reason none of her many brothers and sisters, all of whom were caring and supportive siblings, were able to console her. Helene had turned to Garven, her mother's doctor, for solace. At first, he was the father she had lost when she was a teenager, the priest she had grown away from, then the husband figure she could no longer rely upon. After coming to Garven's office on Wilshire, near the 405 Freeway, several times a week for a month, he became her lover.

The affair was passionate, all the more so because of the great need for discretion they both perceived. They found snatches of time for one another during the day in out of the way places, on weekends at the beach house of a friend of hers, and when both of their children were away. She positively dreaded the possibility of discovery and embarrassment of her children finding out about her affair, even though she was a free woman. For some perverse reason that very fear of being found out added an intense spice to their ardor.

Their encounters were infrequent; and, they thought and planned with the utmost discretion. However, early on, one of Garven's partners, the original and eldest of the neurosurgeons suspected what Garven was up to. He was a man of the world who had married and divorced three times, himself, and had never been without a mistress of his own, even during his periods of legal marriage. He had strong, even absolute scruples about having an affair with a patient. That was his initial impression of Garven's involvement with Helene Eamon.

He confronted Garven.

"Partner, I'd like to talk with you. Please come over to my office for a few minutes," the old gentleman said.

Garven went with him.

"Have a seat. I'll get right to the point. The front office girls, the FROGS, as you young men call them, have hinted to me that you may be having an affair with one of your patients. I need to know yea or nay about that. We cannot have a violation of medical ethics. This town has too many hungry journalists. I don't need to tell you that. So, I ask you straight out, are you having an affair with a patient?"

"Nope," said Garven.

"The rumors persist," pressed his partner.

"The rumor mill will outlive all of us. I have a mistress. Her *mother* was a patient, not her. There is nothing improper or indiscreet in our relationship. Period," Garven insisted.

Frederick Broadhead's face lightened.

"I guess," he said, "every man has to try it. Heaven knows I'm not the one to throw the first rock. You know, Garven, there are three things every man needs to try once in his life to know that he doesn't need them: a boat, a mistress, and a green suit. I have had a trial with all three, and I can vouch for the wisdom of that adage."

The most definable and wearing negative in Garven's life, and the immediate reason for his pensiveness and melancholy, was the accelerating malpractice crisis in California. Interactions with patients were becoming more commonly confrontational. In four years Garven had accumulated five cases against him in his new practice. It was of little consolation that his own situation was typical of the life of a California neurosurgeon. Malpractice insurance rates were skyrocketing, and there was talk of insurance being unobtainable in LA and San Francisco. Garven spent an increasing amount of time in reviewing charts, filling out interrogatives, giving depositions, and huddling with attorneys assigned by his insurance company. None of those activities endeared lawyers to him.

In his residency he had liked his patients and had done his utmost to help them. In private practice he found himself feeling alienated from the very source of his income and his most exciting involvements, his patients. Instead of people coming to find out what was wrong with them and to get it fixed, they now seemed to come in for second opinions and debates. There was always another doctor or aunt or chiropractor who knew better about about the problem at hand or even about neurosurgery than did Garven, it seemed. Threats to report him to the hospital administration, to the county medical society, or to sue him were an almost daily occurrence.

Malpractice suits were becoming recognized as something like the lottery; they were the poor man's only opportunity to become suddenly rich. At least that was the view of the American Trial Lawyers, and they offered that pitch to potential clients blatantly, but dressed in lofty *"pro bono publicum"* terms. The attorneys who before had to skirt the edge of charges of barratry now found a holier-than-thou cause in saving hapless victims of fiendish doctors. One example came to Garven's mind with the same vividness that it did to the attorneys and their clients but for different reasons. For Garven the example served as the height of absurdity, the extreme to which the malpractice crisis could go. For the attorneys and their wishful clients, the case proved that no cause was unjust, no claim too far-fetched to allow it to be the lottery jackpot.

The case Garven thought about involved a woman who sued her radiologist and her referring physician in San Francisco after undergoing a CAT scan of her brain. She claimed that the injection of iodine contrast material for the purposes of enhancing the contrasts of the x-ray study had caused her to lose her psychic powers. The absurdity was not that she was able to find a lawyer to file a suit nor that she was able to have her day in court. No, the thing that incensed Garven was that she won, to the tune of two million dollars. Garven thought that he must have slipped down the rabbit hole and came out in Wonderland when he heard that. After that judgment—to use the term loosely—he expected to hear about a suit from every person in California whose head glowed in the dark, and he knew that was a significant number.

The California civil justice system was so log-jammed with suits that all five of Garven's cases were still open and active after four years. It would be more years before even the first one came to any kind of resolution. He categorically refused to settle any case as a matter of principle; so, he was destined to remain in the system almost as long as he lived.

As a result of these ruminations, Garven was in a foul mood when he left his office to go to the operating room at St. Patricia's. It had been an important hour for Garven, however, because it set him to thinking about what he really wanted to do with the rest of his life.

Karl Oscarssen, an orthopedic surgeon nearing retirement, was scheduled to assist Garven on the multi-level thoracolumbar laminectomy he had scheduled as first case that morning. Karl had referred the patient and was entitled to the assistant's fee by common understanding. Garven would rather have had a different, more adept assistant, or even to have dispensed with having an assistant altogether, but Karl was owed the assistant's fee. That would amount to twenty percent of the amount of Garven's fee as surgeon. Garven knew that he would just have to be a little more watchful to compensate for the older man's slowness and mild lapses of attention.

On a personal level Garven did like to operate with Dr. Oscarssen. He was a good conversationalist. He was sixty-six years old and knew how to navigate through the shoals and sand-bars of the private practice coastline as well as anyone Garven had met. He respected the old Swede's insights and advice.

"Good morning, Garven, you look a little down this morning," Dr. Oscarssen said.

"Thanks for noticing," Garven said, "I guess I let myself think about my malpractice suits or something. That's what we pay the attorneys for, but I can't help getting mad and a little nervous. It is an attack on one's integrity, after all."

"Just one of many nowadays," Karl said, "in case you hadn't noticed. Do you have any plans to do anything about it, or are you just going to let them put it to you until you finally roll over and die in harness?"

"Like what?" Garven asked. "Retire and put my tail between my legs and let them all win?"

He was a bit agitated. The two men finished putting the drapes on the patient's back.

"Knife," Garven requested.

"I have started to do some other things after a career of active surgery. Pay's good, and I don't have to beat my head against a wall anymore. I just see the occasional patient from the old days and scrub in as an assistant to keep my hand in. I have found a way to make a good living without all the pain; that's the long and the short of it," Karl told Garven as the incision widened.

Karl buzzed bleeders, and Garven slipped in the first self-retaining retractor.

"Kind of a skimpy incision, isn't it?" asked Karl. "Seems like you need plenty of room for a case like this. You new guys and your keyhole incisions. Don't you remember that incisions heal from side to side, not end to end?"

"Maybe, but the rate of infection is higher with bigger incisions; and besides, people hurt from side to side. The more side there is, the more hurt. Folks won't put up with a lot of pain these days."

Karl snorted to display what he thought of that kind of reasoning.

"Tell me more about your voodoo practice," Garven said, now hard at work stripping the large back muscles from their connections to the spinous processes.

"My what?"

"Your sure-fire way of making money in medicine without working. I'm interested...Curette, please."

He continued his work.

"Nothing funny or hoodoo about it; just workman's comp," Karl said as he dabbed a bleeding site then electrocoagulated the small open vessel.

"You've got to be kidding. I hate comp patients. Whine and moan, never get better from their phony injuries, never go back to work, all drug addicts. They drive me crazy. I would never be able to work day in and day out with them," Garven said emphatically.

"Rongeur," he ordered the scrub nurse.

She lightly slapped the instrument into the palm of his right hand.

"I think you haven't thought this through all that well, Garven. I am here to tell you that the bureaucrats, and the hospitals, and the lawyers, and the consumer activist groups, and the insurance companies are steadily eroding your choices in running your practice. Pretty soon, they'll be telling you what your can charge; then they'll tell you what operation to do. Then it'll be whether you can operate at all and on whom. Mark my words."

He held the sucker to keep the gutters of the removed bone near the spinal dura free of blood; so, Garven could see.

"Tight, isn't it?" commented Garven as he gingerly worked a fine dissector down the side towards the nerve root.

"What I'm getting at, is there is a lot of money to be made in giving all the therapy and diagnostic procedures for comp patients. They pay a thousand bucks for a final report. The average nonoperative patient can work up a bill of nearly $2500. Add in the occasional operation, and you can make a significant living from workman's comp alone. It's a question of being organized," Karl continued his pitch.

Garven was working with a small sharp curette and fine bone punches now. He was sweating.

"Give me a wipe, Sally," he asked the circulator.

She mopped his brow.

The dura was beginning to bulge normally into the new space created by the extensive laminectomy.

"But, I still can't stand to listen to them moan," Garven said echoing the standard complaint of physicians who saw injured workers, especially those with chronic problems.

"Look," said Karl, "I'm not the one to talk. I see a few patients and send them off to PT, and I write a few reports. That little bit provides me with a comfortable retirement living. I am about to cash even that in and go on a long cruise with my wife. She's got lupus kidney disease, you know. Who knows how long she's got?"

"I didn't know. Sorry to hear that," said Garven.

He nicked the dura with his small sharp curette. Spinal fluid flowed into the dissected portion of the back. Garven swore, then ordered, "Forceps and some 6-0 nylon."

He put a figure-of-eight suture around the small leaking point, and it dried up instantly.

"Anyway," Karl went on as soon as the mini-crisis was over, "what I'd like to tell you is that a man could set up a major clinic with all of his own physical and occupational therapists, radiology equipment, and hire a few young docs or near retirees, even chiropractors, and do everything for the comp patients under one roof. There are a couple of guys down in Southcentral doing that, and I hear they're doing great. State comp practically begs for competent orthopods or neuros to do the work. They have more patients than they know what to do with and more streaming in every day."

He irrigated the surface of the exposed dura; so, Garven could see to do his work.

"And a guy wouldn't have to see every patient himself from start to finish?" Garven asked.

"That's the idea of a big clinic. You see them and do an exam in a few minutes, make the standard range of motion exercises, thigh circumference measurements, that sort of thing. Then you either do the report or see that it is done right. You aren't really the treating physician. No more eight hours a day or night call for you! It is almost unimaginable to have a malpractice suit against you."

"Right angle probe," Garven ordered.

He used it to check to see if the openings through which the nerve roots exited to go to the legs were fully open after his two hour long dissection.

"I have to open this one more foramen, then we're done. They're all pretty much free now," Garven said.

Then he responded to Karl, "I can't remember when I last worked an eight hour day. What're you talking about?"

He laughed.

"That's what I was getting at. You put in less than eight hours any day in this comp thing. Best return on a work investment you will ever see. Think about it, Garven. You're not getting any younger. No use letting the number crunchers take all the money you earn the hard way in your regular practice. This is a chance to get one up on them. And, for that matter, now's the chance to get in on the ground floor before everybody else figures it out," Karl urged.

CHAPTER
Thirty-Five

G arven did think about it. He went down to see Hyman Renninger who
ran clinics on La Brea and on Florence Avenues. He checked the fee
schedules offered by state comp and attended a seminar on report writing put
on by the state. He learned more still from casual conversations with physicians who were doing increasingly more workman's compensation evaluations
and treatment themselves. In a month Garven was well enough informed that
he thought that he knew the system sufficiently to get involved.

He started slowly and simply. He rented Karl Oscarssen's small space; so,
the old man could retire. He bought a few EKG, ergonomic exercise and
performance measuring machines, and hired office staff, several techs, and a
physical therapist to manage them. At first the payments came in very slowly
from the state and from the major insurance companies who served the business community. He had to learn patience and the understanding that he was,
after all, dealing with a governmental bureaucracy for the most part.

He learned from his mistakes. He hired women who had long experience in
dealing with the mountains of paper work involved in the comp industry, and
his return improved. He paid his people well and was able to get better and
better employees, as a consequence. He made it his personal most important
task to see to it that the reports were thick and comprehensive and that they
never failed to get to the workman's comp office before the deadline. After
a year, when the money finally began to come in reliably, he made a serious
shift in his neurosurgery practice schedule out of necessity. Garven began

to commit every afternoon to his new comp business at the expense of his formal neurosurgery practice.

His income from surgery fell off in inverse proportion to the amount of time he spent with his comp clinic, but his overall income was beginning to increase exponentially. His partners in the Los Angeles Neuroscience Medical Group began to notice, then to complain; then the senior partner called Garven to task on his waning production for the group.

"Garven," growled Dr. Broadhead. "I can't figure what's gotten into you. Must be one of those so-called mid-life crises, I keep reading about. First, you get a mistress and get yourself talked about, then you disappear from your real work half of the time. You gone hippie on us? or crazy?"

"No, Fred, neither. I have been starting a work comp clinic, and it has been taking more of my time than I expected," Garven answered.

"In competition with our clinic?" Dr. Broadhead exclaimed.

They had a noncompetitive covenant in their contract, and he was assuming that Garven was committing the unforgivable sin.

"No, all surgery is done through our clinic. The rest are general practice type injuries and stress, all the regular comp kind of things."

Fred Broadhead rubbed his forefinger alongside his nose as he usually did when he pondered a hard question.

"I don't see it that way, Garven. I think that all of the money you have been bringing in should go through our corporation books. You have no right to have a separate personal entity. I suppose that, if push came to shove, we wouldn't be able to make the charge stick that you are in violation of the anti-competition clause of our contract; but the rest of us don't like it. I mean, we don't like it to the point that you are going to have to choose. The rest of the partners don't want the office cluttered up with the low-lives that comp brings in, and we don't want to get involved in all of the headaches."

"Am I hearing an ultimatum?" Garven asked, interrupting.

"I don't like to think of it that way, but a rose is a rose is a rose, I guess," Dr. Broadhead declared. "Either you get out of this silly comp thing and return to full time work and production with us as a neurosurgeon, or we will have to vote you out."

Ordinarily, Garven would have hunkered down for battle with such an ultimatum, on general principles, if for no other reason. But he had thought carefully about what he would say when this predictable confrontation finally came.

"Fred, I have to tell you where I'm coming from. In the past year and a little more, I have made more money from the comp clinic than I did from neurosurgery. I work a third as much. I have not been sued or even threatened with a suit. I don't get called at night, or at home. My blood pressure is starting to return to normal. I think that I am ready for a big change in my life. I will accept your invitation to resign if you and the other partners make it easy and convenient for me to get my share out. Actually, if it's all right, I'd like to maintain a minimal relationship with the partnership, keep my office, keep my name on the door, that sort of thing, all for a fee, of course. I hope we can do all of this amicably. I will offer to stay on until you can get a young associate to take my place."

Dr. Broadhead shook his head; and his white hair, so carefully arranged by his wife that morning, tousled into an unruly thatch.

"Garven, I'm shocked. I never expected this. I am going to die in the harness. I am a neurosurgeon through and through. I don't know anything else. I don't play golf, and I don't have hobbies. I don't have time for that sort of triviality. I will never retire. I find it very hard to understand your thinking."

"Some years ago, I would have said the same thing. I'll tell you, Fred, the intrigues of the university practice and the politics of private practice have about killed off my interest and enthusiasm. Malpractice suits, all the CYA, the brown nosing, and the fee splitting of our practice all leave a very bad taste in my mouth. I am not getting any younger. I see so much of my income going out for the costs of doing business, and I see so little staying with me towards retirement that I feel a pressing need to get as much as I can while I can. And I definitely want to do some living away from the operating room before I slough my mortal coil. I like the corporate practice I'm developing because I am able to maintain an arm's length association with the day to day work. It's a lot easier on the body and soul."

"I didn't know there was living away from the operating room, real living, anyway," said Dr. Broadhead with a wry smile. "I'm a neurosurgeon and nothing else. It's enough. That aside, you think this comp clinic idea does all of that for you?"

"Seems to. Anyway, I would like us to keep on friendly terms, what do you say? I will have my resignation from the group on your desk by tomorrow, if you and I have an agreement."

Dr. Broadhead shook his head again in disbelief but took Garven's hand.

"Of course. All good things must end. I wish you success, Garven. We can have the manager and Terence Enright draw up the papers. Will you let them know?"

"Tomorrow morning, Fred; and thanks for the understanding," Garven said.

"I don't think I would go all the way to 'understanding' because you have me pershimmered, Garven. But I don't see any reason for us to sever our arrangement on bad terms if we don't have to."

As they parted, Garven reflected that he did not feel the slightest remorse. He felt something like being a Phoenix rising.

As long as Garven got the appropriate paper work done well and on time, he had no difficulty getting paid for any itemized bill he submitted to the comp companies. They did not question his medical judgment; if the test or the treatment was ordered by him or his other physicians, it was reimbursable. He bought more machines—electroencephalographs, holter monitors, radioisotope scanners, the best radiography equipment, CAT scan machines, a complete gym loaded with exercise machines. He was able to bill for each of the machines separately as an itemized treatment. The patients were now receiving their entire treatment under one roof, and that treatment lasted three or four months on the average and upwards of a year in some isolated cases. The average bills per patient were now $30,000 with some approaching $100,000. And there were thousands of patients.

Garven had to hire additional staff, including physicians, physical therapists, and chiropractors. He was able to pay these professionals $60,000 to $80,000 a year—significantly less than their potential in the open market place—because they were people who preferred not to have ongoing responsibility for patients, night call, or to have questions asked of their former hospitals or clinic partners.

By the end of the second year of doing the comp work exclusively, Garven added a second clinic with its own complement of machines and staff. By the end of the third year, he had four such clinics, each with its regular staff, and now a neurologist and a lawyer at each location. He gave his professional staff members incentive raises, and his adjunctive staff were paid more than fairly. None of them offered complaints, and he had a remarkably low rate of personnel dissatisfaction or turnover among his employees. He found Hispanics, Asians, and blacks—as they now had to be called—to be excellent workers and quick learners in his business, and many of them were willing to settle for lower wages if questions about their immigration status were soft-pedaled.

By the fall of 1979, Garven had a system of ten clinics in Los Angeles and two in San Diego. He had a small army of technicians, interpreters, attorneys, accountants, and investment brokers. He had a fortune invested in buildings, machines, and personnel. Garven spent his time directing his growing empire like a captain of industry or a military officer. He closeted with his advisors to find tax loopholes and shelters, to manage his investments through holding companies that used off-shore banks, and in buying and selling real estate. In December of 1979, he had grown into a $10,000,000 a year business and had kept $5,000,000 of that for himself, after taxes.

By 1981, the problem for Garven was not how much he could charge nor how many patients he could accommodate through his massive clinic system, but how to keep the numbers of injured workers flowing through his doors. A dozen other entrepreneurial physicians and lawyers and not a few chiropractors had discovered the goose that laid the golden eggs, and they all competed with Garven for a growing but, more or less finite, number of patients. The state was as helpful as it could be in creating more income for the clinics. It allowed more prolonged care, every new diagnostic device, and large awards for stress related problems. Some of the clinics were in direct partnership with attorneys who served the injured people. They made agreements to share the awards among the patient, the attorney, and the doctor. Garven steered entirely clear of that practice—kick-backs—presuming that one day there would be a comeuppance for such associations.

The state was usually generous in its judgments regarding questions about whether or not a worker's condition was, in fact, work related or not. Garven had to hire additional psychologists to handle the workload created by patients streaming in for stress-related cumulative work injuries. He created a clinic with a small operatorium for carpal tunnel syndrome alone because the state could not deny anyone compensation for that wrist and nerve disorder. Best of all, for Garven and his competitors, California, as always in the forefront of expensive social programs, granted enthusiastic approval to a new political school of thought they liked to call "political correctness." The beneficial offshoots of that generous attitude on the part of California was that the state accepted illegal immigrants as bonafide workers and qualified them to receive workman's compensation benefits. Black people—they could no longer be called 'Negroes' under political correctness doctrine—qualified automatically for comp insurance coverage of virtually any health problem, if only they would apply under the aegis of the injured worker's umbrella.

Still, there were not enough workers needing work-comp. Garven hired investigators from 'headhunter' firms who specialized in finding injured workers. Garven knew that many of his patients were being recycled from other clinics, even other cities, and that many of the recipients of his billable care came from contacts made at the gates of major plants. He suspected, but did not very actively seek proof, that workers were being seduced from unemployment office lines to remember their injuries more vividly. It was possible that some of the more zealous of the 'headhunters' were offering temporary financial assistance until the worker's final settlement came in from the insurance company. There was no direct involvement by Garven or his staff in such practices, and he found it best to avoid asking questions regarding methods. He insisted on scrupulous record keeping and monitored all records to be sure that there was no suggestion or taint of kick-backs, bribery, improper influence, or hint of fraud. One of the lawyers' tasks was to monitor the records with a jaundiced eye to make certain that no illegality would ever surface to bring down his empire. The state and the big insurance companies made no complaint, and the service Garven rendered continued to be immensely profitable.

Garven was popular with the patients who passed through his clinic doors and with their comp lawyers because his sympathies lay with the working people and their problems and not with the insurance companies who were paying him. Because of his sympathetic ear, one of the referring comp lawyers sent him a copy of his favorite letter from a client to an insurance company—tongue in cheek.

Chief, Reimbursement Section
Workman's Compensation Insurance
State of California
Sacramento, California

Dear Sir:
I have not received any money for my injuries at work for over three months. My comp worker says he doesn't think I was hurt at work. I am appealing to you. This is what happened: On July 4, last, I was working at my usual job as a hod carrier. My foreman assigned me to work on the fourteenth floor of the new building clearing away a pile of bricks that had been left there. I started to throw them to the ground, but most of them broke, and my foreman ordered me to carry them down. It was very slow to carry them down fourteen floors on the ladder in my hod. I thought of a better way.

I tied a wheel barrow to a rope and put the rope over a pulley on the fourteenth floor. When the barrow was at the top, I tied the rope to the ground and climbed up the ladder to the top and filled the barrow with bricks. I climbed back down the ladder and untied it from the stake on the ground to let the barrow down. I had misjudged the weight of the full barrow. It came down like a rocket. I did not think fast enough and held onto the rope and was pulled up. I met the wheel barrow full of bricks half way up. It struck my right shoulder and broke it. Although the pain was awful, I held on until the weight of the wheel barrow pulled me up to the top where my head hit the big pulley and broke my skull.

I kept my grip even with my injuries and hung there in the air. Then the barrow hit the ground and dumped out half its bricks. I was then heavier than the bricks and started down again fast as you please. I fell to the ground among the broken bricks and broke my pelvis and got a bad concussion. As I lost consciousness, I thought I'd weathered the worst. But I lost my presence of mind and let go the rope. As I lay there out of my head, the wheel barrow with half the bricks rocketed down again and landed on my back. It broke both my legs, three ribs, and my left arm.

And that is why I am not at work. I respectfully submit that I think state comp should take care of me until I can get back to carrying the hod again.

Respectfully,
John Jones.

Garven had to laugh, even though the letter was a recycled joke, because the it was not so far afield from the troubles the injured workers had in getting their claims accepted.

CHAPTER
Thirty-Six

In July, 1981, Garven attended a four day fund-raiser activity for major contributors to the University of California. To that point in time he had been a minor contributor. The soiree was held on Santa Catalina Island.

Leland Stratford, the chairman of the fund raising committee, invited Garven for cocktails on the evening of the second day on Catalina. "I hope you're having a pleasant time, Dr. Wilsonhulme," he said.

"Very," Garven said. "Thanks for having me."

"No, it is the university system that should be thanking you. We know you are busy, and we know that you receive dozens, probably even hundreds of requests for donations every year."

"That's a fair statement," Garven said.

"And time is money," said Stratford. "We don't want to waste any of your valuable time. I will come straight to the point of our fund raising. We have to bring in an additional two hundred million dollars over the next two years. That is regarded as our minimum goal. We would like your help. We are after a few major players from the California scene to give us the boost we need. In your case, we want more than money, to be frank. We would like you take over as chairman of the fund raising drive starting next year."

"You are the premier fund raiser in the country, Mr. Stratford. I can't imagine replacing you."

"My term of office is over at the end of December this year, Dr. Wilsonhulme. I have been at this for ten years. With the upcoming elections, I want to try my hand at raising the money for the Republicans for the next go around.

George Bush will be the likely candidate, and he is not going to get the land-slide victory that Reagan got. We are going to need some long-range strategy, and I have been honored by being included. I'd appreciate it if you would keep this under your hat, by the way," he said.

"Not to worry; who would I tell?" Garven asked.

"If you get into U.C. fund raising in a big way, you will be one of the real movers and shakers in the state, Dr. Wilsonhulme. Behind the scenes you will swing a lot of muscle. Give it some thought. I know you are a decision maker. It would be very valuable for us if you could tell me a yea or a nay before we go back to the mainland. And, more than incidentally, I would like to know if you think you can let us have a million dollars for the fund this year?"

Garven's tax people had told him that he needed to make more contributions. He was entitled to write-off fifty percent of his income for charitable donations. A thought hit him as to how he could benefit by more than just the tax write-off. At his next meeting with Leland Stratford, Garven decided to see if he understood the inner workings of U.C., the donations securing world, and human nature as well as he thought he did.

This time he chose to be direct.

"Leland, I hope you don't mind me calling you by your first name; but I would appreciate it if you would call me, Garven. My friends all do," he said.

"I prefer the informality. It's Leland and Garven, then," Stratford said with a grin that showed perfectly even, dazzling, unnaturally white and overly large teeth, the obvious product of some "dentist to the stars."

"I accept your offer to head up the fund raising drive. It sounds like a full time job. I'll make the necessary shifts to be able to do it," Garven said.

"Great!" Stratford beamed.

"And," Garven paused for effect. "I would like to make a donation to start the ball rolling. I was not thinking of the million dollars you suggested, though."

Leland Stratford almost winced. He could not let the fund raiser chairman-ship go for anything less than a million. He was afraid that he had misjudged Wilsonhulme. This could prove to be an awkward discussion.

"No, I would be honored if you would accept ten million dollars from me," Garven offered in a dry monotone.

The effect was exactly what Garven hoped it would be. Leland Stratford's face was transformed into a look of bliss. That was why he had twisted so many arms and kissed it up so shamelessly for the past year to get this week on Catalina. It was all worth it. Leland was going to go home with more than thirty-five million from the two dozen contributors, and this one gift was the largest.

"Superb!" was all he could muster verbally, but his face radiated the sincerity of his pleasure.

Before Stratford could fully collect himself to speak more verbosely, Garven added, almost soto voce, "There is a little something I would like to have."

Stratford's antennae went up. Way up.

"Well, for that amount, as long as you don't want to change the name of UCLA to "Wilsonhulme U., I think we could accommodate almost any whim."

"Nothing so public or obvious," Garven said. "I am a very private person and insist on absolute anonymity. In fact, I would like to be able to render even more service. I would like to be named to the board of regents of the university system."

"That's a big request, but we do have a vacancy coming up in February. I will run it past the governor. I think he might be persuaded," Stratford said.

"Until February, then," said Garven. "Nice doing business with you."

Leland Stratford was too much of a gentleman and a businessman to ask for Garven's check at that point.

"*It is never easy,*" he sighed to himself.

Garven accepted the chairmanship of the fund raising committee in January after assurances from Stratford that the board of regents position was almost certainly his the following month. Garven decided to be aggressive from the start. He organized parties, local high school drives, heavy contributor retreats by state region, and placed donation cans in convenience stores. He put out a little of the organization's budget money for advertisements in newspapers, magazines, and on TV and radio throughout the state. The results were a dramatic twelve percent increase in donations, and a re-awakened interest in the state's schools of higher education. He started a program of having heavy hitters and even modest contributors taking monthly payroll deductions for the UC system and led the way by having his draw be $100,000 a month over and above his initial contribution. The results were heartening and did not go unnoticed in the governor's office, but they honored his strong request for anonymity. In the February meeting of the board of regents, Garven was officially named to a chair on the board.

Garven had not only been a full professor in a U.C. institution, but he had kept up with the innerworkings of the major administrators and professors since his change to private practice. He was considered, by his colleagues on the board of regents, to be a gold mine of information for decisions about tenure, grants, elevation to department head level, and approval of research projects. Senior level personnel decisions were regarded as being the most bewildering and vexatious they had to grapple with, and the June meeting each year was approached with dread. Over the years, Garven had assiduously gathered data: tape recordings, photographs, movie and video recordings of and affidavits regarding a remarkable number of ranking individuals in the system. His file on UCOMH professors was understandably the most complete and informative in existence. The June, 1982 tenure and advancement meeting proved to be the most efficient on record.

Howard Rosenthal was recommended for elevation to the rank of full tenured professor in the department of pediatrics at UCOMH. His list of publications was impressive. He served on four major national committees, including acting as an advisor to the National Institutes of Health for neonatal matters. He was a sought after speaker, a prime mover in hospital executive committees, and was voted the best teacher in the medical students in 1981. A dozen letters of recommendation from luminaries in the university and from around the world were included with his applications. His students and present and former residents' laudatory statements were bound into a thick book, available for the regents' perusal. He was considered to be the most likely candidate to take the place of the present chief of the department when the current chairman reached the mandatory age of retirement in two years.

Garven knew in advance of the list of men and women who were on the promotions list for 1982. He paid a social call on Emerick Bowden, chairman of the board of regents, when he discovered Rosenthal's name on the list and looked at the neonatologist's impressive credentials.

Bowden lived in quiet regal splendor in Holmby Hills, a new posh neighborhood in Los Angeles that was determined to put Beverly Hills into second place. Garven and Emerick Bowden had known each other for years having played Kamikaze handball against one another in the Beverly Spa Sports Center. They had become respectful acquaintances, short of being real friends; they were too much alike for that. They did have a mutual respect for one another.

"Emerick, I have some information that might interest you. Let me tell you first how I came by it. I attended a university function three or four years ago put on by the department of pediatrics at Osterlund Memorial. Dr. Rosenthal, who is on our list for possible advancement, was being roasted—all in good fun and for a good cause. He had just won a Carnegie Prize for his work on cystic fibrosis in preemies. The roasts were the usual stuff, and I paid little attention. I was sitting next to the number two in the psychiatric department at the time. On of the roasts was, 'Did you hear about poor Howard dropping his wallet in the Tenderloin in San Francisco? He had to kick it all the way to Berkeley before he dared to pick it up.'

"I didn't think all that much about it, but the psychiatrist sitting next to me commented, 'And what do you think he was doing in the Tenderloin?' I thought the laughter about the reference to homosexuality was a bit strained. I asked around casually over the next few months, and got the distinct impression that young Dr. Rosenthal's persuasions were definitely toward the gentle side. One nurse specifically said that the doctor's love 'dare not speak its name'. It occurred to me that such a perversion would not be the best thing for our defenseless children; so, I hired a private attorney to find the truth of it. He produced these pictures."

Garven opened a brown envelope and spread out six enlargements on Bowden's table along with a sworn affidavit for the investigator.

Bowden recoiled from the pictures in disgust. They had been taken in a San Francisco Turkish bath and had remarkable clarity and detail which left nothing to the imagination in their depiction of a vigorous athletic event.

On the same agenda, Steven Chou was to receive the coveted Howard Naffziger Award for Excellence among university neurosurgeons at his upcoming retirement ceremonies. The award carried a $100,000 bonus that could be used at the recipient's discretion. Chou had, for all practical purposes, already retired. He no longer saw patients, did surgery, or conducted research. The retirement program was to be the apex of the social season for Osterlund Memorial for July with invited guests from around the world. The president of the American Association of Neurological Surgeons was the invited guest speaker, and all of Chou's former residents were slated to come. All of that was public information, but the Naffziger Award was the crowning jewel of the evening and was a closely guarded secret. The vote of the regents to approve the award was considered pro forma.

The regents and secretaries filed into the ornate meeting hall. There were no people from the press, no public spectators, and not a single interested person from the many institutions that made up the University of California system, lest there be undue influence on the deliberations and voting of the august body of regents. The discussion and voting proceeded by category and in alphabetical order. When the last fourth of the advancement list was reached, Garven picked up his interest.

Chairman Bowden read, "Rosenthal, Howard. I wish to keep this item totally in camera. I have incontrovertible evidence of criminal wrongdoing in this case. He is not fit to be alone with children let alone to be advanced to a senior position. I will withdraw his name and go on. If anyone is overwhelmed by curiosity about the evidence, come and see me after. Any objections?"

There were none.

Bowden did a quick canvass of the regents with his eyes, then continued, "Shackley, Robert L., candidate for advancement to associate professor in endocrinology at UCSF. You have all read your printouts. Any objections?"

None were put forward, and Dr. Shackley became an associate professor.

The voting went rapidly; and, for the most part, perfunctorily. One pause occurred when Bowden read the four names under the subheading of "Special Awards and Presentations." The first, Sol Abrams, was passed without comment.

"Lets come back to Chou," said Bowden. "Thacker, Lemuel T., Distinguished Service Award for his work with inner city children's clinics in Compton and Watts. Shall I read the noteworthy accomplishments of Professor Thacker?"

There was a universal "no" for the reading of the lengthy laudatory comments and a universal "yes" for his award.

"Now, for Chou," Bowden said after the regents voted to award the U.C. Commendation Prize to Crandall Zimbrovski. "It has come to the committee's attention that there has been an unfavorable development with regards this professor. Emily Sondheim has the details."

The portly spinster from Walnut Creek arose and cleared her voice. It was as deep and throaty as that of most men.

"I received a packet of information from the Los Angeles Police Department regarding Professor Chou. To make a long story short, the LAPD received an anonymous tip that Chou was in violation of landlord responsibilities for a number of his buildings in South Central LA. The law is called the "Slumlord Act" and has to do with serious failure to provide for the health and safety of tenants. He was investigated for an inordinate number of tenant complaints about three years ago; the investigation was finally stopped without formal charges, but the case was left open. Recently, an anonymous tipster sent the LAPD photographic evidence and bank records that indicate that Professor Chou paid off an inspector. That is a felony. Another tipster informed the LAPD of the death of a nine month old black girl who succumbed to carbon monoxide poisoning while asleep in her crib. Her mother had complained twice about smelling a peculiar gas odor, and nothing was done by Professor Chou's management people except to serve eviction papers on the mother. He claims no knowledge of the payoff or of the management company's failures. The district attorney refiled charges just yesterday. They stated that a full investigation would be instigated with no respect as to Professor Chou's high position. There is no knowledge as to the identity of the informant in this case."

"Discussion, please," requested the chairman.

A graying black man stood up to speak. It was unusual for anyone to stand, and Gunther Smith had never made a comment in a June meeting previously to anyone's recollection. He was dressed in a $1200 Saville Row suit, an Italian silk tie; and one could have brushed one's teeth in the mirror shine of his shoes.

"I wish to speak, Mr. Chairman," he intoned in a rich, quiet, baritone voice. Bowden nodded his assent. "This man represents the worst example in the ongoing troubles between my people and the Asian Americans. Because of the racially charged atmosphere in California's inner cities, it would be a serious mistake to honor this man publicly until these charges are put away. I can speak for the NAACP, of which I am the executive director for California, when I say that the people of color in our state would rise up in righteous indignation upon learning that this body knew in advance that a man was guilty of vicious slum lord practices and that man was given this important award."

"Now, to be fair, Mr. Smith, the crimes are only alleged," responded Bowden. Smith's eyes flashed.

"My interest in 'fair' is limited, sir. I am a black man. I've seen 'fair'. Are you accustomed to taking serious gambles, Mr. Chairman?" he asked without betraying stridency in his voice.

"The Chou item is tabled. We can reconsider it next year if the charges are determined to be unfounded," Bowden announced.

"That may be problematical," said one of the regents. "I understand that Dr. Chou has a terminal malignancy. Anyone know anything about that?"

Bowden asked, "Dr. Wilsonhulme, you were in his same department, were you not? What do you know about Dr. Chou's illness that could cast light on this discussion?"

"My understanding was that it was not that threatening. At least death was not considered to be at all imminent. He has a lymphoma, I have heard. They are usually pretty treatable. He seemed quite well when I last law him," Garven responded.

"With that, are there any objections to tabling the question of giving this man an award until next June? Or to adjourning, for that matter?"

The regents were all pleased to have gotten their work done in record time. The voting was unanimous on both suggestions.

CHAPTER
Thirty-Seven

The Los Angeles Times carried a front page story about slum lords the following day. The lead column featured Steven Chou prominently with a lengthy comment by the state and city NAACP leaders. LAPD would neither confirm nor deny the allegations, citing a policy forbidding comment about the substance of ongoing investigations.

At the urging of the board of regents, a major award ceremony for Dr. Chou was canceled by UCOMH, the *Times* had learned from an undisclosed source; the UC board of regents spokesman had no comment. The article commented on Dr. Chou's career and how the ceremony was to have been the crowning honor ushering the prominent brain surgeon and university professor into retirement.

A month later an article appeared on the fourth page of the local section of *The Times*, consisting of three paragraphs, stating that criminal charges had been dropped in the Chou slumlord case after the prominent surgeon agreed to demands by tenants and community leaders to perform major renovations and improvements in his three Los Angeles apartment buildings.

Dr. Chou's wife was quoted in the article as saying, "We are not rich people. My husband's illness has taken everything we have, even our house. Now this. I don't know where the money for these apartment house improvements is supposed to come from. This will ruin us."

A small article in the *Medical News and Views* of that same issue reported that one of the University Hospital's most prominent children's doctors, Howard Rosenthal, was announcing his early retirement from the university and from academic practice. He stated that he was moving to Iowa to open a small pediatric clinic practice in the city of Ames. Dr. Rosenthal cited reasons of health for his abrupt departure. A hospital spokesperson said that Dr. Rosenthal would be sorely missed.

On September 29, Walter Cronkite announced on the CBS evening news that cyanide laced Tylenol capsules had caused the deaths of seven people in the Greater Chicago area. The drug company that manufactured the popular pain reliever recalled 264,000 bottles. Garven turned off the TV and headed upstairs for bed. It was a hot Fall; 1982 was heading towards a record year for heat in LA. He looked at his air conditioning setting and was disappointed to find it as cold as it could be. Apparently the constant heat was overwhelming the air conditioner just as it was him.

He had not been asleep for more than a few minutes when the jangle of the telephone ring startled him.

"Hello," he said trying to shake the cobwebs out of his head.

"Do you know who this is? If you do, don't say, please."

Garven recognized the voice as that of one of the state's workman's compensation treatment facility compliance officers who came by Garven's clinics on a regular basis. Garven had quietly helped the man make the down payment on a new home in Covina. He had loaned him the cash on a no interest basis. The man had paid back every dime over a four year period. There were no records of the transaction; it had been a gentlemen's agreement sealed with a handshake.

"Yes," Garven said wondering at the cloak and dagger quality of the inspector's request.

"I cannot stay on the line long, and this conversation never happened. The state is starting to get very serious about investigating fraud in the workman's comp care industry. California is going broke paying for its workman's comp system, and they are serious about doing something about it. They are going to do stings at unemployment offices to catch stringers who bribe people to act like they were hurt on the job. They are also going to have inspectors go over every patient and the treatment they receive to determine if the care is indicated and if the patients are actually showing up for the treatment that gets billed. In six months they plan to shut down most of the big guys by freezing their insurance payments then the clinics' assets. The word is out that the state thinks it may go into a free-fall financial collapse if they don't act and soon, and they are going to crack down on the comp clinics as an object lesson. A word to the wise..."

"Thanks," Garven said. "I won't forget this."

There was a click on the opposite end of the line.

Garven shook his head ruefully. Another fraud investigation. The insurance companies had the ear of the state. They got their message into the newspapers and onto the TV at will: Mexican worker fakes injury! Alameda clinic bribes workers to pretend to be injured! Falsified records found at Burbank Comp Clinic! 20% of clinic's patients found to be ghosts with no treatment received despite taxpayer expenditures! Garven was altogether familiar with the sanctimonious one-sided litany.

He, unlike most Californians who had only the state and insurance company initiated propaganda to go by, knew more of the whole picture, enough to make him a confirmed cynic. The hypocritical insurance companies cried "fraud!" and raised their insurance rates to compensate every year. The result was a steady increase in after expense income for the insurance companies year in and year out. They had made thirty percent more profit this year than they had three years ago. It made Garven angry—state supported thieves and hypocrites! He railed at the injustice of it.

Nevertheless, Garven was a sane man. He knew he could not afford to buck the system. A bigger and more powerful set of crooks, officially sanctioned crooks, was about to dominate the workman's compensation care system scene—the HMOs. The business of medicine had become a corporate take-no-prisoners battle, and Garven's enterprise, though lucrative, was small-time in comparison to the insurance companies and HMOs. It was time for him to cut his losses and to get out before he became cannon fodder for the avarice of the huge insurance conglomerates. He investigated and planned carefully before contacting the man whom he hoped would buy him out. It was early November by the time he made his choice.

A consortium of family practice physicians and chiropractors who owned three clinics, one each in San Jose, Los Angeles, and San Diego, had previously contacted Garven about the possibility of buying him out. He had politely declined each time they inquired, but never closed the door entirely to the possibility and took pains to keep up an amicable relationship with the leaders of the consortium. You never could tell.

He thumbed the wheel of his private Rolodex around until he found the name he remembered and called the man's office.

"*Buenos dias. Clinica Medica de los Obreros*," the receptionist said.

"Soy Dr. Wilsonhulme, señorita, Esta El Dr. Garcia en la oficina?"

"Si, Doctor. Momentito."

She put him on hold.

"Good morning, Garven," came the slightly accented voice of Daniel Garcia after a few minutes of Hispanic Musak that contained an inordinate number of references to *"el corazon."*

"Good morning, Daniel. How goes the war?"

"SOS. What can I do for you?"

"It's more what I can do for you, amigo. Do you have a little free time today?"

"It's golf at three; otherwise, there's nothing important."

"No work to interfere with the important things of life, eh?"

"You know how it is, the one time people never say, 'It's just a game', is when the're winning in a golf game," Dr. Garcia said with a laugh.

"I'd like to treat you to a shamelessly unhealthful lunch, ply you with liquor, and talk some business," Garven said.

"Best offer I've had in a long time. No Mexican food, though. Hard on my digestion," Dr. Garcia said, the smile still in his voice.

"I'll pick you up at noon, then. Your office still next door to the La Brea state unemployment office?" Garven asked sweetly.

"Very funny. I'll think of some speedy retort by noon. See you then," Dr. Garcia said with a parting chuckle.

Garven had finally chosen Daniel Garcia because he was the biggest crook in the business, with the exception of every insurance company executive. The two men had a long lunch at La Orangerie on La Cienaga, the fanciest place Garven knew about in town that was open for lunch.

The waitress asked if the men wanted drinks. Garcia ordered a gin and tonic. Garven asked for iced-tea.

"Sorry, Sir, it's out of season."

"What do you mean, 'out of season'?" Garven asked.

"It's winter. We don't serve ice-tea in winter. It's restaurant policy."

"How difficult can it be to make me some iced-tea?"

"Can't. It's policy."

Garven laughed and said, "Can I have hot tea?"

"Sure," the waitress beamed.

"How about you make me four pots of strong hot tea?"

The waitress gave him a questioning look, but could see nothing wrong with his request; so, she turned to go.

"And how about a big glass filled with ice and a couple of lemon slices?"

The girl was not sure; but it seemed like something was hokey about his request; he was the customer, after all.

She brought the makings, and Garven made a large glass of strong lemony iced-tea and shared some with Daniel. The two men could hardly stop laughing at the absurdity of the interchange with the waitress. It was clear to Garven that the laughter and the liquor had loosened up Daniel. He made a mental note to leave a generous tip to the unwitting waitress. She had been a god-send.

They came to an agreement in principle over orange roughy and asparagus tips—and the especially flavorful iced-tea.

"We need to have our number crunchers work out the details, Garven; but I think your offer is fair. I wish you luck in your new venture. I can't imagine that it will be as lucrative as the comp business, but maybe you won't have to put up with the constant propaganda in the newspapers from the self-righteous insurance companies. This will be a big chunk of cash and will leverage us to the hilt. I'll have to convince my partners and my accountant, but I think it can be done. Wouldn't you like to have a nice write-off dinner someplace to twist our arms some more? I could get to like this."

Daniel Garcia had an infectious laugh.

Garven had done only a little of the talking during the luncheon meeting and had said nothing about the secretive telephone call he had received earlier. His two ostensible reasons for selling out were fatigue and the need for a change of venue and pace and the desire to see if even more money could be made in the booming hospital ownership business in medium sized communities in California, Nevada, and Oregon. He had no intention of tying up his money in such low turnover businesses, but Garcia and his henchmen did not have to know that.

The following night Garven took his SO Helene, Daniel and Marguerite Garcia, Daniel's accountant, Salvadore Benitez, and his wife, Rolanda, two partners of Daniel's, Ted Stickney and Michael Wong, and their wives Anne-Marie and Mae, and his own attorney, Bryan Hood, and Hood's newest wife, Danielle, to the most expensive restaurant in Los Angeles. The Ginza Sushiko Restaurant was entirely unimposing for the outside. It was located in an "L" shaped strip mall at 3959 Wilshire, and only the initiated would be able to find it. There was not even a sign over its entrance; only a number, A-11, announced its presence. Garven's party of guests were the only patrons in the establishment. There were no reservations for dinner; one made an appointment. Only one group of patrons at a time had such an appointment, and there was a twenty percent mark-up in the price of dinner to have an appointment within one hundred twenty minutes of the dinner hour.

Three silent Japanese girls in immaculate white kimonos embroidered with silk cherry blossoms showed the party to their seats at the sushi bar. The chef greeted them warmly as if they were old friends then snapped his fingers. Two thin busboys hurried out with pots, barrels, and baskets of exotic appearing fresh fish, mushrooms, crustaceans, and mollusks, some of which were still alive. There was not a single item that came from the United States, and not more than a handful that were recognizable by name—such delicacies as *Tako, Amaebi, Anago,* and *Tobikko* (Octopus, sweet shrimp, sea eel, and flying fish roe).

They started with mushroom soup that consisted of a small bowl of hot water in which floated a single button mushroom about the size of a nutmeg and a single herb leaf. The soup had a very delicate aroma and flavor and put the stomachs of Garven and his guests on a ravenous setting. The chef followed with twenty-one more courses that included smoked eel, raw oysters, *Ikura* (salmon roe), puffer fish, sea urchins that were the consistency and color of warm diarrhea but had a heavenly aroma and flavor, and bizarrely configured mushrooms.

The bill was $1400 not including the twenty percent tip. Garven paid with his VISA card since no one anywhere seemed to take his American Express card, and penned in a notation for his tax man that the dinner was for business, and the sale of his California Neuro-Ortho Associates Clinics, Inc. was the sole topic of discussion. Bryan Hood had drawn up a contract, leaving the final sale figure to be filled in at the end of the evening's negotiations. At nine-thirty, he wrote in the number $20,000,000. Bryan signed for the company; and Daniel Garcia, and Michael Wong signed for the *Clinica Medica de los Obreros* group. Garven's name did not appear on the documents.

The twenty million dollar check was wired that evening to the account of The California Rehabilitation Group in the Union Bank of Grand Cayman, and from there, automatically, to the Vanuatu Foreign Exchange Bank in the name of the Fletcher Group, Ltd. The nominal owners of these accounts in the off-shore banks were the attorneys who had drawn up the articles of incorporation for the respective countries. The banks consisted of single small rooms with brass plates over the doors—so-called "name plate banks"—and one or two computer operators and their machines. Garven Wilsonhulme did not appear as owner or executive except on the Vanuatu company and that information was sacrosanct as a matter of national law in Vanuatu. In separate documents, and after a convoluted paper trail, he was finally listed as the sole owner of the Fletcher Group, Ltd., that owned all the rest of the shell companies. The only access to the accounts was by successful communication of a twelve digit number, a computer pass word known only to Garven and the computer, and knowledge of Garven's birth name, Garven Aloysius Carmichael—the most closely guarded secret of all.

Garven Wilsonhulme was out of the workman's compensation care-giving business and on to other things when complete collapse of the industry occurred in 1992 and 1993 in conjunction with the near collapse of the general California economy during the same two years. The corporate workman's compensation medical business never recovered; there was no Phoenix left to rise out of the ashes—unless you count Garven Wilsonhulme.

CHAPTER
Thirty-Eight

Despite Devon Upshire's ascendancy to the neurosurgery department chairmanship at Garven Wilsonhulme's expense, the two men had maintained close social and personal ties over the years from 1971 to 1982. After Devon had been in the chairmanship long enough to look over the hill of his career and life and could see his eventual retirement drawing ever nearer, he was not pleased with what he saw. His pension from the university would afford him a niggardly living of about $50,000 a year starting at age sixty-five, and the addition of social security benefits would only add another sixteen thousand. Devon and his wife, Rachel, had established a life-style that used up $82,000 each year. If they never traveled or remodeled their house, and bought a new car only once each five years, they could possibly reduce that requirement for cash to $59,000. Any further cuts would be into the meat and gristle around their bones, they thought. For that reason Devon was happy to accept Garven's occasional offers of advice on investments. The first suggestion came in 1971, the first time they all got together for a social gathering after Garven's departure from the university.

"You two need about $2,000,000 in dividend yielding investments to be able to enjoy the life you now have. No use accepting a reduced quality of life just because you retire," Garven told the couple, his friends. "You can invest in tax-free municipal bonds at a conservative 9 or 10% yield and have $200,000 a year to live on in perpetuity. The trick, of course, is to get that $2,000,000 in the first place. The nicest trick is to get more than that; so, you can have a few little extras."

Since both Devon and Rachel liked 'extras', they were willing listeners when Garven passed on small tips from time to time.

Two months after Garven was deposed from his neurosurgery chairmanship, he put Devon onto a housing development project in Antelope Valley with the man who was the chairman of the Republican Party of California. The land they were to purchase abutted the section set aside for the future Los Angeles International Airport. Mayor Sam Yorty and several of his councilmen had purchased the airport property itself, it was said around the real estate world that—by the luckiest of happenstances—the deal occurred just before the city and county made the massive land acquisition. A year later, the Upshires' investment of $20,000 had turned into $34,000. On the strength of that success, Devon and Rachel risked half of their $200,000 savings on an investment as venture capitalists, along with Garven, in a small factory in Lancaster, California, again in Antelope Valley. The factory made plastic holders for six-packs of beverages and operated under an exclusive patent. Eighteen months later, they all sold their interests in the company back to the owner per their original agreement. Devon and Rachel were $69,500 richer.

By the time Garven sold his holdings in the workman's comp care clinics in 1982, the Upshires had a little over $3,000,000 in their estate, some from timely investments in gold bullion, some from barrels of aging Scotch whiskey, and some from growth stocks. Devon and Rachel considered Garven Wilsonhulme to have an infallible Midas touch and assiduously cultivated his friendship, glad that he had understood that it was not Devon's doing that resulted in Garven's losing the chairmanship.

At dinner in early May, 1983 at the Upshire's new home in Brentwood, Garven avoided any talk about money and investments. Since that topic always featured prominently in conversations when the three of them got together, the couple were intrigued by Garven's avoidance of the subject.

"Hey, Garven, you've gotten secretive on us all of a sudden," Rachel said jocularly.

"Not really, just cautious," Garven said, vaguely.

That heightened Rachel's curiosity beyond endurance.

"I'd love to know what makes you 'cautious', Garven," she said. "It always has to do with making lots of money, but usually includes your old pals. C'mon, what's up?"

"Look, you guys, you are my best friends. I would be sick if I steered you wrong, seriously wrong, on an investment. I have been given a tip; frankly, an insider's tip, about a small company that has just gone public. I...wouldn't want you to have any risk of problems with the feds, the SEC, or anyone for making too much money," Garven said haltingly, moving carefully from sentence to sentence as if treading through a verbal mine field.

"Garven, there's no such thing as having too much money, being too thin, or having too low of a golf handicap. Boy, this sounds like a real problem—too much money," Rachel laughed. "C'mon, Garven, out with it."

"Now, look Rachel, Devon," Garven looked solemn. "I can't be responsible for what might happen. This is a green banana."

"A what?"

"A new, fledgling company," Devon explained to his wife.

He knew that much, at least.

"That's it," Garven agreed. "The company consists of two people right now, practically speaking, an engineer and his girl friend. They have one worker besides themselves. They have a shop by the little Mojave airport."

"Up in the high desert near Lancaster?" Devon asked.

"Right."

That put Devon and Rachel's curiosity into high gear since they had had two very successful early ventures in the Antelope Valley already. It was a good omen for them.

"What do these entrepreneurs do, Garven? Out with it. This is like pulling teeth," Devon pleaded.

"They make an ultra light airplane. It is invisible to radar, uses about a gallon of aviation fuel every four hundred miles, and can travel at about a hundred to a hundred fifty miles an hour. It can be made for next to nothing. I think it is kind of the airplane version of the Volkswagen. The insider's information given to me was two things. The first is that the plane is going to be launched for sale by the most spectacular gimmick of all time. They are going to unveil it at the Paris Air Show. And that's not the best part. Uncle Sam is going to foot the bill for the whole show—transportation of the prototype across the Atlantic and around Europe and back, hangering while it's there, the whole megilla. The second little tidbit of insider's information..."

He paused. Their rapt expressions told him that they were hooked into his narrative.

"...is that the U.S. Air Force has ordered twenty-four of them on an experimental basis. Who knows what will come out of the Paris Air show?"

"So, where do we fit in?" asked Rachel excitedly. In her mind, she was already in.

"Now, look, you guys; this is the greenest of green bananas. It sounds good and all, and I'm going to back them; but you ought to have a caution. Who knows what will happen? The aerospace industry is a volatile and inexplicable world all to itself. Fortunes are made and lost overnight. I don't know that this is the thing for you. Really," Garven stressed.

"I presume they need production money, right, Garven?" Devon surmised.

"That's it, right now. They all but went broke building the prototype. Both of them quit good jobs in the aerospace industry and worked on their plane full time. In another two weeks they will be evicted for their little hangar factory if they don't come up with some cash. That's the bottom line," Garven said.

"What number goes on that bottom line, Garven?" asked Devon.

"Six million. They need a bigger, better facility, proper aerospace machinery, more engineers, test pilots, attorneys; you can't do anything anywhere without a lawyer or two, or three, accountants, line workers, and the rest of it. One of their main problems is time. If they don't get their money this week, they will go under. I got that straight from the horse's mouth."

Devon and Rachel looked meaningfully and questioningly at each other for a moment. They nodded their heads in an unspoken agreement.

"We want in. It sounds like another winner, Garven, like one of those big computer companies that started out it somebody's garage. We could be fixed for life. Don't even think of trying to keep us out," Devon said.

He sounded almost pleading.

"Or you could be making another typical doctor's rotten investment—the modern day 'there's a sucker-born-ever-minute' scheme. What do we know about making airplanes?" Garven asked rhetorically.

"Tell me, old friend, are you going to invest?" Devon asked pointedly.

"I already have," Garven confessed, a little sheepish, and grinned over at his two old friends.

Devon shook his head in disbelief.

"You sly rascal," he said. "How much?"

"A million to start," Garven replied.

"For once, we want to be major share holders," Devon said. "We are prepared to put in our three million dollar nest egg, right, hon?"

Rachel made an almost imperceptible gulp.

"You bet," she said after a slight pause. "If we think it's worth being in for a penny, then I guess we might as well be in for a pound."

"It's your funeral," Garven said, "but I'll put you in touch. Don't say anything about the insider business. That's a strict ixnay. And don't say I didn't warn you."

"Our lips are sealed," said Rachel conspiratorially and made an unconscious little gesture across her lips.

CHAPTER
Thirty-Nine

In April, 1984 there was an accounting when the "UltraLight Aircraft Corporation" failed to meet its requirement to submit quarterly progress reports to the Securities and Exchange Commission for three quarters running. The involved banks had been screaming for two months. The accounting was conducted by forensic accountants from Washington D.C. Garven did not attend since he did not own stock. The Upshires were the principle stockholders and de facto owners of the corporation by that point. The original designers and engineers of the ultra light craft now resided in Brazil with the bulk of the company's money and were unavailable for the stockholders' meeting.

The rendition of the financial workings of the corporation was long and tedious, but the salient facts that were elucidated by the forensic accounts were of great interest to Devon and Rachel. The two of them were fifty-three years of age, and Devon faced mandatory retirement from the university in a little over a decade. Their original $3,000,000 investment had been increased by $500,000 from a mortgage on their Brentwood house. The house had been theirs free and clear prior to the assumption of the ownership of the exciting new innovation in flying machines. They saw the soaring potential when the United States Small Plane Owners' Association endorsed their project and agreed, in principle, to purchase five hundred of the small efficient craft at $17,000 a copy. Devon and Rachel took out a $1,000,000 loan from a small savings and loan company when they were able to convince the president of the lending company of the truly incredible potential of their investment. They were able to convince the S&L to accept, as collateral, Devon's salary from the university for the next twelve years. The additional loan was crucial to meet the production costs of the huge order from small plane owners'. Devon and Rachel looked at that order as only being the start.

The forensic accountants pointed out the hard facts underlying the great enthusiasms. In two years since the company had gone public, not a single production airplane had been built. The only other plane produced by the company besides the one that went to Paris at taxpayers' expense was one built to permit preliminary testing. That plane had crashed into a small house in the town of Mojave resulting in total demolishment of the plane and the house, a spinal fracture and huge medical costs for the test pilot, and a lawsuit for $10,000,000 that was still slowly winding its way through the clogged California civil justice system. The Upshires had a new working hangar to show for their investment, and nothing else. The machinery had been repossessed; the engineers and workers were now employed by GE and Lockheed. There was no direct proof, but it appeared reasonable to assume that the entire bank account had gone south with the engineer and his wife. The only positive thing about the whole dismal affair was that those two were no longer living in sin. There is no extradition treaty between the United States and Brazil.

Curious about Garven's involvement in the company from the start, the Upshires specifically asked for records of his investment. There was no indication that any person of that name had ever put any money into the project. There was an odd entry in the books. A company called "The Fletcher Group" invested $1,000,000 in May, 1982. The investment had been withdrawn abruptly in July, 1982 immediately before the final contract meeting with the Air Force. The government accountants attributed the failure to secure that contract to the sudden loss of a fourth of the company's working capital and the Air Force's decision that the company was not sufficiently stable to meet the GAO's exacting requirements.

Horst Caesar headed the nation's busiest and most conservative obstetrical unit. It was one of the highest profile departments in the entire country, and Dr. Caesar was, after Everett Koop, the Surgeon General, the best known physician in the United States. Patrons of the department represented the *crème de la crème of* wealthy Los Angeles society. The research done by the department was conservative; the selection of the staff followed guidelines as rigid as those for a church school like BYU regarding moral and ethical character as well as for competence. The care of the young women 'customers' of the department leaned very strongly towards prevention—the major thrust being sexual abstinence and the minor thrust being to instill in the girls a resolve to use contraception failing their full commitment to abstinence. There were no abortions. Girls who had babies out of wedlock were very sternly influenced to give them up for adoption. The few who elected to keep their babies themselves received a frosty reception from the staff.

In the entire history of the department there had never been a public scandal. The only instance known to Anyone—and that to only an inner few—of moral turpitude, involved a junior staff man who confessed to his wife that he had committed adultery. That confession resulted in a quiet divorce and an even quieter termination of the obstetrician's contract with the hospital.

Horst Caesar, as department chairman, was also the de facto guardian of the OB-Gyn staff's virtue, a responsibility that he took very seriously as a few of the residents and student nurses were to learn to their sorrow. Therefore, when Horst Caesar fell from grace figuratively, politically, and publicly; it was a very great fall. To the end of his career, Dr. Caesar insisted that he was entirely innocent of the charges leveled against him, and he spent considerable of his retirement savings in his attempt to prove his guiltlessness.

Garven read about the sordid affair in the *Arizona Republic* on September 1, 1983 at a time when he was establishing residency in Phoenix and making arrangements for his mother to move into a classy retirement center.

The article competed for front page coverage of the news that the USSR had shot down a South Korean Airlines plane that supposedly had strayed over their airspace. 269 people were killed. President Reagan was threatening sanctions against the Soviets. In the other article of interest, an AP report, Dr. Horst Caesar, the prominent head of obstetrics at the prestigious University of California Osterlund Memorial Hospital in Los Angeles had been arrested after soliciting acts of prostitution from an undercover Los Angeles vice officer. The officer produced photographs of the two of them lying naked on a hotel bed with a copy of the front page of the *LA Times* lying casually at the bottom of the bed confirming the date. Her sworn testimony stated that Dr. Caesar had solicited the performance of lewd acts, the nature of which could not be published in the *Arizona Republic*, according to an editor's note.

The article went on to say that Dr. Caesar's lawyer, speaking for him, stated that the prominent physician was completely innocent and had been framed, set-up by the vice officer. When asked if he meant "entrapped", a common defense by men caught in a vice sting, the doctor insisted that it was more than that. He indicated that his client, the famous obstetrician, had been lured up to the hotel room under false pretenses, drugged, photographed, and compromised. He was mounting a suit naming the LAPD, the city, and the vice officer involved. The LAPD and the city attorney responded by saying that Caesar's accusations were "egregious nonsense. The department was professional and such charges were unfounded and made in desperation."

Over the next several weeks, the story remained high profile. There were a series of accusations and counter accusations. The LAPD and DA's office threatened to file a charge of lying under oath to the already serious misdemeanor charges. In the end, Caesar plea bargained. It was, after all, his first offense, and not a major charge, the judge said. The doctor was allowed to pay a fine of $400, and his jail sentence was reduced to time served. He was placed on probation for one year; but, in the end did not have to file as a sex offender. The incident happened to have occurred at a time when the city commission was involved in a crackdown on vice and drug selling, and they could not afford to appear to be soft on a high profile defendant.

The university would not allow Caesar to resign. They went through the tedious process of involuntary termination and were successful in putting Dr. Caesar out the chairmanship of his department, to strip him of his tenure, and to cancel his pension. He was paid a lump sum buyout of his contributions in the amount of $50,000 cash. To his credit, subsequent *Times* articles said, Dr. Caesar did not protest the university's actions nor seek to overturn them. At the age of sixty-one, he entered private practice in Fresno, California. He was granted gynecological privileges at Fresno Community Hospital but no obstetrical privileges. It was felt that that provision was necessary in the best interests of the patients owing to Dr. Caesar's advanced age and to his lack of direct hands-on delivery experience for five years preceding his application. It was the opinion of the members of the OB department of the Fresno hospital that sixty-one was too old to start an OB career at their hospital. The taint of moral turpitude as a factor was never publicly mentioned, but, for the conservative obstetricians on the hospital staff, it was crucial. His being given privileges for a non-operative gynecology practice passed by a single vote. However vigorously Horst Caesar tried to defend his actions and to spin the negative publicity, he was ruined. He retired after a dismal year in the California backwater town.

The furor over the Caesar scandal caused a major controversy in the ranks of LAPD. The vice officer involved, Lt. Amanda Garcia, was openly derided by some of her male colleagues as having faked the entire accusation and evidence. A rank and file blue wall closed around her as a shield. An Internal Affairs hearing cleared her of all wrongdoing since no evidence could be produced against her, but the rumors and jokes around Parker Center continued to circulate. She finally sued the city and the department for mental anguish, gender discrimination, and sexual harassment, and in the settlement, won $30,000. She became a serious political liability. She received a lifetime pension for her medical retirement due to stress which was considered overly generous by the non-union administrators of the nation's largest police force. Lt. Garcia retired to Phoenix, Arizona where it was reported that she became part owner of a major mobile home development as well as the chief security officer for the project. Wags in LAPD said that they had never met a better money manager than that officer. She was able, they said, to turn a measly $30,000 award into $300,000 a year. No one had any facts to back up such wanton allegations, and in a year, no one remembered her nor cared.

CHAPTER
Forty

Helene Eamon, in the fall of 1983, decided that Garven Wilsonhulme would never marry her and that she was tired of being neglected. It did her no good that her boyfriend, if you can call a sixty-four year old, gray haired man, a "boy" friend, was rich. She held to her belief that things always work out for the best, and she decided to move on and find other "bests" for her.

They were attending a fund raiser for the Arizona homeless in the Camelback Inn in Phoenix. Garven had flown Helene in from LA.

On the way back to their own hotel, she asked, "Garven, I need to know something once and for all. I know that men hate ultimatums, and I don't want to put it that way. But...are you and I going to live together? Are we going to get married? It is unfair to me to be made to dangle like this. I need to get on with my life. I need the status of being your wife."

Helene was usually very circumspect and circumlocutory. Garven was caught off guard by her directness. And she was right; he did not like ultimata.

"I thought we had a good thing going for us and were in agreement that we did not want to mess things up by talking about marriage. I'm a two time loser, and you have been through the grinder once yourself. What's wrong with the status quo?"

"Oh, Garven. This isn't enough. Not for me. It's fun at times, but there aren't enough times. I want to wake up by you morning after morning. I want to go out shopping and to movies and for walks. I want to introduce you to my family and friends as my husband. I want a real stable marriage.

Whatever I may have said in a moment of weakness, what I just said now is what I really want."

She looked at him earnestly and expectantly. The ball was in his court, and he had to make the deciding play of the day.

"Well, Helene. I can't say that I'm ready for such a final and long-term commitment. I haven't exactly been a sterling husband or a faithful one. I don't think it's in me to change. I can't help but look at marriage as a ball and chain, to use the old expression, but it's apt. That's the way I look at it, sorry."

"I was afraid that's what you'd say, Garven."

She was crying and was angry at herself for doing so. Her mascara was running, and she got more angry.

"I need to get back to LA tonight. I thought this would happen; so, I bought a return ticket on the red eye."

"And created a self-fulfilling prophecy," Garven said. "You don't even want to stay over and use your regular ticket for tomorrow morning? So, maybe we could talk about this?" he asked, mildly incredulous.

"No, it's best to break off clean. I wouldn't be much fun tonight, anyway. Would you mind having the cabby take me to the airport?"

"I suppose not," Garven said.

His face was set in hard lines. She was already absent from his life, he felt. The drive to the airport was only an incidental. Garven and Helene did not cross paths again.

Henry Kowalski was sixty-three in 1983. He, like most VA staffers, had the countdown to retirement (690 days) figured to the month, week, day, and hour complete with vacation time, weekends, and days off figured in. He was tired of putting up with the anesthesiology residents, let alone the surgery house staff who were so arrogant and pushy. He was tired of walking around the VA corridors with gray old men wearing face masks and coughing pink tinged sputum, men with signs on their backs telling one and all where they should take the old man if he was found wandering around lost. He could scarcely stomach seeing the hundreds of inpatients going about their slow-paced unimportant business in their light blue striped cotton bathrobes. He was tired of working on men who had bad lungs, men with amputated legs, hemiplegics, and the blind. He had to admit it to himself that he did not like the old vets and was tired of being in the company of such losers for the bulk of his life. His memories of his career were none too positive—no significant money, no significant prestige, a drab unrewarding practice; and the change-over to university control of the VA clinical service had been galling. He had had to put up with a series of nasty tyrants from UCOMH. He gritted his teeth when he recalled one such, that Wilsonhulme character whom he had finally bested.

Kowalski had a nice pension coming. He would not be rich like his private practice counterparts, but the pension was over 70% of his present income and was tax exempt. He had one last raise to go, and that would determine the final value of his retirement income. Barring some totally unexpected change, he had calculated that figure down to the last penny. The pension, like his life, was predictable, comfortable, and unexciting. He liked it that way.

The chief of staff called the anesthesiology department secretary and asked to speak to Dr. Kowalski.

"He's not here, Sir," she replied. "He's in the OR, so far as I know. Would you like to leave him a message?"

"I would. Please tell him to be in my office at one o'clock this afternoon. It is a matter of some importance."

Kowalski was on time. One of his virtues was his punctuality.

"What is it Dr. Templeton?" he asked.

None of the career physicians or administrators were on a first name basis. It seemed to maintain a tone of formality, distance, and anonymity; It was more professional, and the physicians preferred it that way.

"Take a seat, Dr. Kowalski. You will need to be seated for this," the chief administrator said.

His voice was solicitous, and that made Henry Kowalski nervous.

CHAPTER
Forty-One

D r. Templeton handed Kowalski an envelope that contained two pages of heavy bond paper. Templeton watched Dr. Kowalski blanch and stay pale as soon as he had perused the first paragraph. Dr. Kowalski was being sued for malpractice, the documents said. It was his first time, and he was affronted, angered, and frightened. He had hoped against all hope to be able to go the last twenty-three months, four days, and six hours of his career without having a malpractice suit on his record.

"We should talk about this, Dr. Kowalski," said Dr. Templeton. "We need to prepare a defense. We'll meet with the lawyers, that sort of thing."

Kowalski crossly wondered who 'we' were; did Templeton have a mouse in his pocket? He knew the drill. He would be all alone out there with his neck laying on the chopping block when the moment of truth came. Thank heavens for the standard malpractice coverage package provided by the VA. At least, he would not be out any of his own money if he lost. That was a consolation.

"It took me a minute, but I do remember the patient now," Kowalski said.

He thought that the old case was long dead and buried. He could not imagine how it had been resurrected.

"This old vet was admitted for resection of a bowel tumor; must have been in '55 or '56. We put him to sleep for the operation, and he never woke up. He must have had a stroke during the procedure. That was the only thing we could figure. He died a couple of days later. That's all there was to it. The family seemed to understand, didn't make any threats or anything. I can't imagine why they are suing at this late date or why at all, for that matter. There's nothing in the attorney's intent-to-sue letter that gives me a clue."

"We'll know soon enough, I suppose," said Templeton morosely.

He hated suits, even if they were against other doctors. They were messy and rancorous, time consuming, and bad for PR. He hated malpractice suits on general principle.

The plaintiff's attorney requested an unusual meeting. Kowalski's attorney was leery, but agreed when the opposing attorney convinced him that it was worth his while. The attorney for the deceased's family met with Kowalski, Templeton, and the attorneys appointed by the insurance company to defend the Chief of Anesthesiology.

The first thing Dr. Kowalski's attorney said was, "I'm surprised to see this suit, gentlemen. It is a very long time past the statute of limitations."

"Not for fraud," said the opposing attorney with a determined set to his square jaw and strong chin.

He had the attention of everyone in the room and had upped the adrenaline levels of more than one of them.

Kowalski leaned over to his attorney and whispered, "I told you there was no statute of limitations for doctors. We just have to bend over and take it. And what does he mean, 'fraud'?"

"Please, Mr. Anthony, what's this about 'fraud'? Isn't that a bit ridiculous, even by California standards?" Kowalski's attorney countered.

The plaintiff's attorney was a hard-faced, pock-marked, ugly man who did not care about anyone's feelings, prejudices, or expectations. It was all about winning.

"Well, Sir, I think you might want to hear and see this. You can save us all a good deal of grief and work. I think you are going to want to settle and quickly once you do," Mr. Anthony said.

"Never!" shrieked Dr. Kowalski. "I will never, ever, EVER settle, you bandits!"

Mr. Anthony looked at the defendant benignly. Kowalski was purple in the face. His attorney thought the man was going to have a heart attack or a stroke or something.

"Please, Dr. Kowalski, you need to calm down. This does no good. None at all. Let me handle it," said the defense attorney.

Mr. Anthony rolled his eyes, and Kowalski's lawyer inclined his own head in acknowledgment of the accuracy of that gesture.

"I think it might be better if you were to go back to your office and take it easy for a while. I will tell you everything that transpires and immediately."

Kowalski hesitated noticeably.

"Please."

"All right," said Kowalski.

He did not feel well. He was having trouble getting control of himself. He felt his pulse and found it racing and pounding. He knew that his blood pressure must be off the manometer.

"I think maybe you're right. I don't know what happened to me. I feel ill. I will lie down for a bit."

He beat a hasty retreat.

"Now to cases," said Mr. Anthony. "Kindly look these over."

He showed the defense attorney a set of nurses notes from the OR. There, in her neat crimped block letter writing was the damning evidence. "Pt. intub. in esophagus. Both nurse Hodges and I tried to tell Dr. K. Pt. turning blue. We officially protested to Dr. K. Pt. covered with drapes. We reported again to Dr. K that pt. was in distress. K. refused to re-intubate. Blood gases - PaO2 58. Re-intubated. Too late. Nurses not at fault."

"A case could be made for malpractice, if all of that's true; but the statute of limitations has run out already. Surely, you don't think you can sell that flimsy documentation as evidence of fraud, do you?" declared the defense attorney emphatically, presuming that a good offense was the best defense.

"No, that's just malpractice. *Res ipsa loquitor*. It's fraud because of this," Anthony said calmly.

He showed the opposing attorney copies of Dr. Kowalski's anesthesia record for the case. In small, difficult to read letters, some that looked like Hindi written backwards, there was a note that read: "Successfully intubated. ABGs ok. PaO2 120. No probs."

On a second page there was a note that said: "Pt. not waking up. ABGs ok. No anes. Probs evident. Possible stroke. Pt. has HBP."

"So, there's no mention of the low arterial blood gas of 58. How do we know that the nurses didn't make a mistake despite their self-serving note?"

Anthony showed the defense attorney the actual chart, the blood gas chit showing "58" was clearly evident."

"Still no more than possible malpractice. No evidence of fraud."

"Read on," Anthony insisted.

He showed the formal progress notes to the defendant's attorney. Dr. Kowalski's note was partially blacked out, almost completely obliterating four lines of writing. The lines below read much the same as the anesthesia record.

"Not all that damning," said Kowalski's attorney, but with a little less assurance. "A little problem with the blacked out area, maybe, but pretty weak for so-called 'fraud'.

"My friend, be a little more thorough, if you would. First hold up the blacked out area to the light."

Kowalski's attorney scrutinized the paper against the naked bulb of the table lamp after removing the lamp shade. It was difficult, but the writing was fairly evident: "Esoph. intubation for over 30 mins. ABGs terrible. Pt. has severe cerebral anoxia."

The attorney paled. The nurses had been right. This would be very difficult to defend.

Anthony was not finished.

"Now go back and look very carefully at the last anesthesia record entry and then again at the progress notes. Use the original chart, not your copies. See if you don't see another connection."

The defense attorney dutifully complied.

It took several comparisons over a period of minutes. Then, as if the proverbial cartoon light bulb suddenly went on over his head, the defense attorney saw it. The latest entry on the anesthesia sheet was alone on a sheet with no indications of vital signs or other evidence of an operation in progress. Unlike the previous page which was penned in black ink, this one was written in blue. He hurriedly looked at the 'blacked-in' segment of the progress note—blue ink, definitely different from the note underneath. One tail from a "P" dangled out uncovered. It was in black ink. The note below was an incriminating blue. Anthony would not have the slightest difficulty proving to even the most skeptical juror or judge that the record had been deliberately tampered with. None of this had been apparent on the Xerox copies that the defense attorney had been working with. The defense attorney felt sick and old right then.

"Now," said attorney Anthony, "we can begin to communicate. Everything I spend will take away from my end of the contingency fee, including my valuable time. If this is made easy for me, I think we can arrive at an entirely equitable agreement. Let me suggest how..."

After hearing 'how', Kowalski's attorney said, "I will have to do a little fast checking. Could you wait here for a bit. I think we can resolve this satisfactorily."

"I have all the time in the world," said Mr. Anthony.

He looked as calm and content as the proverbial summer's morn. All he needed was to be seated on a verandah sipping a mint julep to seem entirely in his proper setting.

"I hope you don't mind if I smoke," he said.

He was already slipping the cellophane wrapper off a cheap fat cigar. The wrapper read: "It's a Boy!"

Kowalski fretted and fidgeted in his office waiting for the negotiations to be completed. He was one floor up from the administrator's office; so, he did not see his attorney scurry in to see the director.

"Come right in. What have you to report?" asked the medical director.

"Dr. Templeton, I will be very brief and to the point," said the attorney, a little breathlessly from his half block walk.

He settled his ample girth into one of Templeton's easy chairs.

"By all means."

"This is it in a nutshell. Kowalski put a breathing tube down the wrong pipe—down the esophagus."

He pronounced the word with long vowels.

"He refused repeated requests by the nurses to change the position of the tube. That gave the patient no oxygen for at least half an hour, and that is malpractice plain and simple."

"But, I thought the statute of limitations..."

"Forget that. For one thing, in this instance, I am sad to say that our cynical Dr. Kowalski is right about one thing, there is no statute of limitation for doctors. There is always a way around that small hurdle."

"I take it there's more…as if this were not enough," sighed Templeton.

"Indeed. He lied, and then he altered the chart."

Dr. Templeton grimaced.

"It is obvious once you see the original chart. It is flagrant. He's dead."

Dr. Templeton took out his handkerchief.

"Is the hospital dead, too?"

Dr. Templeton mopped his brow. It was not a hot day.

"Maybe, maybe not. Mr. Anthony has suggested a deal."

Templeton raised one eyebrow.

"Tell me, who is paying my fee? Precisely for whom am I working?"

Templeton scratched his head.

"I suppose for the hospital, for the VA, if you want to be technical about it. Your firm is hired by the insurance company who is hired by us. I mean the VA itself. I'm not sure where this is going."

"And what if there is a conflict of interest between Dr. Kowalski and the Veteran's Administration Hospital?"

"Then, presuming that as a hypothetical, as you guys say, I guess we would have to hire two attorneys to keep it all copacetic."

"For malpractice defense?"

"Yes."

He looked at the attorney quizzically. It still seemed vague.

"Isn't that what we're talking about here?"

"And for fraud on the doctor's part?"

"Ummmh," Templeton mused.

He took off his glasses and rubbed the sore bridge of his nose.

"I would have to look at the policy."

"Now is a very opportune time, Dr. Templeton. We're talking millions."

Templeton's interest was fully aroused by that. He had his secretary find the policy in the files. He had never been able to understand her system. Maybe that was her way of keeping her job forever—making herself indispensable—he thought. She promptly brought the policy to him. Dr. Templeton quickly ran his finger down paragraph after paragraph then line upon line.

"Here we are," he said finally.

"Let me see, please," the attorney asked.

Templeton had seen all he needed to. The attorney confirmed his impression.

"The VA is expressly not responsible for fraudulent practice on the part of professionals, not for their defense, and does not have to indemnify them against any loss resulting from the fraud. That is a different kettle of fish than plain malpractice."

"Poor Kowalski," murmured Dr. Templeton.

He was glad that he was not in the poor booger's shoes about now, he thought.

"So how do we handle this?"

"Mr. Anthony, the plaintiff's attorney, has offered a settlement; and given the circumstances, I think we should accept his terms without protest or argument. The VA agrees to pay the full extent of the damage coverage allowed by the policy, and no more. That way, the organization does not lose any money. Uncle Sam and his representatives will probably look more favorably on you for that."

Dr. Templeton nodded.

"Fortunately for Mr. Anthony and his clients, the deep pockets here belong to Uncle Sam's insurance company. The amount asked, and just coincidentally available by the policy, is five million bucks."

"Whew! That's pretty steep, don't you think? Do you really think we have to go all the way?"

"The other side of the coin, the price for quibbling, is that the VA joins Dr. Kowalski in the fraud action and in the punitive damages that issue therefrom," said the attorney knowing he was on firm ground for that opinion. "I very strongly suggest that the hospital settle for the full amount and separate itself from the doctor. It's not all that nice, maybe, but it's legal; and it's hardly some arcane principle of the thing, now. It's the money."

Templeton nodded his head in agreement, still reluctant to believe it entirely. It was too much to absorb. And there was poor Kowalski.

"Any other doctors named or likely to be named? Or any of the nurses?" he asked.

"I went over that with Mr. Anthony. It is a much cleaner and simpler case if Dr. Kowalski absorbs the whole shot—wadding and all. The usual thing is to make everybody who ever went near the patient unhappy by naming them, but Anthony is no more interested in that than we are. The surgeon, Henry Winston, I take it he's the chief of the department and the lowly intern, a Dr. Wilsonhulme, if I remember correctly, are altogether peripheral to the case. This is a cut and dried anesthesia case, not a surgery case. The nurses, on the other hand, come across as the heroines. They will get a plaintiff's medal and the key to the city so far as Anthony is concerned. No suit for any of them.

"If you give me the green light, I'll let Mr. Anthony know that he has found the pot of gold at the end of the rainbow. He likely has the papers ready to sign to complete the deal even now if I read him right. He was a thorough attorney and a formidable opponent. I would hate to be in Dr. Kowalski's shoes," the defense attorney said easing himself out of the chair without enthusiasm.

As he left the room, he said, "I don't relish breaking this to Kowalski."

The VA's attorney signed the agreement awarding the patient's survivors $5,000,000 for the wrongful death of their loved one with terminal cancer.

When the formalities were completed he asked, "Would you mind, Mr. Anthony, telling me how you came onto this case. It seems to me that it was buried away in the case files someplace deep out of sight. Did the family contact you?"

"Actually, no, that wasn't the case. I contacted them in order to right the wrong that they had suffered and to send out a message to other doctors."

"Spare me the American Trial Lawyers' rhetoric. How did you learn about it?"

"Funny thing, that. Simplest possible way. Manna from heaven as it were. I received a copy of the chart and a typed explanation of the circumstances right down to the discrepancies in the inks and the improper striking out of the notes as a late altering of the chart. I haven't the foggiest idea who sent the material or why, or why specifically to me? Maybe a disgruntled nurse. I'll tell you, though, I'd like to take him or her out for the best steak in town."

CHAPTER
Forty-Two

D r. Kowalski did not take the news well. He was nothing of an inscrutable. He screamed, literally screamed, that he had been betrayed. He
stamped his feet like a colt being gelded. He was like a child when he learned
that he would have to get himself another lawyer and would have to fight the
VA as well as the plaintiff. He almost fainted when he was made to realize that
he could personally have to pay both the lawyer and any damages awarded
from his own pocket.

Despite his new lawyer's advice, Dr. Kowalski fought the case all the way
through court, refusing to listen to reason, to compromise, or to settle.

He succeeded in quashing Mr. Anthony's final offer to settle for $7,000,000,
screaming that it was "highway robbery. You might as well be wearing a mask
and carrying a gun."

He hated his attorney and sued him for legal malpractice for gross incom-
petence after the judgment was rendered by a jury in Compton that was the
court of jurisdiction after a drawing. The lawyer who sued Kowalski's trial
attorney would not accept a contingency fee. He charged the anesthesiologist
a flat $25,000 and expenses. Kowalski lost that action as well.

The jury in the main trial was not allowed to award for the actual malpractice; that was covered by the $5,000,000 insurance settlement. The jury
did find for the plaintiff's family for the commission of fraud involved in
the wrongful death by medical mishap and awarded them $10,000,000.
Compton juries were notoriously pro-plaintiff when the defendant was a
large company or a rich person such as any doctor.

Chapter Forty-Two

Dr. Kowalski filed for bankruptcy immediately upon being served with the judgment. The insolvency hearing judge required the doctor and his wife to liquidate all of their holdings, bank accounts, and property, even their best car. Dr. Kowalski was left with no equity in a modest home, a five year old station wagon that needed work, two suits of clothing to allow him to do his work, and a shotgun. Those specific assets were permitted under the provisions of the Homestead filing that Kowalski had been farsighted enough to have done when he bought his house in the early fifties. Even then, with $762,000 paid and the couple rendered essentially paupers, the judge, acting in accordance with recently revised California bankruptcy laws, could not allow the debts to be considered discharged. In keeping with the guidelines set down by higher courts, the judge worked out a payment schedule for Dr. Kowalski.

He was to give over all but $400 a month from his VA salary and any other earnings he might have in the future until the remaining nine plus million dollar encumbrance was paid off. Kowalski, in his methodical way, sat down and figured out the length of time required before he would be free of debt enough to retire. It was just over 167 and a third years, not including any interest payments. He would be 230 and a third years old when he was free of his indentured servitude, if he could keep up his present pace of earning.

On Christmas day, 1985, while his wife was visiting their grown daughter, Henry Kowalski put the Bing Crosby *White Christmas* 78 on the stereo and turned the volume up to maximum. He then hanged himself with one of the five neckties he had secretly kept from the forced sale of his personal possessions.

CHAPTER
Forty-Three

In the June, 1984 meeting of the Board of Regents for the University of California, the advancement and awards meeting, Elijah David Shapiro's name was offered as the next chairman of the department of neurosurgery at UCOMH. His name was placed in nomination by Garven Wilsonhulme as Dr. Wilsonhulme's final action as a regent. Garven's term of office expired with the close of that meeting. Dr. Shapiro was the prime candidate to fill the position vacated by Dr. Devon Upshire who left academia to pursue a private practice career because of financial considerations. There were no dissenters to the nomination, and the board wrote a congratulatory letter to Dr. Shapiro wishing him a long and fruitful career in the important position.

At the end of that June, before Garven left Los Angeles to pursue a new position as CEO and President of the Cal/Maxi-Therapy Clinic Group, based in San Francisco, he and Elijah David met for a leisurely lunch. Over coffee and congratulatory snifters of cognac, the two men talked about old times and about the events leading to ED's elevation to the chairmanship.

"I didn't see your hand directly in any of this, Garven; but I know I owe my place to your intervention, somehow," ED. said.

"Nothing of the sort, E.D. You deserved it and got there on your own merits. It was high time that a research oriented professor with a firm background in all of the academic areas was recognized by a chiefship. Once again California is breaking new ground, and it is as it should be," Garven insisted.

"Garven, you are as full of it as a Christmas goose."

He smiled a cryptic smile.

"I can't help thinking that there were a lot of coincidences along the way. Funny thing how each one of the men who got you kicked out and embarrassed came to a bad end. You wouldn't know anything about that would you, old friend?"

Garven's face remained impassive, his eyes as expressionless as ball bearings. He shook his head.

"And you wouldn't tell me if you did, right?"

E.D. did not expect an answer.

"That kind of revenge would have had to come from a white hot core of memory and rage, I would hazard. Don't you agree, Garven? Speaking hypothetically, of course."

"Not exactly, still speaking hypothetically," Garven mused. "I tend to think of vengeance as being like vichyssoise, both are better served up cold. I must have read that some place."

"And I think it was Cornelius Vanderbilt who, when he was screwed out of his position as CEO of one of his own companies, said, 'I will ruin you, gentlemen'. I seem to remember someone telling me that you made some sort of a statement like that at one of the Faculty Executive meetings."

"That was a long time ago, my friend. Who can remember such things from the deep well of our past? Have a little more Courvoisier? A cigar?" Garven said.

"Always ready to celebrate with a genuine Phoenix," E.D. said, unsuccessfully suppressing a wry and knowing smile.

Garven's eyes were half lidded as if he were only paying partial attention to the whole conversation, and his interests were now elsewhere.

Garven accepted the position of CEO of the two year old Cal/Maxi-Therapy Clinics Corporation knowing full well that the rapidly expanding company was headed for trouble in the short term if it was not brought under control. The company was quintessential California—brash, innovative, and heedless of expense, debt, and potential downturns in the economy of the future. The originators of the company, a pair of physicians originally from Sri Lanka, had developed their own clinic into a paragon of efficiency. They were able to see twice as many patients as their competitors at around half the cost. The savings they realized went directly into the pockets of insurance company administrators or stock holders somewhere removed from the people who were doing the work, and that annoyed the hard working physicians. They came up with a plan to establish their own small pre-paid clinic and were able to profit handsomely despite lowering fees by a third. It seemed very easy to do. Shortly, the influx of patients from neighboring communities overwhelmed their facilities; so, they expanded. In a year, they had fifty clinics; and in two years, they had six hundred.

State licensing officials took a dim view of physicians referring their own patients to x-ray and lab facilities that they owned and put pressure on the original physicians to step aside. Although the practice was not strictly illegal, the state assured the two physicians that it soon would be. There was even talk of federal proscriptions being enacted against self-referral. When the Sri Lankans did not make haste to comply, the state came in with an audit of their books. This investigation proved to be fruitful; preliminary accounting was suggestive of skimming. The two entrepreneurs were offered the chance to step aside and to avoid a more thorough investigation and a possible indictment.

They saw the old lettering on the wall: *"Mene mene tekel u-pharsin"* (Aramiac: God has numbered the days of your kingdom and brought it to an end; you have been weighed in the balance and found wanting; and your kingdom has been divided and given to the Medes and Persians).

The two Sri Lankans paid themselves each severance pay of $10,000,000 and gracefully stepped aside, crying all the way to the bank. With the blessing of the State of California and the forces for good in the community, the remaining members of the board of directors cast about for a new CEO and finally selected Garven Wilsonhulme. The state was less free with its vocal blessings when it learned of the board's choice.

To remain in compliance with the State of California's recommendations against self-referral, Dr. Wilsonhulme had to agree by contract not to practice medicine, not to accept any fee or salary for service, or to receive any direct payment from any of the ancillary laboratory services. The board and Garven solved that problem simply and amicably. They gave Garven a salary of $800,000 a year, comparable with that of CEOs of other large corporations. He was also given, at his insistence, stocks and stock options amounting to ten percent of the value of the company. He could not have cared less that he had had to agree not to practice medicine directly through the company.

He had to agree not to sell off any of his stock as long as he remained CEO. In return for that concession, he was guaranteed that his stock could be sold for at least the value of the stock on the day he took office.

Garven's greatest challenge was that the former principle partners had contracted to purchase a large group of free standing clinics in Georgia and Texas from a company called "Health Progress Alliance National." The nearly one thousand clinics under their umbrella had sold for $150,000,000, and Cal/

Maxi-Therapy had been leveraged to its eyebrows to accomplish the buy-out. It was expected that the profits would be counted in billions of dollars once the difficult early period of high debt leverage was past.

His greatest asset was the remarkable capacity of American doctors to roll over and act dead in business matters. They were incapable of joining together to act in any kind of concerted fashion to further their own interests. Garven had known that for years and up until the time of his ascendancy to the position of CEO, he had been frustrated by that observation. Now, he used it to his company's advantage. Doctors of all specialties took the narrow view and squabbled over the right to care for individual patients for a fee, like street dogs over meat scraps. As a consequence, they were all but helpless against organized and determined group health care providers. As soon as the first physician fell in with the Cal/Maxi-Therapy group in a given city, it was no time before the rest of the physicians fell all over themselves to sign contracts to provide health care for payments that were only thirty or forty percent of their former and regular office fees.

This sort of medical economic "block busting"—reminiscent of the past real estate practice of placing one minority family in one house and watching neighborhood property values tumble as a consequence—was enormously successful. The doctors operated under a kind of perverse self-destructive myopic psychology that led them to lose most of their practice income and to increase their work load in order to avoid having another physician sweep up a patient or two from their office. The doctors were like lemmings going over the cliff together. Each year, the doctors involved signed contracts accepting an ever decreasing percentage of the corporation's earnings despite being the ones doing the actual in-the-trenches work. It was strange behavior, but someone was bound to profit from the perversity. Garven reasoned that it might as well be Cal/Maxi-Therapy Corporation and Garven Wilsonhulme.

CHAPTER
Forty-Four

G arven proved to be a highly efficient and productive CEO. He used the financial muscle of Cal/Maxi-Therapy to squeeze doctors, hospitals, and labs into lowering their fees to the level of absolute minimal profit for them and maximal savings for his own company. While he did so, he slowly raised the premiums for the patients, citing increases in costs, and thereby, profited from both ends. Cal/Maxi-Therapy recorded a two year steady increase in profits and achieved a gratifying accrual of new patients signing up for its pre-payment plan. The company was beginning to rival the massive Caesar Permanente Plan in numbers and after expenses income. Caesar functioned on the same ruthless corporate capitalistic plan. The principle difference between the two companies was that Caesar owned its own hospitals, and Cal/Maxi-Therapy merely paid bottom dollar for space in local hospitals for the patients that could not be treated any longer on an outpatient basis and had to be admitted.

Despite the low operational costs and maximized profits achieved by Garven and his executive staff, the outflow of cash to cover the high leverage of Cal/Maxi-Therapy's debts exceeded the income of the company. This resulted in a requirement to borrow more to pay off the debts to the banks and an upward adjustment of the interest rates they had to pay. Garven tightened their policies, pushing the contracting doctors and labs to their limits—just short of them going bankrupt or mounting a mutiny.

He sold off as much of the company's equipment as possible to obtain cash. That required leasing fees to obtain the needed equipment, but postponed the need to pay for a few months. He refused to allow the company to purchase any more high ticket items of its own—CAT scanners, MRIs, fluoroscopic units, or major automated laboratory devices. The financial ledger continued to leak red ink. Garven trimmed back the administrative staff at the corporate level and gained enemies. When that was not enough, he cut back the administrative personnel in the individual clinics. The cost-to-income ratio grew smaller, but it was still a number greater than one.

By the fall of 1987, Cal/Maxi-Therapy was beginning to be late with its payments to banks. The financial people in the corporation desperately juggled payments, stringing out the checks as long as possible to the least squeaky wheels. Physicians were reimbursed the latest and the least because they paid the least attention to business matters. Many of them blithely accepted the lack of payments or ignored the situation as merely being part of doing business in an increasingly hostile business climate. The very least attentive of them were not paid for a year or more. Hospitals were only a little less naive and patient, feeling themselves trapped. Almost every business involved with Cal/Maxi-Therapy regarded the huge medical conglomerate as to large to be allowed to fail since they were likely to go down with them. Vendors were more business minded and pragmatic. They sent demands, even threats.

Garven looked over the stack of demand and attorney letters and said to his number two in his San Francisco office, "I have a basic plan, Lewis. Every day there are more demands for money than there is money. I sort out the letters into polite demands and nasty attorney threats. I put the payments that need to be made into a hat and draw out two or three to pay that day. If the demands are phrased in unpleasant language or if the attorney is really nasty, I don't even put their claim in the hat."

Lewis Sackett could only manage a thin lipped smile. There was little to smile about around corporate headquarters.

Banks were not the least bit naive, and they were demanding, but they knew that if they were too exacting; or if they sought help from the courts, they might bring down the whole house of cards. By necessity, the banks became witting accomplices in the decrescendo march toward bankruptcy with their own escalating indebtedness. The prevailing philosophy from top to bottom was that the system, at least as it pertained to Cal/Maxi-Therapy Corporation, was too big to fail.

Garven held meetings with the physician heads of the major clinics under the Cal/Maxi-Therapy umbrella to explain the deteriorating situation and to enlist their patience and understanding. He offered to sell off significant portions of the ownership of the clinics to the physicians who worked in them and to barter off most of the contracts with individual patients and industrial companies. This resulted in decentralization of Cal/Maxi-Therapy and slowed down the descent. He slashed the salaries of the remaining central executives, including his own. Many of the affected executives abandoned the sinking ship, selling off their promised stock options at a fraction of what they had been worth when the executives had started with the company with such high expectations. As he personally collected the undervalued stock options from the departing executives, Garven collected more enemies.

Garven cut his own salary to a dollar a year as an example to everyone else at a personal cost of $800,000 annually; most were not impressed. The obliquity of the graphic line of the business' downward trend flattened somewhat with all of these Draconian measures, but remained on a downhill slant. Garven was severely stressed, particularly since he had virtually no one in whom he could confide.

For all of the heavy responsibility of his position, Garven did not have to put in a great deal of time in actual work. He traveled to Europe and to Japan on vacation, and he attended the reunion of his high school class at Burton-Cagle School for a week in late April. While he enjoyed seeing most of his old classmates, Devon and Rachel Upshire were there to put a damper on his enthusiasm and to underscore for him the degree to which he had become alienated and isolated. Despite their protestations that they did not hold him responsible for the collapse of their finances, they no longer saw Garven socially.

Lyle Durche and Edward Sespootch still kept up Garven's house and grounds in Phoenix after a fashion. Mainly, they hired boys to do the outside work and women to tend to the house and did not bother Garven about the details. The two men became Garven's only friends, and the three of them rarely discussed Garven's business woes that depressed him and bored them. Lyle persuaded Garven to go with him back to Arizona to the Cipher High School reunion for what would have been Garven's class had he not been sent off to prep school in California. He and Garven even persuaded Edward to go with them, something of a social coup given Edward's ingrained reticence. The return proved to be the most positive thing Garven did all year.

One of the few people he remembered at the reunion held on the dusty playing field-park west of the Cipher town boundaries, was a woman named Sarah Carlisle. That was her maiden name; the name of the girl Garven remembered. She was now a mature, handsome woman, named Sarah

Knighton. She could once have been beautiful, Garven thought, but the years had been hard for her, as they had been for him, he surmised. Many of his other former classmates were standoffish, even rude, towards Garven because of his being 'rich'. To be 'rich'—which included anyone or any family that earned $50,000 a year or more—made the person or family a relative social pariah so far as the perennial inhabitants were concerned. They, like their counterparts throughout the rest of the state, refused to vote for candidates deemed to be 'rich'. They did their business with small mom and pop establishments in strong preference to patronizing large 'rich' concerns.

Sarah responded to Garven's friendly overtures with smiles and genuine interest in what he had to say. She talked to him as well. Of all his former classmates, she alone appeared not to hold his financial success against him. Garven found that refreshing, and her attractive, as a result.

She went out of her way to sit beside him at a table for the class picnic that held the worst reprobates in the history of their class. Besides Garven, the table accommodated Lyle Durche, Edward Sespootch, Steve Ranklin, who was now the sheriff, his father having retired, Tadd Stricklin, Clark Denton, Hyrum Jones, and Teddy Sorensen. Sarah was the only woman and the only churchgoer at their table. Garven found himself shushing the rest of the men when their language got too raunchy for Sarah's tender ears, a bow to chivalry that made her laugh. The assemblage of his oldest friends took Garven back to the old sandlot football games that he had thrived on and where he had sharpened his competitive teeth when he and his mother had first moved to Cipher when he was ten years old. He had a small flash of memory about a young coyote silently watching the boys' brutal games. The presence of Sarah as an adult sitting close beside him kept Garven's attentions in the present most of the time.

"Weren't you named something else when you were here, Garven?" she asked.

"Yes. I was adopted by the doctor," he said.

Her question had not felt to him like prying and seemed benign, affable, like her.

"Oh, yeah, I remember. You were Rachel Carmichael's son. She was the school teacher, right?" she queried, sure that she was correct.

"That's right," Garven answered between bites of ripe corn on the cob and hot chilies.

"Tell me about yourself, Garven. I'd really like to know what became of you," Sarah asked later in the day when the small crowd of classmates began to disperse.

Garven gave the keys to his car to Lyle and walked with Sarah. When they came to her house, she suggested that they take an evening horseback ride. It had been ages since he had been on a horse.

"That would be great," he answered when she asked. "I'm not sure that I still know how."

"Like riding a bicycle. And you were a great rider back when. Everyone said you liked to go out at sunset and ride with the coyotes. A few said that you used to howl at the moon with them," she laughed, "that's one thing I remember about you for sure. I think you can still do anything you want. You look fit enough. Not like the beer bellies I see on the guys who never left," she commented.

Garven liked the fact that she noticed him. He looked at her face for evidence of flattering guile and found none.

It was past dark when they came back. On the ride over still familiar old trails the two of them learned all about each other. Garven surprised himself by speaking so freely. She listened well and uncritically. In turn, Garven listened to her life as well. Sarah had had four children; one died, and the others had flown the nest, left Cipher like practically every kid who came of age. She had been widowed by a mine accident nearly fifteen years ago and never remarried. The town's population had not varied one percent a decade since Garven had lived there, and the general attitudes of anti-science, anti-intellectualism, anti-evolution, and anti-progress had not altered either. By the end of their ride, Garven was taking notice of Sarah Knighton as someone more than a chance acquaintance at a reunion.

Garven spent as much time as he could with Sarah during the three days of the class reunion. When everyone else left, he decided to stay on for a few days. Edward and Lyle clucked at him and raised their eyebrows and rolled their eyes lasciviously, but Garven paid them no mind. A week later, when it was time for him to get back to work, he realized how little he looked forward to getting back to the rat race in San Francisco and how much he liked being in insignificant little Cipher.

He tallied up Sarah's advantages and disadvantages on an unwritten ledger sheet. Many of her attributes and characteristics defied placement on the ledger because they could fit into either column. That aspect of his scrutiny of her reflected more the changes in his own needs and preferences than it did any real standard, he recognized. She was middle-aged and looked it, plump and graying. Her eyes were active and curious, friendly and warm. She had wrinkles and smile lines. She had not had a face-lift like half the women he knew that were her age. Her tendency to being overweight acted to smooth out some of her wrinkles. She seemed to be more attractive than Garven had remembered her as a girl; but, then, Garven was looking through a different prism.

Sarah was intelligent but had a limited education and was woefully inexperienced by worldly standards. She had been to California and did not like it, to Utah for church activities, and to New Mexico on brief excursions; but she had lived out her life almost entirely within ten miles of the house where she was born. Her second best trait was her quality of common sense. Her best trait was that she understood Garven Wilsonhulme and accepted him despite that understanding.

By the time Garven got into his Mercedes to drive back to Phoenix, he had made a decision. He meant to have Sarah in his life. He knew that would have to mean marriage, even in the short run. Sarah was a devout Mormon and would have rejected him instantly had he proposed intimacy on any other basis. Their only physical intimacy had been to hold hands; a randy touch or even a kiss would have been out of the question, he knew instinctively. He was not sure how she felt about him; and when he stepped back to look at his own feelings objectively, he could scarcely understand his own emotions. Objectively, he was rich, fit, intelligent, strong, and reasonably apt socially. It was not braggadocio to think that. On the obverse side of the coin, he was short, had a twice broken nose, and a hint of cauliflower ears; in short, he was not a heart throb. In the world where mature single women lived, he was something of a prize since he was not a homosexual as were so many of the men those women encountered. In truth, he could have, with or without marriage, any of dozens of fine women, even trophy women. He had to scratch his head in wonderment that what he wanted was the paradigm of a home town girl grown up.

He and Sarah corresponded by letter and by telephone. Garven had to do the telephoning because Sarah was uncomfortable about calling long distance because of the cost, and about the propriety of the woman calling the man in the first place. Everything she did charmed him because of her unaffected, straightforward, gentle, innocent, and practical ways. He dropped all pretense within himself of objectivity and pursued her openly and boyishly. At first, Sarah was put off by his ardor, knowing his reputation for worldliness, for being the 'natural man' that her Sunday School teachers had warned her about as being the 'enemy to God'. The genuine respectfulness with which he paid her court gradually won her away from that misgiving. He rekindled the dormant feelings she had reserved only for her husband and put her off balance. It had been a long time since a man had done that; and she found that she rather liked it.

He came to see her again in Cipher, and she traveled to Phoenix and to San Francisco to see him. He scrupulously avoided even the least hint of impropriety. He made it obvious by not staying in the same hotel where he had her rooms booked. He took her to see operas, plays, and to restaurants where the food was as foreign to her as if it had been flown in from Mars. She was willing to try everything, rejected nothing until she had given it a real effort. She liked Chinese, Japanese, and Thai food and did not prefer heavy French sauces and creams, the peculiar breads of Ethiopia, or the hot curries of India. In the end, she still preferred simple things—meat and potatoes, vegetables she could recognize, and bread she made herself. She had to admit that she did not understand opera and asked why it was impossible to have one in English. She loved legitimate theater and Broadway musicals, especially old ones that had been made into movies; and, when all was said and done in the way of entertainment, she preferred country music and her small town. In all of those preferences, Garven recognized a growing compatibility between them.

He proposed marriage and offered her the sun, the moon, and the stars. To his astonishment, after nearly a year of wooing, she refused his first bended knee offer.

"Why?" he asked disconcertedly, "I thought you cared for me."

"I do; I do," she said sadly. "I just don't know. It has all happened so fast. I could handle the changes in my life, but the real problem boils down to the fact that we don't have the same religious beliefs. Religion is very important to me. I swore that I would never even date a man who wasn't of my faith. Now, I'm very confused. Give me a little time, please. Don't reject me. Ask me again. I'll give you a signal."

CHAPTER
Forty-Five

In a meeting in Chicago in November of 1988 with representatives of every merchant bank that Cal/Maxi Therapy owed, Garven was told flatly that they had come to the end of the line. He would have to file for Chapter 11 at least or for Chapter 7—out-and-out bankruptcy—more likely. Their lawyers and his lawyers would hammer out the details. Garven was not surprised; but he was depressed by the final failure of the company; but in his usual habit of not indulging in self-recrimination for things out of his control, he recognized that the overwhelming burden of debt with which he had been saddled at the very outset of his chairmanship had predetermined this outcome. It was the height of frustration to him that business was excellent; the company raked in a great deal of money. Had the former owners not overstretched themselves and bought the Georgia and Texas company and yoked Cal/Maxi-Therapy to an improvidently high rate of interest for their loan, he would have been presiding over a phenomenally lucrative enterprise.

The decision about how to end the days of Cal/Maxi-Therapy worried at Garven. The only room to maneuver that he had lay in the fact that his personal finances and even his contract were not completely locked into the maintenance of the company. He mulled his decision over in sleepless nights and weight losing days. He kept his own counsel, not even sharing his concerns and decisions with his or the company's attorneys or board of directors. As the date of enforced bankruptcy loomed closer, Garven made up his mind and called an extraordinary meeting of the remaining four member of the board after a week of consideration on his own.

"You are all aware of the critical nature of our finances," he said without preamble or even passing the amenities. "We had the potential to make this into a multi-billion dollar company, but we over leveraged ourselves and do not have enough money to keep up with our debt burden. That is the plain and simple truth of it. We have over $250,000,000 in liquidatable funds against $2,100,000,000 in outstanding debts. We can liquidate all our holdings and come up least $10,000,000 short of even paying the most pressing immediate loan payment calls. Neither we nor the banks can hold on long enough to get us over the hump and into the black. The parent company—the central organization of which you are the board of directors, and I am the CEO—can erase more than two-thirds of our debts by frankly declaring bankruptcy and letting the separate clinics go their own way. The law will still require that each clinic and every doctor in each clinic honor the contracts with the patients and the companies. With the parent company out of the way, everyone of them is going to be in deep trouble, but the financial burdens will be spread over a wide area.

"And what about the money we have coming per our contracts, the severance pay and stock options?" demanded Lewis Sackett.

There was fear and anger in his face.

"Good question," replied Garven. "And I have the answer. I have gone over my contract with a magnifying glass. Because of the way the original two Sri Lankans set up this business to benefit themselves, I have ultimate authority. I can exercise whatever option I choose so long as I don't violate the law, and so long as I do it before we are served with bankruptcy closure orders. For example, I can allow bankruptcy to take place as a matter of inevitable course and be a nice fellow and give all of the assets presently on our books to the court to divvy up."

"And screw all of us, including yourself," Lewis interjected. "What about 'nice' to us, for a change? We've all put more into this venture than anyone else."

"Now that you mention it, there is another option," Garven said patiently. "I can elect to pay each of us off in the form of a yearly corporate bonus. No one has received such a bonus this year, and there is no law to prevent me from being generous or to base that bonus on the bottom line of the profit-loss column. It's perfectly legal until the court takes over; then we, that is, I, will no longer have a say. I think this is the last meeting we will be able to have before the court does assume authority, incidentally. Chapter 11 is not an option; our debts are too big to be handled with a restructuring," Garven said with sobering candor.

"So, what do we do?"

"The contracts and the articles of incorporation and establishment of this board as well as past established policies of doing business require me to propose and you to dispose. I am going to make a recommendation that is perfectly legal but will be extremely unpopular outside this room. This is it."

Garven passed around a single sheet of paper to each of the four board members.

"You will have to vote by written statement. Let me strongly advise you to make your vote unanimous in favor of the proposal—united we stand, and all that. That will help defend against any future challenge; and, mark my words, there will be a challenge. You'll have to be tough; the fire that melts the butter hardens the egg. Try and keep that in mind."

As they read what was written on the sheet, Garven made a last comment.

"Forget about cashing in on your stock options. The stock is, for practical purposes, worthless; and the SEC would be down our throats if we tried to dump it."

The paper Garven circulated had the names of the four board members and the CEO and a dollar figure beside each name. The concept behind the figures listed was as shocking as the figures themselves. Garven was proposing that each one of them be given a six or seven figure bonus, the amount of which was determined by seniority in the business. The company's treasury would be almost entirely denuded once the bonuses were awarded, and the company would fold immediately after the last bonus was paid.

"Agreed?" asked Garven with a voice and face free of the cynicism implicit in the proposal.

The sheer magnitude of the departure from any reasonable business transaction took a minute or two to digest. Garven had indicated a sum of $10,000,000 for Lewis Sackett, and corresponding but somewhat lesser payouts for the other three. He had allotted himself $100,000,000. Their heads all nodded, reluctantly at first, but finally unanimously in the affirmative since each of them had failed to find anything clearly illegal in the proposal or in the amounts to be disbursed.

"Good," said Garven, matter-of-factly, "I think we can all agree that it would not be in our best interests to alert the stock holders, clinic managers, patients, or the public just yet of our private transaction here today. We will pay out the bonuses over the next two weeks. Today you are going to fire me and appoint Ralph Smothers as CEO. He will preside over the demise of the company and the termination of each of you from the board of Cal/Maxi-Therapy. Now, it may seem a small point, but you and I must be fired; we don't have the privilege of bowing out with a graceful resignation, if we are to collect our severance pay and bonus. Sorry if that puts a negative note on your résumé."

The other three men gave an appreciative but nervous laugh.

Few of the board members had ever even spoken to Ralph Smothers, although they all knew who he was. Mr. Smothers was the head of the accounting department and had held that position since the company was run by the Sri Lankans. He was a colorless functionary. Mr. Smothers knew to the penny about Cal/Maxi-Therapy's shaky financial position. For a million dollar bonus of his own, authorized by the outgoing CEO, Mr. Smothers would take the heat from the outside, from the banks, the doctors, the investors, and from the contracting patients and patient groups. All along Garven had regarded the man as having the soul of a calculator. On his last day as CEO, Garven decided that that quality made Ralph Smothers the perfect man to succeed him.

The board vote that evening was unanimous, and there were no dissenting comments. Garven left the room out of a job. He stopped at the nearest telephone and arranged for a wire transfer of his $100,000,000 to the Cayman Islands and then on to the Vanuatu Fletcher account. The following day, he left on the early flight to Cipher, Arizona for a two month vacation from telephones. Garven was not troubled by his lop-sided transaction. He knew that he had lost his conscience about the same time he lost his religion. It was the day just before he turned ten when his biological father deserted Garven and his mother. He neglected to leave a forwarding address or telephone number and made no attempt to contact any of his former colleagues in the large health care provider industry. He made it a point not to read a magazine or a newspaper, to listen to the radio, or to watch television for the entire two months. It was a very therapeutic and restful vacation.

Garven's presence in the town made the final difference to Sarah Knighton. She talked over Garven's proposal of marriage with the ecclesiastical authority in her church. He was an eminently practical man as well as a devout believer. It was better that she find happiness, and that she not be alone, he told her. Perhaps in God's own time and in His wisdom, the 'gentile' Sarah loved would see the light and join the fold. Garven did not press her. She became frustrated with his politeness and careful hands-off courting.

Garven was staying in two rooms at the town's motel.

His telephone rang insistently.

"Hello," he answered.

"This is Sarah," she said.

"Sarah who?"

"Garven Wilsonhulme," she stormed good naturedly, "you know it is difficult for me to call you."

"I would never have recognized your voice," Garven teased.

"I know I'm a little old fashioned," she said, "but I am going to be downright brazen. Dr. Wilsonhulme, Sir, would you be my guest at dinner this evening?"

The formality amused Garven since the two of them had eaten together nearly every evening since he had come to Cipher. He laughed.

"I would be honored," he said affecting an upper-crust accent.

"The dinner will be formal," she said. "I have something special in mind. Would seven suit your schedule?"

"It would be perfect."

In keeping with her cryptic enthusiasm and with the letter of her invitation, Garven dug out his old tuxedo and was pleased that it was not too dusty from its stay in the motel closet. He spruced up the best he could and waited as impatient as any boy on prom night until five of seven.

She greeted him at the door and laughed out loud at his formal attire and expression. However, she, too, was in a formal gown, one that Garven had bought for her at I Magnin's in San Francisco and that he particularly liked.

"Please come in. The dinner is almost ready. Sit down, and I'll bring it in."

She left for the kitchen where enticing aromas of bread and garlic wafted towards him.

He sat at the table, curious at its sparse setting. There were not even plates or utensils. In the center of the shining wood table top sat a small vase in which stood a pair of perfect red roses in full bloom. Their stems were tied together with a white bow.

Sarah walked back into the room, her hands empty. She looked shy and insecure, as one who had made the first gesture in a world where everyone waves and no one waves back. Garven was no romantic, but he did recognize a signal when he saw one. He stood up and walked over to her. He reached out and took both of her hands in his. Then, still holding her left hand with his right one, he reached in his pocket and took something out which he palmed.

He knelt on one knee and said simply, "Will you honor me by becoming my wife, Sarah? Without you it will be a lonely life."

"I will," she said. "I thought you'd never ask."

He shook his head in confession of his ignorance of how women think. She helped him to his feet because his knees had stiffened up. They embraced for nearly half an hour. She cried.

The wise and practical Mormon bishop performed the ceremony in the local church with her family and friends from the town and around the country in attendance. Lyle and Edward stood on his side of the aisle. To his delight, both of his children attended and were obviously taken with Sarah. For all the excitements and pleasures of his urbane life, and for reasons he could not then nor later articulate satisfactorily, it was one of the best days of his life. He remembered from one of his history classes at Stanford, the story of one Abd-Er-Rahman III of Spain.

The powerful Islamic conqueror and occupier of Spain, in about the year 960 AD, said; and Garven had committed his words to memory:

> "I have now reigned about fifty years in victory or peace, beloved by my subjects, dreaded by my enemies and respected by my allies. Riches and honors, power and pleasure, have waited on my call; nor does any earthly blessing appear to have been wanting to my felicity. In this situation I have diligently numbered the days of pure and genuine happiness which have fallen to my lot. They amount to fourteen."

Garven felt a kinship with the words of Abd-Er-Rahman, a man who failed to mention wife or family in his account of his personal history. Garven Wilsonhulme counted his wedding to Sarah Knighton as one of his own fourteen days of pure and genuine happiness.

CHAPTER
Forty-Six

Garven was bored with retirement. He was almost fifty-nine years old. Having money, a great deal of money, certainly had its advantages; but Garven had discovered that, for him, it did not substitute for purposeful endeavor or satisfying work. He grew restless. He missed the jousting of business, the intellectual stimulation of research, and the satisfaction of sitting in the seats of power. Most of all he missed operative neurosurgery, which came as a slow-growing surprise to him. He had come to grips with that facet of his personality that caused him to compete so vehemently. He knew that his acquisitiveness had exceeded all rational bounds and was little more than a contest against other highly motivated and competent players. In and of itself, the value of the money he had accumulated so far exceeded his needs, which were rather simple, or even his ability to spend it, that Garven had lost his desire to get more. Much of that attitude he had absorbed from the soothing sameness of life in Cipher, Arizona where he now spent the majority of his time. The people in the town had an ingrained attitude that 'enough' was definable in terms of having 'sufficient for my needs'. Garven had settled into a way of thinking that embraced that philosophy. But, nonetheless, he needed action and involvement.

He and Sarah set out to travel, to yacht, to snorkel in the Caribbean, to deep-sea fish in Chesapeake Bay for blue fish and off San Diego for albacore. They partied, entertained, and donated their time and money. Garven enjoyed it all, and yet wanted more. Sarah watched her new husband's restlessness and could not come up with a solution for it. He looked at an assortment of business enterprises to occupy his active mind—thorough-bred race horse breeding, cattle ranching, owning an exotic Phoenix restaurant, being a part of a new computer company just getting started in Orem, Utah, and dabbling in the Chicago futures market. None of them captured his interest effectively enough to keep him involved in them.

Knowing that he was casting about for an investment of his energies and money, one of his old friends for the Cal/Maxi-Therapy days came by his small home in Cipher with a proposal.

"Garven, my friend. You need to be a major player in a good health maintenance organization. HMOs are the health care delivery vehicle of the future. They are just getting started. Clinton and his wife are going to make everybody in the country join up. That's their new plan, I hear. People in the know are all saying that this the last chance to get in on the ground floor. If you thought Cal/Maxi-Therapy was a great idea, you ain't seen nothin' yet, as they say. There is so much money to be made with the right HMO that you would have to hire a company just to count your earnings. It is the greatest cash cow since the Midas touch.

"Can you imagine having the federal government on your side to make your business go? It's as good as affirmative action for the rich. It'll be like the old days of Medicare before the bean counters took over. I'm telling you, Garv. this is the greatest scam in the history of health care. Take money from the patients and doctors and give it to the HMO administrators and investors. Sort of a reverse Robin Hood idea. Let the folks out in Podunk think they're getting a bargain because the docs' fees are being squeezed down to nothing. What do the people know? They think doctors' salaries are the beginning and the end of health care costs, and the feds are helping to convince them of that. It's a great scam, my man. How about taking a look at my proposal. With your money and expertise in running these kind of programs, we can't lose."

"I don't think so, Jack," Garven said to his old acquaintance. "I'm not up to it any more. The fun has gone out of that sort of thing for me just like most docs think the fun has gone out of medicine. There are plenty of young guys out there that can milk that cow for you. I wish you the best. Really, I do; but I don't want to get back into it."

Jack's parting shot was, "Okay, it's your loss; but it's also your life, Garv. This looks like a happy arrangement. I hope you can stand it. I would be bored outta my skull. Hang in there, old buddy."

Sarah watched her husband for months without overtly commenting on his activities or his state of mind.

Finally, she said, "Garven, apparently, I know you better than you know yourself. You are a brain surgeon. That's the long and the short of it. That's what you need to do. Forget about making money from it or getting prestige or power. Just go and do it. Complain about the patients; worry about malpractice suits; get tired. Maybe even do medical humanitarian neurosurgery. It's time for you to get out from under my feet and back into it."

As usual, Sarah's calm deliberative common sense carried Garven's thinking. He called Elijah David Shapiro at UCOMH and asked him to set up a six month refresher residency course for him. It had been years since he had had a scalpel in his hand. He needed the practical toning up as well as the certification he could present to one of the Phoenix hospitals to be able to get staff and operating privileges, and then maybe hook up with a care-giver outfit going to the Third World.

"It has taken me a long time, a life-time, if the truth be known, E.D., to come to grips with what I am. I have been a lot of things, most of them bad, but beneath it all, I am a neurosurgeon, pure and simple. I want to get back into it for the relatively short period that I will be able to do it safely for the patients," Garven said soberly.

E.D. had laughed when Garven made his request and took more than a little persuading to be convinced that the one-time professor and pope was serious. Once Elijah David saw neurosurgery through Garven's sincere eyes, he agreed, and had something of a renewal of his own enthusiasm.

§§§§§

On July 1, 1990 Dr. Garven C. Wilsonhulme, the balding and graying new resident, walked through the front doors of U.C. Osterlund Memorial Hospital with butterflies in his stomach like every other intern and resident who had ever walked through those doors and into that cacophonous and cavernous waiting room. It made no difference that so much experience lay behind him; there was something of a cleansing effect on the man, a feeling approaching absolution. There was a throng of people milling around him— the halt, lame, blind, crippled, and crazy—saints and criminals—leathery faces lined in pain, all gathered in the great leveling cauldron of the big city hospital anteroom.

The room was exactly as he remembered it—large and hollow enough that the voices and clanging carts and trays produced echoes. There were a few benches, presumably the same ones that had been bolted to the floor when he first walked into the place forty years previously. Most of the people still sat on the grimy floor picnicking, scolding squalling children with their drooping diapers and runny noses. The names might have changed, but Garven knew he was looking into the same faces of despair, the corps of harried tired women, shambling addicts, and lost looking derelicts carefully hiding their brown paper bags. Paint peeled here and there; the walls and floors were splotched with a variegated array of stains; and there were areas of wall denuded with plaster. He saw a line of what looked like bullet holes pocking one wall at abdomen level. Garven's pulse quickened. He felt the same sense of pressure, that there was more work to do than he could get done; and he had yet to start his refresher course. He felt more alive than he had in years. He felt like a brain surgeon. The old coyote from Cipher, Arizona would have smiled, he thought.

> "…life is such a brief span at the longest, one should put self and self-interest on one side. In the first place, one should put duty to the Master. How best can I work for the good of others should be a supreme question."

> -Harvey Cushing, M.D.,
> Doctor of Science Pioneer Neurosurgeon

In Greek and Roman legends, the Phoenix is the symbol of immortality and resurrection. The Roman poet, Claudian, told the classical story, as translated by Henry Vaughan:

Chapter Forty-Six

THE PHOENIX

He knows his time is out! and doth provide
New principles of life; herbs he brings dried
From the hot hills, and with rich spices frames
A Pile shall burn, and Hatch him with his flames.

On this the weakling sits; salutes the Sun
With pleasant noise, and prays and begs for some
Of his own fire, that quickly may restore
The youth and vigor, which he had before.
Whom soon as Phoebus [Apollo's] spies, stopping his rays

He makes a stand, and thus allays his pains......
He shakes his locks, and from his golden head,
Shoots on bright beam, which smites with vital fire

The willing bird; to burn is his desire.
That he may live again; he's proud in death,
And goes in haste to gain a better breath.
The spice heap fired with celestial rays
Doth burn the aged Phoenix, when straight stays
The Chariot of the amazed Moon; the pole
Resists the wheeling, swift Orbs, and the whole
Fabric of Nature at a stand remains.
Till the old bird anew, young begins again.

www.phoenixarises.com/phoenix/legends/greek.ht

-The End-

The Vulture and the Phoenix author, Carl Douglass, a former neurosurgeon turned successful author, has included elements of his own and others' experiences into two of his novels, Saga of a Neurosurgeon series, and All In Jest. He is a voracious reader and an assiduous researcher--a set of passions which have led him to write novels about assassins, irregular warfare, medico-legal entanglements, and the impending apocalypse. He works to achieve realism and avoids fantasy genre in his works. Writing has been a great ride occupying the autumn of his life. His wife puts up with it as she has done with his other enthusiasms.

HONORS, AWARDS, AND MEMBERSHIPS
Phi Kappa Phi University Honor Society
Alpha Omega Alpha Medical Honor Society
BS (Medical Biology) degree—magna cum laude
MD—magna cum laude
CDR/MC/USN

American Medical Association
American Association of Neurosurgeons
Congress of Neurological Surgeons
Fellow of the American College of Surgeons
The Association of Military Surgeons of the United States
Life Member of the Medical Society of Vienna
Diplomate of the American Board of Neurological Surgery

Past President, Our Community Foundation, Wasatch County, Utah
Past Medical Liaison Officer, Deseret International Foundation
Past Chief of Surgery,
Antelope Valley Regional Medical Center, Lancaster, California
Past Member-at-Large, Central Medical Committee,
Utah Valley Regional Medical Center, Provo, Utah
Past Member, Utah State Foster Care Review Committee